Colliding Tastes

Ray Davis

Contents

The man glared at me even as I smiled at him. "I don't," he said, as if it were obvious. "I just couldn't stand watching you get cheated."

"Cheated? I don't think I was being cheated."

"Fine. Whatever, I don't care. You're going to end up homeless from giving people too much, and then don't come crying to me!" He spun around, stomping his boot clad feet to the exit, a sour expression on his handsome face.

"Wait!" I called, waiting for him to turn around or at least stop. He didn't, ignoring my shouts as he left in a whirlwind of anger. "How can I come crying if I don't even know your name?" He left before I could even finish.

I wonder why he helped me? He seemed so reluctant, but he'd done it anyway. He couldn't be too mean if he'd helped me, even though he'd acted despicably to that poor woman.

Oh cheese and crackers, I should've scolded him for doing that, but talking to him made me forget. He had a very mesmerising voice...I wonder how it sounded when he-

"Excuse me, miss? One strawberry cupcake, please."

Chapter 2

My hands were twitching involuntarily as I leaned against the wall of that stupid bakery.

"Goddammit," I muttered under my breath. "Where the hell is Clark?" Clark was the closest thing I had to a best friend. He was practically family.

"Hey man," I heard from beside me, followed by a hard slap to my shoulder.

"You're late," I said, but I wasn't really angry. Clark was too good to me for me to treat him horribly.

He simply laughed loudly, used to my grouchiness by now. "I saw you come out of that shop. What were you doing in there, don't you realise you're fat enough as it is?"

"Piss off!" I groaned, shoving him away from me.

"No, really, what were you doing in there?" he asked curiously, raising an eyebrow. He was my complete opposite; with blond hair, light skin, and blue eyes. "I thought you hated sweets."

"I do," I agreed as I slumped further against the wall.

He was still confused. "So...?" I glared at the ground as I remembered that girl from the bakery. She was beautiful, but she had pissed me off. "Whoa!" Clark laughed at the look on my face. "What got your knickers in a knot?"

At the sound of a tinkling, cheery laugh, we looked up to see my worst nightmare walking out of the shop. My glare deepened as I watched the carefree smile on her face grow. What a child.

Clark made a low whistling noise. "She's stupid," I grumbled, looking away so I wouldn't keep staring at the sincere grin on her face, or the way her eyes twinkled.

He looked at me incredulously. "What are you talking about? Do you even see her?"

"I see her, alright," I said. "I went in there because I had to save her sorry ass."

Clark let out a low laugh. "How so?"

I shrugged. "I've seen her before. She's such a fucking pushover, it's unbelievable. She lets customers walk all over her like a bloody welcome mat and she doesn't even care."

"Huh," Clark grunted, looking thoughtful. He turned and smirked at me. "What did you do?"

"Don't look at me like that, mate," I protested, raising my palms in defence. "It wasn't my fault. She was going to give money she earnt fair and square back to some cheating dick."

"Wow, you must really like her," he teased. "What's her name?"

"I don't fucking know," I muttered.

He made a humming noise and got one of those devious smirks on his face that told me I wouldn't like what he was planning. "Hey, sweet cheeks!" he bellowed.

"What the hell, Clark!" I hissed, grabbing his shoulder.

He shook me off and shot me a pleased look when the girl turned around. When she spotted us, her smile widened instead of faltered like what usually happened when people saw us leaning against a dark wall next to a dumpy little bakery. "Are you talking to me?" she asked politely.

"Yeah," Clark replied, waving her over.

She smiled wider and scampered over to us immediately, which ticked me off to no boundaries. Was she seriously so unconditionally trusting? Did she have no common sense?

"Hello!" she greeted Clark, stretching out her palm in welcome. He shook it vigorously, earning a small giggle from her. It was the sound of pure joy, and it made me feel really uncomfortable to be around such a sweet-natured, girlish person.

"What's your name?" he asked, shooting me a sly look. I snorted.

"I'm Charlotte," she replied, entirely too cheerfully, before her doe-eyed green gaze slid over to me. If possible, her grin stretched even wider, and she bounced on the tip of her toes. "Hi, stranger!" she trilled enthusiastically.

I grunted, fighting the urge to flip her off. Too much fucking nice for me. "Have you met?" Clark asked slyly.

"Oh yes!" Charlotte answered eagerly. "This guy helped me out, he was super nice!" I made a face, wondering if she was mocking me, but then I realised that she wouldn't know how to mock people if I told her exactly what to sya.

Clark bit his lip hard to keep the laughter in, and I just let the disgust seep into my expression. I expected her face to fall, but she kept smiling at me.

Bitch.

"Nice to you?" Clark replied smoothly, teasingly. "You must be mistaken. This guy's a grumpy old dickhead."

Charlotte glanced at me in amusement, causing me to clench my teeth. What was so funny about me, huh? "He is," she agreed. "But he saved me some money and I didn't get a chance to say thank you! So thank you!"

Clark elbowed me in the ribs. I glared viciously at him before staring straight at Charlotte. I expected her to squirm, or blush even, but she just continued to smile her little smile at me, thinking I was her hero or some crazy shit like that.

Clark elbowed me again and I shoved him away. "You're welcome," I said angrily, turning away.

"What's your name?" I heard her ask kindly, but I ignored her, assuming she was talking to Clark.

"That's Ben," Clark chuckled. "And I'm Clark."

"Dude," I hissed under my breath. "Why the fuck did you give away our names? This girl could be a psychotic stalker, for Chrissakes!"

Clark shot me a look, and then slowly moved his eyes back to Charlotte. I followed his line of sight to the girl, who was watching us with wide eyes, a faint grin tickling at the corners of her pink lips. "Really?" he said under his breath. "You're being ridiculous."

I humphed and turned away again, crossing my arms. I heard that tinkling laugh again, which made me itch to move and see the joyful expression on her face as she giggled away merrily. But I restrained myself because she was more annoying than anyone I've ever met before.

"Well, thank you for the help, Ben!" she teased gently, but with sincere undercurrents in her soft voice. "Thank you very, very much!"

I continued to ignore her until I heard a weary sigh from beside me. "Let's exchange numbers," Clark suggested to her.

I could literally hear the bouncing she was making as she agreed. What a complete fucking idiot. She was way too trusting to be safe. She really didn't have a bloody clue how the world worked if she just gave out her number willy-nilly to random strangers.

"Okay, bye, Clark! Bye, Benny!" She waved cheerfully and started skipping away from us, humming a tune under her breath. Clark watched her go with a soft smile on his face, and I knew that her charisma had reeled him in without a doubt.

Wait. Hold the fuck up.

Did she just call me Benny? Does she have a death wish?

"What a sweetheart," he commented, turning to me with a wide grin even as I still fumed at her nickname. My name is Ben. B-E-N. Not Benny, for Chrissakes. I'm not a child.

I watched him with an unimpressed look on my face. "She's way too innocent for my taste."

Clark snorted. "Your taste? You mean nobody, since you're a total grump?"

I glared at him. "I'd probably turn her into an asshole like me." It was true. She was much safer staying away, or hanging around a good guy like Clark.

He laughed. "When have you ever cared about that?"

I paused, then frowned. Wait, he was right. When have I ever cared? "Well, it doesn't matter. I don't like her," I told him angrily.

His mouth dropped. "How could you not? She's a fucking angel!"

"Exactly. She's too happy! I mean, does she even have other emotions? Does she not get embarrassed or angry or jealous? Because it doesn't seem like it!" I argued.

"You're impossible."

"And you're lovesick," I retorted, noticing how he was getting a sort of glazed look in his eye like he always did whenever he found a girl he liked.

"I'm not lovesick!"

I started making whipping noises with my mouth. "Lovesick!" I said mockingly.

"Mate, c'mon. How can you hate her? Just because she's a pushover? Is it bad to want people to be happy?"

"Dude, she seems like the kind of girl who'd forgive you if you intentionally cheated on her."

His mouth dropped open. "What kind of demon would do that to her of all people?"

"I would to see if I could get a reaction." I grinned. He let out a chuckle and shoved me.

"You just can't admit that you like her," he said, eyeing me up.

"How can I like a person I barely know?" Especially when it's an overly cheerful pushover like her?

"You can when it's Charlotte," he said, nudging me. "I mean, she's gorgeous, she's funny, and she's got a wonderful personality!"

"Nauseatingly so."

He finally gave up on me, throwing his arms in the air. "Whatever. You'll change your mind soon."

"We won't even see her again," I replied, grinning widely at the prospect. We'd never have to see that hyper, happy ball of positivity ever again.

Clark smirked, waggling his eyebrows tauntingly. "Ah, ah, ah, don't you remember I got her number? And I fully intend on using it!"

"You fucker!" I groaned, aiming a kick at his shins.

"You'll thank me some day!" he cried as he ran away.

"Doubt it!"

Chapter 3

I watched Barry as he came to a stop in front of me, just as I was leaving my room for class. He was in my Composition class, but I'd never really spoken to him before.

He looked rather flustered, and so I narrowed my eyes in concern. "Alright, Barry?" I greeted politely, smiling at him.

"Hi Charlie," he mumbled, his face going bright red.

I cocked my head at his actions, my smile slipping slightly. Was he alright? "How are you?"

"I'm j-just fine," he stuttered, leading me to believe that he was not, in fact, 'just fine.'

"You sure?" I prodded, frowning at the way his hands twisted nervously together, like he was having a mini seizure.

"I just w-want to tell you something."

Now I was utterly nonplussed, because he was a good student - I doubted he needed my notes. Nor did I think he wanted to copy my homework. What else could he want to say? "Yes?" I prompted, encouraging him with a smile.

"I...eh, I l-like you," he shoved out, looking absolutely mortified.

I frowned again. Why did he look so embarrassed to tell me such a simple thing? I wasn't cruel, I did have a nice answer for him. Ginny, my roommate and best friend, had told me he might let me know something like that. "I like you too, Barry," I finally said.

The poor lad brightened up tenfold, making me grin at how he suddenly seemed so much better. "You do?" he almost squeaked.

My grin widened and I nodded my head enthusiastically. "Yeah, you're a good friend!" As soon as I said those words, Barry's face grew darker than a thundercloud and I almost gasped.

Why did this always happen? Whenever I made acquaintance with a boy and they said they liked me, this always happened! I wouldn't make friends with somebody I didn't like, so why did they insist on stating the obvious? And why didn't they like that I was happy being friends with them? I didn't think led them on. In fact, I always made sure to explain that I wasn't up for dating.

Boys think they deserve too much sometimes.

Just then, I heard a bark of amused laughter, and glanced over my shoulder to see the mysterious stranger - Ben, was it? - with his hands on his knees, almost choking on his spit as he laughed hard and loud.

My eyes lit up at the sight of him for reasons unknown to me. "Sorry, Barry, I have to go!" I exclaimed, deciding to explain the circumstances to him next time. As I scurried away, he stared after me, as though his eyes would somehow magically transport me back to him. Sorry Barry, but getting to see Ben was rare, so I had to take the chance while I could.

Soon, I reached Ben and grinned in triumph. He snorted loudly and said, "What was that?"

I frowned, wondering if he could help me understand the mind of the male gender. "I don't get it, Benny," I started, wringing my hands just like Barry had previously. "These boys keep saying that they like me, and I always say I like them too because they're all so nice. But then they get so disappointed when I say that they're good friends, even though I always say that we're just friends!"

As I finished speaking, he began chuckling again. I would've asked what was so funny if I didn't find his laugh to be so amusing. It was a cross between a smoker's laugh and a lion's roar, if that made any sense. "Exactly how many times has this happened to you?" he finally asked, once he got a hold of himself.

I thought about it for a minute. "There was Timmy and Harold last term," I mused. "Derrick, Andrew, and Finley in September...Terrence last month, and Barry today!"

Ben's mouth fell open as I spoke and he looked incredulous. "Did you seriously shove that many people in the friend-zone?" he demanded in his regular rude tone. But I didn't mind. I had the patience of a saint. "Oh hell, those poor guys."

"Friend-zone?" I repeated, still puzzled. For pete's sake, I didn't understand why boys couldn't understand when things were completely platonic.

"Did you not recognise those as confessions?" He made a noise in the back of his throat like he thought I was being unbelievably moronic and then raised his eyebrows.

My eyes suddenly widened in shock as I realised what I had done. "Cheese and crackers," I gasped, smacking my forehead with my hand. "I am such a headcase! Was I really leading them on?"

"I agree with the headcase part," Ben stated flatly, before turning around to walk away.

"Hey!" I called, unsure as to why he would just leave like that without saying goodbye. "Where are you going?"

"Away from you, Shortcake," he threw in without a backwards glance. Shortcake?

"Not even a goodbye?"

"Not even a goodbye."

I stared at him until he disappeared from my line of sight and then shrugged. He was such a strange, strange man. I wasn't used to dealing with people like him, but there was just something about him...maybe it was the way he seemed to dislike me already, or maybe it was the fact that I'd never seen him smile, but I wanted to know more.

Hostility be damned, I'd become his friend even if it was to be the hardest thing in the world. And judging from his personality as I've come across him, it probably was going to be the hardest thing in the world.

"Charlie!" a feminine voice cried.

"Ginny!" I teased back as she raced to catch up with me. "Where did you disappear off to last night?"

Ginny smirked as she fixed her already perfect hair and clothes. "I decided to go pay Zachary a visit," she said slyly, throwing me a dirty wink.

I raised my eyebrows at her unabashed behaviour. Honestly, she was such a little hussy. I needed her to teach me, actually, how to differentiate between flirting and just being friends. "Where'd you get the new clothes to change in?"

"I came prepared!" she held up a black leather purse and winked. "Here - let me just chuck this in our room and we'll be off."

"Hurry up, we're already late!" I said as she scurried into our room.

"Jesus Christ, loosen up!" she called from inside. "Professor Pierce isn't gonna give a fuck even if we ditch and you know it!" She purposefully walked slower just to make me laugh at her. "Hey, Charlie, is that guy you were just talking to who I think he is?"

"You mean Barry, or Benny?" I asked absentmindedly as we headed to our class.

Ginny stifled a laugh as she sidled up to my side. "So Sir Bartholemue finally told you he fancied you?"

I swivelled to face her and swatted her arm lightly. "Virginia Richards!" I exclaimed sternly. "How come you told me that the poor lad liked me as friends, not that he actually fancied me?"

She snickered while I continued to frown. "You're so thick, Charlie, but I thought you'd figure it out!"

"Obviously I didn't."

"That's because you're stupid." Ginny rolled her eyes and pulled a breakfast bagel out of her backpack, along with a spoon and a carton of yoghurt.

I stared at her as she casually began eating her breakfast as though she didn't just pull it out of her schoolbag. "What are you doing?"

"What, you think I'm going to skip breakfast? Do you know how many calories you burn playing the horizontal tango?"

"Do you know how much I didn't want to know that?" I closed my eyes and shivered. I didn't mind that my sex monkey of a best friend was a little promiscuous, but I did mind when she described her encounters to me.

She spooned some yoghurt into her mouth and flung the spoon at me. "Hey, if you actually looked for a guy, you wouldn't be complaining about your lack of a romantic life."

"Where's your romantic life?" I challenged, throwing the spoon back. She expertly caught it in her mouth and wriggled her eyebrows conceitedly. "I thought last week, you went to visit Tyler at midnight."

"Sex is good enough for me. But since that's clearly not an option for you, you should find a man."

"Well, I'm not going to be able to do that if you keep chasing away all the guys who come to me," I told her.

"Good thing too, 'cause none of those tossers who confess are worth your time."

"Oh come on, Andrew was pretty nice," I defended.

"Nice, but stupid," she replied remorselessly.

"You called me stupid as well, you know?"

"But that's okay, because you're cute. He's not cute. At all."

I felt guilty for laughing, I really did, but I laughed anyway. "You're so horrible!"

"I know. But at least I get some action."

I shook my head. "Well, it's a good thing that Benny told me that they were confessions, otherwise I would've been completely clueless!"

Ginny choked on her laugh and almost tripped over her own feet. "So I wasn't mistaken - did you seriously just call Benjamin Fisher Benny?"

"Yeah, so?"

"So, you just called this big, scary guy a cute nickname! He's probably digging your grave already!"

"Don't be dramatic," I clicked my tongue and swatted her again. "He's not scary."

"Trust me, Charlie. That boy will destroy you, and he will do it without a single regret."

Chapter 4

"**I** had no idea she went to the same uni as us!" Clark revelled in a low voice, the happiness obvious in his tone.

I grunted, not opening my eyes. "Who the fuck are you talking about this time?"

"Why don't you open your eyes and see for yourself?"

"Because that requires effort."

"But Ben, it's your best friend!" he mocked.

I cracked open one eye to look at him. "Then what does that make you?"

Clark's smile became suggestive and he slid down the bench we were sitting on until our elbows were pressed together. "What else but...lovers?" he purred mockingly, running a finger down my arm.

I grabbed his head and shoved it towards his knees. "I swear to god, you touch me like that again and I will end you," I growled. "Are we clear?"

"As glass," he replied cheekily, his voice muffled by his jeans. "Jeez, Ben, I get you're straight but why are you this straight?"

I released his head and crossed my arms, reattempting to get some shut-eye before class. And if my nap just so happened to stretch throughout the lesson...well, nobody had to know, right? "Who were you talking about earlier?"

"Charlotte! Over here!" Clark suddenly bellowed, and even with my eyes shut, I could feel how energetically he waved his hands.

I groaned in embarrassment for his sake seeing as he probably didn't care, until I realised what he'd just said. "Did you say Charlotte?" I hissed.

Clark smirked. "Maybe you can take this as a chance to mind your manners."

"What manners?" I wondered.

"Exactly."

"Hello!" I heard the voice of my nightmares greet us.

"You never replied to my text," Clark teased, and I almost told him that he sounded like a clingy girlfriend, but decided to keep quiet. If I spoke around that chick, I'd only say hurtful things and then Clark would shoot me in the balls.

I kept my eyes closed, but I could hear the way she stammered out her reply and internally cringed. "Uh-I...eh-"

"She's trying to let you down easy," I interrupted, not even flinching when Clark kicked me in the shin. Hell if I was going to sit here and listen to my idiot best friend flirt with a girl who was trying to get away without sounding mean.

"Oh no, no, I wasn't-"

I let out a heavy sigh and opened my eyes. "If you don't want to date him, just let him know now. He won't be offended and he'll get over it. He's a big enough boy."

"Ben!" Clark exclaimed in exasperation.

I waved him away and stared accusingly at the pushover in front of me. "So?"

She turned a light pink colour and glanced between Clark and me. "Well...I don't know you all that well," she murmured to him in a soft voice. "So I didn't know what to say." She gave away her number within minutes of meeting us, so what else did she expect? Idiot.

I turned my head so that Clark wouldn't see me snicker at how awkward the two of them were being. But he noticed and not-so-subtly punched me in the gut. "Don't be such a wuss," I mocked.

"Oh wow," I heard the girl gasp, and I looked up to see her eyebrows furrowed. "I just think I'll leave-"

"Wait!" Clark cried, springing to his feet. Thirsty bastard. "I'll walk you to class. Is that okay with you, Charlotte?"

She stared at him for a moment as though he confused the fuck out of her and then shrugged. "You can call me Charlie," she offered after a pause. She smiled at him, and I swear to god the lad got a bit starstruck at the sight of her dimples. And, not that I'd ever admit it in public, but the happiness of it dazzled me too. It had been a while since I've seen someone smile with so much feeling.

Jesus, I was losing it.

Clark shot me a triumphant look and I rolled my eyes. She didn't say yes or no, dork, don't get too excited. "Okay,

Charlie, shall we go?" he asked. I heaved a sigh, hoping that with those two jabber-mouths gone, I'd finally be able to get some sleep.

"You're going to leave Benny here alone?" the girl asked worriedly.

I slid my eyes to her and glowered harshly, making her shift uneasily. "Don't call me Benny," I ordered. "I am not your pet, I am not your toy, and I am not your friend, got it?"

"Ben." I ignored Clark, and continued to stare at her angrily.

"It's okay, Cl...Clark, is it? It's alright." She turned to me and smiled wider, causing me to frown deeper. What was her problem? Did she want me to rip up that prissy backpack of hers into shreds? "I'm going to keep calling you Benny, because I like it," she told me. "So you can call me whatever you want as payment!"

"Not whatever you want," Clark interrupted, piercing me with his eyes. He was trying to get me to be nicer to this chick, but I didn't want to. Why the fuck would I when I didn't even know her? And now she was ordering me around?

"I am not giving you a nickname," I finally said.

"Why not?" she pushed. "It's only fair if I call you Benny."

Fair? She must be a primary schooler masquerading as a university student, because there is no way that someone like her was a young adult. I pretended to think about it. "How about this? No."

"Come on. Please?" She blinked at me and tipped her head, her eyes widening pleadingly. I blinked back, wondering how such a small girl could be so good at persuading people.

Maybe it was her big eyes. Maybe she was a demon, and that was why I felt myself weakening.

I glared at her for making me relent, and then at Clark for involving me with such an annoying girl. He just continued to watch her with this soft glow in his eyes. He was so whipped. "Fine!" I barked. "Fine, only to get you to stop complaining, goddammit."

She winced a little at my tone of voice, but then beamed at me. "What do you have in mind, Benny?"

Fuck, what did I get myself into? Now, every time I saw this demon, I'd have to endure her calling me that emasculating name. Benny. God, just thinking it gives me shivers. "I'll call you Shit-fac-"

"Ben," Clark warned.

I groaned slightly and rolled my eyes to the sky. No peace. No more peace, Ben. That was what happened when you tried to do something good, it just bit you right in the ass. No more good deeds for me. "Lottie," I finally grumbled. "I'll call you Lottie."

"Wow, no one's ever called me that before!" she exclaimed excitedly, before turning to Clark. "Lottie such a good one, isn't it?" He nodded agreeably with her, but I knew he wasn't really listening to her.

"Wow, you must feel so accomplished," I bit sarcastically, wishing to god she would just leave already. "Now go to cla-"

"Why would I feel accomplished, you're the one who came up with it!"

Oh my god. I couldn't do this. She was driving me insane. I needed to leave before I stick my head in the fountain and never come out. Fuck me.

Chapter 5

Even as Clark walked me to my next class, my mind wandered over to his friend. Ben, was his name.

I had so many questions about him. Like why was he so standoffish? I probably annoyed him with the whole 'Benny' thing, true, but he didn't have to be so rude, right? There was definitely something else that was the problem.

"Charlie? Charlie!"

I glanced up at Clark and smiled. "Yes?"

"You didn't listen to a single word I said, did you?"

I bit my lip in embarrassment and turned my head. "I didn't even realise you were speaking," I mumbled.

He let out a bark of amused laughter that made me smile. What a patient guy, he didn't even mind my blatant ditziness. "I'll take that as a no, then?"

"I'm sorry!" I apologised quickly. "What did you say?"

"I asked you how in Davy Jones' locker am I supposed to take you to your lessons when I don't know what you have?"

I paused and then pivoted on my heel to grin at him. "Did Mr Manly just quote Spongebob?" I teased.

His cheeks slowly turned a light pink. "Ehm...I h-have two little brothers," he stammered, and upon seeing my amused face, he mock-glared. "Hey, you understood that reference, that makes you just as bad!"

I looked down at the Spongebob pendant I had hanging on my charm chain that my baby cousin had gotten for me, alongside my other lucky pendants. "Now, how is it possible that I know about Spongebob?" I asked slowly, purposefully dangling my necklace in front of his eyes.

Clark narrowed his eyes and pointed his finger at me. "Will you just tell me where your class is?"

"What's the matter?" I baited.

"I can't see my forehe--oh fuck!"

I wiggled my eyebrows. "Yes, Patrick?"

He waved me away. "Forget you," he grumbled, stomping ahead.

"Wait, Clark!" I called, taking longer strides to catch up with him. "I'm sorry, I was just teasi-"

"Chill, Charlie. I know." He flashed me a toothy grin. "Are you trying to avoid the question?"

"What question?"

"Where is your next class? I swear, I won't stalk you if it makes you that uncomfortable." He grinned.

I smiled sheepishly. "Oh! Ehm...I have English Literature now."

Clark's eyes brightened, and I took in how happy he appeared that I was still following him - oh wow, he was so nice.

He took my elbow and began dragging me off. "I know where that is, let's go! Quickly, my History of Theatre lesson starts in five minutes!"

"Then why'd you offer to walk me? I don't want you to be late!" I said guiltily. I hated it when people went out of their way for me. It was never necessary, and they could be helping themselves instead of me.

"Because I want to, Charlie, Jesus Christ."

I cocked my head and stared at the back of his blond head. He seemed sincere enough, and that was good enough for me!

"That boy likes you, Casanova," Ginny tittered, knocking me with her shoulder.

"Why would he?" I asked, highly confused

"Oh, I don't know." She pretended to ponder it for a minute. "Maybe it's because you're pretty?"

"That's shallow though, and he doesn't seem shallow." In fact, Clark was the absolute opposite of shallow.

"Shut your yapping mouth, did I say I was finished speaking?"

"I wasn't yapping!" I exclaimed defensively.

"Charlie, maybe he likes you because you're sweet, or because you're funny, or because you're a disgustingly positive son of a bitch-"

"Was that a compliment?" I wondered.

"I'm not done speaking yet!"

"You're never done speaking." I looked at my best friend incredulously, watching as she casually brought out an apple and industrial size jar of Nutella from the depths of her tiny backpack. "Where are you getting all this food?"

"They're all gifts from admirers, Charlie, don't look at me that."

"Ginny, that technically means that you're a prostitute."

Ginny rolled her eyes. "You're just avoiding the subject."

"What subject?" I asked, tipping my head curiously.

She stared at me for a minute. "Charlie, have I ever told you that you're a brainless centipede?"

"Yes, but like all the other times you've called me that, I still don't understand why you had to choose centipede of all things."

"Wow, shit, you don't even know that you're avoiding the subject, do you? You honestly forgot what we were literally just talking about."

I smiled weakly. "What were we talking about again?"

Ginny groaned out loud and shoved the Nutella jar in my face. "Take it! Just take it, you're probably hungry."

"I can't eat when I'm on the job. And by the way, you can't either."

She glanced down at her uniform and waved her hand airily. "Diana's not here to complain, so who gives a shite?"

I just shook my head at her. "You're an awful employee. Put that food away, and take this Nutella back!"

"You're not you when you're hungry, Charlie!"

I laughed at her. "I'm not hungry, though."

"But it's Nutella," she sang, waving the jar in front of me.

"I'm allergic to hazel nuts, you cheesehead."

She pouted and took an exaggerated bite of her apple before shoving both things in her purse and stowing it under the counter. "Where's Diana, anyway?"

"I'm right here, and I need one of you to take the truck and deliver the raspberry-cream cake to this address."

Diana heaved an enormous red box up and out of the display case and placed it on the counter. She peered at us expectantly through her glasses, her eyes piercing even in her old age. "I'll do it!" Ginny announced, pulling off the Good Eats apron and throwing it at me. "That way, I can eat on the ride," she added to me in a whisper.

"Okay, Virginia, just be prompt about it, don't leave Charlotte by herself like last time."

I smiled reassuringly at Diana. "Oh, that was no problem, I can handle it."

"Suck up," Ginny coughed. I lightly pinched her side and she stuck her tongue out.

Diana scowled at us. "I know you can handle it, but I want to make sure Virginia here is doing her share of the work at well!"

"Of course I am!" Ginny exclaimed in outrage. "Jesus, Di, get your knickers untwisted already."

"Ginny, keep quiet," I whispered, watching as Diana's fluffy white hair puffed up more from her frustration. It was a wonder she hadn't fired Ginny already.

"Just go, Virginia, please," Diana sighed, before waddling back into her office in the back.

"I hate it when she calls me Virginia. It's like she's calling me vagina, or virginity," Ginny grumbled, grabbing her purse and the cake box. "I'll see you in ten...maybe twenty if I stop to get some Starbucks."

"Okay, bye, Virginia!" I teased. She flipped me off and skipped to the front door.

"The fuck," I heard her exclaim just outside the door. "What the fuck are you doing, just standing in front of here like a freak? Jesus Christ! Go the fuck inside if you want to see her!"

I raised my eyebrows at her language, but then my eyes widened as she shoved a certain growling someone straight head first through the door. "Benny?"

Chapter 6

Why the fuck would I stalk a chick that I didn't even like? I wasn't stalking her.

Lottie had dropped her wallet when Clark pulled her away to her class, and there was money and her student ID and her worker's badge and license, so obviously she would needed it at some point, right?

And even if I'm some arrogant asshole, I'm not just gonna leave the wallet for another bigger ass to steal it when I was perfectly capable of bringing it to her.

When that brunette bitch screeched at me and then bodily tossed me inside that stupid little bakery, I was pissed. I planned to just drop the wallet outside and throw something at the door to get Lottie's attention, but no.

Some fucker had to come out while I was contemplating what to do, and make my entrance that much more notice-able.

"Benny!" Lottie exclaimed when I straightened, my face screwing up with anger at her nickname for me.

"Here," I muttered brusquely, striding up to the counter and slamming her wallet next to her.

At the sight of it, her eyes lit up tenfold and she let loose a thousand-watt beam that unnecessarily astonished the grimace out of me. "Hey!" she said happily, turning her shining eyes on me.

"Whatever," I mumbled, turning my eyes away so that I wouldn't have to see that cheesy smile of hers.

"Thank you, thank you, Benny!" She clasped her hands together and jumped over the counter, flinging her arms around my neck.

"Whoa, whoa, what are you doing?" I snapped, my arms raising slightly, refusing to wrap them around her.

"I'm thanking you!" she replied cheerily, her feet swaying as she hovered off the ground, since I was a bit taller than her.

"Well, stop it," I grunted, pulling her off of me. Her smile didn't drop even as I shuffled away from her, and I frowned at that.

Why was she always so happy? It fucking pissed me off. Did she even have any other emotions?

I glared at her to make sure she would stay away, and then turned around to leave. All I wanted to do was leave that fucking wallet for her to find, and then run away. If she didn't even find it, I couldn't care less, at least I tried, right? But that stupid friend of hers had to catch me.

For Chrissakes, if that was happened every time I did a good deed, then fuck everything.

"Wait!"

I ignored her and kept walking away. In fact, I had even gotten outside, except she somehow dashed in front of me and spread her limbs so that she was blocking my path. "What do you want, Shortcake?" I hissed. "I brought you your goddamn wallet, now would you just bloody leave me alone?"

Her expression flickered from happy to upset to happy again so quickly that I thought I might've hallucinated the hurt on her face, except that the smile was a little bit smaller.

I would've felt guilty if I wasn't satisfied that I'd gotten her to show an emotion other than joy. "Thank you," I enunciated a moment later, when I realised she wasn't replying.

She looked away for a moment and then glanced back at me with those big doe-like eyes of hers, and I almost found myself speechless when she cocked her head with a soft expression on her face. Like she didn't even mind that I had just snapped at her. "You just...you dropped your phone," she spoke softly, stretching out her hand.

I furrowed my eyebrows when I saw it in her outstretched palm. She would actually give me back my mobile even when I was so rude to her?

Of course she would. It was Lottie, for Chrissakes.

Okay, now I felt like a first class son-of-a-bitch. I took my phone from her and hesitated. She still had that kindly look on her face, and it did nothing to make me feel less mean. But why the hell was I feeling mean? I didn't even like this girl, so why was I feeling bad?

"Thanks, Lottie," I said slowly.

She smiled slightly and stretched out her hand as if to pat my arm, but quickly retracted it and waved. "See you later, Benny," she sang, before skipping away to the inside of the bakery.

My eyebrows furrowed again and I looked down at my hand to see that it was outstretched in her direction. Okay, what was going on with me?

That was it. I was officially crazy. I let out a low groan and ran a hand through my hair in frustration. "Girls," I cursed.

I stomped into the bakery again, startling Lottie out of a daydream. She blinked at me and smiled, though she still looked confused. "Did I drop anything else?" she asked jokingly.

I didn't say anything, I just walked up to the counter and stared down at her little bell. I couldn't quite look her in the eye with her staring at me with those well-meaning grass green eyes.

I sighed and dug inside my jeans pocket to bring out a packet of gummy sweets my friend Queenie had given me. I laid it on the counter as some sort of peace offering and then glanced up at her. She was - no surprise - smiling at me. Before she could comment or hug me or something even more ridiculous, I high-tailed it out of there before she managed to make me doubt myself even more.

I let out a deep breath once I was home clear and looked over my shoulder at the tinted windows of the bakery. At least now I felt a little bit better, and that was good enough. My phone rang at that moment and I picked up without checking caller ID. "Hello?"

"Benjamin!" a familiar voice sang.

"Hey Ms. Wallace, need me to pick up Queenie?" I answered, trying to catch my breath from running up the stairs.

"Oh, how thoughtful of you to ask! I didn't want to trouble you, but..."

"It's no trouble," I replied mechanically, used to these conversations. "Want me to head up to the school now?"

"Oh, yes please! I have a hair appointment now, and I cannot miss it!"

"Of course, I'll take her to my place and you can pick her up whenever you're ready, sound good?"

"Thank you so much, Benjamin! I know I can always count on you!"

"Yeah, it's no problem Ms. Wallace. I'll see you later."

"Bye bye!"

I hung up. Looked like I would be missing my Psych lecture.

Even though Ms Wallace meant well, she didn't really know what being a mum entailed, and so those responsibilities fell on me - a near stranger who just happened to help her one day with her groceries and ended up being her makeshift-nanny.

If anybody ever found out about that, I would be finished. My reputation would be over, and people would start to think of me as approachable. I couldn't have that. I needed everyone to leave me alone. That was why I needed to stay away from Lottie. Because if I let myself be nice to her, she'd keep expecting it. And it had been a long time since someone had expected good will from me, and it was too late to change that.

For now, Queenie and Clark were my only exceptions.

Chapter 7

Once I got off work, I drove over to a park nearby where I could eat Ben's sweeties without Ginny snatching them away like I knew she would. I grinned at the packet. Even though he didn't know it, gummy worms were one of my absolute favourites, and that was what he had given me.

Add that to the fact that Benjamin Fisher had given me sweets, and I was on Cloud 9. I mean, sure it had been out of guilt, but that must've meant that he'd felt at least a little compassion towards me, right? And that compassion was enough to satiate me for the time being, since he obviously wouldn't have changed his attitude towards me completely.

Why did I even care about getting on his good side? I didn't really know, all I knew was that when I saw that glimmer of amusement in his eyes, it made me very, very happy, and I knew I wanted to see it again. Maybe even a smile if I was lucky.

But I had to be very, very lucky.

I sat down on the cool metal bench of the swing and gently pushed myself back so that I was swaying as I ate the gummy worms - savouring each sweet, chewy bite. First the head comes off, then each notch of the body, and then finally the tip. "I love sweeties!" I sang loudly, propelling myself higher off the ground.

"I love sweeties, too," a small voice cheered, and I felt the swing set rattle as someone plopped down in the other seat.

I turned my head with a worm dangling out of my mouth and blinked at the small girl rocking next to me with something sticky covering her mouth. "Hello!" I greeted with a smile. "How are you doing, sweetheart?"

She grinned a red-toothed smile at me and gave me a thumbs up. She had a bright red lollipop hanging between her lips and was sucking on it happily.

"Wow, you're a messy one, aren't you?" I stopped swinging and placed my hand on her rope to get her to stop. "Why don't I wipe your face, eh?" I knew it was weird that I was cleaning random children's faces, but who cared? I took out one of my travel-size wet wipe packs from my purse and used one of the wet wipes to scrub all the sugar off her face.

The cute little girl squirmed and batted away my hand. "No!" she squeaked, her little feet kicking at me energetically.

"I'll give you a gummy worm if you stop moving," I compromised, showing her my precious packet. As if I'd flipped a switch, she became as still as a statue, her spine stiff and her wide-eyed expression hilarious. It was almost comical how quickly she stopped moving.

I smiled, pleased, and knelt down next to this child, wiping away any last trace of lolly, and winking when I realised her big brown eyes were staring at me. "There we are!" I exclaimed cheerily, standing up and patting her head of unruly blonde curls. "And here you are!" I presented her with my beloved sweeties as promised, and laughed delightedly when her eyes bugged out in shock.

"I have these same sweeties!" she declared loudly, jumping up and down. She was so bouncy that she began smacking my thigh, kind of hard for a five year old. I grabbed her hand to get her to stop and she began shaking around the gummy worms instead.

"Oh really?" I asked lightly, cocking my hip. "Where are they?"

"They're right here!" she squealed, waving around the bag I had just given her.

I laughed again, and then frowned. "Where's your mummy, darling?" I asked curiously, glancing around the park. There were quite a few parents and kids lolling about, but none that I would've guessed to be this sweet little girl's.

"Mummy has gone out!"

"Then is your daddy here?"

She cocked her head, looking confused. "Daddy?"

"Queenie, would you stop running off?"

The little girl and I turned around and I spotted a very annoyed Ben stomping towards us.

"Benjy!" Queenie squeaked, taking off towards him.

My widened eyes were quickly accompanied by a gaping mouth when he opened his arms and caught her mid-jump, the momentum forcing him to stumble back. Queenie laughed loudly and hugged Ben's neck with one arm, the other tightly clenching the packet of sweets.

At the adorable sight in front of me, I couldn't help but let out a quiet "aww." Big, bad Ben was currently hugging a little girl. I didn't even think he knew what a child was, much less be so good at handling them. Was that his baby?

"What are you doing here?" he abruptly asked me.

I blinked twice and shook myself out of my daze. Ben gave me a weirded out look and set Queenie on her feet, before glaring at me.

"What are you doing here?" he repeated in a low, angry voice. "Are you following me?"

I was taken aback at how mad he seemed. What did I do this time? "Why would I be following you?" I replied, puzzled. I hardly knew him, how was I to know where he went on a daily basis?

He looked down at Queenie and frowned. "Where did you get those, Queenie?" he asked, taking the packet of sweets from her small hands.

"Hey!" she complained, batting at his knees. "Those are mine, the nice lady gave them to me!"

"Queenie!" he scolded, holding the bag out of her reach. "Why would you take them from her?"

"I gave them to her," I interrupted, grinning slightly at how fatherly he was behaving. "It was a reward for keeping still."

"Yeah!" Queenie exclaimed, stomping her foot and wrinkling her nose. "The nice lady gave them to me for staying still while she cleaned my face!"

Ben snapped his head to me, and I widened my eyes at how cross he still was. "Do you ever keep anything for yourself?" he asked crossly.

I shrugged and smiled. "I had a few and then gave it to her if that makes you feel any better."

Ben scrutinised me, causing me to squirm slightly under his gaze. "It doesn't," he said brusquely, before passing me the gummy worms.

"Hey, it's okay, just let her have them-"

"I'm taking her out for ice-cream, she doesn't need any more sugar," he interrupted, waving me away. "Come on, Queenie, let's go."

I sighed and turned around to leave. He really didn't like me, did he? That shouldn't have hurt as much as it did. I mean, I'd only known him for three days, and he glared at me every time he saw me. It was kind of down-heartening.

"Wait! Can the nice lady come?" Queenie pleaded suddenly.

I swivelled around, and upon seeing Ben's horrorstruck face, I smiled widely, even though I was beginning to feel my self-esteem be crushed. "No, honey, I can't, I'm already set." I waved around the sweets and gave her a thumbs up.

She frowned at me, and then tugged on Ben's sweater. I knew it was going to be a problem, and I didn't want to bother Ben more than I already had, so I waved quickly and turned around again to walk away.

"You can come."

My head snapped up and I stared at Ben, who appeared quite as ease as he regarded me. "I shouldn't, I can't," I tried. It wasn't helping that I was really craving ice cream right now.

"Queenie likes you for some reason, so would you just stop being so stubborn and come?"

I hesitated and looked down at the ground. "I don't want to be a burden," I replied, almost silently.

Ben sighed heavily. "Would you just come? Jesus, it's ice cream, I'm not taking you out to dinner."

My cheeks flamed up, but I managed to meet his look with a wide smile. He was willingly letting me come with him and his little friend? Willingly? Okay, maybe it was for Queenie, but still. My smile widened and I clasped my hands together. "Okay," I agreed a little breathlessly. I wasn't sure why I was so happy, but it didn't matter at all. Benjamin Fisher wasn't glaring at me for once. It was something to put in the history books!

I'd probably been standing still for too long, because Ben's easy expression became a glare again. "Hurry up, we have to go now."

I ran after him and Queenie, who was currently eyeing my sweeties with a hungry look on her face. I bent down to her level and whispered, "Maybe I can hide some in your ice cream."

She beamed widely at me and began running faster. "Come on, Benjy! I want to eat ice cream now!"

Ben scooped her up in one swift movement and silenced her with a stern look. "Keep your mouth closed, Queenie, otherwise I'll lock you in the boot!"

I smothered a giggle at his tone, and bit my lip hard to keep from smiling, but when Queenie started complaining, I couldn't help it. Ben glanced at me at the sound of my laugh, and when I thought he was going to snap, he didn't. He didn't even frown. In fact, he actually sort of smiled. It was a hidden one, and it was one that looked like he didn't want it to surface, but nonetheless, it was an upturning of lips. It was a tiny little baby smile.

Now I knew why I was working so hard to be his friend.

Chapter 8

Yes, my friend Queenie was a six year old girl.

"Why does it take so long to pick out ice cream?" I grumbled, crossing my arms as I shook my head at the two girls who had their faces pressed against the glass.

Lottie glanced at me and smiled nicely. "It's a very important decision, Ben! Cookies and cream or cookie dough, that is the question."

"That is the question," Queenie repeated, giggling. Since she wasn't tall enough to see through the glass at the ice cream, she was perched on Lottie's hip.

"Alright, poppet, which one do you think looks good today?"

"They look the same every day!" I interjected, throwing my hands in the air. Jesus, it was just ice cream.

Lottie and Queenie glanced at each other and then looked at me with identical playfully pitiful expressions. "Oh man, he doesn't know the art of choosing the perfect ice cream, does he?" I heard Lottie whisper. I raised my eyebrows at her and.

"Benjy doesn't even like ice cream," Queenie replied in a tone that was just short of horror.

Lottie gave an exaggerated gasp and looked at me. "He doesn't?" she exclaimed.

I crossed my arms defensively. "Why is that so bad?Just pick already!" I groaned in annoyance. We'd been standing around for five minutes, and the lady at the cashier was staring at us.

"Hm...what'll you be having, princess?" Lottie asked Queenie, propping her more securely on her hip.

I noticed her arms shaking slightly from the weight of Queenie's body and I rolled my eyes. Jesus, was it that hard to ask me for help? I plucked Queenie from Lottie's grasp. Lottie stared at me, looking a little shocked. "Pick!" I demanded, holding Queenie away from my body and dangling her almost above the counter, trying to ignore Lottie's penetrating green gaze.

"Benjy, will you buy me a cho-co-lutt ice cream?" she pleaded, widening her cute little eyes at me.

I narrowed my gaze at her. She was already using these tactics to get what she wanted? I was almost impressed. "One chocolate on a cone, please," I told the worker, who nodded brightly. "Now what about you?" I added to Lottie.

She smiled at me and then turned to face the counter. "One cookie dough in a cup, if you please!" she chirped brightly, that constant smile of hers not wavering. "It was a cookie dough kind of day, you know?"

I couldn't meet her happy look. "I guess."

She laughed that tinkling laugh of hers, and I was so put off by the way the sound startled me that it took a minute to realise that she was paying for the ice cream.

"Hey!" I said quietly, my eyebrows furrowing crossly as she accepted the change from the cashier. "Who said you could pay?"

"You didn't want me to?" she asked in confusion, looking taken aback as though she didn't think it was morally right to allow me to pay.

"Of course I didn't want you to, what told you otherwise?" I replied. I watched her confused face and huffed. "Who's been making you pay for them?"

Lottie's green-eyed gaze softened and she shrugged. "Well, I've always been the one to pay, except around Ginny, and nobody's complained before."

I took in a sharp breath. Honestly, how'd she make it this far in life without accidentally selling off her soul in exchange to help a man cross the street?

"Why're you so mad?" she asked quietly, looking down at her feet.

I groaned softly. "Of course they never complained. They wanted to save their money because people are greedy assh-"

"How's the ice cream, Princess?" Lottie interrupted brightly, and I almost threw her ice cream at the wall before I realised she'd stopped me from cursing in front of a little kid.

I walked outside and gripped Queenie tightly, trying to exhaust some of the anger in my body. I wasn't sure what it was about her, but Charlotte Carter had shaken me up, and I wasn't sure whether that was a good or bad thing.

"Ben?"

I snapped my eyes to her, but she didn't seem scared in the slightest; in fact, she even seemed a bit amused. "Why are you calling me Ben?" I growled in frustration, not even sure why I was annoyed that she wasn't calling me by that repulsive nickname.

"Isn't that your name?" she teased lightly, smiling that smile of hers. I gave her a flat look to show her that I wasn't impressed. "Well, I figured since you didn't like it, I'd stop."

"When have you ever cared about what I do and don't like?" Because if she had, I wouldn't be forced to put up with her right now.

Lottie grinned brightly. "I do care about what you do and don't like."

I pointed at her. "And that's your problem!" I said. "You care too much! Have you ever cared about yourself before others?"

"Of course!" she replied immediately.

I glanced at Queenie. "Oh yeah?" I challenged. "When was the last time you did something for yourself without thinking of the benefit of others?"

Her eyes widened and a flicker of hurt passed through them, sending a strange shot of pain through my chest. What was going on with me? "I do respect myself," she argued weekly.

"Whatever," I said. "It doesn't matter because I don't care."

I turned to walk away and take Queenie home, but her next words froze me stiff.

"If you don't care as much as you say you don't, then why are you getting so angry with me?"

My eyes closed and my breathing grew raspier in irritation. She was right. Why was I getting so angry? I needed to get away from her.

I needed to stay away before she buried herself any deeper than she already had.***I ran my hand through my hair and glared at my carpeted floor.

Clark watched me, a sleeping Queenie stretched across his lap. "Why'd you call me over?" he asked, the mirth in his voice obvious.

I moved my scowl to him. "Why the fuck do you sound like that?"

Clark grinned widely, which only made my scowl deepen. "Well, Benny, it's just that I've never seen you so torn up about something before."

I pointed my finger at him. "Don't call me Benny!" I snapped, struggling to keep my voice low so as to not wake up Queenie.

He raised his hands in surrender, but that teasing glint was still in his eyes. "What, Charlie's allowed to, and I, your bestest friend in the entire world, isn't?"

"Who the hell is Charlie?"

"Oh, I'm sorry." Clark smirked. "I meant Lottie."

My hands curled into fists at the sound of him calling her that, and I had no idea why. "Shut up," I said, turning away so that he wouldn't see the red on my face.

"What's she done, Ben? I've never seen you so on edge before." He dropped the cheeriness and sounded a bit worried. I breathed deeply. If there was anyone I could count on, it was Clark, no matter how annoying he got.

"Maybe I'm so on edge because I need to punch something." That was probably it. It explained the flush my face got around her and the way my muscles tensed whenever she smiled that smile that made it seem like she could fix the entire world.

"I don't think that's it," Clark mused, tapping his chin.

"Then what?" I growled. "I'm tired of being around her and getting like this every time!"

"Well, first of all, you need to calm the fuck down. It's not even her making you mad, is it?"

"It's her whole existence," I insisted. "She's so annoying, how do you like her? She lets people step all over her and then smiles that fucking smile like she doesn't even care! She wouldn't care if all of her limbs got taken away as long as some stupid oaf got a nice meal!"

Clark stared at me for a long time before he grinned this insanely creepy grin that made me scoot further away from him. "That fucking smile?" he repeated in a sing song voice.

"I didn't mean it like that, Jesus-"

"I see the problem," he injected confidently.

I crossed my arms, interested to know what exactly he'd come up with. "Oh yeah? And what is it?"

"You care about her because you're just a big ol' softie, aren't you?"

"Nope! There's no way I could care about some lass I've only known for a few days."

"We're not in fucking Egypt, Benjamin. Stop being in denial and is it even possible for you to not be so stubborn?"

I closed my eyes tightly. "Nah. There's no way I care."

"You obviously don't hate her if you're all torn up about what happened in the ice cream shop."

"I do," I replied instantly, but it sounded weak, even to my ears.

Clark threw his hands up in the air. "Whatever you say, Benny. There's no getting through your thick skull."

"Don't call me Benny!"

I don't care about her.

Chapter 9

"Charlie!" I heard Ginny screech as she entered the dorm, followed by the sound of her taking a swing at anything that stood in her way.

I peeked my head out of our room and grabbed her arm as she stomped down the hallway. "Oh wow," I said, a slight crease forming between my eyebrows. "What's gotten into your knickers?"

She stumbled inside and almost collapsed on the floor, but I took her arm and guided her to her bed.

"Are you drunk, Virginia?" I asked sternly, staring at her. It was ten in the morning!

"I am not called Vagina," she muttered indignantly.

I raised my eyebrows. "Uh huh," I said, nodding.

"I'm not drunk," she protested, swatting away my fluttering hands. "Jesus, stop hovering!"

I bit my lip. I always worried about her - she tended to hook up spontaneously when she got drunk, and there was only one reason why she would drink in the first place. "What happened?" I asked softly, taking her by the elbow so she would stop smacking me.

"Nothing!"

I stared at her stuttering and bright red face. "Are you sure?"

"Yeah..."

She had something she was trying to hide. I sighed. "Which guy was it?" I asked.

"Zachary!" she suddenly wailed, throwing her arms around me and burying her face in my neck. "I went to a party to break up with him, but he kissed another girl before I could!" At ten in the morning?

I rubbed her back soothingly, but at her words, my eyes widened. She never got upset when one of her boyfriends cheated on her, and she was never this teary over being dumped first. It hurt her pride whenever it happened, but never reduced her a mess like right now. "Do you...do you like him?" I asked. I was treading on thin waters here. Ginny didn't do crushes.

"Of course I liked him! He was fucking fit and the sex was incredible!"

I winced slightly at her words. "That's not what I meant. I mean, do you...fancy him?"

The hands that clutched my neck tightened almost imperceptibly, but I still felt it. "No," she replied, a bit too quickly to sound like the truth.

"You can tell me, you know?" I said quietly, massaging her back. "You don't have to, but you can if you want to, whenever you want."

"Thanks, Charlie. You're the best friend ever," she mumbled.

I smiled and released her, gently pushing her on her back. Now that her tear ducts were dry, she needed rest. "Here, have a little kip, my shift starts soon. When I come back, I'll bring back some films and we can have a movie-and-cupcake marathon!"

She blinked at me. "Pride and Prejudice and double chocolate chunk?" she ordered more than asked, already almost like her usual self.

I laughed at her. "Of course, I'm in the mood for some Darcy, myself. I'll just leave some aspirin for you and be off."

"Yeah, okay," she said, snuggling under her covers and turning to face the wall.

I grabbed the aspirin bottle from a bathroom cabinet and placed it at her bedside table. Then I picked up my keys and locked the room, before skipping over to my car and starting the engine. When I reached the bakery, I frowned when I realised that it was locked. I unlocked it, flipped the sign to 'Open,' and checked in.

While I tied on my apron, I popped my head in Diana's office to see if she was in. A little note was stuck to the desk. It said, 'Charlotte, I won't be in until late this afternoon. Be a dear and pop the cream puffs in the oven and fill them with cream later. Don't forget the powdered sugar on top!'

I almost jumped up and down with excitement. I loved cream puffs, especially the ones she made.

Working at the bakery was really the best thing for me. It always smelt like fresh bread and sweet frosting, and it was a bright and open space. I pattered over to the back room where the cream puff dough had been rising and smiled giddily.

Once everything was in the oven and I'd whipped the cream and put it in the fridge, I walked back to the front counter and waited for customers.

Later, when the cream puffs were done and cooled, I set them on the counter and started filling them using the piping bag filled with cream. My god, they looked so good...good enough to eat, in fact.

I grinned widely and pulled two fifty pence pieces from my pocket, placing them in the till. "You beauty," I whispered to the cream puff that was now in my hand, and I took a huge bite.

The dough was slightly sweet and chewy, and the cream was light and smooth, and it was so delicious that I couldn't help but scarf the five inch thing in a matter of seconds.

A cleared throat brought me down from my high, and I almost choked on the last bite. My eyes watered slightly while I glanced up, and then I almost passed out when I realised who it was.

My face probably lit up to fifty shades of red before I smiled widely. "Hello Benny, Clark!" That was so embarrassing. It literally took all I had to not run away from embarrassment.

"Those look delicious," Clark said without replying, a hungry gleam in his eyes.

I laughed - everybody looked like that when they entered the bakery. "Would you like to try one?" I asked, wiping my hands on my apron.

"How much?"

"One pound per each."

He quickly shoved a five pound note onto the counter, grabbed five completed puffs, and hurried over to one of the little tables at the front. As soon as he sat down, he was stuffing his face.

My grin widened, until I realised that Ben was still standing there awkwardly. "Do you want one?" I asked kindly.

He immediately scowled, and I wondered why he wasn't moving to sit with his friend if he disliked me so much. "I don't like sweets," he replied. "You know that." I did know that.

"These aren't sugary, I promise," I said. "They're not too plain, not too sweet! I think you'll like it."

He paused and stared at me. I shifted around, not knowing where to place my gaze. "You're seriously good at that."

"Good at what?"

"Persuading people to eat that shit - I don't even want it but you're making me want it."

That was the closest I've ever gotten to a compliment from him. The thought made my smile turn into a beam. "Does that mean you want to try it? I made it myself! I mean, I didn't mix the dough, but I baked it and filled it with cream and I would be so happy if you'd just give it a try!"

"Do it, Ben," Clark said over a mouthful of cream. I laughed when I saw the powdered sugar dusting his chin, making him look years younger.

"Fine."

I almost exploded with happiness with that one word, and lightly bounced on the tips of my toes as he handed me the money and took a cream puff from my hand.

"Christ. Stop jumping around, Lottie," Ben said, glaring at me. I loved it when he called me by that name, for some reason.

I tried to keep still for him, but the sugar may have already hit my blood, because now my whole body was trembling. "Try it!" I said excitedly, my eyes shining. My hands clasped together as I watched him, and he became sort of uncomfortable.

I heard Clark laugh. "Go ahead, Ben. Make her smile and eat it."

Ben shot him a glare. "I don't even have to eat this thing to make her smile." He shoved the cream puff in his mouth and chewed.

I stared and watched as his expression changed as he ate. I couldn't tell whether he liked it or not, but he didn't look disgusted, which I supposed was a start.

A tiny flickering of a smile lit at my lips. I loved watching how people's moods changed because of a simple treat, and the way Ben seemed a little floored made me strangely triumphant.

"How was it?" I asked eagerly. The pause he made as he contemplated his answer was enough for me to die and be reincarnated from the apprehension.

Ben smiled.

Chapter 10

I don't think I'd like it - I really didn't. It wasn't only because I'm a dickhead, but I just don't like sweets. But Lottie was staring at me with stars in her eyes and I could hear Clark's obnoxious laughter coming from behind me, so I had to do it.

When I took a bite, I was shocked. It was like biting into a creamy, fluffy cloud. The sweetness came mostly from the powdered sugar on top - just the right amount for someone like me that didn't do sugar. I couldn't stop the lazy smile that stretched across my face, because Lottie knew what I liked before even I did.

Once I finished the entire thing, I looked up and immediately wished I hadn't. She was staring at me, and if I thought her happiness had reached its limit when I said I'd eat the damn thing, I was dead wrong.

I almost wanted to cover my eyes, because it seemed like the way she smiled should be private, shown only to the most special people. It made me a little angry, but I wasn't sure why. But this was Lottie we were talking about - I had no idea where her Happy Metre let off. "You liked it?" Her voice went up about three octaves from her excitement. I would've winced, except with Lottie, it just cute.

Oh god, I was getting soft.

My eyes narrowed as she began bouncing again. "It's not bad," I said. Her smile didn't dim at all, and the slight annoyance I felt became apparent in the scowl on my face. I wondered if she could be serious.

"Good," she replied simply. Her green eyes twinkled and two bright red spots appeared high on her cheeks. She looked like a woman who would give you the world on a platter if it would make you happy.

Without another word, she gathered the remaining puffs, arranging them neatly in the display thing that lay below the front counter.

I sighed and walked over to Clark, collapsing on the chair across from him. He grinned creepily at me, and with the sugar coating his chin, I felt the need to run away. "What?" I said.

He shook his head and stared at Lottie weirdly until she straightened, tossed us a polite smile, and disappeared into the back room. "I saw that!" he sang obnoxiously, as soon as she was out of earshot.

"What?" I pressed, my expression darkening.

"It's funny, actually," he said, ignoring me completely. "When I see her by myself, she's sweet, but she's so calm. But the second she sees you, she gets super excited. Care to explain?"

I hated that all-knowing smirk he wore. The words he spoke were untrue. It was impossible. "I can't take you seriously when you look like you tripped and fell on a line of cocaine," I said.

Clark rolled his eyes and dusted off his chin. "I think she fancies you."

I couldn't answer straight away, because my brain was shouting obscenities at my heart for finding the idea of Lottie liking me satisfying. "Don't talk to me," I told Clark angrily. She didn't fancy me. I was a dick and she was the opposite of that.

"I thought you wanted her," I said, annoyed. "Why do you have to push me on this?"

"I do like her." Did I just want to punch my best friend? "But not romantically. In a platonic way." And now the urge was gone.

I nodded absentmindedly to Clark, wondering where the relief was coming from. I thought back to Lottie and her beaming smile, and felt myself get annoyed again for absolutely no reason. Her smile made me so mad that my breathing got shorter and heavier, and made me feel warm.

"Why do I get so mad at her?" I blurted out. If there was one thing I hated, it was talking feelings. That shit made me feel sort of filthy.

Clark leant forward and stared at me gleefully. "You're jealous," he stated matter-of-factly. "You're absolutely jealous!"

I grimaced. "Of what?"

He grinned, as though he was thoroughly enjoying psycho-analysing me. "Charlie smiles at anyone she sees - you're annoyed because they're not rare smiles, so it's not all that special when you get one."

I blinked, slightly short of completely shocked. "When did you become such an expert?"

"I'm going for my degree in Psychology, remember? Why don't you give her a chance?"

I stared at the table and scowled because I didn't want to be discussing this. I didn't like feelings. "I think I'm more worried about her not giving me a chance."

"You shouldn't worry about what she'll think of your family, dude. And, sure, she smiles at everybody, but the difference is she smiles at you like she puts you up on a pedestal."

I couldn't for the life of me understand why. I'd been a bastard to her this whole time - was she masochistic or something? They was no way she could brush off my horrid words each and every time. Right then, Lottie returned from the back room, and so we immediately shut our mouths and looked at her. She seemed to have forgotten we were there, and was cheerfully humming a little tune.

I stayed quiet and just watched her. She was really quite pretty, and her face always had a friendly, approachable look about it. I always thought that she was all smiles and that there was nothing else there, but as I watched, I noticed how her mouth puckered in worry, or how her eyebrows furrowed as though she was upset.

For some reason, I felt my chest ache and wondered what was going on with me. I barely knew the girl, so why was I feeling so protective? Like whoever bothered her needed to come answer to me.

Oh Christ. This couldn't be happening. That satisfied feeling I got from the fact that maybe Lottie looked at me differently had to be something else. Christ. No. This was so new to me, and I didn't like it. I didn't want to be all caught up over some girl, but at the same time, I wanted her to see me. Not Ben the Bumface, but Ben...just Ben.

"Go ask her to have coffee with you," Clark whispered to me, and I looked at him as though he was stupid.

"No," I replied firmly. She was still annoying, and I had no desire to see her when she was all bubbly over caffeine.

"Do it," he ordered.

I shook my head stubbornly. "I don't want to," I said.

"Why not?"

"I barely know her."

He scoffed quietly. "That's what dates are for, you idiot. You get to know each other."

"I don't want to go on a date with her!"

"Did I ask you what you wanted to do?"

"You can't order me around."

"Do it or I'll do it for you."

My eyes narrowed. "You wouldn't."

There was that creepy smile again. "Try me."

I didn't want to try him, so I abruptly got out of my seat and walked over to the counter, trying to act as casual as possible.

Lottie was currently drying off a metal bowl, so I waited until she was done and then cleared my throat. She almost fell over in surprise, but when she saw me, a smile enveloped her face. My words died in my throat at the sight. Was this really different than the way she smiled at other people? Because it really looked the exact same to me.

"Hey Benny," she chirped. Why did I let her call me that again? "I thought you left already!"

"We were going to, but Ben had something to ask you, Charlie," Clark said mischievously. I shot him a glare, but he just winked and made a shooing motion.

"Is there anything you want?" she asked, and I seriously couldn't speak because of the way she sounded. It was almost unreal how much friendliness she could project into her words.

I cleared my throat again. "When's your break?"

She looked confused and glanced at the clock. Her expression brightened. "It's actually in five minutes!"

I nodded, and tried to find the words to say. Why was I doing this again? "Come have coffee with me," I blurted. I heard Clark's muffled laughter behind me and discreetly flipped him off without turning around.

"Pardon?" Lottie asked, cocking her head. Normally, I would think she was just teasing me to get me to say it again, but this was Lottie, not some other girl. She wasn't sly or flirtatious at all.

"Would you like to have coffee with me?" I repeated, a little calmer, but still quite nervous.

Lottie seemed to process my words, and when she understood, her expression seemed somewhat reserved. "Are you sure?"

It kind of bit me in the ass when she said that, because that meant she wasn't used to me not being rude, and so she wasn't sure whether I was fucking with her or not. Honestly, that made me kind of annoyed at myself. "I'm sure," I said, trying not to sound too dismissive like I usually did.

She bit her lip, and I had to force myself to look at the crease in between her eyebrows. "Then I'd love to," she said, smiling this warm smile that made my stomach feel like it was overflowing with acid.

"Okay," I said awkwardly. "I guess I'll just...wait for you to be done."

She nodded happily. "I'll be ready in a couple minutes!"

I returned her nod and immediately turned my back, not wanting her to see my flushed face. I was a mixture of emotions, but when I saw Clark's smug face, I mostly felt the violence coming out. Making sure Lottie wasn't looking, I smacked the back of his head. "You, sir, are an asshole," I hissed.

"You're going to thank me," he replied cheekily.

And the sad part was, I was pretty sure I would.

Chapter 11

I was sitting in a coffee shop, directly across from the one known as Benjamin Fisher.

I was more excited than was normal. It may not have been a big deal to most people, but he'd asked to have coffee with him. Was it a date? He hadn't given me any clue, so maybe we were just hanging out.

Whatever it was, I didn't care, because I was here with Ben. I hadn't known him long, but he made me smile, even when he was being rude. The only problem was, I didn't know what to talk about.

The waitress approached our table and deposited our coffee in front of the respective person, flashing us a large smile.

"Thank you!" I exclaimed cheerily.

She nodded once. "Would you like anything else?"

I glanced at Ben. He stared at me, and then looked at the waitress. "Could you bring us a slice of the chocolate lava cake?" he asked.

The waitress beamed at him, jotted it down on her writing pad, and trotted off. "Why did you order that cake?" I asked curiously. He'd even managed to pick the thing I'd been eyeing since we came inside. "I thought you didn't like sweet things."

"I don't," he replied. I nodded, prompting him to say more. He wouldn't say more than necessary unless you practically forced it out of him. "You...you just looked like you wanted it," he explained quickly, and then turned his head.

I had practically bit my lip in half from trying not to smile like a creeper, but those few awkward words were enough to make me want to hug him. "You're so nice!" I said, pleased by that aspect of his personality.

"Right," he said and made a weird face.

I wanted to laugh because he seemed like he was forcing himself to be rude to me. "You are," I said, nodding my head enthusiastically.

"Okay," he said, obviously not believing me. "You're a bit of a weirdo."

This time, I actually did laugh. "I know," I agreed good-naturedly. "It's a genetic trait - my mum was weird too."

Ben looked at me carefully. "Was weird," he repeated.

I was taken aback, because he was observant enough to pick up the past tense. I automatically reached for a napkin and began moulding it with my fingers. "Yeah," I said absent-mindedly. "She passed last summer."

Ben nodded once, and didn't say anything for a couple of minutes. "Why are you still smiling?" he asked suddenly.

In my surprise, my smile shrank. "Am I not allowed to?" I asked, my eyebrows furrowing. My mum was dead, okay, yeah. I loved her to pieces, but she wouldn't want me crying every day. That was why I smiled instead.

"That's not it," Ben said. "I mean, you're allowed to, but you smile like you have no care in the world. Like nothing matters but you." His tone was almost accusing.

"Actually," I said, "I have many cares, but I'd rather not be a bother to others." I smiled because my mum said it made her feel warm. I figured other people might want to feel like that too.

For a moment, Ben squeezed his eyes shut. "You're weird," he said finally, cracking his eyes back open

I shrugged. "So I've been told."

He shook his head and gulped his coffee. I wondered why he wasn't choking from the heat, because I could only take small sips at a time.

I didn't want to talk about myself anymore, so I leant on my elbows and waited for him to finish drinking. When he noticed my position, he raised an eyebrow skeptically. "How old are you?" I asked him.

"Twenty," he said, seemingly surprised by my question.

I smiled. "Me too! Actually, I turn twenty next month."

Ben looked uncomfortable. I hoped I wasn't bothering him with my chatter. "When's your birthday?"

"The third," I replied. "The third of November!"

"Then this is your second year at uni?"

My grin grew. "Nope, this is my third year. I just started school a bit young."

He nodded. "Cool," he said simply.

I took a deep breath - it was a good thing I was pretty talkative, otherwise this would've been a disaster. But then, the waitress glided our way with an enormous plate of chocolate lava cake, and my words died in my throat. "Oh," I said, my eyes widening. "Thank you very much, miss!" She shot me a smile and peeked at Ben before scurrying off. I couldn't blame her for looking - Ben was really handsome.

"You're drooling," he said and snorted, a faintly amused look on his face.

"I'm not!" I cried, but smiled anyway, because I loved it when he wasn't scowling at me. He was a handsome guy even when he frowned, but when his face was all kind, all bets were off.

"You are," he argued, gesturing to my chin.

I knew he was trying to bait me, so I crossed my arms and leant back in my chair. "Not," I said childishly and even stuck my tongue out at him. But let's be real, I was also making sure I really hadn't drooled. It was possible, though, because that cake looked more beautiful than anything I have ever seen before in my life.

I worked at a bakery, sure, but that didn't stop me from admiring creations from other places. I wasn't cheating on Good Eats, not at all. Just...checking out the competition.

Ben's forehead wrinkled as he watched me. "You were checking for drool, weren't you?" he asked after a beat.

I looked away. "No," I squeaked. When I peeked back at him, it seemed like he was struggling to hold back a smile. I bit my lip. I wanted to hear him laugh again. "Okay, I was,"

I said, throwing my hands up in the air. "Go ahead. Laugh it up."

He took one look at my pout before he began roaring with laughter, his shoulders shaking with how much he was laughing. It made me happy to see him laugh like that, and the sound was such that as soon as I heard it, I had to giggle along with him. When the noise died down, I still had a faint half-smile on my face.

"Oh Christ," Ben said, wiping a stray tear from the corner of his eye. "Why did that make me laugh so much? You're such a dummy."

I didn't even mind that he'd called me dumb, because he definitely didn't mean it. "I know," I said. "My mind tends to dim when I'm around others of higher intellect."

Ben did that tough-guy thing that guys do, you know? The one where a half-smirk lifts up one corner and they crack their necks, looking unbelievably cocky.

"The waitress looks like she's studying at Oxford," I continued innocently. He froze and glared at me, but there wasn't much heart behind the look. I snickered behind my hands.

"You're funny," he said.

"I know you want to smile," I said, wiggling my eyebrows.

And for some reason, he did.

"Thank you for paying, Benny!" I said, as we made our way outside the coffee shop.

He nodded, burying his hands inside his jeans' pockets. "I invited you, of course I paid," he muttered.

"Well, I'm happy anyway," I told him. "That means I get to buy more packs of mini M&M's at the market today."

He half-laughed and half-huffed, following me down the sidewalk. "How are your teeth not rotted from all that sugar?"

I laughed. "I brush my teeth, genius."

"I don't think I like it when you make fun of me."

"Don't be sensitive," I teased, nudging his arm. "That's what you get for inviting me out." Now, since I knew Ben better, I felt comfortable enough to be a bit cheekier than usual.

"Maybe I should just stay at home," he said, using his hand to push me further away from him.

I held back a laugh. Every time I walked too close, he'd awkwardly reach around and scoot me about two feet away. A safe distance, I suppose. "But you'd miss me."

"Most likely not."

"Probably," I agreed. Ben didn't really need me, 'cause he was all tough guy and whatnot.

This time Ben was the one nudging me. I was so surprised that I wobbled off balance and would've fallen if he hadn't caught my arm. "Did I push you that hard?" he asked, his eyebrows furrowed.

I laughed at his annoyance. "No, I'm just clumsy," I said, allowing him to help me.

"Okay," he replied warily.

There was silence for a moment. I needed to fill it up. "Do you live at school?" I asked.

"No," he said.

He wasn't one to offer up information, but I was getting used to it. "If you don't mind my asking, where do you stay?"

"Clark and I share a flat nearby."

"Yeah?" I said curiously. Jesus, he took a man of few words to the next level. "That's pretty cool."

He nodded at me. I wished he would smile a bit more, because I absolutely loved it. It made his whole face light up. But I supposed that was why I liked his smiles so much - because I rarely saw them. It made them special.

Since the coffee shop was only a couple of blocks away from uni, Ben just walked me to my room, since he had a lecture to attend.

"Hey, Benny?" I said, right before he walked away.

He inclined his head to me, acknowledging my words.

I smiled at him. Not like my regular cheesy grins, but one that tried to tell him something. "Thank you," I said.

His voice rough when he replied, "Alright," and then quickly walked away.

Ben was strange. He didn't speak much, nor did he smile, and he was extremely snappy. I didn't mind too much, though, because that little blush I caught as he turned away seemed to make all my efforts worth it.

Chapter 12

Over the next few days, I saw more of Lottie than I ever thought I could've handled before. I wouldn't call us friends because she still annoyed me. But I was slowly becoming used to her peppy self. Queenie loved her too, but I suspected that was more due to the fact that Lottie always brought her something from the bakery.

"Can we visit Charlie today?" Queenie begged. I was babysitting her again, because her mum apparently had some 'urgent, unavoidable meeting' or some shit like that. Personally, I figured she just wanted to get a facial or pedicure or something.

I groaned at the little girl. "I'm too tired," I tried to say, because I really didn't want to see Lottie. Christ, whenever I saw her, I realised I didn't know what to say or do. I had to hold my tongue, because even though she took my horrid temper like a champ, I knew I'd feel like absolute crap if I swore at her or called her names. She didn't deserve my shite personality, honestly.

But then I wondered why I second-guessed myself around her when I didn't care to do that around anyone else.

"Come on, please?" Queenie pleaded, skipping over to where I lay on my sofa. She patted my face, reminding me that I hadn't shaved yet and probably looked like homeless man.

I grabbed her hand to stop her from feeling the beginnings of my beard. "Go away," I said gruffly.

"Benjy," she whined, her already high voice going up like five octaves. I winced.

"I don't want to," I said, crossing my arms. You'd think that as the one in charge, I could say something and have her listen, but then you would be wrong. Because the truth was, that girl knew exactly what to do to make me agree to her demands.

Clark entered the room at that minute and laughed at my annoyed expression. "Just go," he told me while he walked over to the kitchen. "Stop being lazy."

"You take her, then" I said, scowling at him.

"Am I the one who desperately wants to see my lover? No."

"She is not my lover!" I snapped, struggling to rein in the plethora of insults that wanted to stream out of my mouth. Censoring myself for Queenie's benefit was exhausting. "And I don't desperately want to see her!"

Clark smirked knowingly at me. I knew that look, and it made me even more irritated. "Yeah? Is that right, Benjy?"

"Stop psycho-analysing me, freak."

"I'm not taking Queenie," he said, ignoring me.

Queenie, who had perked up upon hearing her name, pouted. "Oh, come on!" she squeaked. "I wanna see Charlie!"

Who didn't? Besides me, of course.

Of course.

"Ben will take you," Clark said. He winked at me and sprinted away before I could leap up and throttle him.

I rubbed my hand all over my face in defeat. "Fine, let's go," I muttered, standing up and grabbing my keys and wallet off the table. Lottie would just have to deal with my trashy appearance, because I wasn't changing my clothes for her.

I paused and then quickly sprayed on some cologne that was lying around before Queenie could notice.

"Yay!" Queenie squealed. I may have been frustrated, but the sound of her happiness as she scrambled to put on her shoes made my angry face smooth out. When she was ready, I ushered her into my car and drove off to Lottie's bakery.

When I unlocked the doors and helped her cross the street to the kerb, Queenie pelted head-on inside. I grimaced at her enthusiasm as I trudged along behind her. I didn't know why I'd conceded when I felt so weird coming here. It wasn't even like it was our first time visiting Lottie in the past few days.

I pushed open the entrance door, and the first thing I noticed was Queenie sitting on the floor, her mouth down-turned and her arms crossed. "What are you doing?" I asked, bewildered.

"Charlie's not here," she said and pouted even harder, practically curling into a ball. I glanced up and wasn't too sure of the disappointed flutter I felt upon seeing that Lottie wasn't standing behind the counter to greet us with her bright smile. A brunette girl was there instead and she looked immensely bored, but when she saw me, her eyes lit up in recognition.

"Hey! You're Charlie's friend, right? I'm Ginny - her best friend."

I furrowed my eyebrows at her challenging tone. "Er...good for you," I said, feeling a bit annoyed that she was talking to me. I'd come all this way for Queenie to see Lottie, and all we got was her?

"Charlie should be here soon. Her shift starts in fifteen minutes," the girl told me, seemingly peeved by my abrupt tone. I didn't know why she was mad, it wasn't even like I knew her. Christ.

"Whatever," I said, and turned away to help Queenie off the floor. "Let's just go, Queenie. Lottie's not here."

"Lottie?" the girl interrupted. "That's such a cute nickname for her. I can almost overlook your asshole-ness!"

I glared at her and her loud mouth, and was about to give her a piece of my mind when I felt something soft rest against my forearm. It was too big to be Queenie, so I opened my mouth to hiss at the person when I realised it was Lottie. She stared at me, a calming smile on her face, her eyes asking me to stop being so rude. As quickly as my hackles raised, I deflated.

The girl at the counter smirked at me, and I tried to ignore the knowing look she had on. I was calmer now, thanks to Lottie. She didn't even have to use words.

"Hey Ginny," Lottie grinned, and then jumped in surprise when she felt Queenie attach herself to her leg. "Oh my! Hello, princess."

Queenie grinned adoringly at her. "Charlie!" she said. "Did you make that special thing for me you promised you would make?"

I groaned at her shamelessness. "Queenie-"

"Yes I did, little lady," Lottie cut in, and gave her a kind smile. "Did you bring the payment?"

I was admittedly amused when Queenie brought out a mini packet of M&M's and handed them to Lottie, whose eyes sparkled happily. I almost smiled.

"Good girl!" Lottie exclaimed, bending over to pat Queenie on the head. "Let me go change into my uniform and I'll bring out that special something." She winked at me and I looked away, forcing myself to breathe as she hugged the so-called Ginny hello and disappeared into the back room.

I was too busy staring at the floor to notice Ginny smirking at me until I heard her clear her throat obnoxiously. "What was that little scene?" she asked, raising her eyebrows.

I scowled and crossed my arms. "What scene?"

Her devilish smirk widened. "Y'know, the goo-goo eyes you were giving my best friend."

"I was not giving her goo-goo eyes," I snapped. Was I? Oh god, I hoped I wasn't, because that would be so fucking embarrassing.

"Oh, sure you weren't."

"You're obnoxious."

"And you're rude, so we're even."

I would've said more, but Lottie entered right then, a pan of something in her hands. She looked excited and beckoned for me and Queenie to sit at one of the tables. She followed us and set the pan down. When I glanced inside, there was just a batch of unassuming mini vanilla cakes. They were nothing special, to be honest, but Lottie looked fit to burst. "What are these?" I asked slowly, not really wanting to hurt her feelings.

She grinned at me, and took out a box of sprinkles and a can of chocolate frosting from her apron pocket. "I've been experimenting," she started enthusiastically. "We sell sweet and savoury things here, but I wanted to make something for people who only like a little bit of sweet, not too much!"

"But I like a lot of sweet!" Queenie interrupted, pouting.

"I know, princess," Lottie said patiently. "That's why I brought the frosting and sprinkles. I want you two to be my first tasters - besides Ginny and I!" Her eyes twinkled cheerily; she seemed eager to please, eager to make something we would like. "Try them!"

I looked at her cautiously. I really wasn't the biggest fan of sweet things, and she knew that. But she made something that was only very slightly sweet. Did she...do that for me?

I forced myself to not be so full of myself and picked up a cake while Lottie slathered Queenie's with frosting and sprinkles. It was innocent-looking, spongey to touch and golden brown, and when I broke it open, the inside was fluffy and smelt like vanilla.

"Try it," Lottie urged. "I promise, it's not that sweet."

For some reason, I trusted her, be it because of her wide, honest eyes or her smile. So I stuffed the whole damn thing into my mouth. It was still slightly warm and it was almost like it was melting in my mouth. And Lottie was right - it wasn't that sweet. I could taste the vanilla and a little bit of sugar, but it was the right amount for someone so adverse to it like me.

"Do you like it?" Lottie tried to mask it, but I could see how hopeful she was under her steady smile. Like she really, really wanted me to like what she made.

All I knew was that as soon as I heard her hesitancy and saw the careful look in her eyes, I was done in. "It's pretty good," I acknowledged, trying to appear nonchalant. I could hear Ginny scoff somewhere behind us, but I ignored her.

The way Lottie's face lit up joyfully would make you think that those cakes of hers had won a Nobel Peace Prize. "Pretty good? That's a big step up from 'not bad'!"

I felt bad for always brushing her off. Her words just reminded me of how much she seemed to treasure anything pleasant I had to say to her. But it made me feel like I needed to do a lot better, which was such a foreign feeling to me, especially towards someone I didn't know that well.

"I like it too!" Queenie said, chocolate frosting smeared all over her fingers and mouth.

"How do you know you liked it when it's all over your face and not in your mouth?" I asked, her.

Queenie laughed as Lottie reached into her apron pocket again. "Here, Princess," she said, pulling a packet of wet wipes out. "Let's clean you up."

"Okay, Charlie!" Ginny suddenly said from the front counter. "Enough socialising, now come get your cute bum over here!"

"But there's nobody here," Lottie said, frowning slightly. I frowned too before I realised what I was doing.

"Diana texted me and said she would be here soon, so I suggest you stop flirting and come here before she whips your hide."

Lottie laughed, but gathered up her things and moved next to Ginny. "I'll miss you, Benny," she teased. "You too, princess."

"Yeah, you're too far away," I said. She smiled at me and disappeared into the back room to put the cakes away.

I stood up suddenly, knowing that this was my chance. I strode up to the front counter and extracted my wallet. "How much?" I asked, knowing that Lottie would refuse my money the second she came back.

"She didn't slave over those things for you to make you pay," Ginny scoffed.

My chest did this weird seizing thing before I cleared my throat. So she did make them for me. "How. Much?" I repeated, glaring.

For a moment, she just scrutinised me. "Two pounds fifty pence, but just put it in her tip jar. Charlie does the till counting at the end of the day and she'll know you paid."

I nodded and shoved a five pound note into Charlie's tip jar, which was marked with her name. "Thanks," I said.

She smiled, even though I'd been kind of a jerk. "You're a rude guy, but you seem to Charlie kindly and that's all I care about."

"We're not dating," I hissed, in case Lottie managed to overhear.

Ginny shrugged. "You don't have to date someone to care about them, but you hear what you want to mister!" I ignored her and went back to my seat to sit down, and by then, Lottie had returned. Upon seeing that Queenie and I were still there, she smiled and blew me a kiss.

And I realised that maybe Ginny was right.

Chapter 13

I stood outside the coed dorms, wondering if what I was doing was right. I was about to intervene in Ginny's love life, something she'd warned me to stay away from.

"Hey, Charlie, is it?" a girl in my English Lit class, Fiona, called. "What are you doing here?"

I smiled broadly, thankful to see a familiar face. "I'm just looking for Zach. Do you have any idea where he could be?"

"Well, I think his dorm number is twelve, I'm not sure if he's in though." Fiona looked at me worriedly. "Why do you need him, Charlie?"

I smiled. "I just need to pass on a message from Ginny."

"Oh. Okay. Well, be careful, alright? Zach's been drinking a lot lately, causing a freaking zoo in our dorm."

I nodded and waved goodbye. I knew Zach loved drinking, but was the reason for his overconsumption because of my best friend? I'd have to find out.

People stared at me as I walked through their dorm. I stayed in the girl's dorm at all times, but I'd been in the coed one before. It was a lot bigger, but smelt like men. Not even attractive men, like Ben, but like sweaty undergraduate men.

I knocked on the door marked 'twelve' and heard an unintelligible groan from the other side. "If that's you, Reina, go away!"

I winced. "It's not Reina," I said softly. "It's Charlie."

Ginny and Zach had 'dated' for the better part of a month, longer than I'd ever seen either of them before. Zach had come from my old high school and we were good friends, which was how he met Ginny. She and Zach didn't start dating until this month, though.

The door opened, revealing a shirtless Zach with week-old stubble and a disgruntled look on his face. "Why is it that you take forever between your visits to me?" he grumbled.

I smiled at him and pushed past into his room. The place was a mess - clothes everywhere, bed in disarray, bottles and pizza boxes cluttered on the desk. "Nice place," I commented.

Zach groaned again and slammed the door shut, shuffling over to stand next to me. Even though he smelt like he hadn't taken a shower in a couple of days, I hugged him. I had been so busy that I hadn't talked to him in couple of months, and I'd missed him. He was like a big brother to me.

His arms squeezed me gently and I saw his face light up. "Missed you, pest," he said.

I let go and patted his chest. "Missed you too, now go take a shower, you smell kind of like you've been sitting in a dumpster."

Zach never argued with me, because everything I told him to do was for his own good and he knew that. He grabbed some clothes from his closet before shuffling away.

While he took his shower, I gathered up all the rubbish and threw it in a big, disposable bag. Then I took all his discarded clothes and dumped them into his empty laundry basket. I had to pinch my nose because the place smelt disgusting.

I took a bottle of air freshener from my bag, always fully prepared when it came to Zach. It seemed like every time I visited him, his room got more and more nasty. He was so lucky that he didn't have a roommate, otherwise the poor guy would've died from the stench.

When Zach entered, his dark hair dripping onto his blue shirt and looking refreshed, his carpet was somewhat visible. I smiled at him from where I sat on his still messy bed. "Hey, Cheesehead," I said. "I did a little cleaning, but you better do the rest, okay?"

He smiled at me. "Thanks, Charlie."

I nodded and patted the spot next to me. "C'mere, Zach."

"I know that face. What have I done this time?"

I beckoned to him and he came and sat down next to me, making the bed dip. "Zach," I began seriously. "Do you like Ginny? Because if you do, I need you to please go fix whatever you did. She's my best friend," I said gently.

"She doesn't like me, Charlie."

I grinned at him.

He blinked, huffing out a confused breath. "I mean...she doesn't, right? I thought she hated me and just liked the sex."

I coughed awkwardly. I didn't like picturing my old best friend and new best friend doing anything. "Why don't you find out? If it gives you a hint, she's been kinda down since you broke up with her."

A small smile blossomed on his lips. "Are you sure?"

I patted his shoulder. "I'd give it a go. She might punch you a few times, but she's worth it."

Zach rested his elbows on his thighs and turned his head to look at me. "Okay," he said. "I'll try."

I nodded and stood up. "Don't hurt her, Zach," I said. I did something very out of character and grabbed his collar, bringing his face close to mine. "You make her cry again and I will kill you," I whispered. I let go of him and waved. "Bye, Zach."

"Bye, Charlie," he said weakly.

I skipped to my next lesson, a smile on my face. I couldn't wait until Zach talked to Ginny.

The door to Ginny's and my room slammed open, and I was greeted with her completely red face. I sat up in my bed, my lips turning up at the sight of her pissed-off face. She was so funny when she was mad.

Ginny stalked towards me. "Charlie," she said darkly.

I stood up. "Yes, my wonderfullest bestest friend ever?"

"Did you or did you not talk to Zach about getting me back?"

I edged around my bed, my smile not dropping. I knew she would be mad because her pride was the most important thing to her. She never wanted to feel like she needed someone to do her work for her. But I'd rather her be happy than lonely.

"As a matter of fact, I may have done something like that," I said.

"Well, Charlie," she said. "I need you to do something for me."

"Yes?"

"Run!"

I yelped and pelted out of the room, dodging around the girls in our dorm. Ginny chased me, yelling things that I'd really rather not repeat.

I ran outside and glanced over my shoulder to see her slowing down. I may not have been the most athletic girl around, but I was a mite more fit than Miss Couch Potato. Because I was too busy laughing at her sweaty face, I didn't notice when I was about to hit someone until I slammed into their chest.

The person grabbed my arms before I could fall and I smiled a dazed smile. "I'm so sorry," I said, and then looked up. "Oh, hey Ben!"

Ben looked at me in annoyance and set me upright. "What are you doing, Lottie?"

I peeked behind me and squeaked, twisting in his grip until I was hiding behind his back.

"Lottie-"

I hushed him and waited for Ginny to race past us. Because he was much larger than me, he hid my entire body. I heard her heavy breathing as she approached Ben.

"Hey, jerk!" she called. I giggled and bunched his shirt under my fingers, pressing my face into his back.

I felt him stiffen and giggled again. "What do you want?" Ben asked her - and quite rudely, might I add.

"Have you seen Charlie? She was just here."

I whispered, "No," into his back, hoping he'd hear me.

"No," I heard him say, and I sighed in relief. Ben's back stiffened even more and I waited until I heard her footsteps jog away.

"Is she gone?" I whispered.

"Yes, you can let go now," he said, his voice oddly strained.

I slowly let go of him and he turned around, his expression tight. I smiled gently. "Thanks for hiding me!"

His face twisted into a strange grimace and his hand reached behind him to smooth out the crumpled fabric of his shirt. "What were you doing?"

My smile became turned sheepish and I scratched the back of my head. "Well...I kinda sorta...set Ginny up?"

Ben looked at me funny. "So why is she so mad? You didn't pick some creepy, ugly guy did you?"

I laughed. "Of course not! It was her ex-boyfriend."

He rolled his eyes. "That's even worse."

I shook my head earnestly. "No, they really like each other, Benny. I couldn't let them just wallow in self-pity!"

Ben stared at me for a minute, and I could've sworn I saw affection in his eyes. "Wow," he said, but his voice was flat. "I can't believe you."

I cocked my head. "What?"

His hand came and brushed against my cheek for a split second before he snatched it back. I felt a heat flush my face.

"You're such a..." He stopped in the middle of his sentence and his face went kinda pink.

I smiled and patted him on the cheek. "I agree."

Chapter 14

Lottie's doe-eyed gaze was fixed on me, a fond smile on her face. I stared at her. I could still feel the warmth of her breath fanning against my back, the way her laugh vibrated against my shirt. Thankfully, I was good at not showing how affected I was by the simplest of gestures.

"Charlotte Carter!" that brunette from the bakery screeched, and Lottie turned, a panicked look on her face.

"Bye, Ben!" she cried to me, tossing me a smile before she turned on her heel and pelted away from her friend.

The brunette whose name I'd forgotten stopped in front of me and made a face. "I knew she was behind you," she said.

I raised an eyebrow. "So why didn't you say anything?"

"Because all she did was touch you and you got all hot and bothered," she said smugly. "And it was fucking hilarious."

My fists clenched up and I glared at her. "I did not!" I protested angrily. Lie.

"Do you think I'm stupid? Your face went from normal to white to red in two seconds flat."

"Not."

"It actually did."

I pointed in the opposite direction Lottie had taken off to. "You know what? Why don't you stop fucking talking to me and go find her?"

The girl flipped me the bird and said, "Denial isn't healthy, you know," and sprinted off in the direction I pointed to. I smirked; she didn't even suspect a thing. That was what she got for being an annoying little pest.

"Boo!"

Without turning around, I rolled my eyes. "You're not scary, Lottie."

She trotted over into my line of sight and pouted. "I thought I'd got you this time."

"Maybe if you were more frightening," I suggested. "But you're about as frightening as a little baby."

She giggled. "Except in the mornings," she joked. "You never want to see me before I've had my chocolate milk."

Christ. Chocolate milk? I thought she was going to say coffee. "I actually never want to see you anyways," I said. Lottie's face fell slightly and I immediately felt guilty. I was so used to saying the rudest thing I could, that I'd forgotten how much it bothered her. My eyebrows furrowed and I stretched out my hands before quickly dropping them. "I was just kidding," I said.

She peeked at me with her wide green eyes, and she perked up. I felt a little better when I saw her smile. "You are so weird," she said, her eyes crinkling at the corners.

"I'm weird?" I said, affronted. "What about you?"

She giggled into her hand and glanced over my shoulder. "Good afternoon!" she called, waving energetically at a girl who was making her way past us.

When Lottie smiled at the girl, I felt my heart stutter when I realised that it was a different smile than the one she gave me. I frowned, thinking about it. When she smiled at the girl, it was sweet and welcoming, polite, if anything. But when she smiled at me, no. Stop it. I internally shook my head.

I couldn't think about stuff like that, because it most likely wasn't true. Lottie was a friendly person, of course she would be nice to me. No use getting my hopes up when anything more was impossible.

"Benny? Are you okay?"

I looked at her and automatically took a step back at the sight of the warmth in her expression. "I'm fine," I managed to say.

Lottie didn't look convinced, but she glanced at her watched and squawked. I had to bite my lip to keep from laughing at the sound. Lottie seriously made some of the strangest noises I'd ever heard.

"I'm late!" she cried, her arms flapping around like a mad-woman. "Oh jeez, I'm so late, I'm going to be late for work!"

She twirled around in the spot as though it would magically transport her to the bakery. "Lottie, are you late?" I asked sarcastically.

She let out a quick, bright laugh before patting my arm and darting away. "Come visit me later, okay? I have a long shift today!"

"Probably not," I called.

Another lie.

Three hours later, I got out of my car and noticed Lottie washing the windows of the bakery, swaying side to side.

I chuckled to myself when I noticed she was squirting water onto the windows using a huge Nerf water gun that was almost as long as her torso.

I tiptoed closer until I was right behind her, close enough to hear that she was humming the Spongebob Squarepants theme song. She still hadn't noticed me, so I leant forward until my lips were right at her ear.

"Boo," I whispered.

Lottie let out the single most adorable squeak I have ever heard in my entire life and swung around, her hand automatically spraying me with her water gun. I spluttered and spat out the water, wiping some of it from my eyes. I groaned when I saw the wet drops staining my shirt.

"Oh!" Lottie exclaimed, her face flushing pink, her hands hovering over me as though she wanted to do something but didn't know what. "I'm so sorry, Ben!"

I pushed away her fluttering hands and lifted up the corner of my shirt to wipe off my face. I grinned to myself when I saw her determinedly looking away from my stomach. I laughed into my shirt and then let it fall back over me. "Don't worry about it," I said, striding through the bakery doors.

She pattered after me and smiled as she positioned herself behind the front counter.

Don't think too much of it, I scolded myself.

"Thanks for visiting me!" she exclaimed. I could tell that she was genuinely pleased to see me, and for some reason I felt myself becoming more pleased at the thought of that.

I leant against the counter. "I had nothing else to do," I said casually, trying to play it off. It was so hard to keep calm around her when I kind of just wanted to hug her. Just then, the door to the bakery opened, and I heard the clicking of expensive high heels. My eyes snapped up and widened as I realised who it was.

Lottie, meanwhile, smiled brightly. "Good evening!" she trilled.

I could feel a hard expression creep up my face, and my eyebrows furrowed. Mrs. Wellington saw me at the same time I saw her, and we death-glared at each other.

"Is this who you serve here?" she spat. "I thought this was a respectable place!"

Lottie's eyebrows fairly disappeared into her hairline, and her smile immediately dropped. "Pardon?" she said faintly.

I felt a familiar anger crawl up my spine. I hated this woman and her family. They were all a bunch of gold-digging, snobbish aristocrats - and good friends of my parents.

"Seeing how you behave towards your parents, it's a wonder you can still strut around like you own everything," Mrs. Wellington said, her voice cold as ice. I didn't care a whit for the woman.

My hands clenched up into fists. I felt something touch me, and glanced at Lottie to see her hands covering one of my own. Her gaze was focused on Mrs Wellington.

"Excuse me, ma'am, but I have to request that you be a bit more polite to my friend," Lottie said in the firmest voice I had ever heard her use. Friend?

Mrs Wellington glared at me with a hatred so fierce that I stepped back. She had no right to be such a complete and utter bitch to me. "Polite to whom?" she hissed.

"Ma'am," Lottie said, her tone still firm, but her eyes were now flashing. It surprised me, because I didn't expect anything like this from her. "There is a strict no-unwanted-negativity in this bakery, so I'm going to have to ask you to leave."

I didn't speak, too shocked by Lottie's anger, even when Mrs Wellington slammed her fist on the counter and twirled around. She was just as bad as my parents, and seeing her sent an unwanted reminder of them to me.

Lottie frowned as Mrs Wellington left the bakery, and I felt something gnaw at my stomach. Something that felt overwhelmingly like fondness. It made my gut clench up and my face flush, and try as I might to deny it, I had to admit that that girl had done what I thought was impossible. In the span of a few days, she had dug down and managed to settle herself inside my heart.

Because of her, I didn't really care how shitty anyone else thought I was. 'Cause if that sweetheart liked me, how bad could I be?

Chapter 15

My fingers curled into fists as that...woman strutted out like she owned the place. I took a deep, calming breath and closed my eyes, my mind whirring. Who did she think she was, coming in here and insulting Ben?

I felt my anger building up once again at the memory, and I squeezed my eyelids shut so as to banish the image of his stone-cold expression and emotionless voice. I hoped I'd never have to hear such a detached and heart-breaking sound ever again.

I'd never been mean to someone before - at least not intentionally. It didn't feel right to make somebody feel bad, but now, defending Ben? Well, I'd never felt so good in my life as when I told that woman off.

It was exhilarating - I didn't believe I could ever do something like that. But since it was Ben whom she was berating, I couldn't help myself. Nobody, nobody was allowed to say such horrid things to him. That was where I drew the line.

And, I'll admit, seeing that shocked and impressed expression on his face was worth a million of 'Mrs Wellington's' disdainful looks.

When I had calmed down enough to open my eyes, I noticed Ben's gaze fixated on me. I smiled sheepishly and scratched the back of my head, my cheeks flushing. I realised I'd probably made a fool out of myself in front of him.

"I'm sorry you had to see that," I said softly. "I didn't meant to lose my temper. But I'm not sorry for doing it."

Ben cleared his throat. "Don't be sorry. It was fucking awesome."

"Yeah?"

He cleared his throat again. "You shouldn't be embarrassed, you kind of needed that."

Okay, now I was confused. "Needed what?"

Ben was quiet, thinking about it. "You need to be well-rounded," he said finally. "It can't be healthy to be smiling every minute of the day."

"So I should take breaks every hour to shout at nasty old battle-axes?" I teased, but I knew he was being serious. I wasn't sure if it was out of concern for my emotional well-being or annoyance at my supposedly stagnant character, but he was serious about me needing time to not be such a pushover.

"If it comes to that," he said, an almost invisible smile tugging at the corners of his lips. My eyes shined at the sight, because even such a faint amusement made my heart beat wildly.

I paused. And then I said, "I don't smile all the time."

Ben raised his eyebrows. "Yes. You do."

"I actually don't," I argued. I couldn't help but grin at the conversation we were having.

"You're smiling right now!"

I laughed. "That's because you're so funny."

"What was so funny?" he said, outraged.

"Your face," I said automatically. I closed my eyes slightly and shook my head at my stupid response.

Ben stopped, his mouth half-open. His expression flattened. "I see the appeal," he said, unimpressed.

I laughed again. It was really hard to show emotions other than joy around him, because that was what I felt around him! "It's your fault," I told him. "I can't stop smiling when you're around."

"Because I'm just so funny," he said, rolling his eyes. He was annoyed, I could tell.

My eyebrows furrowed; I didn't mean to bother him or make it seem like he was a joke. I just...didn't know how to be calm around him. I liked him. At least as a friend. I didn't know him well enough to fancy him, but I liked him well enough to want the feeling reciprocated. "No," I said slowly. "Because..." I stopped speaking, because I realised I didn't know how to explain.

He raised his eyebrows, as though prompting me on.

I cleared my throat and looked at my hands resting on the counter.

"So am I just your personal puppet show?" He spoke lightly, trying to seem casual, but I noticed the way his chest seemed to puff up in attempt to realign his bruised ego.

Just like with Mrs Wellington, I felt my blood rush to my ears. I blinked furiously, the same sensation that was what gave me the courage to defend Ben cropping up again, this time against his own self-destructive behaviour. "No!" I said adamantly. "Is it that hard for you to see that I smile around you maybe because I'm happy to see you?"

He stared at me blankly. I almost groaned, because he was so hard to read. I almost never knew what he was feeling, and he definitely wasn't the type to speak his feelings.

I sighed and looked away when the door opened. For the first time in my life, I had to force the welcoming smile onto my face when I greeted the customer. "Hello!" I said to the man.

He smirked slowly at me, and my smile faltered at the sight. I was used to these kinds of customers, but that didn't mean I enjoyed serving them. "Hey," he replied.

Ben looked at the guy and immediately scowled. I wasn't sure what was going on, but he moved around the counter until he was standing beside me.

Even though it was against the rules for him to do that, for some reason it soothed me, and my smile became more cheerful. "Is there anything in particular you'd like to have?" I asked.

The man's smirk widened. I had to stop myself from cringing. "Food or otherwise?" he asked in a suggestive tone.

I bit my lip hard, because suddenly I found him hilarious. His hair had too much gel, I could smell his cologne three feet away, and I could literally feel the desperation oozing out of him. "Let's start with food," I said, the laugh clear in my voice.

I saw Ben look down at me, wondering why I sounded like I wanted to start guffawing. The man, meanwhile, pouted slightly, and his ridiculousness almost made me lose it. "I'd like a dozen dulce de leche cupcakes," he said glumly.

I nodded, trying to keep a straight face. I trotted over to the back room to grab a to-go box, and Ben followed me.

"Why are you flirting with that guy?" he asked gruffly.

I glanced at him while I ruffled through a cabinet. "I'm not flirting," I said, amused. "I'm trying not to laugh at him."

He leant against the cabinet I was kneeling in front of, and he crossed his arms. "Just like with me, huh?"

"No," I corrected, rolling my eyes at his inability to believe that I wanted to be his friend. "With you, it's different."

"How different?" he pushed.

"You know, I've never heard you talk so much without pushing you," I said, and stood up. I smiled at him, and he looked away.

"Shut it," he grumbled, and I giggled.

I patted his shoulder and started to walk back to the shop. "Don't worry, Benny. I laugh at you because I'm just really happy. I want to laugh at that guy because he looks slimy."

He didn't reply, but I knew he heard me. I knelt in front of the counter where the guy was waiting impatiently. I swept twelve cupcakes into the box I'd found and stood up.

"Twenty-four pounds, please," I said, laying the box on top of the counter.

The man slapped some notes into my hand and grabbed the box, quickly rushing away. As soon as he exited, I started laughing loudly. Poor guy was embarrassed at his horrible flirting attempts.

"Don't be rude," I heard, and tried to kerb my giggles as I grinned up at Ben. I felt my face flush with embarrassment when I looked at his handsome face, realising that I'd told him twice that he made me happy.

I was shameless. Ginny would sort-of be proud.

"I wasn't being mean," I said, and then realised that it was a little mean to laugh at guys who weren't very good at flirting. "Okay, I was being mean," I admitted.

Ben let out a deep breath. "Man, I've seen you angry, annoyed, and happy all in the space of ten minutes. It's like Armageddon."

"Because you've seen all of that, that automatically means we're best friends."

He looked taken aback. "Whoa, who the hell said anything about being friends? We're not friends."

"Best friends," I corrected. "And I said it. Just now. We're best friends."

"No, shut up, get away from me," he said, walking backwards with his hands up as if to defend himself from me.

"Come on, best friend!" I said, clasping my hands together. "Say it, come on."

"You're the Antichrist," he snapped, and whirled around to stomp away.

"Okay, bye, best friend!" The door slammed shut behind him, and I started laughing. I felt light, and I knew my eyes were twinkling.

It was weird. I mean, before it was easy to smile and stuff, but every time I did, I would think of my mum and feel myself deflate. But around Ben, the joy just surfaced and shone out and I couldn't hide it because I didn't really want to.

Okay. I take it back, I didn't like Ben as a friend. I kind of, sort of...fancied him. Okay, I admit it. He was rude and cold, but I still couldn't help from blushing and smiling and laughing in his presence.

Maybe I was a masochist.

Chapter 16

"You know, lately I've had to ask you what's the matter an unnecessary amount of times," Clark said, sighing painfully.

I whipped around from where I was pacing and scowled. "Here's a thought," I said flatly, "how about you stop asking me that?"

Clark grinned, looking way too pleased with himself. "Now, where's the fun in that? I find amusement in your little tantrums."

I was already annoyed, and now my best friend was just adding fuel to the fire. "I'm not having a tantrum!" I thundered.

"I'm not sure why I even ask you why you come back in such horrible moods. It's obvious it's to do with Charlie."

I paused, my anger coming to an abrupt standstill. I'd known the girl for what? A few weeks? And I realised that Clark was right. Lottie was the cause of my rising temper.

"What happened this time?" Clark asked patiently.

I looked at him, rolling my eyes. He looked like an eager therapist the way he was sitting. "You looking at me like that doesn't make me want to tell you," I said.

Clark gave me an unimpressed look. "What happened this time?" he repeated more forcefully.

I stared at him. "I went to the bakery and Mrs Wellington came in."

His nose wrinkled in disgust and understanding. That's why I managed to stay close with the bastard - he understood my situation better than anyone. "God, I always wondered how that crabby old hag managed to change the Miss to Mrs, but the Mr is just as bad as her." I nodded in agreement. "Did she act like her usual self?"

I nodded again. "Like she cuts the throats of puppies in her spare time."

Clark winced. "And in front of Charlie? How'd she handle it?" he asked curiously. Because that was always the deciding factor - people who agreed with my family and their horrid friends just to make a good impression on wealthy people, or even listened to their demeaning words with frightened rabbit eyes, pissed me off. I couldn't stand those types of people.

But Lottie...

I strode over to the sofa and sat down heavily, burying my face in my hands. I heard Clark groan. "Oh god, did she cry or something? Or did she offer Mrs Willy-ton free cupcakes to get her approval?"

I gritted my teeth. "No. Worse."

Clark sighed. "I really thought she was different. What did she do?"

"She stood up for me."

I glanced up, and noticed Clark gaping at me. "What the fuck, man? How is that worse? You scared the shit out of me, I thought she'd acted like a dickhead!"

"You don't understand!" I snapped, my fists clenching up. "It's worse because now I know that she really isn't a dickhead!"

"And how is that worse?" he asked, looking like he wanted to smack me upside the head. And I could totally understand why.

I gritted my teeth. "Lottie, the bird who lets customers walk all over her and offers her sweeties to small children, stood up for me!" Why couldn't he understand how bad this was? She'd even said I made her happy, and I couldn't let that happen.

Clark rolled his eyes. "Don't be such a dickass, Ben. That means she likes you, which is definitely a good thing."

"It's not. I'm a dick. She needs to stay away."

"And even though you're a dick, she's still kind to you."

"Well, she's weird."

"Look, Ben. I know you're hyped up on the 'I'm not good for her' shit, but she's good for you. She could help you be a better person."

Ladies and gentlemen, my best friend, who thought I wasn't a good person. Not that I could blame him.

I sighed. "She wants to be friends." Best friends.

Clark started laughing, and I stared at him in irritation. He had absolutely no sympathy for me whatsoever. I crossed my arms and raised my eyebrows, waiting for him to stop braying like an ass. When he stopped, he still had a cheesy grin on his face. "What did she do?"

I grimaced. "Laughed. All she ever does is laugh at me."

"Oh man. Never did I think I'd see the day when my Benny would be so mad that a girl friend-zoned him. Hell, I never thought I'd see the day that you were the one being friend-zoned! Man, this is rich."

I stood up and walked over to him, slapping the back of his head. "I fucking hate you. You're a horrible excuse for a friend."

He rubbed his hair and wiggled his eyebrows, not fazed in the slightest. "At least you don't have romantic feelings for me, friend."

Out of pure frustration, I kicked the back of the armchair he was sitting in. He went toppling forward, landing on his face with a muffled exclamation. I smirked to myself.

"Sometimes I really do think you're in love with me."

"Boo!"

I sighed and laid my Multivariable Calculus textbook onto the table. I raised my hands and wiggled the fingers. "Ooh, so frightening, ahh, save me, help," I said, my voice devoid of emotion.

Lottie laughed and sat down across from me, not at all offended. "Why is it so hard to catch you unawares?" she asked with a teasing smile.

"'Catch me unawares'?" I repeated, raising my eyebrows. "Hello, Miss English Major."

She rolled her eyes and gestured to my textbook and graphing calculator. "Hello, Mr. Smarty-Pants. I didn't know you were taking maths."

I shrugged, avoiding her gaze. I knew if I looked at her, she'd be smiling, and I couldn't deal with that so early in the morning.

"But it kind of explains your big head," she continued. "I mean, your brain must be huge."

My eyebrows furrowed. I wasn't sure if that was a compliment or an insult. "I have a big head?" I repeated, bringing up my hands to cradle my head. It wasn't big. Was it?

She simply grinned, and I knew she was teasing. Of course she was. I bet she'd never said a cruel thing in her life, even as a joke.

Just then, my stomach grumbled loudly, and I closed my eyes, completely embarrassed. God, of course it would roar like a beast the second she sat down with me. I hadn't had breakfast that morning, because Clark had kept annoying me about Lottie, and I couldn't take it anymore. So I came to the library to study, but apparently I can never find peace.

Lottie looked at me, amused and concerned. "Do you want something to eat?" she asked, not even waiting for my answer before rifling through her bag.

"No," I said, my eyes narrowing when she brought out two apples and a tub of yoghurt. "Is that your food?"

She brushed her hair out of her eyes and smiled at me. "No. I started to carry around spare food because Ginny is always hungry. I swear, she's like a bear in the springtime."

"So give it to her," I dismissed, trying to ignore when my stomach howled again.

Lottie shook her head and pushed the food towards me. "No, eat," she said stubbornly.

"We're in a library!" I hissed quietly.

"Yes, we are," she said, raising her eyebrows. "But nobody cares. See, that kid brought Starbucks and that other guy is eating cake." I glanced around, and true to her word, people were eating all over. I looked at the food she was presenting me with. I really was hungry. "Take it," she said encouragingly. "You need to eat breakfast."

God. She was literally sunshine. "Are you sure it's not yours?" I asked again. I had to make sure, okay? She wouldn't lie to me, but if I ate her breakfast, I'd be guilty. She probably needed it more than me.

Lottie stood up and leant over the table, grabbing my hands. I was in such a state of shock from the feel of her soft skin, that I didn't even notice when she placed the yoghurt in one hand and an apple in the other.

"You're so difficult," she said as she sat back, her eyes twinkling. "If it makes you feel any better, I'll keep one of these apples."

I frowned at my hands, wondering when exactly she stopped touching me.

Oh my god, I was going insane.

"Oh yeah!" she squeaked, and I had to hold back an amused grin because the sound she made was so high-pitched and just plain weird. "Here's the spoon!"

She brandished a large, metal spoon, and I accepted it, not even bothering to ask her why she carried silverware in her bag. I paused just as I was about to rip the top off the yoghurt. "Blueberry," I read off the label. Blueberry was my favourite flavour, because it was more tart than sweet.

She grinned. "Because Ginny makes me carry her food around, I buy all the ones I like and she hates. Blueberry is my favourite."

I stared at her kind, open face for a minute, and then at the food she'd given me. For some reason, I felt my face slowly become warm. "Thanks," I blurted, unable to look at her.

There was a pause, and out of the corner of my eye, I saw the way she looked at me. It scared the fuck out of me, because sweet, friendly girls weren't supposed to hang around assholes like me.

But I was too far gone to care anymore.

"You're welcome," she said, in a voice softer than cotton.

Charlotte Carter was probably the first human in existence to succeed in the impossible - making me blush.

Chapter 17

Right as I spotted that completely adorable red flush on Ben's cheeks, my phone began to sing the theme song of Dragon Ball Z Kai.

He raised his eyebrows and shot me a pointed look. "Dragon Ball? Really?" I could tell he was mentally replacing how old I was with how old I should be.

"You're the one who recognises it," I said cheekily.

Ben's mouth opened, but he had no words to say. He simply rolled his eyes and went back to his maths homework.

I looked at my phone and then at Ben. He stared at me blankly. "Can I answer it?" I asked, not wanting to be rude.

Ben nodded. "By all means." I beamed at him. I didn't care what anyone said, including himself - he was a nice person.

"Hello!" I greeted into the phone.

"Charlie!"

My grin widened until my face almost split in two at the sound of the familiar voice. "Papa! You haven't called me in so long!" Ben was now staring at me in curiosity, but this time

I wasn't fazed, because I was talking to one of my favourite men in the entire world.

"Ah-ah," he scolded, "it doesn't work that way, poppet. You can't just make up some excuse about how you're busy with college work, so I should always be one to call. It makes me feel like you don't wanna talk to your old man!"

I laughed. Man, I missed him so much, and I didn't even realise how much until now. "Don't be absurd, Papa," I said, amused. "How's Husky?" Husky was my dad's best friend's.. .husky. But I loved the beautiful puppy like she was my own, since our little house was too small for a big dog like her and I was never allowed any pets.

"She's great," my dad said in his hearty voice, the kind that filled up a room whether you wanted to hear it or not. "I taught her how to pee outside, so she doesn't use her water bowl to empty out that humongous bladder anymore."

I paused to breathe out a silent laugh. I loved my dad, but sometimes he gave out too much information. Way too much, to be clear. "That's...good," I choked out. He laughed his big belly laugh, and I could just picture him and his slight pot belly jiggling from the force of it. I took a deep breath and then said, "So how's Delia?"

Delia was my...nothing, as of yet. I knew my dad wanted to court her, but was still hung up over my mother. It was so tragic, and I was so proud of my dad for chugging along and not letting himself fall into any sort of trouble.

I guess Delia was nice enough. I'd known her for about a year, but was usually at uni during that time. She made my dad smile though, so I wasn't complaining. Much.

"Delia's great!" he said enthusiastically. He sounded so happy. "She's great."

"Er..." I trailed off, sounding extremely unintelligent. "I, er...good. That's good. Tell her I said hello."

"Of course, poppet. She's coming over for dinner, so I'll tell her then."

I felt my stomach drop to my shoes. She was coming over to dinner? I mean, of course she was allowed to, I just...I don't know. Maybe I was being selfish or something. "Well, my class starts in ten minutes, so I've gotta go, Papa," I said, not as reluctantly had I not brought Delia up. Now I was eager to get off the phone. "I'll come home for the Christmas holidays."

"You better, Charlie."

"Okay, Papa. Cheers!"

"Cheers, poppet."

I hung up quickly and let out a breath I didn't know I was holding. My eyebrows furrowed slightly. I should be happy for my dad, because he'd found someone else who made him happy.

But as my fingers touched the heart charm that hung from the chain around my neck, I felt myself sobering up. I guess it wouldn't really hit that my mum was gone until Papa had completely moved on. Which could very well be soon.

"Okay. You're creeping me out."

I jumped, my gaze flickering over to Ben. He was watching me carefully. "Why?" I asked curiously.

Ben licked off the spoon that was covered in the yoghurt I gave him, his eyebrows furrowed like he was thinking. His dark eyes were hooded. "You looked really sad for a moment," he said, nodding at my necklace.

My hands unconsciously reached up again, but I clenched my fist and let it drop. I smiled, but it felt fake on my face, so my expression smoothened. I didn't want to lie to Ben and say that I was okay when I wasn't really, but I didn't want to tell him the truth and seem pathetic.

"Okay, seriously, Lottie, what's wrong?" The odd part was, he sounded like he actually cared. The worried tone of his voice soothed me, and I saw my mum's smile behind my eyes.

"Don't worry about it," I finally said. The smile eased on a little bit better, because the way he was looking at me was doing strange things to my insides. It wasn't even the multiple emotions that made it so intense, it was just a blur of feelings I could only hope existed in him for me.

Ben sighed angrily and chomped into the apple, almost violently. "Who called you?"

Oh my, he was nosy today. "My dad," I said. Did he not hear me say 'Papa' multiple times? But maybe he was one of those uninterested people who didn't care about others' phone conversations.

I definitely wasn't like that. I listened to everything around me, and my ears always picked up some sort of gossip. I didn't mean to pry...I just liked to pay attention.

He opened his mouth to say something, but I was tired of talking about myself, so I said, "Is the yoghurt too sweet?"

Ben glared at me. "No," he said shortly. I frowned and my hands started trembling. I'd been getting longer answers from him lately, and now he was back to only a few words.

"So is fruit sweetness okay for you then?" I prompted, clasping my hands together. Now my leg jiggled, but at least he couldn't see that under the table.

"Lottie," he said firmly. "Stop that."

"Stop what?"

"Stop that. Whatever it is you're doing."

I looked at him with wide eyes. "It would be really helpful if I knew what I should stop doing," I said nicely.

"I don't know," he said, frustrated. He seemed to be grabbing for words, unable to string together something to say. "Stop being so...thoughtful."

"What am I doing that's so thoughtful?" I asked, confused. Ben looked extremely annoyed, and whether it was with himself or with me, I didn't know.

"You're asking me if my yoghurt is too sweet when you just got off a conversation with your dad looking like your puppy just died!"

He was concerned? I stared at him, and I felt my heart fill up with something unfamiliar from the sight of the awkwardly angry man in front of me. "Don't look at me like that," he snapped, looking away.

I spotted his neck turn red, and it made a small smile appear on my face. "Ben, you're a kind person," I said solemnly. "You really are very kind."

He took in a sharp breath and crossed his arms, determinedly not looking at me. I glanced at my watch, realising that my English Lit class really did start in ten minutes. I didn't want to leave Ben, though. At least not when he seemed to be in such a bad mood.

"I'm sorry," I said. "I'm sorry, Benny. I didn't mean to look upset."

"You're not supposed to apologise for feelings. You're supposed to talk about them if you need to."

I blinked. I wasn't used to telling my problems to anyone except Ginny. And really, they couldn't even be classified as problems, since it was just me being selfish. "Do you-do you maybe want me to explain them to you?" I asked softly, hesitantly.

"Why do you think I asked?" he said in exasperation. I would've laughed had I not been feeling so subdued, and it seemed that Ben realised that. His expression grew pinched as he waited for me to talk. "Well?" he said, but not impatiently. This time, he was the one prompting me.

I closed my eyes briefly, and then looked at him. I opened my mouth to speak; to tell him that my dad was probably going to start dating Della, that my dog was all alone, that I'd have to go home during the Christmas holidays when I really didn't want to, that my dad had completely forgotten that my birthday came before Christmas. But what came out was definitely not what I expected.

"I miss my mum."

My eyes widened as soon as I said those words. I couldn't believe it. I spent the past few months trying to move on, and here I was still wallowing after her?

I expected Ben to sneer at me, to laugh or call me names, to do something to show me how childish I was being. But he did something that surprised us both, probably him more so than me.

He stood up, walked around the table, and folded me in a hug.

Chapter 18

She was small and warm and she smelt like a sweet perfume.

I could feel her surprise in the way she stiffened upon first feeling my hug. I was surprised too.

Why did I do that again?

I didn't know. I mean, Lottie had told me things I never thought she would ever tell me. She was a deeper person than I'd originally thought. She could feel and be hurt, she didn't just smile for the hell of it.

When I looked at her as she told me that she missed her mum, I realised that I'd never seen a more lost or lonely person in my life. Including myself. That was what drove me to initiate that hug. That expression on her face goddamn near cracked my front. I couldn't stand it any more.

Lottie held onto my shirt as though it was her anchor, her hands clenching the fabric between the fists. Her chin was resting firmly on my shoulder, the back of her head pressed against my neck and her cold-tipped nose nestling itself into the exposed skin of my upper back.

She felt fragile in my arms, but not the way a porcelain doll feels...more like a teddy bear. I could feel the subtle tremors of her body despite the lack of tears leaking from her eyes, and the fact that something was upsetting her was doing weird things to my head.

"My mum," she said, her tone of voice low, as though she was thinking hard. "My mum liked my smile a lot. She said it made her feel happy whenever she was upset, and I didn't like it when she was sad, so I began to smile all the time."

My arms tightened around her and she let out a protesting squeak. The funny sound softened my hard expression, and I loosened my arms so that I wasn't suffocating her. "I'm sorry," I said gruffly.

Lottie pulled back and furrowed her eyebrows at me. "Why are you sorry?" she asked, puzzled.

I could understand her a little better now. Before, I was a horrid bastard, assuming that nothing went on inside that head of hers apart from her cheesy smile. "I judged you wrong," I told her. "I'm sorry," I repeated. "I get it. A smile can sometimes turn a person's day around, and that's why you always have one on."

Lottie smiled, and she tapped my nose. "Bingo," she said.

Ah fuck. She was an absolutely wonderful human being. I mean, what kind of person would willingly do something like that and actually mean it?

"Ben, I really have to get to class, but I'll come find you later, okay?" she said.

"Okay," I forced out. My hands clenched into fists at my side and I had to take a deep breath to calm myself down.

How did she get to be so beautiful?

It wasn't her looks; it really wasn't. It was in her Beauty with a capital B. It was her friendliness, her kindness, that pleasant aura that always hung around her. She was a person you could spill your secrets to and she wouldn't judge you one whit. She could smile at you and it would be like all your problems were gone.

"Bye-bye, Benny," she said cheerfully, grabbing her bag and ruffling my hair. And then she was gone, running out of the library on her way to her class.

I brought my hand up to my head and was about to fix my no doubt unruly hair, but then I decided to leave it the way it was.

I'd become a complete and utter pansy. I didn't fix my hair because the touchy part of my subconscious demanded that since Lottie had touched it, my hair was suddenly sacred.

I scowled. "I am a man," I told myself sternly. "Fix the fucking hair, it's just hair, goddammit!"

I didn't fix the hair.

I spotted her sitting on a bench near her classroom around lunchtime, earbuds in her ears, her head bopping to the tune of her music. I almost grinned, because it was such a funny sight. Her hair bounced with every movement of her head, and at random intervals, she would stick out her tongue rocker-style and play the air guitar.

I started to make my way over to her, but stopped when I saw some guy swaggering towards her. My eyebrows furrowed when Lottie looked at him and removed her earbuds. My only consolation was that her expression was polite, but anyone could mistake her stranger smile for something more. I know I used to.

I wasn't close enough to hear what he was saying, but I could tell from his body language that he was a complete slime ball. He was smirking at her, smirking! I almost lost it when I saw him reach into his pocket, hand her a scrap of paper, and then saunter away, looking extremely pleased with himself.

I was stuck in place, my face probably flushed with anger and my jaw ticking. Lottie stared at the paper in her hands, and I kept my eyes on her to see what she would do next. A happy smile grew on her mouth, and it was a smile so amused that I would've walked away right then and there had she not let out a high, clear laugh, crumpled up the paper, and tossed it over her shoulder.

Just like that, all the pent up fury left my body in a second, and I was left feeling awkward from my own thoughts. I'd acted like a jealous boyfriend. Why had I acted like a jealous boyfriend?

I took a deep breath to calm myself down and began to creep up behind her as she put her earbuds back in her ears. I reached her and bent at the waist, yanked out one earbud and said, "Boo!"

She let out a girlish squeak and jumped violently, her bag falling off her lap. When she saw me, her cheeks turned a light pink colour. She frowned, but it didn't escape me how she was holding back a smile.

Lottie didn't look at him like that, I thought.

"I believe that's two-nil," I said smugly, taking a seat beside her. I kept a safe half metre away from her.

"Yeah?" she teased, but I detected an embarrassed undercurrent in her voice. "Well...y-you have furry eyebrows!"

I couldn't help but laugh when I heard her comeback, and I saw her eyes shine at the sound of it. I cleared my throat, abruptly halting my laughter. "How dare you," I said drily.

"I dare."

"Yeah?" I struggled to find something to say that would make her laugh. "Well, no one likes you."

She giggled. "No one likes you," she returned easily.

"Whoa, that insult is so unoriginal, it's almost as if I said it three seconds ago," I said sarcastically.

Lottie paused, looking confused. "But you did say it a few seco-" She stopped speaking, and a look of comprehension dawned on her face.

"Try-hard," I said.

"Have you been reading the How to Insult Like an Eleven Year Old manual again?"

"Actually," I said haughtily, "it's How to Insult Like a Twelve Year Old."

She laughed. "Ah, my bad.""Yeah. Your bad."

We fell into a silence then, and I wasn't sure if I knew her enough for it to be comfortable or not. I didn't know what to say to her to keep on hearing her voice. I wasn't used to speaking first, or even to speaking very much at all, but for some reason, I felt the need to do so with Lottie.

I didn't have to, though. She turned her head to look at the huge gap between us. "Are you scared of me?" she asked teasingly, sidling closer to me.

I tensed when she leant towards me, and my leg began bouncing nervously. "You are the least scary person on the planet," I managed to say.

"You haven't seen me in the morning then," she said and laughed.

She wasn't looking at me, but then she did, and she seemed surprised at our close proximity. She didn't move away though, and neither did I. We were both completely still, just looking at each other, evaluating each other's moves.

Lottie looked down and then peeked at me shyly, her cheeks turning red. I slowly placed my hand on her neck, moving at such a pace that she could move away if she so wanted to.

She didn't move away.

Chapter 19

I was not a lip virgin. I was nineteen years old, but the last time I was kissed by a boy called Seamus Ronan. Back then, Seamus Ronan was a cute guy in my co-ed grammar school, but he kissed like a dog. Overeager, wet, and sloppy.

I liked to think that he didn't count, because it was a pretty juvenile kiss at that. But he was, and it saddened me to think that he was who I had to set standards with.

I knew Ben could surpass that, because all he had to do was keep his tongue to himself unless he knew how to use it. I turned into Ben when he shifted and felt my face heat up. Ben stared at me and leant in very slowly, giving me the opportunity to move away if need be.

I didn't though.

I knew that I liked him. He was gorgeous, but that wasn't all. He was kind in his own way and treated Queenie like his baby sister. He was mysterious and calm and kind of ill-mannered, but when he smiled or laughed...oh God. It was the best gift in the world.

I peered into his eyes, pursing my lips. "What do you think you're doing?" he asked gruffly.

"Huh," I said in surprise, mesmerised by the colours swirling in his eyes. "I always thought your eyes were brown, but they're not." I squinted my own eyes.

Ben's mouth quirked up and it made me smile. I loved his smile. "Lottie, I really, really want to   "

"Yeah?" I asked hopefully.

His face smoothed out into an indecipherable expression. Almost as if a switch was flipped, he scooted away and turned his head in the opposite direction. And suddenly, the old Ben was back.

I cocked my head, the lack of warmth glaringly obvious without him next to me. I was confused. "What do you want to do, Benny?" I prompted.

"Don't call me Benny," he said simply. My eyebrows furrowed. It had been a while since he'd said that to me, and to be honest, it made me feel really awkward.

"Oh, okay. S-sorry." His abrupt change in attitude was messing with my head, but I had to stop being so lame. I took a deep breath and smiled slightly. "I need to get to my next class," I said after checking my watch. "Bye-bye, Ben."

He turned back to me, a slight frown marring his handsome features. I let my smile become lighter, happier, and I shoved my earbuds in my ears before moving out of his way.

I sighed. "Nice work, Charlotte."

Ginny threw her arm around my shoulder. "What's wrong with you, poppet?"

I glanced at her from my job of wiping down the counters and flicked soap at her nose. "Oh yuck, I have a thing on my back. Get it off."

She smirked. "That's the repressed sexual tension I hear, isn't it?"

I laughed. "All I hear is 'fwa fwa fwa fwa,' from a snuffy little pig!"

"Don't distract me with your nasty snorting, I did notice that you're lacking enthusiasm, you know," she said sternly. "Now, tell Auntie Ginny what the matter is."

I shrugged my shoulders. "I don't know, Ginny. Nothing really. I'm being stupid?"

"Was that a question or a response? Because either way, I agree."

I giggled. "Don't worry about it, Ginny. It's just some school troubles."

"Babe, don't lie to me. It's Ben isn't it? Goddamn, I knew that that boy was PMS in a well-sculpted package. What did he do?"

My eyebrows furrowed. "He didn't do anything."

She threw her hands up in the air. "Well that's even worse. Fuck, what happened, was he gonna kiss you and then chicken-shitted out?"

My eyes practically bulged out of my head and I almost choked on my spit. How did she know?

Ginny pumped her fists and let out a wild animal screech. I cringed back. "I was right? I was right! Holy shit! He almost kissed you? What in the actual fuck?"

"I agree!" I said enthusiastically. "Moving on-"

"Wait, no! Don't do that to me, Charlie! Ben almost kissed you? I knew there was something going on between you two!" she yelled, latching onto my arm.

I laughed at her and pulled away from her crushing grip, but I didn't like where this was going. I didn't want to talk about it. I didn't want to talk about Ben wanting nothing to do with me. "Please, Ginny, d-"

The bell to our bakery dinged, and both of us looked up. A brown haired teenager walked in, his hands shoved deep inside his pockets, a vacant expression on his face. When I noticed Ginny's eyes becoming predatory, I made a face at her and shoved her into the back room.

"Good afternoon!" I greeted the boy. He looked at me and grinned quite a friendly grin, and I smiled right back. His smile reminded me of something, but I couldn't quite put my finger on it.

"Hi," he said. "I'm looking for an anniversary cake. Maybe vanilla? I dunno. It's for my parents."

I pursed my lips. "Are two layers enough? I think we have one in the back. I can pipe on some frosting for the names and date if you'd like."

He shrugged. "Okay."

I held up one finger to let him know to hold on, and I walked into the back room. Ginny was sitting on one of the counters, eating whipped cream from a can. "Ginny, stop it," I said good-naturedly. "You'll become ill."

"Don't tell me what to do," she muttered, and kept licking cream off the sides.

I wrinkled my nose, but let it go and walked over to the fridge. I took out a pre-prepared, two-layered vanilla sheet cake and let it rest on the top of the fridge while I shuffled around, gathering up frosting and piping bags.

"Ben! Ben! " I heard a shout, and I whirled around, surprised. It wasn't Ginny who had shouted, it was the boy. "What are you doing here?"

I grabbed the cake and walked back to the front counter, only to see the boy staring at Ben with wide eyes, while Ben stood stock-still, his jaw ticking. I knew that that meant he was extremely uncomfortable. "What are you doing here? Your house is two hours away," he said gruffly.

I cocked my head, very confused. "You two know each other?" I said, wanting to ease the tension some.

The boy turned to me, an eager smile on his face. "Yeah, Ben is my brother! But he never comes to visit." The last part was accusatory, and he spun back around to glare at Ben. "Why don't you ever come to visit? Or even call?"

My brain was already melting from the fact that Ben had a wee brother that was in the bakery at this very moment. But not only that, Ben was here too, even after our awkward encounter a few hours ago. "Archer, not here," Ben warned, glancing at me.

I, meanwhile, was processing his words in my head. I bit my lip hard, trying not to smile. "Pardon?" I asked, the laugh hidden in my tone. Ben noticed and shot me a look which I promptly ignored.

"My name is Archer?" the boy said, his eyebrows knitting together like he was confused as to what I was laughing about.

"Is it short for anything?" I replied, unable to help the grin that slowly crept up my face.

"Lottie," Ben warned. "If your words aren't necessary, don't say them."

Archer stared at me. "Er...no?" It came out as more of a question than an answer.

"Are you sure?" I prodded cheerfully.

He raised an eyebrow. "And what would it be short for, exactly?"

A laugh escaped my mouth and I pressed a hand to keep myself calm as I thought of the very obvious possibility. "Archibald?" I suggested, before slapping my hand against the counter and laughing to myself. Oh man, I loved that name. Archibald. It was just too good.

Ben pinched the bridge of his nose at my easily-entertained self and let out a low groan while Arched watched me in amusement as I continued to laugh at the thought of knowing someone named Archibald.

"My mum doesn't dislike me quite that much," he joked.

I laughed again and looked at Ben with a wide smile. He returned my look impassively. "Your brother is so polite - what happened to you?" I teased.

Ben's face noticeably soured and I frowned, hoping I hadn't offended him. "Shut up," he grunted, kicking the floor like a little kid.

"Ben, why haven't you come to visit us?" Archer asked again. My forehead creased because of the innocent way Archer asked the question, and I felt a pinch in my throat.

The way Ben was holding himself, I knew there was something the matter that didn't need to come into light. "Oh, don't be silly," I said quickly. "I go to the same uni as your brother. It's so hard to find time between working and lessons to call my dad. If he didn't call me first most of the time, I'd never speak to him."

Archer was in no way convinced, but he simply shrugged and glared at Ben again. "Whatever. Can you put 'Happy 25th anniversary, Harrison and Carrie' on the cake?"

"Carrie Fisher," I said, grinning. "Star Wars, huh?" Archer grinned and snapped his fingers at me. "In what colour would you like it?"

"Er...blue? And red?" I nodded and began piping out the letters in a fancy, curly way. Archer watched me work, and without turning around to look at his big brother, he said, "You're coming back with me to celebrate. Okay?"

I peeked up from the cake and saw how Ben stiffened and how his face paled. My heart pained for him, and I was about to open my mouth to butt in when Ben said, "Fine. But only for a couple of hours."

Even if it made Ben upset, getting his brother to agree to come home with him made Archer so happy that his eyes danced and his hands clutched the front counter until his knuckles turned white. His excitement made me smile, but I was still worried for Ben. I didn't know what was the matter, but I knew that despite him being a little cheesehead a while ago, I still cared what happened inside his head.

"There, it's finished," I said, straightening up. "You like?"

"Yeah," he said. "How much?"

"Oh, don't even worry about it-"

"Archer, don't listen to her," Ben growled. "She wouldn't let you pay if you paid her to let you pay her. Just give her the money and run."

"Ben-" I protested.

"Lottie," he said firmly. "Shut up and let the boy pay." I pouted at him, but he remained firm.

Archer glanced between the two of us, but seemed to decide he didn't care enough to enquire. "Whatever. Here's a twenty. Can you put it in a plastic box, not cardboard?"

I sighed and shoved his twenty pound note into the till, and then I nodded. "Of course. Just give me a minute."

I ducked down and grabbed a plastic box for the cake, and when I straightened back up, I almost collided with Ben's chin. "Lottie, listen," he said, in a low voice so that nobody but me could hear him. "Come with me."

I started. "What?"

"I can't go there alone. Please. Can you come with me?"

Chapter 20

Lottie looked completely flabbergasted, and I knew why, of course. I was an ass to her right when we were about to kiss and ruined any chances of doing that ever again.

I had been so close. And then I had remembered that Lottie deserved someone better than me. Someone that could take care of her. That wasn't me because I couldn't even take care of myself. Why would I destroy a girl's chance of making something of herself by being with me?

"Come with you?" she echoed, her big eyes dazed by my question.

I was already embarrassed enough from having to plead with her to come, I wasn't repeating myself. "Yes," I said quietly, not meeting her eyes.

"Are you sure I'm allowed?" Lottie said. "Because I'd never want to intrud-"

"Hey," I interrupted, my hand tilting her chin up so she would look at me. I dropped my hand down when I saw her maintaining eye contact. "Don't worry about it. I'm inviting you. Hell, Archer's inviting you." I raised my voice slightly and said, "Archer, you're inviting Lottie over, right?"

Archer walked over to us and I fought the urge to grab the kid in a bear hug. I hadn't seen him since he was fourteen years old. Three years. That was how long it had been since I'd been disowned. But Archer didn't know that. And he couldn't know either.

"You know her that well?" he asked, nudging me suggestively with his shoulder. I flicked his forehead and scowled at him, and he scowled back.

It made me feel a bit better to know that he was just as excited to see me as I was to see him. Fuck, I missed the kid. Alright? I'd missed my baby brother. Three years. Fuck.

"I'm his friend," I heard Lottie pipe up. I looked at her and her smiling face, and knew that my expression was slowly becoming pained. Friends?

Fuck me.

"Just friends?" Archer questioned after throwing a sly smirk my way.

Lottie nodded, her big eyes widening with excitement. "Maybe even best friends!"

I cleared my throat and fought back my depressed sigh. "Let's not get ahead of ourselves, Lottie."

Archer shrugged and grabbed the cake that Lottie had packed. "Whatever. I'm gonna go wait in my car, and I swear Ben, if you run away, I won't let you get away so easily this time."

I glanced at him and realised that he was genuinely worried that I would leave him again. I wished he knew that the first time I left wasn't by choice, and it wasn't by choice to not be in contact either. I ruffled his hair. "Don't worry kiddo, I'll be there in a sec."

"Don't call me kiddo, old man," he grumbled, frantically trying to smooth his hair back.

"Three years apart is not that big of a gap," I said, twisting his ear.

"Older than me still," he said, pulling away from my grip. "Let go, you boob, I need to go put this in the cooler before it melts!"

I released him and watched as he walked out with that awkward teenage strut of his. He was just as I remembered. Tall and gangly, wearing cargo shorts and V-necks because apparently the ladies dig the V on men as much as they dig the P. But he'd grown up some, and it frustrated me that I'd missed three years of his life.

When I glanced back at Lottie, she was looking at me warmly, with a smile that softened the already smooth edges of her face. I could feel heat creep up my cheeks, and I didn't want her to see it, so I turned away.

"Last chance - you sure I can come?" she asked. I noticed that she phrased it in a way that made it seem like she was the one who wanted to come and not the other way around.

I nodded, my frown fading. I couldn't be angry when I looked at her. She made it impossible to.

Lottie clasped her hands together. "Oh, this is exciting!" she said.

I scoffed. "Oh, come off it. It's my parents - not exciting in the slightest." I felt my lip curl and I scowled to myself. I didn't want to go back there.

Lottie didn't reply, she just bounced in place and then squeaked. "Wait here, I need to tell Ginny to cover for me!"

She ran into the back room and I sighed. It wouldn't be so bad if she was there. Right? Lottie would help me get through it without even thinking about it. Now that I was thinking about it, I could've asked Clark to come, but I didn't. I could've just pulled out my mobile and told the lad to get his bum here are quick as possible.

But I didn't.

"You fucking jammy sod!" I heard her friend - Winnie? - yell. "And it's Friday too! Fuck this job! That battle-axe Diana will never let me leave now! Where are her other workers, fuck's sake!"

Lottie laughed that bright, clear laugh of hers and skipped back into the shop, her uniform gone and replaced with a floral dress. My eye twitched.

"Shall we?" she asked, her eyes twinkling brightly. She bent her elbow and looked at me expectantly.

I stared at her arm and raised my eyebrows. What the fuck was she waiting for? "What are you doing?" I asked.

She pouted and dropped her arm. "I was trying to be posh, but you wouldn't take my arm like a proper English gentleman!"

I spun around to walk outside. "I never said anything about being a gentleman."

Lottie laughed and scurried to catch up with me. "Can't even pretend for a second to keep me happy, can you, Benny?"

I looked down at her and frowned. Did she like gentlemen or something? So I had to be gentleman to make her happy? God fucking dammit. Why did this always happen? I was the furthest possible thing from a gentleman, and that was one of the reasons I was alone.

At my silence, Lottie tugged on my elbow. "Come on, Ben, I was just joking. I know you're not into that kinda stuff, come on!"

Calm the fuck down, Ben. You're acting like a little twat.

We were almost at my car when I flung my arm across her shoulders. She stumbled a little from the pressure, but I caught her and helped her straighten out. Out of the corner of my eye, I saw Archer staring at us and making kissy faces. I flipped him the bird and kept walking with Lottie .

She was kind of small, quite a few centimetres shorter than me. She only reached halfway up my chest, but in a strange way, she fit.

And don't think I didn't notice the adoring smile she shot in my direction. Because I did and it made my stomach twist up. I really had to stop letting myself feel these things. I also really had to take my arm off of her. But I didn't.

"Get in," I said to her.

"Please!" she sang out playfully.

I narrowed my eyes as she stepped out of my grip. "Sorry?"

"'Get in, please, Lottie!' is what I should've heard." I stared at her until she laughed at me and swatted my arm. "I'm just taking the Mickey, lighten up, will you?"

I rolled my eyes and got in the driver's seat. "You make terrible jokes, Lottie."

She gaped. "You lie!"

"No, I truth." It was getting harder and harder to keep the smile from showing around her.

"I do not make terrible jokes, I actually wonder why I decided to study English instead of becoming a freelance comedian."

"Because you wouldn't have made any money?" I suggested.

"Gosh, Ben, stop ruining my dreams," she said, poking my cheek.

I simply pushed away her hand and pulled up next to what I presumed was Archer's car. I rolled down the window and said, "Nice ride. Birthday present?"

He looked at me and nodded. I could tell he was still kind of angry at me. Lottie leant over me and beamed at Archer. Her sudden movement shocked me, and my back slammed against the seat in an effort to keep from touching her. "Archibald, I really like your car!"

Archer laughed at her. It made me happy that he liked Lottie, because I wanted my baby brother to like my...friends. "Thanks. Lottie is it?"

"Don't call her Lottie," I said before I could stop myself.

"Why not? Isn't that what you call her?"

"My name is Charlotte, you can call me Charlie," Lottie offered weakly.

Archer's eyes widened, and then he smirked. "Why can't I call you Lottie like Ben does?"

My grip on the steering wheel tightened. "Just call her Charlie, Jesus Christ."

"Charlie Jesus Christ is a mouthful, you can stick with Charlie," Lottie piped up.

"Stop making bad jokes and sit down," I said, using my arm to push her back on her seat.

"That was a pretty good joke, you have to admit," she cooed.

I pointed at my straight face. "Do I look like I'm laughing?"

"That depends on what your definition of laughing is."

"I'm pretty sure laughing has a solid definition."

Lottie just looked at me with amusement. Why I was amusing her, I had absolutely no clue. I looked at her like that because she was being ridiculous.

"Lead the way, little brother," I called to Archer. He shot me a thumbs up and drove out of the car park, me trailing behind him. "The drive's pretty long," I said to Lottie. "Maybe two-ish hours - three if we get in a jam."

Lottie frowned. "Why did Archer come all the way to my bakery if he lives two hours away?"

I frowned too. "I have no clue."

Suddenly, Lottie let out a loud "Aw!" and clasped her hands together. "Maybe he was looking for you!" she exclaimed. "Aw, that's so cute!"

I rolled my eyes at her excitement. "Oh stop," I said. "That's a bad theory."

"You think everything of mine is bad," she said and then frowned.

I glanced at her out of the corner of my eye, at how, even when she was trying to be angry, there was still that telltale sign of a smile on her mouth and a twinkle in her eyes.

Not everything.

Chapter 21

I bit my lip and turned my head to look at Ben. My brow furrowed worriedly. For the past half an hour, he'd been silent, his hands slowly growing whiter and whiter from how hard he was holding the steering wheel.

I was about to stretch out my hand towards him, but then I remembered how he'd snapped at me before. I breathed out and cracked my knuckles.

Do it, Lottie. When have I ever bothered about his snappiness anyways?

"Ben?" I said softly.

He didn't acknowledge me in the slightest. Did he not hear me?

"What's the matter?" I said, raising my voice. I gently touched his shoulder.

Ben jumped. He glanced at me, and his hands relaxed on the wheel. "Nothing," he said tightly.

"Then why do you look constipated?" I asked.

Ben relaxed some more. "Just, can you just keep talking to me?" he said in a low voice.

"Stupid stuff or deep stuff?"

"Anything. Just...talk."

I hummed under my breath and stroked my chin. Anything, he said. "I like to write," I told him.

"Is that so, Miss English Major?"

I laughed and shoved his shoulder. He barely even moved because of how little my force affected him, which made me laugh harder. "No," I said. "I mean, I really like to write. I like to create characters and give them a personality. I like to see what they would do in any given situation and then write it down because I want to get to know my own creation. They're like little people thriving off of me and I like it when they develop and then I become so proud of them, like I'm their mother or something. It's really cool to me that when you step back and look at a piece of writing, and you realise that you wrote that, and you see how your babies have lived their lives, and you cry for them, and laugh at them, and when their story is over, it's really sad because it's almost as if you haven't been making them up, but they're actual people."

I paused for a breath, and looked at Ben, who wasn't speaking at all. I thought back to what I said and realised that maybe I just painted myself as a total lunatic. Plus, my smile was as large as my face, and I think it creeped him out a bit.

"I'm sorry, I'm just really weird about this kinda stuff," I said. "I'm not crazy, I don't think my characters are actually real, I just-"

"Hey," Ben interrupted. "Don't apologise."

And he didn't even have to say anything else, because that was enough to get me blushing like a tomato. It made my insides twist up whenever he spoke to me, because even though he didn't say anything particularly sweet, it still made me happy. I could catch his underlying meaning despite him not saying anything.

He was driving one-handed, his left hand resting casually on the mini-table between our seats. I glanced down at it and flexed my own hands. Should I do it? What if he just pulled away and made me feel super awkward?

Brush it off if he does that, you wuss. No risk, no reward.

I took a deep breath, calming myself. I looked at Ben, and was once again floored by his good looks. My goodness, he was such a good looking guy. Stop it, Lottie. Focus. No, not on his pretty eyes.

Before I could chicken out, I reached out and laced our fingers together, my breath bated for when he would pull away and glare at me. I actually almost passed out when he didn't move away. He actually held on tighter.

I ducked my head because my face was becoming unbearably hot, but was it me, or was his face turning red too?

Oh jeez.

"Are you hungry?" Ben's asked me some time later. I was beginning to worry that my hand was sweaty or something, because he kept flexing his fingers before tightening his grip on my hand.

"Actually, yes," I admitted

"Okay, because there's a garage at the next exit. You can go snag something from inside while I buy some petrol, yeah?"

I glanced at him and noticed that he was determinedly staring at the road. I smiled slightly. "You really are kind," I said solemnly. "I don't see why anybody would think otherwise."

He didn't say anything, but his jaw locked. I frowned. I hoped he wasn't one of those "I'm so tough, I don't have feelings, grrr, roar, meat," guys who couldn't take sissy compliments from peppy girls.

Ben let go of my hand so that he could turn into the exit, and we smoothly rolled up to one of the petrol stations. I went to open the door, but he laid a hand on my shoulder and shook his head. "What's wrong, Ben?" I asked, but he didn't reply. He just opened his own door, sprinted around the car, and opened my door.

"I can be a gentleman too," he said, with a ridiculous grin on his face.

I bit my lip to keep my already ginormous smile from becoming super creepy. "Aw, Benny!" I exclaimed. I climbed out. "You don't have to be a gentleman, I swear, I was only teasing you!"

"Hey," he interrupted, flicking my nose. "It's whatever, okay? Just shut up." The grin was gone, but I was satisfied, because the sight was imprinted in the front of my mind.

I beamed at him. "Ben," was all I said. I couldn't even bring my feelings into words, because all my heart was saying was Ben, Ben, Ben.

"Yeah?"

I didn't say anything, I just hugged him extremely tight around the waist and ran away to the garage's store before he could even comprehend what was going on. "Good afternoon, love," called the old man manning the till.

I waved energetically at him, still feeling an adrenaline rush from when I hugged Ben. He was really cuddly for such a large person, and I wanted to keep hugging him and never let go because he gave the best hugs.

"Looking for anything in particular?" asked the old man.

I glanced at him and almost laugh out loud at his funny hairstyle. He was completely bald on the top of his head, but at the back were long, white hairs gathered into a teal hairband. "Where are your sweeties and crisps?" I asked politely, only seeing a rack full of lighters and beef jerky.

He smiled a half-toothless smile and pointed to the left. "Along the wall is where you should find them, lass."

"Thank you!" I said.

I went out to where he pointed and grabbed a humongous packet of my favourite Haribos from the chocolate rack, and then moved onto the next one.

I stood quietly for a minute and pondered the different flavours of Walker's crisps. "I wonder what kind Ben likes?" I said out loud. I was thinking so hard that I didn't even notice the presence that came to stand behind me.

"Salt and vinegar, or ketchup," someone whispered into my ear.

"Oh!" I squeaked, nearly jumping out of my skin. I spun on my heel and pouted at the amused Ben. "You gave me a fright," I said.

"I know," he replied smugly. "Three-nil now, or am I counting wrong?"

I couldn't stay angry at him, so I just lightly smacked his upper arm and turned around so I could grab the ketchup crisps. "The ketchup flavour is good?" I said curiously, staring at the red packet.

Ben looked shocked at the words that had escaped my mouth, so surprised that I furrowed my eyebrows, trying to think about whether I had said something more offensive than I had meant.

I stared at him and raised my eyebrows. "Are you constipated?"

Ben rolled his eyes and took the food from my arms. "My bowel movements are doing well, thanks for the concern," he muttered.

I laughed, trailing behind him like a puppy. My laughter faded when I noticed him striding towards the till. "Hey, I can pay, Benny!" I said, jogging to catch up to him.

He glanced down at me and shook his head. "Don't argue with me," he ordered.

I poked him. "Don't command me to do things," I replied, slightly miffed at his austere tone.

He froze mid-stride. There was an awkward silence between the two of us before he sighed and said, "You're right, I'm sorry."

I smiled. "It's alright." He shot a ghost of a smile at me before dumping the food on the counter.

The old man grinned at us, not at all fazed by all the racket we were making. "How's everything going, you young lovebirds?"

My eyes widened. "Oh we're not-"

Ben shook his head at me, placed a five pound note and a two pound coin on the counter, and took the food and water in his arms. "Keep the change!" he told the old man, and then he grabbed my hand and sprinted out.

"Wait!" we heard the old man call.

My heart was in my throat, because I usually went through a mental preparation before touching him in any sort. But here he was, blindly grabbing me and giving me heart attacks. We reached the car and slid into our seats. Ben put the crisp, sweets, and water on my lap.

I looked at him and his flushed face, and it was crazy how innocent he seemed. "Ben," I said. "You're really quite lovely, aren't you?"

"Lottie," he said. "I think that's you."

Chapter 22

As we got closer and closer to our destination, I was trying to think of what drug I must've taken that would've made me be stupid enough to agree to this.

I didn't want to be anywhere near those people. There was a reason I left, and even though it wasn't of my own free will at the beginning, it made me happy to leave. But I was happy without them.

Fuck. I wasn't even sure if I knew what 'happy' was anymore.

A small squeak had me glancing to my left, where a sleeping Lottie sat. I frowned. She may act like she did, but did she really know how to be happy?

In her sleep, her nose scrunched up and her forehead wrinkled worriedly. A gasping noise escaped her mouth. I wondered what was the matter. Was it her mother? Her father?

"Lottie," I said to myself. I liked saying her name. It reminded me of things I used to forget. It reminded me of determination and stubbornness and friendliness. It reminded me to be kind.

She moaned in her sleep, almost like she was in pain, and, as if by second nature, I reached out and grasped her hand in mine. It was small and soft and warm, and when we made contact, she let out a tiny sigh and relaxed.

"I'm sorry," I muttered. "I'm sorry, Lottie."

My phone rang at that moment, and I scowled. I wanted to just be alone for a while. I wanted to just soak in Lottie's company. But fuck if I could.

I connected my phone to my car and pressed 'accept call.' "Ben," came Archer's voice, all staticky through the speakers.

I sighed. "What's up, kiddo?"

"We're almost there. Are you ready?"

No. I wasn't. "Yeah. Don't worry about me, buddy. I'm fine."

I heard Archer let out a relieved sigh. "Okay."

I knew the kid was still worried I would leave him again. "Hey, don't worry, Archer," I said. "I'm still going. Besides, Lottie would get really upset if I turned back."

"Lottie?" he asked, confused. "Oh, your Lottie. The Lottie who is your Lottie and only your Lottie, but is everyone else's Charlie."

"Oh shut it," I said quietly. Lottie stirred next to me, but I didn't want to her to be woken up.

"Chill oooout, Ben. I had no idea that she already had you at her beck and call. And you're not even shagging, are you?"

"Jesus Christ, kid, keep talking and I'll feed you worms, got it?"

"Yeah, but Lottie might get upset, won't she?"

I huffed in frustration and ended the call. Lottie wasn't controlling me. I glanced at her and her slightly heaving chest. She was one of the only people who didn't try and change me.

I glared at the roads that were taking me back to the place I never wanted to go back to. As I drove, the farmland that enclosed the roads was soon replaced by buildings. It occurred to me that Lottie should be briefed before meeting my parents. I didn't want her to get hurt by their callousness. I wanted to make sure she understood that what they said didn't matter.

I removed my hand from her tight grip and shook her shoulder. "Lottie," I said loudly. "Lottie, wake up."

A slow groan escaped her mouth and she jolted up, rubbing the sleep from her bleary eyes. "Wha-" she said, her voice thick and fatigued. "Benny?" She glanced around quickly, and upon seeing me beside her, she relaxed.

I held back my amused smile at the sight of her tangled hair. She looked like a doll, but I knew she needed to clean up before she met my parents. "We're almost there," I informed her, my hands unconsciously gripping the steering wheel tighter.

She yawned and stretched her arms, and I almost laughed, because she couldn't even yawn like a normal person. She yawned like a panda. "Okay, Ben," she said agreeably.

I gritted my teeth. I'd have to tell her someday, wouldn't I? Just suck it up, Ben. Tell her. "Er...Lottie?"

At my tone of voice, her head popped up and she furrowed her eyebrows in concern. It baffled me how quickly she could detect sorrow in somebody - even before they could themselves. "Yes?"

I closed my eyes for a fraction of a second. "Er, there's probably something you should know about my parents." She remained quiet, but urged me on with a soft touch to my forearm. Why was this so hard to say? "They disowned me," I said quickly. The words felt like tar in my mouth.

When I didn't hear anything from Lottie, not even a gasp like I expected, I looked at her. My eyebrows raised when I saw that her face had turned a bright red - she wasn't blushing, she was...angry? Her fists clenched, and it reminded me of that time in her bakery, when Mrs. Wellington had come and Lottie had sent her away.

"Lottie?" I said worriedly. She looked like she was about to explode, to be honest. "Lottie..."

I had to look back at the road, but I heard her take in a shuddering breath. "Disowned," she repeated.

My jaw clenched. "Yeah," I said.

"Is there a reason, or do they simply not see what a stud of a son they have?"

A small smile quirked up my lips at her words, and it shocked me. She knew exactly what to say. "Three years ago," I said, "I told them I didn't want to inherit my dad's company - I didn't know what I wanted to do, but I didn't want to become my dad. And so they thought I was just wasting my life and was a screw-up and would never do anything good with my life. So when I didn't change my mind and started getting into trouble, they told me I could either get out, or I could follow in his footsteps."

I wasn't sure why I was telling her. We hadn't actually known each other for a long time, but she'd already made me more comfortable around her than I could remember being around anyone, besides Clark.

"I don't mean any offence," she said, "but I'm not really 'feeling the love' towards your parents." She shook her head. "That's such a stupid reason, Ben, seriously. Disowning you for that? Stupid. You're their kid."

I chuckled. God, that was what she did to me - she made me laugh. She made me happy. Even when she was insulting someone, she seemed kind. If that was even possible.

"Aw, yay," I heard her say, and her finger poked my bottom lip. "I love it when this happens."

To cover up the fact that my cheeks were heating up, I cleared my throat obnoxiously. "Anyway. They're not going to be happy to see me, so I'm just warning you. And they're extremely posh, so they might also take stabs at you. Don't take it to heart, okay? Because I know that nothing bad they're gonna say to you is true."

Without replying, Lottie loosened one of my hands from the steering wheel. "Relax, Ben," she said. "You're hurting yourself."

"Promise me you won't mind what they think of you, Lottie," I said, even as I turned to mush from her light touch.

"Ben, you keep smoothing down your shirt and patting your hair. If anything, you're the one who minds what they think."

I scowled. "I do not."

"You are. You've been doing it the entire car ride. Relax, Ben. You're a wonderful person, and they should know it. You are better than anything foul they're going to say to you, okay? Don't worry about me."

My mind raced at her words. Every syllable was punctuated with a sincere tone, and I knew that she thought what she said was the truth. But was I really? Was I really a good person? I couldn't believe that.

"Benny!" she exclaimed. "Stop that!"

I wrenched my eyes off the road for a second so I could look at her. "Stop what, Lottie?" I asked.

"Doubting yourself. Stop doubting yourself."

Goddammit. God motherfucking dammit. Why did she have to do that? Why did she have to know me better than anyone ever has in the span of a few simple weeks? "Jesus Christ, Lottie. Have you ever considered being a motivational speaker?"

She laughed. But even her soothing words and vote of confidence weren't enough to hold back the nerves that began to settle in my stomach as we got closer to my parents' mansion. "Hey, Ben," Lottie said, five minutes later.

Images of my parents kicking me out swirled in my mind, and I had to force myself to reply. "Yeah?"

"I'm here, okay?"

"I know," I said. I knew I'd feel embarrassed later because of how needy I'd projected myself to her, but as of now, I was grateful for her. I glanced at her and felt myself slightly comforted at the sight of her closed eyes and calm expression. God, she was heaven-sent.

"We'll do this together," she said.

"I'm grateful for you," I whispered low enough that she wouldn't hear me. "I'm very grateful that you're in my life."

Precisely twelve minutes later, my car rumbled to a stop behind Archer's. Lottie and I got out and approached him. He was busy carrying the cake.

I swallowed when I looked at the large, white brick mansion and the unnaturally green lawn surrounding it. Everything was how I remembered. Nothing had changed. My stomach churned and I froze mid-step. I couldn't do this. I had to go back. They didn't want me here.

A hand touched my elbow. "Ben," Lottie said, her tone more caring than I could've imagined possible.

I breathed out. "Thanks for coming, Lottie," I said.

"You're welcome!" she exclaimed, smiling at me reassuringly. My heart rate decreased as I looked at her, and I felt more calm.

"Ready?" a voice said from behind us.

I took a deep breath to compose myself. "Hold on," I said. I combed my fingers through her wavy brown hair, untangling the snarls and smoothing down loose hairs. As much as I thought she was beautiful, I wanted there to be as little snarky comments directed towards her as possible.

She smiled her thanks and I nodded.

"Now let's go," I said. Archer grinned at me and bent his head for us to follow him. I pulled Lottie to my side and rested my hand on her back. Touching her had a calming effect on me, and it made me feel better about entering the dragons' lair.

"As soon as you want to leave, just say the word," Lottie said to me.

"It'll be fine," I said. She nodded and patted my cheek and told me she was proud of me. I felt like a little puppy from all her attention, but to be honest, I didn't really mind.

"It will be fine," she repeated.

Chapter 23

y head tipped back. "Your house," I said, awestruck. "It's not a house..."

"It's not mine, either," Ben muttered.

I glanced at him. His back was stiff and straight and his expression was pinched. It was obvious how much he didn't want to be here, and I really wished that we could leave. But he needed to do this - face his demons and make peace.We stood on the lawn that lay before the mansion, and I was just looking up at it. It was huge and extremely beautiful.

Archer nudged me. "The cake is melting, we should go in," he said.

I glanced at Ben again. He didn't look as though he was ever going to move. "Ben?" I asked tentatively.

"What?" he said, his voice tense.

I didn't like this. "Let's go in, okay?"

Ben nodded and began walking, his movements jerky and his strides long. Archer and I looked at each other and hurried to catch up to him. I didn't like how upset he was, and I didn't like how hard he was working to cover up that sadness with harshness. I ran up beside Ben and laced my fingers with his. His grip on my hand tightened, and I smiled.

At the front door, Ben abruptly stopped, and I slammed into his back. "Oh," I squeaked in surprise, stepping back and rubbing my nose.

"Sorry," he said, but sounded extremely distracted.

I waited for a moment, and when Archer started jumping impatiently, I tapped Ben on the shoulder. "Ben?"

"What?"

"Could you please look at me?"

When he turned to me, his expression was distant and cold, and I could tell that he wasn't really looking at me - his mind was somewhere else.

I frowned worriedly. "Ben, come back to Earth."

His mouth twisted into a scowl. "What, Lottie? Why do you always want something from me?"

I was taken aback. "What do you mean?"

"You can't just say stuff like that," he said loudly and un- kindly. "You can't just pretend that you can fix everything, because you can't!"

I gulped. "I-I know that-"

"No you don't! You don't know how hard it is for me to do this, and yet you pretend that you do! I don't need your help, okay?"

My self-defence mechanism was to smile - it had always been like that. I couldn't help that whenever I felt hurt, I hid it with happiness. My mouth wavered into a shaky smile as

I took a few steps back. "I'm sorry," I tried to say. "I didn't mean for-"

Ben turned away. "You don't care," he said. "God, Charlotte, don't you have the decency to know not to look so happy to see me this mad?"

The smile dropped. I didn't know he felt that way. I didn't know he thought I was just pretending to care. I thought I'd made it clear how much I liked him.

My heart stuttered when I realised that he'd called me Charlotte. Even though his back was turned to me, I lifted my chin and pressed my lips together so that an outsider wouldn't know that anything was wrong. I didn't say anything in response to Ben, because it seemed that anything I said just made him angrier and more annoyed. He didn't need more stress right now.

Archer's mouth was wide open when I looked at him. He was shocked. I tossed him a small smile. Maybe I was just overreacting. Maybe I didn't mean as much as I thought I had. I took a deep breath. Don't cry, Lottie.

Lottie. Only Ben called me Lottie.

Don't cry, Charlie.

I was just overreacting, like the silly little girl most people thought I was. How could I possibly feel such things over a few simple sentences? The only answer was that I was being stupid. Silly.

I needed to get over myself. Stop being so lame. Stop overreacting. Take a deep breath. He was just upset. Maybe he didn't mean what he said. My thoughts jumbled into each other until my head hurt. I shuffled backward.

Ben wouldn't turn around to look at me, which led me to believe that he meant every single word he had said. But I had told him that we would do this together and I wasn't backing out. I wanted him to know that I wasn't in it just for the ride.

Archer put a hand on my shoulder and gave me a sympathetic look. I just smiled and nodded towards the door. "Open it," I whispered. I gestured to the cake and he handed it to me while he searched for his keys.

I kept my distance from the brothers as Archer walked up beside Ben and clapped him on the shoulder. "Ready?" he said to Ben. Ben remained silent as the pristine white door swung open. "Alright, come on in."

I felt utterly insignificant as I stepped through the doorframe and into the beautiful mansion. The floors were smooth white and black marble, and the halls were lined with beautiful landscape paintings and thousand pound vases.

I had barely stepped inside and I was already lost.

It didn't look like a celebration of any kind was going on. I stood awkwardly on the foyer, waiting for some sort of direction. Archer strode forward, and so I followed him after a quick glance at Ben. He stood in front of one of the paintings, and I couldn't see his face.

I figured he needed some alone time, so I kept following Archer. "We should put this in the fridge," I said quietly.

He waited for me to catch up and then threw his arm around my shoulders. "I don't know what's up with him, Charlie," he said sadly. "I bet he's just really stressed."

I shrugged. "Don't worry about it, kiddo," I said, even though he stood a foot taller than me.

I guess something in my expression made Archer rethink his next words, because he just sighed and ushered me forward. I decided to change the subject.

"How did you end up in my bakery?" I asked. Good Eats was fairly popular with the locals and the uni students, but I didn't know that city dwellers had any idea about us.

Archer paused. "I heard Mrs. Wellington tell my mum about seeing Ben over there," he said. "I just wanted to try my luck."

 I smiled, and it was a little more real this time because I was so happy for him. "I'm really glad," I said. "I'm glad you found him, and I know he's glad too."

Archer patted my head. "I think it was a bad idea to bring him here, though. But I don't know what the big deal is."

I frowned. Did Archer not know about Ben being dis-owned? "No, it was a good idea," I assured him. "Ben needs this."

Archer shrugged and continued leading me down the white marbled floor and through different doors until we reached a large, metal door. "Here's the kitchen," he an-nounced, letting go of me in order to open the door.

When he did, I jumped in surprise. The kitchen was bustling with people dressed in white and black, plates of food in their hands while others stood in front of stoves and ovens, doctoring the cooking food. My eyes travelled across the hot room, and I noticed a huge, four layer cake perched on top of the fridge, decorated with white fondant and covered in silver flowers.

"Archer, what on Earth?" I said, shocked. I looked at the cake in my hands and frowned. "What was the point of this?"

He grinned sheepishly and rubbed the back of his head. "I didn't want to be that douche who walks into a store and walks right out without buying anything."

"So you wasted money on something you weren't even going to eat?" I said in a scolding tone.

Archer rolled his eyes, reminding me largely of Ben. Ben looked exactly like that when he rolled his eyes at me.

I pursed my lips. I hoped Ben was okay. "Where should I put this, then?"

Archer led me over to the fridge and opened it up. "Just shove it anywhere," he said.

There was absolutely zero space. Every inch of every shelf was covered in cold cuts and condiments and vegetables and bread and cream. I had to balance the now useless cake on top of three jars of raspberry jam, where it wobbled precariously as I shut the fridge door.

I looked at Archer, who was watching me carefully. "What now?" I asked. I definitely wasn't dressed for any fancy occasion. Maybe I should just-

"Miss Carter!" a shrill voice screeched from the entrance of the kitchen.

I jumped and turned around, my eyes finding a tall, thin white-haired woman running over to me. She was dressed in a black pencil skirt and white blouse - professional enough to be part of the staff, but not fancy enough for a guest.

I furrowed my eyebrows and looked at Archer. He shrugged. "I'm Charlotte Carter," I said to the woman.

She eyed me up and down, her nose wrinkling in surprise. "Where is your luggage?" she asked.

"Luggage?"

"You are Mr. Fisher's girlfriend, are you not? I was informed that you two would be staying the weekend. Mr. Fisher's room has been prepared for you two-"

"Oh, I'm not staying the weekend!" I said, my eyes widening in horror. I looked at Archer again, and he blinked nervously. "What did you do?" I mouthed.

The woman frowned. "You must, Miss Carter. Madame Fisher has already been informed and is eagerly awaiting your arrival."

"B-but I can't stay that long," I stammered. "I have work, and school-"

"That can be easily taken care of, Miss Carter."

I was running out of excuses. I didn't want to stay here the weekend. I wanted to go back - back to Ginny and Diana and Queenie. Diana would kill me for missing a shift. Ginny would kill me for leaving her on her own. "I didn't bring any spare clothes," I said desperately. My hands clasped together so that she would know how much I wanted to leave.

She cocked her head. "You don't want to be with Mr. Fisher, Miss Carter?"

I blinked, taken aback. Why would he not leave? "Is he staying?"

"Yes, miss."

I could feel myself wavering. I didn't want him to go through this by himself. But on the other hand, he didn't want me to be here. And he had Archer. I could just hire a car and ride back home. Forget that this ever happened.

Archer tapped me on the shoulder. "I asked him to stay," he said. "And I think you should, too."

"Why?" I asked, feeling myself wilting down. If I was a flower, all this negativity would've turned me dry and brown. "You heard him. He doesn't want me here."

He scoffed and waved a hand around. "Don't listen to that fucker. He's just being stupid. I would've thought you'd be used to it by now."

I tried to smile at his attempt at cheering me up. "Hey, it doesn't matter. It's your parents' anniversary, it's got nothing to do with me."

Archer grabbed my arm and looked over my head at the woman. "Laura, I'll take care of this."

The woman, Laura, nodded stiffly and turned around, seemingly eager to get out of the stuffy kitchen. "You'll take care of this?" I parroted, raising my eyebrows. I didn't want to be taken care of. I kind of just wanted to go home and eat lots and lots of cookie dough ice cream.

Archer put his hands on my shoulders and bent down to my eye level. "Look, Charlotte, I need you to stay. Nobody in this whole place knows jackshit about my brother - even me."

I shrugged, my head falling down so that I wouldn't have to look at him. "You know, Archer, I don't even know if I know him. God, the only personal things I know about him are that he likes blueberry yoghurt and doesn't like sweets!"

Archer shook his head. "I don't think you understand, Charlie."

"What don't I understand?"

"Him and you - you don't see it, but from an outsider's point of view, there are no two people more right for each other than you and my big brother."

Chapter 24

The door to my old room flew open and my brother marched in, his face red and his expression furious.

"What is it?" I asked dully.

"You're a stupid motherfucker!" Archer yelled, storming up to me and punching me in the shoulder.

I let out a grunt from the unexpected impact and then glared at him, my nostrils flaring. "What the fuck, kid?"

"Hey, don't call me kid, Benjamin!" he said angrily, pushing me. "You're the one who's acting like a kid!"

My fists clenched. "Get out," I said. I was in a God-awful mood, and he was doing nothing to help me out.

Archer matched my glare and crossed his arms over his chest. "What's wrong with you?"

I turned my head, my jaw beginning to tick. I knew what he was talking about, but I didn't want to think about it. "Get out," I repeated.

I heard him sigh, and then he said, "Why did you say those things to Charlie?"

My chest tightened painfully when I recalled the stunned and hurt expression on Lottie's face when I spoke cruelly to her. "I don't know," I said. I didn't know why those horrible things spewed out of my mouth. I had no excuse.

"That's not an answer."

I scowled. "It is a fucking answer."

"So you're telling me that you don't know why you were such an arse to her?"

When he said it like that, I sounded like a complete moron.

Okay, so I was.

"She should be used to it by now," I said, feeling a vein bulge in my forehead. "I told her so many times what a big jerk I was, and she didn't even listen to me. It's her fault."

I wanted to take it back as soon as I'd said it.

Archer's mouth opened noiselessly, and he raised his eyebrows incredulously. "Ben!" he said, sounding like he wanted to hit me again. "You're three years older than me, and I know what a dumb thing that is to say!"

I looked away. I wanted nothing more than to find Lottie and tell her I was sorry and that I didn't know what was wrong with me; that I was just a bad person and that she shouldn't take it to heart. Nothing I said to her back there was true, and I wished I could take it back.

But hell if she'd ever want to look at me again. Unless I was being selfish and assumed she liked me more than she did. I probably was.

Archer sighed again. "I just have one more question."

"What?" I asked reluctantly.

"Does Charlie, I dunno, does she become Mr. Clean when she's upset?"

I furrowed my eyebrows and looked at my little brother. My confusion caused my anger to simmer down a bit. "What do you mean?"

He scratched his head, just as confused as I. "I can't get her out of the kitchen. She kind of took over making the pastries, and then she started scrubbing the stove, and I just..."

I closed my eyes and took a deep breath. "Fuck," I muttered. I sat down and buried my face into my hands. "Fuck," I repeated.

I should've known better than to lash out on her. Just because she made it seem like she absorbed the pain of each blow, didn't mean she was invincible. After all, she was still a human, and she still had a heart. And in her case, it was a huge heart.

"Can you do something about it?" Archer asked. "I know you probably want to stay away from her, but nobody else can get her away. I figured you'd be able to."

I looked up and stared at my brother, wondering when he grew up so fast. "What makes you think that?"

He gave me a look like I was being stupid. "Isn't it obvious? Even I've noticed."

I hissed impatiently through my teeth. "Noticed what, Archer?"

Archer rolled his eyes. "That girl would do anything for you, Ben. And you better fucking man up and believe it before some other guy starts treating her right."

The kitchen held some of my fondest memories of this stone cold mansion, although that wasn't saying much. In the kitchen, there was always life and activity and warmth even when every other room was empty and cold.

I stepped inside and was instantly hit with a gust of hot air that smelt like baking bread. I inhaled deeply. God, I had missed that scent.

"Is that...little Benjy?" a surprised female voice exclaimed.

I looked up, my eyes finding a somewhat stout, fair haired woman staring at me, her face weathered and wrinkled from hours of working near stoves and gardening under the sun. "Miss Franny," I said, nodding at her. My worried expression softened slightly at the familiar sight of her. Miss Franny, the head cook and my old tutor, beamed at me.

"Benjy!" she said louder, and rushed over to me. I opened my arms and she hugged me tightly, her aroma of yeast and flour rising to my nose.

"Hey, Miss Franny," I said. I felt myself twitch slightly, because I had been scanning the kitchen and couldn't find Lottie. Where was she?

She stepped back and used a hand towel to swat my arm. I winced and rubbed the now aching spot. "I can't believe you!" she said accusingly. "You didn't bother to visit dear old Miss Franny once! Don't you have a considerate bone in your body, boy?"

I grimaced. If there was one thing that stood out about Chef Francine, it was that she was exactly like a mother hen over her charges. And she became somewhat violent during long periods of distance between herself and said charges. Meaning me.

"I'm sorry," I said honestly. I really was glad to see her, and I wanted to catch up, but I really needed to find Lottie before she worked herself to a faint. "But Miss Franny, I came here to look for someone."

She stopped shaking her finger at me and frowned. "Are you talking about that brown haired lass with the green dress on?"

I nodded, my eyebrows furrowing. "Where is she?"

Miss Franny pointed towards a row of counters. "The poor thing is on her knees behind the third drawer, scrubbing the floor to death. Who is she, Benjy?" But I was already hurrying over there, so I didn't have a chance to answer. Besides, I wouldn't have known what to say. Girlfriend? No. Friend? Most likely not, after what I did.

I stopped in front of the cabinets and peered over the other side of them, and I saw Lottie's form shaking as she vigorously used a small sponge to clean the tiles. I sat on the counter and swung my legs over the side, landing right behind her.

Lottie didn't hear the thumping sound I made, and she didn't seem to notice when I knelt next to her, my eyes trained on her face. Her big eyes were dim and her mouth was pursed into a thin line. I felt my chest tighten.

Why did I have to be such a douche-ninny?

Just because coming to my old house made me nervous didn't give me the right to snap at her like she meant nothing.

And knowing her, she'd probably be beating herself up over it, believing that my harsh words were her fault.

At that moment, I really hated myself.

I tried to think of a way to announce my presence, but not scare her. I didn't want to scare her. I took a deep breath and tapped her shoulder. She didn't flinch. She didn't even stop working. "Please leave me be, I'm fine-" she started to say.

"Lottie," I said. Her hand stop scrubbing and she jumped, nearly tipping over backwards. I used one hand to stop her from falling. "Lottie, please stop working," I said. "It's your day off."

Instead of answering me, she leant back on her heels, dusted off her dress, and stood up. I frowned, but stood up with her. Even though I was a head and a half taller than her, when she tilted her chin up like she was doing now, she seemed miles taller.

"We should probably go meet my parents now," I said after an awkward pause in which I realised she wasn't going to acknowledge me. I deserved it, to be sure, but I didn't like it. I was too used to having her whole attention on me whenever we were together.

Lottie began walking, and I hurried to catch up to her. I felt like a naughty little boy, just trailing behind his angry friend and feeling very sorry for himself. "Lottie-" I said, and then stopped. I didn't know what to say.

She kept walking, acting as if I hadn't spoken. I bit my lip at the way her jaw ticked and her eyebrows arched, her nose up in the air. Was she being...proud?

I didn't know she could be like that.

For some reason, I felt myself become proud of her for holding her ground. I was proud that she wasn't going to let me walk all over her - but I wouldn't have anyways.

When she turned into the wrong hallway, I cleared my throat, fighting back an amused smile. "Wrong way, love," I said. My smile surfaced when she made no move to respond, but turned around and pranced in the other direction anyway.

I followed behind her and could feel my nervous self becoming soothed from the mere sight of her - however angry she was at me. My breathing steadied and I figured that I could get through this day if I just focused on the way Lottie's hair fell on her cheeks, or how her green dress flowed down her figure.

I wondered how she knew the way to go, because the mansion was extremely large and even I used to get lost as a kid. But then I realised she was following the noises that grew louder the closer we got. I caught up to her and walked beside her the rest of the way, even though she drifted away the second I got too close. To be honest, that hurt my feelings a bit, but I ordered myself to suck it up, considering that I was much, much worse.

We reached the large sitting room my parents had dedicated as the room to entertain guests in, and I stopped in front of the gleaming mahogany door. I didn't want to go in. I wanted to go home - my home. This wasn't home anymore. I didn't want to see my parents. I wasn't sure why I'd agreed to this. I didn't want to see those disappointed faces again.

I felt something small touch my elbow, but when I looked, Lottie's hands were by her sides. But that ghostly touch gave me the little strength I needed, and so I pushed open the door.

We were greeted by a room full of classily dressed, rich snobs, all chatting about vapid topics or politics. I recognised a lot of them - all from back in the days when I attended the benefits and charities that my parents forced me to go to. Nobody noticed Lottie and I standing awkwardly near the front at first - they just went about drinking their champagne and twittering about God-knows-what nonsense.

Then Archer spotted us, and a smile stretched across his boyish face. He loped on over, and at his movements, people began to turn their heads to us. I didn't like the way some of the men were looking at Lottie, so I inched closer to her. She didn't move away which meant she was just as nervous as I. I badly wanted to draw her into me and protect her from the predatoriness of the wealthy prats in this room, but I knew she wouldn't be okay with that.

I heard my name in the renewed chattering of the crowd, except this time they whispered, as though that made it less obvious.

"What is the older boy doing here?" someone asked.

"Finally decided to show his face to his poor parents?" someone else said in an especially nasty tone.

"And who is that girl?"

I would've lost it had Archer not reached me and clapped me on the shoulder. "Hey, bro!" he exclaimed happily. "Glad you brought Charlie! Mum and Dad just went out for a moment, they should be back here in a few."

I hadn't known just how much I'd wanted to hear Lottie's voice again until she spoke then. "I'm just going to pop on round to the loo," she said quietly, tiredly. My chest squeezed. She quickly escaped outside, and I cursed. I didn't like this at all. This ignoring thing had to stop. I had to fix it.

She flounced away, even as I called after her. "Lottie, wait!" I said, feeling myself become desperate. "Lottie, please! I'm so sorry for saying those things to you, okay? I didn't mean them at all - I'm just a dick! A dick who doesn't deserve you, I don't deserve anything you do for me, and I'm just so fucking sorry."

I spun around and punched the column that stood in front of me. The plaster crumbled underneath my fist, and I hissed in pain. Tiny scratches and beads of blood dotted my knuckles, but I still felt angry. Disgusted at myself. I had messed up.

I should never take a gem like Lottie for granted.

I jumped when a soft hand grazed my hurt fingers. Lottie stared at my hand, her expression puckered in worry. My heart started thundering around when I realised that her eyes weren't distant anymore, but warm and open.

She sighed. "I just needed to hear that I actually meant something to you."

Chapter 25

ave you heard the news? I meant more to Benjamin Fisher than I had originally thought. I didn't know exactly what that entailed, but it was enough to make me giddy with joy. I meant something to him!

Benjamin Fisher cared about me!

He stared at me while I prodded at his hand that he'd used to punch through a wall. God, he was such a cheesehead sometimes, I didn't know why he insisted on hurting himself. "You need to get yourself cleaned up," I said, letting go of his wrist.

I looked up at him when he didn't respond and realised that he was staring at me vacantly, his mouth slightly open in shock. I smiled in amusement. He looked absolutely frozen.

"Hello!" I said, waving my hand in front of his face. "Does this head have an occupant?"

Ben seemed to be rendered speechless. I figured he was just surprised that I was talking to him. I'll admit, it was incredibly hard to keep a straight face a while ago when all I wanted to do was run straight at him and cry.

But I wanted to keep my head. A few words shouldn't have been able to hurt me so much. He shouldn't have such a hold over my emotions. I shouldn't let him have such a hold over my emotions. I have to be my own person before I start to rely on another. "You're really dopey sometimes," I said. I smacked his cheek lightly. "Get a hold of yourself!"

Ben blinked. "Don't hit me," he muttered.

I laughed and smacked his cheek again, but very, very lightly. "What was that?"

I raised my hand again, but this time he caught my wrist. "Don't hit me!" he exclaimed, his tone bordering on a whine.

I raised my eyebrows. "Sissy," I said teasingly.

Ben's eyebrows furrowed. "What did you call me?"

"I called you a sissy."

"Take it back."

"No."

"Take. It. Back."

I laughed. "Are you twelve?"

A mischievous grin overtook Ben's face that overjoyed and frightened me in equal parts. I backed away slowly. "When I was twelve, I did track and field," he said.

I scoffed. When he was twelve? As if that talent would carry on over eight years...right? "Which area did you specialise in?"

"400 metre sprint." The grin became almost wolfish and I let out a surprised squeak.

"Awesome, brilliant, incredible, fantastic," I said enthusiastically. "Well, goodbye!"

I took off running, well aware that he could catch me in three seconds flat. "Lottie, I have something for you!" he sang loudly in the creepiest voice I may have heard in my life.

I started laughing uncontrollably and clutched my stomach, stumbling over my feet. "Stop it, stop, Ben!" I yelled. "I'm gonna pee!"

"Nobody's stopping you!" he yelled right back. He sounded really close, so I panicked, turning sharply into the nearest corridor.

"Go away before I pee on you!"

"Lottie, where are you going?" I heard the sound of him sliding on the floor, followed by a thump as he fell.

I stopped running then, laughing so hard that tears fell out of my eyes. I worried a little for Ben though, so I ran back to him while still laughing. He lay still on his back, a disgruntled expression on his face. I knelt beside him and tried to kerb my chuckles for his sake, but found it increasingly hard, as every time I looked at his face, I burst into fresh peals of laughter. I literally almost peed myself. "Ben, are you okay?" I said between giggles.

"Laugh it up," he muttered, indignant. "It's really funny, isn't it?"

I clamped my mouth shut and managed to stop myself from laughing some more. "It really is," I confessed. "Ben, did it hurt when you fell? Wait, oh no, what about your hand?" I snatched up his hand before he could hide it, and realised that his fall caused him to scrape it up even more. I frowned. "Can you take me to the loo, Benny? I want to clean this up."

He scowled and turned his head away from me as he sat up. "I can clean it up myself," he said childishly.

"I'm sure you're a big boy, but I feel bad and I want to clean it up for you. Is that okay, sweetheart?"

Ben looked at me, the scowl replaced by a slight blush. I had to contain my coos at how adorable he looked with his cheeks all cherry red and his eyebrows furrowed like a little kid. "Whatever," he said.

The sound of approaching footsteps hit my ears, and I stiffened, looking around the hallway. A man's and a woman's voices reached us and I stood up. Ben straightened so that he stood slightly in front of me, his body angled to block me from view.

"Who is that?" I said, balancing on my tiptoes and trying to shove Ben out of the way. He refused to move, however, and used one arm to stop me from moving.

"Benjamin?" the woman's voice said, saturated with shock. "Benjamin!"

I yanked myself out of Ben's hold, and my eyes widened when I saw the couple standing before us. A rather tall, blonde haired woman and an even taller dark haired man, both middle aged, but both bearing a striking resemblance to the bloke standing next to me, stood still. The woman was beautiful, with a kind face and creases around her eyes which hinted that she smiled a lot. The man seemed older, however, because he was more solemn than his wife.

"Hello, Mum," Ben said, his voice stiff and his body tense. "Hello Dad."

"We...we didn't know you would be coming," his mum said, tears filling her eyes. I was alarmed at the tears and instantly started towards her. Ben jerked me back, reminding me that I didn't know this woman well enough to comfort her, not to mention she was one of the two that turned Ben out of his own home.

"I didn't think I would be either," Ben said. His father had yet to say anything, yet to do anything besides stare at us intimidatingly.

His mum looked uncertain, like she didn't know whether to hold back or come running to him, and that surprised me. I had thought for sure they'd want him gone. "Benjamin," his mother said again, almost despairingly. Her eyes darted to her husband and then back to us.

I narrowed my eyes, trying to figure out what Mr. Fisher was thinking so hard about. "Hello," I finally said, trying to ease the tension in the air.

Mrs Fisher looked surprised, as though she hadn't noticed me. "Hello," she replied politely. "And you are?"

I stepped forward, extending my hand and smiling. "My name is Charlotte, I'm Ben's friend."

She shook my hand. I was pleased, because her grip was firm. "I'm Benjamin's mother, Carrie."

"Pleased to meet you, ma'am," I said with the same, fixed smile on my face.

"Carrie," Mr. Fisher said suddenly. He had a voice as rough as nails. My smile faltered.

Mrs Fisher looked at him and seemed to read his mind. "No," she said firmly. "Not again, Harrison."

My smile fell. Ben caught me by my shoulders and I reached behind me, taking hold of his hand. "Is there a problem, sir?" I asked Ben's father.

He eyed me. "Yes there is. Two problems, actually."

Chapter 26

I felt my jaw click from the effort I was going through to keep from yelling at the man in front of me.

Lottie's hand squeezed mine tightly, and she stepped back so that she was standing next to me and not in front of me. I focused on her hand, not on my anger. I focused on how her hand was so little but felt really strong from the time she spent working in that bakery of hers.

"What are those two problems?" I heard Lottie ask. My grip on her hand tightened, because I knew what my father would say, and I didn't want her to feel hurt.

"I'm looking at them," he said.

I scowled and straightened, about to let him have it, but Lottie beat me to the punch. She let go of my hand, and her hands formed fists. "How dare you!" she said in the loudest voice I have ever heard her use. To be fair, it wasn't even that loud. But for Lottie, it was noteworthy.

My father raised his eyebrows. "Excuse me?"

I couldn't see her face, but I heard her furious tone of voice. I'm going to be honest - angry Lottie turned me on just as much as regular Lottie. "How dare you treat Ben like that? He's your son!"

My father let out a huff of air and straightened his back. "He is no son of mine," he snapped.

"Harrison!" Mum exclaimed, visibly distraught.

I blinked and stepped back. Of course he'd say that - he'd disowned me, hadn't he? Of course his feelings wouldn't have changed.

Lottie let out a small, frustrated sigh. "Why?"

"Why what?"

"Why isn't he a son of yours? Because he doesn't want to be like you? I'm glad he doesn't, because I like him just the way he is, and I already don't like you!"

Mine and my father's eyes widened in surprise. Maybe he was surprised that such a slip of a girl stood up to him, but I was surprised at how ready she was to defend me, as if I mattered at all.

"Show some respect, young lady."

"My name is Charlotte, and I will show some respect when you say sorry to your son and mean it!"

His gaze flickered to me and I met it evenly. I was embarrassed that Lottie had to listen to this bullshit. I shouldn't have brought her. "He is not my son."

"Why is he not your son?" Lottie asked.

I took her shoulders and pulled her into my chest. "Calm down, Lottie," I whispered. "It's okay."

"It's not okay," she said. She tried to get out of my hold, and while we struggled, my father strode off.

Mum looked at us helplessly. "I'm sorry, Benjamin," she said, wringing her hands. My mum never used to fidget. She must genuinely be upset, but that did little to comfort me. "I'm sorry. I'll go talk to him, okay? Don't worry."

"Ben," Lottie said when my mum had walked off. My ears pricked up worriedly at the hoarseness of her voice, and I spun her around. Her big green eyes shone with tears.

I furrowed her eyebrows, unsure of what to do. "Why are you crying, Lottie? I'm sorry my dad's such a bastard, but don't listen to anything he says, okay?"

She furiously wiped at her eyes and turned away from me. "It's not okay, Ben," she said, and I could tell she was trying to get rid of any evidence that she was sad. "Why can't you see that? He's your dad, he shouldn't treat you so badly. You don't deserve it."

I shrugged, feeling really awkward in my skin. She cried for me. She didn't even cry for herself, but she cried for me. I shoved my hands into my pockets, because they really ached to hug her, but I didn't know if I should. "Don't worry about it, babe," I said.

She shrugged her shoulders tiredly, and it made her look extremely small. My frown deepened. "I'm still going to worry," she said.

Ah fuck. I wrapped my arm around her shoulders and pulled her against my side, and that immediately made me feel better. "I'd rather you not."

"But I still am going to. You can't force me not to."

Jeez, she was so stubborn. I really didn't want her to tire herself out for me, but the fact that she did...I felt myself well up with affection for her, so much so that I felt compelled to swoop down and peck her forehead. A tiny smile curled up the corners of her lips. "That's what I wanted to see," I said.

She took my free hand and started walking. "I'm not really sure I want to go back in there."

I nodded. "Same."

Suddenly, she stopped. "Wait. I know where I want to go."

"Where?"

"The toilet."

I snorted. "You said you've been needing to go for the past twenty minutes. Did you forget about your bladder?"

She laughed, and I relished in the sound. "My pee controls itself when it needs to."

I shook my head. "Okay. Let's go, then."

As we began to walk again, Lottie's expression crumpled in confusion. "Ben," she said.

"Yeah?"

"I seem to remember something about that lady butler saying that we would be sharing a room. Tell me I'm wrong."

I froze and looked at her. "You're joking."

"I swear, I'm not."

I blinked and my jaw ticked uncomfortably. "Ah fuck."

Chapter 27

"This is my room," Ben said awkwardly, unable to meet my eyes. He stood at least three feet away from me.

I rubbed my arms and coughed. "I like it." The room was spacious, and the only pieces of furniture present were a bed, a desk and office chair, and a bookshelf. "It suits you - boring and plain," I added.

"Rude," he said, a hint of a smile on his face. My face relaxed - I loved his smiles. They were like flowers peeking out during a thunderstorm. They made me feel warm and cosy on the inside.

I sat down on the chair and looked around. The bed frame and desk and bookshelf were made of the same dark brown wood, and his walls were beige. I couldn't see any decorations besides a wall clock. Even his desk was free of pencils or paper. I ran a finger across the desk and a streak of dust came off with it. My brow furrowed and I said, "It's like-"

"-I was never here to begin with."

I looked down and willed myself to relax. I had lost my temper back there, and I couldn't afford to do it again. But the way his parents treated Ben...it made me sick to my stomach. "Yeah," I said with a sigh. I used my hand to feverishly push off all the dust until the surface of the desk was shiny and clean. I smiled. Better.

There was a pause. "You know, there are other rooms you can stay in," Ben said, his eyes on the floor.

I bit my lip, trying to hide my devilish grin. The poor guy felt incredibly awkward because we had to share a room. I couldn't torture him, no matter how much I wanted to. "I could just sleep on the floor," I suggested. "I'm not sure I want to be alone in this huge place."

Ben scowled. "You're on the bed, I'm on the floor," he said.

"I refuse. Your germs have been festering in those sheets for years."

That comment loosened him up a little, and he walked over to me, sitting on the desk. "I'm sure they're clean."

I looked up at him and smiled. His handsome face was free of suspicion for once, and that made me happy. "Wanna bet? If dust comes flying up when you sit on the bed, I win."

He raised his eyebrows and crossed him arms. "What are the odds?" he asked.

"I haven't decided yet. Just go." I pushed him off the desk and motioned over to the bed. "Go on, then."

Ben rolled his eyes but walked over anyway, flopping down on his back. "See?" he said smugly. "It smells like lemons, and there's absolutely no dust. I win."

I laughed at his self-satisfied expression. "Okay, I lose, whatever. What do you want in return?"

He propped himself up on his elbows and eyed me carefully. "I'll think about it," he said, "but when I figure it out, you have to listen to me, whatever I say."

"Within reason," I chirped.

He nodded. "Within reason."

I sprang off the chair and launched myself on the bed, landing on my stomach, above and perpendicular to Ben, my limbs spread-eagled. I sighed in delight as I sank into the soft mattress. "It's like a feather."

Ben rolled over onto his stomach and looked at me. When I reached out and patted his head like a dog, he just rolled his eyes.

"You've got lovely hair," I said softly. The patting gradually became stroking, and then my fingers threaded into his dark, silky locks and combed through the tangle. He was one of those guys who wore a bed-head proudly, and it suited him.

Ben's eyes closed as I continued to comb his hair with my fingers. I scooted around the bed until I was lying beside him, and kept my hand in his hair. A small noise escaped him that almost made me squeal. He had literally purred.

I couldn't handle the cuteness. My smile was so wide that I felt my cheeks begin to ache. Before I could talk myself out of it, I ducked my head and planted a kiss on his cheek. "You're so cute!" I squeaked.

Ben's eyes opened and he furrowed his brows at me, frowning. "Cute like a puppy or cute like a man?"

Of course he'd bring that up. I just shook my head playfully and said, "Like the manliest man I know."

"Which is me, right?" he asked, concerned, turning his head towards me.

I giggled, and then I stopped when I realised how close we were. I didn't want a repeat of last time to happen, so I rolled onto my back, stretching my arms and legs out. My right arm collided with his back, but I didn't move it. I was too comfortable. "Not that your head needs to get any bigger, but you're brilliant, Benny."

He made another noise. "You haven't called me Benny in a while."

I grinned sheepishly. "Yeah, I know you don't like it, sorry."

There was a pause. Then, "I don't mind when you say it."

A few hours later, I lay on my back on Ben's bed while he worked on something on his laptop. Despite how much I stretched my limbs, I barely took up half the bed. It had to be even bigger than a king, but what was bigger than king?

We'd spent the time watching The Breakfast Club on Netflix on his laptop, because there was nothing else to do. Now I was tired and hungry, but it wasn't even past six.

"What are you doing?" I asked Ben. "I'm hungry. We missed the party. I want food."

He spun the chair around and looked at me with raised eyebrows. "Did you want to go to that party?"

I threw my hands up. "I saw cake," I said sadly. "It looked really delicious." I felt insides twist in disappointment at the thought and a really embarrassing growl escaped from my belly. I laughed nervously and clasped my stomach, looking up at Ben with big eyes. His expression darkened, and then he shook his head and stood up.

Ben beckoned to me. "Let's go scavenging then, Lottie."

I cheered as I leapt off the bed. "Sweet!"

Ben and I walked out of his room quietly. Nobody lingered in the halls, but we could hear sounds of couples that would be staying the night talking in the extra rooms. "Let's take care to not run into anyone," Ben said.

I nodded agreeably. "I'm not really fancying the idea of meeting any more high society prats."

He chuckled humourlessly. "No kidding."

I winced. "Are they all..."

"Snobby, posh, condescending? Maybe not all, but a good few are."

"I'm sorry," I said.

He sighed. "Me too." I could feel my heart melt for him, and I glanced at him before slipping my hand into his. The good thing was, he didn't mortify me by letting go.

We made it to the kitchen without seeing anybody. Thankfully, Ben remembered all the detours that nobody who was visiting would know, and so we managed to avoid everyone.

"Benjy!" a loud, female voice said in a scolding tone. I looked up and jumped, and our hands disconnected. For a moment, I was disappointed, but then a woman was stomping over to us, and my eyes fixed on her.

I'd seen her when I was helping out in the kitchen some hours ago. She reminded me of my granny with the stern yet loving expression on her face, and I knew right away that she meant a lot to Ben. "Hey, Miss Franny," Ben said weakly, cringing into me. I would've laughed, had the woman not begun to eye me up.

My back straightened immediately and I smiled. "Hello, ma'am," I said, holding out my hand. "Nice to meet you."

She frowned, and my brow dipped worriedly. "Hello," she said politely, shaking my hand suspiciously.

I didn't lose my smile, but I felt my head dipping down slightly. "Miss Franny," said Ben, "what's wrong?"

I then noticed the wooden spoon in her other hand, and she began whacking Ben with it. "Every day you lived here, I told you how important it is to eat! And yet you skipped your meals! What were you doing, Ben? Were you with this girl?"

I flinched slightly at her words, but shrugged it off. Over-protective mother-like women were not my speciality. Ben glanced at me and stepped forward, bending over to whisper something in her ear. I didn't hear what was said, I just knew that what he said made his Miss Franny beam like a little girl.

When Ben stepped back, Miss Franny brought her hands up and cupped my cheeks, as gently as my own grandmother. "How lovely!" she said.

My eyes widened and I looked at Ben's smug expression. What had he said?

Chapter 28

Watching Lottie devour practically all of the leftover cake was like watching a kid meeting Mickey Mouse in Disneyland for the first time. She was surprisingly tidy for someone who ate so quickly.

I stared at her until she stopped and glanced at me, an embarrassed expression on her face. A splotch of pink icing had somehow ended up on the bridge of her nose. I shook my head in amusement and handed her a napkin. Lottie sheepishly wiped her mouth until I moved forward and directed her hand to her nose. Her entire face turned a bright crimson, which made me chuckle.

"You wouldn't happen to be looking at me like that because you want cake and not because you think I'm being a greedy pig, would you?" she asked, almost shyly.

I leant over the counter and rested my chin in my palms. "Do I like cake?" I asked, raising my eyebrows.

She laughed that laugh I adored, despite how embarrassed she was. "Sorry, Benny."

"Don't be," I said. I felt a sharp pain on the back of my head and groaned, reaching around to cradle it.

"Benjamin!" Miss Franny scolded, a large, metal spoon in her hand. "Did you just call the poor girl a greedy pig?"

My eyes widened in terror. "What? No, I didn't!"

I glanced at Lottie for help, and saw that she had a hand covering her mouth to stifle her giggles. "Benjamin," Miss Franny said sternly.

"I swear to God, ma'am, I didn't!"

She shook her head and looked at Lottie. "Don't listen to a word the boy says, dear. He's quite dense - doesn't even realise half the things he says."

My mouth opened and I looked back and forth between my old tutor and Lottie. Lottie's eyes twinkled with mischief, and Miss Franny winked at me. "Miss Franny," I moaned. "Don't put words in my mouth!"

"You don't speak enough, dear, I'm just helping out."

My palms flattened on the counter and I willed myself to not turn red. "Maybe you should just let us eat in peace," I suggested. She patted my head with the spoon and smiled before walking away. I let out a quiet groan, slamming my head down, and Lottie giggled softly. "I didn't call you a greedy pig," I said, my voice muffled by the smooth marble.

"I know, Ben."

I looked up and noticed that she had her gentle smile on, which made me gulp nervously and turn my gaze to the platter of food and plate of cake Miss Franny had put together for us. I picked up a fork and speared one of the mini bangers. "The food is delicious," Lottie said, and I knew she was trying to ease my mortification.

I nodded and popped the banger in my mouth. "Miss Franny is really talented," I said, and then froze when the entire sausage fell out of my mouth.

Lottie and I locked gazes. To her credit, she managed to keep a straight face for all of two seconds before she lost it. Her mouth contorted and she burst into a fit of laughter that had her leaning on her arm, using the other hand to bang at the counter. I sat there, fighting between a grin at how sweet she was and a scowl because she was making fun of me.

"I'm sorry!" she managed to gasp. "Don't be embarrass ed...I just - your face!" She started giggling again, her face turning pink from how hard she went at it.

I raised my eyebrows and waited for her to calm down. It took several minutes of which I spent finishing my mini sausages and starting on the casserole dish of poutine.

Suddenly, someone slapped my hand away from my fork. "Hold up, Scooby Doo, let me in on this poutine, yeah?" Lottie smiled at me and picked up her fork.

"Scooby Doo?" I wondered. I frowned. "Was that a crack at my food eating?"

"It wasn't a crack, it was an ode."

"That was not an ode, do you even know what odes are?"

"I know that they exist," she said brightly.

I scoffed. English major, my ass. "Of course they exist, and an ode is supposed to be like a mmfmffm-" Lottie had shoved her fork into my mouth, succeeding in both silencing and almost choking me.

"I think that's the first time I have had to shut you up! I don't care what an ode is while my tummy is empty."

"How is your tummy empty? It's got to be only the size of my fist, and you've already eaten most of the cake," I said.

Lottie giggled into her hand. "What did your Miss Franny say about calling me a pig?"

My mouth opened. "Who called you a pig? Not me. Don't put words in my mouth, not where Miss Franny can hear you," I said, whispering the last part intently.

"I'm just teasing, Benny," she said cheerily, patting my cheek. "Here, want some more poutine?" She held her fork out to me, and I glanced from her fork to her encouraging expression.

"I can feed myself," I muttered, grabbing the fork from her hand. I ate the potatoes and then realised that this was the second time I'd touched her fork with my mouth. That thought made me freeze, and my movements were stiff when I handed the fork back to her.

She just regarded me with amusement. "You're weird," she said, "but sort of in a good way."

I gulped to make myself not act like such an idiot. "Sort of?" I asked, glad that my voice had its regular amount of brusqueness in it.

"Yup, only sort of." She smiled at me and ate her own forkful of poutine. I internally cringed because I had also used that fork. God, I was such a mess. Get your dumbfuck brain out of the clouds, Benjamin. "Are you full?" she asked.

I shrugged awkwardly. "Not really."

"Then stop staring off into space and eat some more, Ben."

"Thanks, Mother," I said with a roll of my eyes.

"Sassy," she said, laughing. "You're so sassy."

I pulled a plate of cheese filled pasties towards me and started scarfing them. Anything to stop me from becoming a total and utter idiot in front of this girl.

Although I was almost one hundred percent sure that she didn't care about that one whit.

"I think I just ate my body weight in cake," Lottie groaned, flopping backwards onto my bed.

I sat down on my chair and spun it around to face her. "Was it worth it?"

She grinned. "Yes it was."

I chuckled and turned back to my desk, opening my laptop. I had a maths assignment to turn in, and since we'd be here for a couple days, I had to do it online.

"Ben?"

"Yeah?"

"I don't have anything to change into," she whispered. "Also, I don't have anything - not a toothbrush or a towel or even a comb!"

I frowned and then stood, feeling guilty. It was my fault she was stranded here with no supplies in the first place. If I hadn't have asked her to come, she'd be at her room, happily chilling with her best friend. "We can go get some stuff if you want. I'm sure there's some markets nearby."

Lottie rubbed her arm and mumbled something. I raised my eyebrows. She grinned sheepishly and said, "I don't have any money, Benny boy."

I held up two fingers. "Don't call me Benny boy," I said, putting down one finger. "And seriously? Obviously I'm gonna buy it for you."

"I really can't let you do that," she murmured, sounding uncomfortable. "Don't you have some spares around here?"

"I can get you clean towels and toothpaste, but not any of the other stuff. Unless you wanna wear..." I trailed off and scratched my head, wondering why now of all times I had to run my mouth.

"Wanna wear what?"

I gulped and looked at her curious face. "Obviously you don't have to, I mean, it's totally your decision. We can go to Safeway or maybe BHS and see if they've got something."

Lottie giggled at my stammering. "What were you going to say before, Benny?"

I shoved my hands in my armpits and blinked hard. "Well, you can always wear my shirt if you want. And maybe we can borrow some trousers from Archer. He might also have a spare toothbrush."

It took a few moments before Lottie responded. "Well, I'm all about being cheap and avoiding paying for things," she said cheerily. "I hope you didn't sweat too much, Benny."

My mouth opened at her teasing. "Oh, shut up, Lottie."

She laughed and my frown melted off my face. "I'm shutting up."

Chapter 29

I turned on my phone and cringed. "Oh dear," I said, my hand going to my face. "Oh dear, oh dear, oh dear."

Ben poked his head out of his closet and raised his eyebrows. "What happened?"

The bright text scrolling across my phone's screen made me gulp. I was in deep trouble. "Seventeen missed calls and twelve texts," I whispered.

He rolled his eyes. "The brunette?"

I thought it was quite funny that he and Ginny didn't really like each other, but at the same time, it disappointed me. I wanted them to get along. "Yeah, it's Ginny," I said, feeling exceptionally guilty. I'd been here for the past, what, eight hours? Ginny thought she'd be covering for me for two to three hours at most.

Ben looked at me blankly. "Aren't you going to call her back?" he asked, his tone questioning my state of mind.

I laughed in embarrassment, covering my face with both hands. "That may be something I should do, huh?" Too bad that I didn't really want to.

"Probably," he agreed, emerging from the closet, a towel draped around his neck. "At least if you want to keep your life."

I plopped onto the bed and sighed. "You're remarkably sensitive to my well being, Benny. I think you're the one who should be the motivational speaker," I said with a grin.

"Tone down the sass, Lottie," he said, but I knew he was just teasing. It was a bit hard to tell, but he definitely was. "I'm going to take a shower, and you are going to call your friend."

I laughed. "Okay, Your Majesty," I said. Ben pulled an immature face that made me laugh again, and then he disappeared into the bathroom.

I looked at my phone again and lay down on my back. I should call Ginny and stop being a scaredy-cat, but on the other hand, do I really want to go home only for her to rip out my small intestine and choke me with it?

I giggled at myself and dialled her number. "Charlie!" a deep voice that certainly was not Ginny's exclaimed.

I frowned and rolled over so that I lay on my stomach. "Yes, who is speaking?"

"It's Zach."

I pursed my lips, my brow furrowing in confusion. "Zach, what're you doing answering Ginny's phone?"

There was a pause. "Oh. Well here's the thing, Charlie..."

"If it's dirty, I'd rather you not tell me," I said. Ginny thought I wanted to hear all the details of her adventures, and I didn't want Zach to think that as well.

I heard choking on the other end. "What - oh whatever, it doesn't matter. I just thought you should know that Ginny is currently passed out on my bed."

I let out a worried groan. This was why I couldn't leave her alone! "Are you serious?" I said. "God, does she have alcohol poisoning? I hope you made her drink water before she fell asleep! Did you check and see if she was breathing? Is she lying properly?"

"Calm down, Charlie, she's fine. She was just tired."

"Then what's she doing at your place?"

"I'm not exactly sure."

I raised my eyebrows. "What so you mean, you're not sure?"

I heard a knock on the door and turned to see Archer poking his head in. I motioned for him to come in but be quiet, and he walked over, sitting next to me on the bed.

"I am speaking English, pest. I meant what I said," Zach said sassily.

I chose to ignore that. "Why'd you call me seventeen times, then? Shouldn't you be talking to her?"

"Sleeping people generally do not respond to queries given to them; I'm not sure if you go the memo, though, Charlie."

I groaned again. "Zach! Why did you call?"

"I need advice," he said. "I haven't really spoken to her since I talked to you, and that's because when I said 'hi,' she responded with, 'go suck on a dead goat.'"

"You're hopeless," I said. I looked over at Archer, and saw that he was staring at me.

'Zach?' he mouthed. 'Does Ben know about this?'

I laughed quietly and shoved him away. "Listen, Zach, you already know what Ginny's like. All you can do is pray she doesn't get violent."

"That is shit advice."

"The fact that she came to your room to crash instead of some other random person's means something, Zach. Just do whatever you did to keep her around the last time."

"But Charlie, there was more physical stuff involved-"

"No, I do not need that kind of information," I said, closing my eyes tightly. I swallowed exaggeratedly. "Don't speak anymore. Please."

I heard Zach laugh on the other end, before he quieted and became serious. "Charlie, I just want you to know that the only reason I kissed that girl in front of Ginny was because Ginny's the only girl I've ever really liked, you know?"

I didn't understand how that worked. "Then why did you do it?" I asked softly.

"It scared me," he said.

I didn't accept his excuse - in fact, I thought it was pretty stupid - but I respected that he was going to be trying to win her back. "Don't be a baby, Zach," I said. "Mature a little, okay? And take care of my best friend while I'm gone."

"Okay, pest. Wait, where are you anyway? Ginny said something about your boyfriend, but you don't have a boyfriend, do you?"

I felt my cheeks heat up at his words, and I didn't know why. "No, I don't have a boyfriend," I said slowly, avoiding the first question. Archer winked at me, which made me turn even redder. Oh my goodness.

"Whatever," Zach said, losing interest. "See ya later."

"Bye, Zach. Take care of Ginny, remember!"

"Okay, bye Charlie."

I hung up and pointedly looked at Archer. "What did I do?" he asked, laughing. "I'm not the one who got caught talking to Zaaach while my...masculine friend showers in the bathroom."

I pointed my finger at him. "You better hope you never get caught with any 'masculine' friends," I said.

"I am not gay!" Archer protested. "And even if I was, then that would still be okay, right?"

I smiled at him and ruffled his hair. "Yes, of course it would be, Archibald," I said, laughing. He pushed my fluttering hands away and leapt off the bed to go sit in the office chair.

Ben found us like that a few minutes later, with me lying on his bed telling off Archer who was spinning nauseatingly fast in the chair.

"You are going to be sick!" I said. I should've gotten off the bed to stop him, but Ben's bed was just too comfortable.

Suddenly, the door to the bathroom opened and Ben walked out, but I didn't glance up at him. I stayed in my position on the bed. "What the hell are you doing, punk?" I heard him say.

I chose to believe he said that to Archer, because out of the stupid people in the room, he was being stupider. "You know," I told Ben, "you take a long time to shower."

"First of all, who cares," he said, and I heard him stride across the room and over to Archer, where he put a stop to the whole chair-spinning thing.

"Please tell me this is my head being fucked up and not just you, you know...not wearing clothes," Archer said groggily.

I choked on nothing and immediately covered my eyes with my hands, my face turning three shades of red. I heard the thump of Ben's hand whacking Archer, and had to bite back my laugh. "Get out, Archer," he growled.

"Sir, yes sir!" I heard the door slam closed but kept my eyes covered. I really hoped Archer was joking when he said Ben didn't have any clothes on.

There was a pause. "Lottie?" Ben said curiously. "What are you doing?"

"Please put on some clothes!" I squeaked. I wasn't sure if I could keep from embarrassing myself if I saw him...without clothes on.

Ben scoffed. "I'm wearing sweatpants. Don't listen to Archer."

I slowly removed my hands from my eyes and peeked at Ben, who was staring at me in exasperation. My cheeks reddened slightly when I saw that he only wore sweatpants. There was a white towel around his neck and his hair was dripping water onto his chest.

I cleared my throat awkwardly. Focus, Lottie. Focus. I blinked hard and coughed.

"You are so weird," Ben said, rubbing at his hair with the towel. I took in a sharp breath of air and force myself to look away.

Get your mind out of the gutter, woman. I laughed slightly and tried to get over myself. "I know. What time is it?"

"It's almost nine. Do you want to take a shower and then maybe watch another movie?"

I smiled delightedly at the awkward way he spoke, like he was unsure of himself. It was so cute! "Okay!" I agreed. "Can I have a towel?"

His worry lines melted off his face and he nodded, grabbing a clean towel and his shirt from his closet. "Here. The shirt is kinda big for me, so it should be decent for you to wear without...er..."

"Trousers?" I said cheekily.

His cheeks tinged pink and he swallowed. "That's right. Trousers."

I smiled and took the towel and shirt from him before heading over to the bathroom. It was warm and steamy from his shower, and it smelt like soap. It was a clean, strong smell. A Ben smell.

The only soap was his manly brand, so I ended up washing my hair with his cologne-scented shampoo and scrubbing my body with a bar of soap that smelt like lemon.

I dried and pulled on Ben's shirt, which was slightly wrinkled, but was still clean. He was right - because it had been slightly loose on him, it fell down my body unflatteringly, and reached as far as my dress had, which was good. The fabric was soft and worn, and I stood there grinning like an idiot for three minutes before exiting the bathroom.

Ben glanced at me while I wrapped my hair in the towel to dry it off, and then immediately looked back at his laptop. I folded my dress and placed it on the floor, then padded over to him. He sat on his bed with his back against the wall, the pillows strewn around him.

I paused when I reached the edge of the bed. "Can I sit next to you?" I asked.

Ben coughed again and cleared his throat. "Oh...er, yeah. Sure."

I grinned and jumped on the mattress, pulling a soft pillow with me and placing it on my lap. My shoulder touched Ben's, and my knee knocked his thigh when I crossed my legs. "What are we watching?"

"What do you want to watch?" he asked, not looking at me.

"I don't know. Oh, hey, is that Lilo and Stitch?" I beamed when I saw the little icon - I loved that film.

"Lilo and Stitch it is ," Ben muttered, pressing play.

I scooted closer to him to better see the screen and then leant forward. I heard Ben's breath catch, and that made my heart beat faster. Just watch the film, okay? I told myself.

"Just watch the film, okay?" I heard Ben whisper to himself.

The grin barely left my face the rest of the night.

Chapter 30

I woke up to the feel of a crick in my neck, an object pressing into my hip, and a body huddled against my side. With a large yawn, I blinked open my eyes and realised that I had a crick because I was slumped against a wall, that the object was my laptop, and the little body that clutched onto my torso was...Lottie.

I scrubbed the sand out of my eyes and sort of froze when I realised that I had a Lottie cuddling me in her sleep. The shirt she wore, my shirt, had risen almost to her hips, and I gulped hard before stretching the arm that wasn't curled around her head and tugging the shirt it back over her legs.

I rubbed my face and shut my laptop, putting it back on my desk. Then I shuffled down on the bed until I was actually lying down, and I pulled Lottie with me. She made a cute little sleepy noise, and then smashed her face against one of the pillows that I had awkwardly put near her head.

I breathed in and out and tried to focus on anything other than the little sleeping beauty I had attached to my body. She wasn't even doing anything sexy, but I could feel my face grow hot anyways. I needed to calm down.

I made the mistake of looking down at her just nestled against me, and my heart started beating like a pair of drums in a rock band. Her face was planted into the pillow, but I could hear the little sigh she made every time she breathed out and I could feel her body moving up and down as she continued breathing.

She was so kind and caring and she stuck up for me, and she got angry from me (twice). I didn't want to scare her off, because besides Clark and my brother, she had become one of the most important people in my life. And if I scared her off with my advances, I wouldn't know what to do with myself.

Remembering all those poor guys she unknowingly friend zoned, I didn't want to end up bitter like them. I have to be okay with what I already had, because at least I had something.

I breathed out, and Lottie's head rose on my chest. She smiled in her sleep, and then made another one of her weird noises.

Maybe I should just go back to sleep before I hurt myself.

A hand smacking me in the jaw woke me up next. I jumped and opened my eyes to see Lottie stretching.

"Oh, I'm so sorry," she said in a sleepy voice.

I hoped she would move her head away from my chest, because my heart was beating out of control. "How are you doing?" I asked her. I cleared my throat when she raised her head slightly, her mop of curly brown hair falling in her eyes.

She smiled with her eyes closed and fell back on her pillow. "I had a fantastic sleep, Benny, what about you?"

"I did too," I said quietly. I'd had the best night's rest I've gotten in months, and it was most likely because of my cuddle buddy.

"What time is it?" she asked, her voice still heavy with sleep.

I shuffled out from under her and sat up, grabbing my phone from my desk. "It's nine."

"Not too shabby," she said. "I'm so sorry, did I suffocate you in your sleep?" she asked worriedly, using one hand to comb through her hair. It was taking real work to keep myself calm, but fuck, she looked so cute just sitting there awkwardly.

I snorted. "As if you're big enough."

She smiled. "I hope you didn't mind me last night. I'm a hardcore cuddler, and it seems like you got the brunt of the impact. You should've just shoved a pillow at me to leave you alone."

"It's fine," I said. I hadn't minded in the slightest. A knock on the door made me scowl. "Who is it?"

"It's Archer."

Lottie got out of bed and padded over to the door, wrenching it open to reveal my little brother. He grinned at her. "Had a good sleep?" he asked, eyeing my shirt which she was still wearing.

"Shut up," I said.

He moved his gaze to me and smirked. "Mum wants to see you. Oh, and Charlie."

I worked my jaw and took a deep breath. I noticed Lottie glance at me with drawn eyebrows. "Just Mum?" I asked.

"Yeah, just her."

"When?" Lottie said.

"As soon as you're ready. She's in her office."

"That should be fine. Right, Ben?"

I looked at her hopeful expression and felt myself nodding. I couldn't say anything, though. I didn't know what to say. What did my mother want to talk to us about? And why without my father?

"Well, okay. I'll leave you guys to your...devices then," Archer said, winking at Lottie. She giggled as she closed the door, and I rolled my eyes.

"Ben?" Lottie said, walking up to me. I stared down at her and raised my eyebrows. "How's your hand?"

"It's fine," I said, shrugging. There were a few scratches and some bruising, but nothing big. I've had worse.

I blanked out when she grabbed my hand to examine it. "I'll put some ointment on it later," she promised.

"No need." I gently removed myself from her grip. "What are you going to wear, Lottie?"

She smiled. "I'll just wear my dress again. It doesn't smell that bad. Ben?"

"What?"

She beckoned, and I bent my head so that she could whisper whatever she was going to in my ear. But instead, she turned her head and kissed my cheek, and then dashed into the bathroom.

And she just left me there to stand like an idiot, a vacant expression on my very, very red face.

There was an uncomfortable silence. Mum shifted in her chair, and Lottie scooted closer to me on the sofa we sat on.

"How are you, Mrs. Fisher?" Lottie asked to break the silence.

My mum smiled politely at her. "I'm doing well, Charlotte. And you?"

She grinned broadly. "Oh, just grand."

Mum leant back in her chair and regarded Lottie thoughtfully. I frowned. What was she thinking? "Yes? And why is that?"

"Because I figured something out that makes me very happy."

"And what did you figure out?"

Lottie winked at my mother. "Secret," she stage-whispered.

My mum laughed, and I knew that Lottie had won her over, like she did with literally everyone she met. "I have one question, Charlotte."

"You can call me Charlie, Mrs. Fisher."

Mum smiled, and it surprised me. It had been a long time since I'd seen her smile like that, with her eyes all crinkled up.

I took a deep breath. "Mum, why did you really call us in here?" Lottie's gentle hand touched one of mine, which I didn't even realise had been clenched in a fist. I relaxed enough for her to slip her fingers through mine and squeeze reassuringly.

Mum sighed, and the worry lines appeared again. "Benjamin, I just wanted to talk to you about your father."

I closed my eyes at her words. My chest felt tight. "Okay," I said. "Talk away."

"Look honey, I know he's been hard on you in the past, and I know that-"

Lottie's obnoxious ringtone interrupted my mother. "I'm so sorry, Mrs. Fisher, but I really think I should take this," she said, smiling apologetically.

My mum waved her off. "No worries, darling. Take your call."

Lottie shot a wavering smile at me and squeezed my hand before darting outside. My gaze followed her and I frowned. I knew that squeeze wasn't just to comfort me, but her as well. All thoughts of my father flew out of my head.

"Ben? Ben."

I jumped and looked at my mum. "Pardon?"

Mum pursed her lips. "If you're so worried about the girl, go check on her. We can talk in a minute," she said in amusement. My eyebrows raised in surprise, but I surged to my feet.

"Thanks, Mum," I said, bending down to kiss her on the cheek. I strode over to the door and opened it quietly. Lottie's back was to me when I stepped outside.

"O-okay, I'll be right there," I heard her say, before hanging up.

Her voice had cracked while speaking, and I was so worried that I took her shoulders and spun her to face me. "What's wrong?"

Lottie looked up at me, a couple of tears trickling down her cheeks. My heart fairly cracked. "I need to go," she said. "Delia called. My dad's in the hospital, I need to go now."

"I'll take you," I said immediately, my hand moving to rub the tears off her cheeks. This had never happened to me before, the whole aching because of someone else.

"No," she said, just as quickly. She stepped away from me and I frowned. "No, Ben, you need to stay here and sort things out with your dad. But I need to go see mine, okay?"

"I can take you," I said firmly. I needed to take her. I couldn't let her go like this.

She rubbed her eyes quickly and looked at me. She smiled, and that was the little gesture that hurt the most. "Stay with your family, Ben," she said softly.

"I'm not comfortable letting you go in this state." We stared defiantly at each other for a minute, me crossing my arms and Lottie trembling ever so slightly.

"I'll be fine," she said.

"I want to make sure of that myself."

"I'm happy you feel like that, but I want to go alone!" Lottie stopped speaking and looked down, wiping at her face again. Her small frame seemed even smaller when she curled into herself like that. Like she was trying to protect herself from me.

I felt strange inside. My chest tightened and my head hurt and I knew I didn't want her to leave without me. "Lottie," I began.

"Ben," she said. "Please."

Maybe it was the heartbroken look she gave me, or the way her hands trembled, or how her big eyes glistened, but I felt myself weakening. "Make sure to call me when you reach," I said.

She smiled, and it was genuine this time. "I promise," she said.

"Don't talk to anybody, don't look at anybody, and if anybody looks at you funny, call the police, okay?"

The look in her eyes softened and it made my insides flame up like a campfire. "Okay."

"And for heaven's sake, don't you dare ever-"

Lottie cut me off in the middle of my sentence, but not with words or by smacking me or anything like that. She took a step forward, pulled my face down to her level, and kissed me.

I was so shocked that I completely froze, but then she moved her hands to my hair and made this small squeaky sound and I just lost it. There was only one coherent thought in my mind.

I think I was in love with Charlotte Carter.

Chapter 31

"You think I can let you leave after that?" Ben snapped, trailing behind me like a lost puppy.

I sped up as I walked down the hall, trying to get away from him. "Your mother wants to talk to you, Benny," I said patiently.

"Are you going to pretend like that didn't just happen?"

Truth be told, I still felt dizzy and I knew the red hadn't faded from my face. I didn't know why I kissed him, but I was glad I did, because that kiss was amazing. It blew my other ones with Seamus out of the water, and not because Ben was a much better kisser.

Okay, that was part of it.

"Lottie, are you seriously going to pretend like that didn't happen?"

I kept walking because I knew I needed to get to my dad as soon as possible. "But it did happen."

"I know!"

I smiled at his frustration. I didn't know why he was so upset. I just wanted to go see Papa, and alone. "So what's the problem?"

He sighed deeply. "You're going the wrong way," he said in a patronising tone.

I frowned and stopped. It looked like I'd passed this corridor before...oh man. Ben caught up with me and I looked at his annoyed expression. "Where should I go?" I asked.

"I'll take you."

"Ben, for the last time, I want to go mys-"

"I'll take you to the front, Chatty Pants," he interrupted, rolling his eyes.

I blinked, wondering why he didn't put up a bigger fight. "Oh. Okay. Er, do you-?"

"Do I...?"

Without asking, I poked his hand. He was angry at me, so I didn't know if he'd want to hold my hand or not. Ben snorted and scooted closer to me, wrapping his arm around my shoulders. I smiled at the floor.

After a couple minutes, we reached the front door, and the smile slipped off my face. I clenched my phone so tight that my knuckles turned white. "Bye, Ben," I said. "I'll see you soon, okay?"

He looked at me blankly. "I hope you know I'm not happy."

I rubbed my arm and stepped away from him. "You made that quite clear."

"And I don't want you to go without me."

"I know."

"And you better listen to my rules, alright?"

I laughed. "Why are you still speaking and not kissing me?"

At that, Ben cracked one of his heart-melting smiles which just made my insides fall into a puddle on the ground at the sight. He stepped forward and touched my cheek before bending down and giving me one small kiss.

My eyes stayed closed as he kept standing there, our foreheads touching. "Bye, Benny. I'll see you soon, promise."

"Alright, Lottie. You better keep that promise."

I grinned and punched his arm lightly. "You can trust me, Benny."

He shrugged and watched as I walked backwards from him. I kept smiling and waving and walking, even as his expression screwed up and he opened his mouth. "Would you watch where you're going?" he snapped, just as I smacked into the gate.

I scratched my head sheepishly and patted it as if to say sorry. "My bad, Mr. Gate," I whispered, flicking the bolt open so that I could walk outside. "Goodbye, Benny!"

Ben frowned at me but raised one hand up in farewell regardless. I felt an ache in my chest, but I shrugged it off. I was just being childish.

I'd see him soon.

"You can sit here," I said to the elderly man who'd just gotten on the bus. I sprang up and gestured to my seat with a big smile.

The man smiled and patted my back before falling heavily onto the seat. I sighed and tried to find somewhere to grab onto, but there wasn't any room. There were too many people.

The bus took a sharp turn and I stumbled, crashing head first into some poor guy wearing a backpack. "I'm so sorry," I gasped, straightening and backing up. "I'm really sorry!"

The guy smirked, and I realised he was dressed expensively. "No worries. But you should probably come hold this bar in case it happens again." Him and another bulky man were already holding it, but a quick glance around told me I had no other option. I blinked at him. He seemed familiar, but I couldn't for the life of me remember where I'd seen him.

"Thank you," I said softly, grabbing onto the bar a decent number of inches under his hand. My scrawny height didn't make it that uncomfortable, but the position I was in caused me to bump into the guy multiple times. I felt like my face was going to burn off from embarrassment. I clutched the bar tighter and looked steadily at the floor and not at the guy's staring eyes. He was making me feel extremely violated.

I sighed shakily and scooted a little further away from him, only to bump into a woman and her child. I blushed and murmured my apologies, and then I noticed the guy's smirk widen when I had to scoot back near him.

My heart was beating furiously and I felt more and more like prey every passing second. I took out my phone and dialled, then waited impatiently for the answer.

"Lottie, it's been ten minutes, don't tell me you're already lost," came Ben's voice, clear and deep and soothing.

I sighed, feeling my tensed muscles relax just at the sound of his voice. "I'm not lost," I said. "I just missed you."

There was a short pause, and I was almost certain that Ben had frozen. He was weird like that when people expressed emotions around him. It was quite funny, to be honest. "You missed me? I saw you ten minutes ago." He said it like I was a chore, but I figured it was just one of his manly ruses.

"Yeah, I know," I said. I wanted to keep talking to him so that he would distract me from this guy's creepy looks.

I heard Ben knock something over on the other end, and that made me smile. "What's really the matter, Lottie?" he asked seriously.

I furrowed my eyebrows in confusion at how he knew I wasn't just calling him. So Ben was intuitive now, was he? I was impressed and felt my heart swell up at how concerned he was. I glanced at the creepy guy and saw that while he wasn't looking at me, he was definitely listening in.

"Lottie, what's wrong?"

"Nothing," I said quickly. "Did you talk to your mum?"

He snorted. "That was very subtle, Carter, but I get the hint. I did talk to her - I'll tell you about it later."

I kicked at the dirty bus floor and braced myself when the bus turned again. This time, the guy's hand touched my back as I straightened myself out. I stiffened. "Please don't touch me," I said politely.

"We're talking on the phone, how the hell am I touching you?"

I squirmed and stepped back. The guy raised his eyebrows. "I was just helping you out," he said patronisingly. I didn't like how he spoke to me like I was a child. It was different from the way Ben teased me.

"Please don't touch me," I repeated, more firmly this time.

"Lottie, who the hell is touching you? You better fucking get out of there or at least beat his ass, I swear to God!"

The guy nodded and smiled as though he was so charming, but I felt a chill go down my back. Who was he? The bus stopped then, and people started to file out, so I took that opportunity to snag the back seat next to a middle-aged woman and her kids.

"Lottie!" Ben said loudly. "Are you okay?"

I jumped and realised that I hadn't been answering his calls. "Don't worry, nothing happened," I tried to assure him. "Just a misunderstanding."

"A misunderstanding?" he said dubiously.

"Yeah." I started nodding vigorously before I realised that he couldn't see me. My phone started beeping, so I frowned and looked at the screen. Delia's name flashed as a waiting call. "Can you hold for a second, Ben?"

"I actually have to go, Lottie - Miss Franny needs something. Make sure you call me when you get to the hospital, okay?"

I grinned, suddenly feeling shy for some reason. "Okay," I agreed. I hung up and switched to Delia. "Hi, Delia. How's my dad?"

"He's doing okay. He hasn't woken up yet," she said in a subdued version of her normally peppy voice.

I sighed in relief and closed my eyes, massaging my forehead with my fingers. Papa was okay! "How okay is he?"

"Okay as in he would've been perfectly fine if he was twenty years younger."

"But since he's not...?"

"The doctors are waiting until you get here to tell me what's going on, Charlie. How much longer will you be?"

I peered up at the board that said where the bus would be stopping next. "Maybe an hour?"

I heard Delia sigh. "Okay. Try and hurry."

She hung up before I could say bye, and I frowned at my phone. She normally wasn't so rude. Maybe she really was worried about Papa?

My lips puckered. It wasn't that I didn't like her. It's just that...once my dad met her, he started to forget about me. I didn't doubt that he loved me, but...aw man, I was just self-ish. She made Papa happy, and that was all that mattered. Even though she wasn't Mum, she still made him happy, which was more than I could say about myself.

I cast my eyes up towards the dingy blue ceiling. "Are you okay, darlin'?" the woman sitting next to me asked with a thick Brummie accent.

I smiled reassuringly and nodded. "I'm doing well, thank you," I said.

The woman patted my arm, then went back to scolding her kids, who were squabbling about something indistinct.

I sat stiffly in my seat for the rest of the ride. The guy from before hadn't left yet, even as the bus emptied and filled again and again. Sometimes out of the corner of my eye, I would see him look at me and smirk knowingly, which made my stomach clench up. I wished I could call Ben, but he would question it and probably track me down, and I didn't need that right now.

Finally, the bus stopped near the hospital, and I surged to my feet. As I scurried to the front, I felt something grab my arm, causing me to stumble.

"Whoa there, clumsy." I frowned. Clumsy? He was the one who make me fall.

I tried to subtly extricate myself from the guy's hold, and then stepped back. "It was lovely to meet you," I said, lying through my teeth.

"My name's Rick, hen," he said, the pet name making me dislike him even more. What respectable man called a woman hen? Was he not taught any manners? "And yours?" But I could tell he already knew it. Rick. Oh my god, it was Rick.

I felt bile rising in my throat. I had to get out of there immediately. Not only was it Rick, but I was also really worked up about Papa, and I didn't really like things getting in my way.

"I need to get off now, I'm sorry," I said, panicking. I turned around and ran off before the bus could drive away again.

When I entered the hospital, I immediately felt sick. The scent of disinfectant and the bright white of the walls brought back memories of Mum and her last days. She'd had colon cancer, and we didn't catch it until it was too late. She died last summer, and thinking about it was too painful. It was too soon.

I gulped once and sniffed two times to get rid of the incoming tears, and then pressed my palms against my eyes. "No," I whispered. "Don't do that now."

"Miss?" a man in pale green scrubs asked me, looking concerned. "Do you need something?"

I breathed in and blinked a few times. "Do you know which room Charles Carter was assigned to? I'm his daughter."

He beckoned me to the front desk. "Can I see some ID?" he asked as he looked through the computer. I fumbled with my purse and showed him my driver's licence, and he nodded. "Okay, he's in 21B - if you walk down that hall and take a right, it should be the second door on the left."

I smiled gratefully and spun around. "Thank you!" I called as I walked as quickly as possible in the direction he had pointed.

My body tensed more as more as I ventured further into the hospital. The sight of gurneys and the rolling beds and the carts of medical supplies and noises varying from screaming to crying wasn't unfamiliar to me. I stopped in front of 21B and raised my hand to knock on the door. I stopped midway. I breathed in and willed myself to open the door and get inside to where I was needed. Open the door, you cheesehead.

I couldn't. I felt a tear roll down my cheek. My chest began to ache, and my hands turned white. I didn't know why. Papa was okay. What was wrong with me?

I clasped a hand over my mouth to stop the sob and grabbed my phone, dialling Ben's number once again.

"Lottie, you've reached?" he said immediately upon answering.

"Yes," I whispered.

I could literally hear him frown. "What's wrong?"

"I don't know. I can't go inside." My hands began to shake.

"Why not? Do you want me to teach you how to open a door or something?" That made me giggle softly, and the relief in his next words was almost palpable. "Lottie, all you gotta do is twist the handle. Your dad's waiting for you."

He was right. I needed to see my dad. "I know."

"Then why aren't you?"

"I don't know. I don't know, okay? Ben, my tummy hurts and my head aches and my chest pains and my eyes burn and I don't know why because I'm perfectly healthy and I just-I just-"

"Lottie, babe, you're okay. You're fine. Your dad's fine, too. This isn't like your mum, your dad is gonna be fine. Alright?"

I blinked and rested my head on the door. His voice was the most gentle I had ever heard it, and there was no sign of his usual gruffness. "Alright," I said quietly. My muscles started to relax again. He was right. Papa was okay. He'd be okay.

There was a pause. "Are you okay?"

I smiled. "I am now."

"Good," he said, and I almost laughed at how manly and brusque he made that one word.

"Thank you," I said sincerely.

"Yeah, okay. So are you going inside or what?"

Even the least romantic things he said made me blush. He made me so happy. "Yes, I am. Benny, you're a lovely person." At my words, I heard a large thud and the sound of Ben cursing extremely vulgar things that I really don't feel comfortable sharing. "Are you okay?" I asked, holding back a laugh. That was how easily he could turn my mood around.

"I'm fine," he snapped, but the annoyance didn't seem to be directed at me. "I'll talk to you later, okay? Go check on your dad first."

"Okay, bye," I said softly. He said it in return and I hung up.

I took a deep breath and opened the door, my eyes blinking hard to get used to the dimmer ambience of the room. I saw Papa sleeping peacefully on a small bed, and Delia was sitting next to him in one of the chairs, her face solemn.

She glanced at me when I walked, and then did a double-take. "Charlie," she said. "You look so beautiful! Like you're glowing."

I may have been mistaken, but at that moment, I only knew one thing.

I was in love with Benjamin Fisher.

Chapter 32

"**Y**ou're going to run a hole in the ground from all that pacing you're doing," Archer observed from his perch on top of my desk.

I glared at him, my phone clutched tightly in my friend. I felt anxious and coiled, like I was going to spring any second. "Oh, shut it, you."

He smirked and wiggled his eyebrows, but I was already so done with him that I began pacing again. I tried to get rid of all my nervous energy, but none of it was going away.

Why wasn't she calling again? Not that I wanted her to call.

Fuck, who was I kidding? I wanted her to call me. I wanted to see how she was doing.

"Seriously, Ben, if you're so worried about her, why don't you call?" Archer said after a while. "You're making me tired with all this walking."

"Why don't I call?" I repeated slowly. I looked at my phone. Lottie's name was listed under my recent calls, and it sort of made me grin when I saw the ridiculous picture she'd set as her contact image. She had taken my phone and had been trying to make me laugh with all these weird faces, but then accidentally took a picture and loved it so much that she told me that's the face she wanted me to see whenever she called me.

"Yes, Ben. Call her," Archer said, even slower than me. I scowled at his mocking expression. "You are capable of that, you know."

I hesitated, practically gnawing off my lip. "But what if she's talking to her dad or the doctor or something?"

Archer jumped off my desk and rolled his eyes. "Fine, don't call her. Let's just go to the kitchen or something, because I can't really stand you right now."

I shoved him as he walked past, and he stumbled before straightening and making an immature face at me. I sighed and followed him out the door.

One of the doors was open as we walked by, and the lady inside was talking very loudly on her phone. "Yes, yes. Two in the afternoon on the third? Yes, that should be fine. Thank you, good day."

I furrowed my eyebrows and caught up to Archer. "What's the date today?" I asked.

"It's the second of November. Why?" he asked curiously.

I swore under my breath. That mean tomorrow was Lottie's birthday, and I'd gotten her nothing. What the fuck? Why was I so stupid?

What was I even supposed to get her? I didn't really know what she liked. Well, she'd once told me she was a big fan of Teenage Mutant Ninja Turtles. And I knew she liked sweet things. But I wanted it to be meaningful. What was I supposed to do?

I took out my phone and dialled Clark's number. "What's up, homeboy?" he said in an upbeat voice. "Cheers for not telling me you were leaving without me for two days."

I cringed. "Sorry Clark. I didn't think it would take this long."

"You're not sorry, you sketchy bastard. You know, it gets very lonely without my bestest friend around." I could pretty much hear the pout in his whining voice.

"Aw poor baby," I said in a monotone. "Suck it up."

Clark huffed. "Did you call me to bully me or do you have another agenda?"

"I don't have an agenda. I have a problem," I said.

"Ah! A problem! I'm good at those."

I massaged my temples with my fingers and debated on whether or not it was a good idea to tell him about Lottie. Because he would definitely blow it out of proportions and then pester me so much that I would literally find a way to transport my hand from my phone to his just to throttle him.

"What's the dealio Benjamin Button?"

"It's Lottie's birthday tomorrow," I said, and then immediately yanked the phone from my ear, because Clark had started screeching.

Archer glanced at me and then at my phone. "Your friend is a weirdo."

I nodded and stared at my phone, wondering how his lungs had that much capacity. "Are you done?" I asked flatly.

"Why didn't you tell me?" he said loudly, affronted. "Why'd you wait until the day before?"

"Because I forgot!" I snapped.

"You're a horrible boyfriend."

It took me a minute to process that, and my entire face became hot. "I am not her boyfriend!" Archer nudged me at that and winked. I flipped him the bird.

"Yeah, you wish you were."

I refused to respond to that. Anything I could say wouldn't help my case at all.

"Okay, so you forgot her birthday. Who cares? It's tomorrow, not today."

"I didn't get her anything," I said through gritted teeth. "That's the problem. I need your help."

Clark hummed on the other end. "I don't know. A necklace or something? Maybe a locket, and put my picture in it."

"Why the hell would I put your picture?"

"She likes me more," he said, chuckling.

I snorted. "No she doesn't. And I don't want to do that. That's too cliché."

"Ah, so Benjamin Fisher wants to get his beloved something unique. Because that's an original thought."

"You're no help, I'm hanging up!"

"Okay, bye best friend!"

I muttered a bye and ended the call. Archer darted into the kitchen and started yelling for Miss Franny.

"Benjy," she said, materialising in front of me. "Why the long face?"

I looked at her and pouted. "Miss Franny," I said, my tone bordering on a whine, "I don't know what to give Lottie for her birthday."

She laughed. "Are you joking? That girl is so kind. Even if you get her a box of dog treats, she'll treasure it because it's from you. It doesn't matter what you get."

"But I want it to be special!" Of course I wanted it to be special. I fucking...I fucking loved her, okay? It couldn't be just any old thing.

Her eyes twinkled and she smiled mischievously. "How cute!" she cooed, jumping forward to pinch my cheeks. "That's so cute, my Benjy is flustered over how to shop for a girl!"

I pried her hands off of me and massaged the redness out of my face. "None of you are any help," I muttered.

"Well, what does she like, Benjamin?"

I frowned. "Sweet things. She's a writer as well. Uhm...she likes things that cuddle. And Cartoon Network." I'd thought about getting her a kitten or a puppy, but I couldn't when she lived in a dorm.

"She likes sweet things?" Miss Franny asked thoughtfully.

I scoffed. "Oh yeah. She would live off sugar if she could."

"Then why don't you bake her something?"

I leant against the countertop and frowned. That was a really good idea, but... "I can't cook for shit, Miss Franny."

She rolled her eyes. "You can follow instructions, can't you?"

"Yeah."

Miss Franny beckoned to me and I followed her over to the back counter where she kept all her cookbooks. She took one of them out and frowned as she flipped through the pages. "What flavour does she like most?"

"Chocolate."

She grinned and handed the cookbook over to me, which was open to a page that had a picture of a chocolate cake covered in fancy chocolate frosting and chocolate flowers.

"I can't do this!" I said, shaking my head. "I can barely even toast my bread in the morning. How am I supposed to make this?"

"The cake is simple, Benjy. And I'll help you make the frosting. Don't worry about it, I know Charlotte will love you for this."

My heart did the equivalent of a stammer and I shook my head. I'd worry about if she'd like the cake first. I'd worry about her liking me later. "Okay," I said quietly. I could do this, because it was for Lottie. She deserved it and much more.

Miss Franny stared at me for a moment. "You were right, that girl really does make you happy, doesn't she?" Because that was what I had whispered to her that time when she first met Lottie. That Lottie made me happier than anybody else I knew.

I turned my face away so she wouldn't see my constipated expression. "Yeah," I said, shrugging nonchalantly. I laid the book on the counter and scanned the ingredients. "Do you have all of this stuff?"

"Of course I do. You just wait here and I'll bring it to you."

"But Miss Fra-"

"Just wait here!"

Twenty minutes later, I squinted at the instructions. "What does 'cream the butter and sugar together' mean?" I muttered. "Isn't cream a noun? Why is it being used as a verb?"

Archer leant over the book. "I think it means mix it or something."

I stared at the solid chunk of butter just sitting casually in the middle of the mixing bowl. "How do you mix butter?"

Archer shrugged. "I don't know, man. Ask the Franster."

I looked over at Miss Franny, who was cooking dinner. "She's busy."

"Call Charlie then."

"That's suspicious though. Why would I call her just to ask how to cream something?"

He rolled his eyes. "God, you're acting like such a girl! Give me your phone."

"What? N-" Archer cut me off by yanking it out of my apron pocket. Yes, I was wearing an apron. Yes, it was Miss Franny's. Yes, it was covered in flowers. Who cared?

"Hello? Charlie? Hey, what's up?" He listened for a while and glanced at me, winking when he saw how furious I was. What the fuck? "Yeah, I just have a question for you. What does it mean to cream sugar and butter?" He listened for a bit more, and I scowled darkly, crossing my arms. "Okay, sweet. Thanks Charlie. I'll see you soon. Yeah, okay...bye!"

He clicked off my phone and handed it back oh-so casually. "I'm gonna fucking eviscerate you," I said.

"Charlie said that creaming means when you kind of mash up the butter and the sugar together until it becomes super smooth and creamy. She said to do it with a fork."

"Anything else?" I asked, raising my eyebrows at the cheesy grin he wore.

He laughed. "This is really lame for me to say, but she said to remind you that you're a lovely person."

I uncrossed my arms, blinking sheepishly. I felt the anger roll out of me. Fuck, I missed her. She hadn't even been gone that long and I missed her. I was going soft. Fuck. Damn.

My eyebrows furrowed and I sighed slightly. I grabbed a fork from one of the drawers and started mashing up the butter and the sugar. "This is nasty," I said to distract myself. But her pretty face kept popping up in my mind, and I kept remembering what it was like to kiss her.

"It looks like...I don't know what it looks like, but probably something gross."

I finished creaming the butter and sugar and pushed it aside. "Now what? Er...dry ingredients. Okay, okay, flour-fuck!"

Archer laughed at the powder that now coated the front of my shirt. I muttered curses as I brushed it off and tried to open the flour bag again.

"This is so annoying! It's getting everywhere!"

"Maybe start with salt?" Archer suggested.

I made a face and grabbed the teaspoon measurer and the salt. I tried to nudge in only a small amount, but OF COURSE I HAD TO SPILL OUT LIKE A WHOLE CUP.

By now, I was super pissed off and didn't want to do this anymore, and the way Archer was trying to hold back his laugh made me want to smash his face into that nasty butter-sugar thing.

"How's it coming along, Benjy?" Miss Franny called from across the kitchen.

"Just splendidly," I said through gritted teeth. I closed my eyes and clenched my fists. Why was I doing this again?

A warm smile and a pair of big green eyes popped up in my mind.

Oh. Yeah.

I breathed in deeply to try and get rid of my impatience, and then looked at the cookbook again. Once all the dry ingredients were in a different bowl, I tried to mix them together, but I must've jerked too hard or something, because a good amount of the ingredients jumped out. How did Lottie do this shit?

"God fucking dammit!" I growled, slamming my hand against the counter.

"Ben, calm down."

I stared at my brother and tried to breath. This wasn't going well. I didn't enjoy this. I wanted to stop.

But I didn't, because I wanted to make Lottie something for her birthday, or so help me I would strangle myself.

I breathed in deeply and cracked my knuckles. "Okay...okay, okay, okay. Milk? I can do milk. Milk is good. Okay, okay, okay, sweet."

"Wow, you didn't spill any of it," Archer said, impressed.

I felt a little bit better now that I had managed not to drop at least one of the ingredients.

But then finally, finally, everything was mixed and put into two prepared pans and shoved into the oven, and I collapsed on the floor in one big heap. I let out a loud, relieved groan.

That had been the worst hour of my life. I would never do this again.

Archer peeked at me. "Miss Franny said you can use the prepared frosting if you'd like, and she'll just show you how to make the roses with it."

"Okay," I said tiredly. "If you say so." He grinned at me, and then wandered off to who-knows-where.

When the timer dinged half an hour later, I opened the oven and stared at the two trays. The cakes looked pretty good, to be honest. I was proud. But then I frowned. How was I supposed to take it out?

I turned off the oven and waited for a couple of minutes to see if it would cool. "How do I do this?" I said to myself.

A towel was thrust at me, and I grinned at Miss Franny before carefully pulling out the trays and putting them on the counter. "Wait for them to cool, and then you can decorate it," she said. "I made some chocolate ganache, and there's some raspberry jam in the fridge for you to put in the middle."

I stood up and scratched the back of my head. "Thanks, Miss Franny."

She shook her head affectionately and patted my arm. "They look great, Benjy. Now take them out of the trays."

I pursed my lips. "How?"

"What do you mean, how? Just flip it upside down and it should slide right out. You did butter the trays, didn't you?"

I stared at her for a minute until her face changed into an annoyed expression. I started laughing. "I'm just playing. Of course I did."

Miss Franny smiled widely. "I haven't seen you like this in years."

I cupped my elbows with my hands and shrugged, looking away. My face grew hot at her words. "It's whatever," I said.

She decided to drop it, and just showed me the small conical bag in her hand. "This is a piping bag. It's got a little tip so that you can make designs, like those roses in the book. Here, let me show you."

She took out a piece of parchment paper and held the paper like a pen, but with both hands. She gently squeezed, and moved it in a circular motion, and when she pulled back, there was a perfect little chocolate rose just sitting there.

I gaped. "Wait, can you do that again? I blinked."

Miss Franny rolled her eyes and did it again. "Now you try."

I took it, but it was really small in my hands. I tried to hold it like Miss Franny, but I didn't know how to hold it and squeeze at the same time.

"Wait, wait, wait," I said, when my first try turned out like a demented looking version of hers. "Let me try again."

Miss Franny waited patiently as I tried and tried and tried again, and subsequently failed and failed and failed again.

"This one doesn't look too bad," I said unsurely, pointing to one that was a little too big and a little too crooked, but was still recognisable as a rose.

"Benjamin, it's fine. You know how to do it. The cakes should be cooled now, so you just have to put it together." Miss Franny patted my arm and walked off to go finish making dinner.

I bit my lip and looked at everything in front of me. There was a carton of fresh raspberries, a jar of raspberry jam, a bowl of chocolate ganache, a bowl of whipped cream, and a bowl of chocolate frosting. I cracked my knuckles and gently put the first layer of cake on the cake stand.

First I awkwardly spread some raspberry jam on it, but I accidentally stabbed the cake a good few times. Then I kind of flung the whipped cream on top of the jam and spread it out with my palm. I might've accidentally melted it with my body heat, though. Oops.

"Benjamin!" I glanced up from drizzling the chocolate ganache on top the cream. It was my mother. I'd sort of forgiven her after she'd spent all of about ten minutes apologising to me and asking for my forgiveness. I figured she meant it. I knew it wasn't her who had a part in kicking me out. Dad was a force to be reckoned with, and I didn't blame her for not being able to convince him otherwise. Plus, she was my mother. She'd given birth to me. Raised me.

"What's up, Mum?" She looked confused when she saw me in the apron, but I just raised my eyebrows. I didn't look that bad. In fact, the florals looked really good on my skin tone.

When she didn't reply for a solid minute, I went back to my masterpiece. I really carefully placed the second layer of cake on top of the first and almost yelled in rage when part of the filling squeezed out of the sides and dripped down.

"Shit," I muttered. I glared at it for a few seconds, but then got over it and started the dump all of the chocolate frosting on top.

"Benjamin," Mum said again. "When you're finished, could you come back to my office?"

"Why?"

"Your father wants to talk to you."

I froze and almost stabbed the cake with my knife. He wanted to talk to me, did he? Well I didn't want to talk to him, not after all that shit he'd said to Lottie. "Whatever," I said.

"Will you come?" she pleaded.

I could feel a vein pulsing in my forehead. "Yeah," I said, trying my hardest not to be short with her.

She was quiet for a minute. "I'm sorry, darling," she said softly, and then I heard the click of her heels as she walked away.

I bent my head down and felt my eyes burn. "Me too."

Chapter 33

"So he's okay?" I repeated for what seemed like the eighty-ninth time.

The doctor sighed in a way that offended me how annoyed he sounded. "I've told you, Miss Carter, your father has diabetes and is at high risk for heart disease. He needs to learn to control his diet and take care of himself."

I raised my eyebrows at his tone. "Yes," I said, ever-patient, "but if he takes your medication and starts exercising and eating healthy, he'll be okay?"

The doctor pursed his lips, as though he thought I wasn't thinking about this enough. He was my father, of course I was thinking about it! "Yes, he will," he said finally. "And make sure he cuts down on the beer. If this happens again, he might not be so lucky."

I nodded and glanced over at Papa, who still slept peacefully on the bed. Delia sat beside him, her ears cocked towards our conversation, but her eyes trained on his pale face. "I'll leave the prescription with my nurse, and she can go to the pharmacy if you'd like," the doctor, whose name I neglected to learn, said.

I smiled gratefully. "That would be wonderful, thank you, sir."

He nodded stiffly and stood there clutching his clipboard for a moment before he nodded again and strode out of the room. I laughed to myself at his weird behaviour. I sat down in the chair next to Delia and rested my chin in my palm. The doctor had told me that Papa would wake up as soon as the sleeping pills wore off. He wanted him well rested, or something.

"He'll be okay," Delia said softly. She reached out slightly as if to take my hand, but then clenched her hand into a fist and pulled back.

My mouth puckered at her actions. She was never normally like this. My dad must have seriously scared her. "Yeah, he will," I agreed, leaving no room for argument. "I'll stay home for a few days to make sure that he's okay."

"No longer than Wednesday," she said. "You can't miss much more of school."

I frowned. "But this is my dad," I said.

"And I'm here to take care of him, Charlie, you don't need to worry. You need to get your education."

I sort of scooted away from her and her angry face. Her words hurt me slightly. I didn't need to be there for my dad? Did she mean I wasn't welcome? "My dad is more important than uni," I said quietly.

She sighed and looked away. "I know he is, but you heard the doctor. He'll be fine. And I'm here to take care of him."

My fingers clutched the underside of my chair until they turned numb. She wouldn't look at me, so I couldn't see her expression, but her voice was steely and firm. I gulped, feeling my chest constrict. "Do you love him?" I asked hesitantly.

"I do," she said immediately.

I bowed my head. This was so hard for me to grasp. I knew that she cared about Papa, but it was just hard to think about when my mum died only a year and a half ago. It didn't seem right. It didn't seem fair.

But Delia really did seem to love my dad, so I decided that I had to make an effort to try like her.

Mum would have wanted that, right? It was her daily goal to make people happy, and because of that, it was now mine. And I guess if Delia made Papa happy, I could deal, right? Well, I needed to deal - it wasn't even my decision. Mum's mantra echoed in my mind: "if it's somebody you love, there's no limit to how hard you work to make them happy." And that includes myself as well.

Once I came to that conclusion, I felt as if a small weight had been lifted off my shoulders. I wasn't used to shying away from people, and it had taken me an extreme effort to keep away from Delia. I wouldn't do that anymore. Because I was one hundred percent sure that Mum would be so happy that this woman was making Papa happy.

"Okay," I said. "I'll only stay until Wednesday. But can you call me every day and tell me how he is?"

She smiled slightly, and I was relieved to finally see her laugh lines. She had worried me with all her stoicism. "Of course, Charlie."

I nodded and grinned. It was okay. Everything would be fine.

"Charlie, you look really tired. Do you want to go home? The doctor said your dad can go home as soon as he wakes up, but if you want, you can go ahead of us."

"I'm not tired. I want to be here when he wakes up."

She shrugged. "Okay, love."

Just then, my phone rang, and I already knew who was calling. My face lit up, because usually I was the one who called, not Ben. "I'm going to take this," I said to Delia, springing up out of my chair and hurrying outside.

In the hall, I leant against the door and pressed answer. "Hey, Lottie," Ben said. Like it always did, my body immediately relaxed at the sound of his voice, and I felt myself unconsciously smile.

"Alright, Ben?" I said, staring at the floor so that I wouldn't hurt myself by grinning too much.

"Yeah, hey, Lottie. I was just wondering, are you gonna be back at uni soon?"

I puzzled over the question. Why did he want to know? Wasn't he still at his parents'? "What is your definition of soon?"

"Like in a couple of hours."

I bit my lip. "Er...if by a couple of hours, you mean a couple of days, then yes."

There was silence over the line, and I thought he'd hung up until he spoke again. "Why the hell would I say hours if I meant days?" he asked in a flat tone.

I shrugged, even though he couldn't see me. "I'll be leaving on Wednesday."

"Wednesday?" he repeated, and it may just have been me, but he sounded slightly anguished. I wondered why. "Charlotte Carter, what is the date today?"

I thought about it for a minute. "The second of November."

"Good girl. Now, that means that tomorrow's date is..."

I wondered if he was trying to trick me. "...The third?" I said slowly, expecting some sort of a catch.

He sighed in exasperation. "Come on, Lottie! What happens on the third?" he tried again.

I pouted. "I don't know, Ben! Just tell me!"

"Lottie, tomorrow's your damn birthday!"

I froze.

My birthday?

"Oh," was all I could say.

"Oh," he scoffed.

I couldn't believe I'd forgotten. I usually looked forward to my birthday, because even if Papa was sometimes forgetful, Zach and Ginny usually made it special. I suddenly found it hard to breathe. Ben had remembered my birthday? When had I told him? Like a couple of months ago, probably, and he'd remembered! I pressed my palm against my hot cheek and smiled so hard that I felt my chest tighten.

Then I furrowed my eyebrows in confusion. "Why are you so annoyed?" I perked up. "Aw, Ben, did you want to hang out with me?"

"No," he said quickly, adamantly. I laughed cheerfully, feeling the remaining weight on my shoulders disappear. "I just...I-I...wanted to..."

I decided not to tease him any further. The poor thing sounded so flustered that it made me inwardly squeak. "I guess I'll just stay here. It's not that big of a deal."

"Oh," he said blankly. "What about Ginny?"

"She won't mind. My dad's more important." I wondered why he was pushing this.

He was quiet for a while. "But what about you?"

I made a small noise of confusion. "What do you mean?"

"Nothing," he said cryptically. I frowned, wanting to know what he meant. What was there about me? "Well, er, I guess I'll see you Wednesday, then."

"Yeah," I said, not even attempting to hide how forlorn I was. It was only a few days, but I would miss seeing him like crazy. I already missed him.

"Cheers, Lottie."

"Bye Benny. Take care, alright? Tell Miss Franny and Archer that I send my love."

"Okay, bye."

I hung up and clutched my phone to my chest. Bless him, he was so awkward! It made me want to bury my face in my knees and just squeal. Lord, I loved him so much.

I went back inside the room, and Delia glanced up at me curiously. "Who is it that you talk to that leaves you looking so lovely?" she asked, cocking an eyebrow.

I smiled weakly and tucked my hair behind my ears. "I'm not sure what you mean?"

She patted the chair next to her, and then started wiggling her eyebrows at me. Back before I met Ben, I would back away and stay quiet, but this time I laughed softly. "It's a boy, isn't it?" she asked knowingly.

I looked away, but grinned and nodded anyway. "It's a very wonderful boy."

She cooed like a bird. "How cute. What's he like? What's his name?"

She seemed eager, her brown eyes alight with mirth and sincerity. I decided that I could talk to her. "His name is Ben," I began shyly. "And he's extremely gruff, but I...I think he's a very, very lovely person."

Delia squeezed my forearm. "It sounds like you really like him."

Like was most definitely the wrong word.

"But those are my favourites!" Papa complained.

I tossed the value pack of fried bacon bits into the box for the food bank. "Make carrots your new favourite," I suggested, hopping up onto the counter so that I could read the top shelf.

He chuckled, but I could tell he wasn't a happy camper, what with me emptying the house of all his disgusting junk food. And that came from a girl who lived and breathed sugar.

I pointed accusingly at a pack of sugary doughnuts he'd gotten from the store. "The quality of this is just terrible!" I said. "Why couldn't you have gone to a bakery instead? At least they don't put in all these random chemicals."

"But they're my favourite type of doughnuts!"

I laughed because my dad was acting like a child. "Good. When you share your favourite thing with other people, it makes it ten times better."

Papa looked at me and raised his eyebrows. "How can that be when I'm not getting any of it?"

"Doctor's orders," I said. I grabbed a box of frosting-coated animal crackers and put them in the food bank box too. "Don't worry, I'm leaving all the good stuff - the Cadbury's and the Jaffa cakes and the digestive biscuits."

He squinted his eyes. "Are they the chocolate covered digestives?" I nodded and he beamed, throwing his hands up in the air. "Wonderful. Thank you, poppet!"

"You're welcome, Papa." I jumped off the counter to give him a hug right as the doorbell rang.

"Charlie-" he began.

"I'll get it!" I sang, picking up my skirt and hurrying over to the door.

The person rang insistently, relentlessly for dozens of consecutive rings. I grimaced and slid across the wooden floor to move faster.

"Coming!" I said. "I'm coming!"

I reached the door and yanked it open. "You're a persistent little thing, aren't y-" I stopped short because of the sight that lay before me. I raised my eyebrows in surprise.

A bouquet of roses hid the person's face until he lowered it and smiled that devastatingly breathtaking smile of his that made my heart go absolutely mad and had my face turning red in milliseconds.

My eyes widened.

Ben stepped forward until we were toe-to-toe and leant down, his nose scrunched up playfully.

"Hey Lottie."

Chapter 34

Back when I was in high school, I hadn't known how much my father's approval had meant to me until I lost it in the worst way possible.A lot of people take for granted what their parents give them. I don't mean the material things, but things like pride and love and faith.My father had never been the emotional type.

He liked to keep private, and basically only smiled at my mother.

He never let Archer or I know when he liked what we did. The only giveaway was the fact that he didn't say anything. But when he didn't like what we did?God, that was another story.In fact, that story was so long that it ended in me being disowned and tossed out of my own house. The only reason I made it out without killing myself was because of Clark.

I owed him so much.I don't know how to make what my father had done seem justifiable, because it was pretty fucked up. But, I'll be honest: I hadn't exactly been a...golden child. Far from it.In fact, let's just hover under the assumption that the only reason I had gone to public school, despite my family's grand fortune, was because they had kicked me out of Claudius' Grammar School for Boys. And that was even with the substantial donation my father bestowed upon them each year.Get me now?I had been a fucked up kid.I had come home high and clutching a bottle of scotch at around midnight the night my father decided he had had enough of me. He had told me that if I didn't buck up and get my act together, I should damn well be sure to never show my face around him ever again.

He had told me that if I didn't start working with him to get ready for my inheritance, then I was dead to him.So I told him that I was already six feet under, and I walked out.I shouldn't have lost my temper. I shouldn't have acted like an idiot. I shouldn't have started smoking. I shouldn't have done a lot of things that I did, but I think the one thing I did right was making that stupidly wonderful bakery my hangout place.And most days I would see the small girl with the big smile allow customers to use her as a welcome mat, and I would want to march in there and fucking shout at every single heartless bastard who tried to cheat their way into saving a couple of quid.The day I finally did march in was the day I decided to quit smoking, and without the subdued effect it gave me, I couldn't ignore when that woman was bothering Lottie.And I was perfectly okay with that, because I would gladly give all the shit I used to be into just to be able to make Lottie this happy with my mere presence.

Before her, I had thought nobody would ever really want me. That nobody needed me in their lives and that I was better off staying away.But a girl named Charlotte Carter changed that.I lowered the roses from my nose because they tickled, and I smiled at Lottie. I wanted to laugh, because she looked so surprised that I thought her eyes would pop out. I shuffled forward and leant down. "Hey Lottie," I said.It took all of one second for realisation to hit her, and her gaping mouth closed into a thousand-watt smile that I swear to God was filled with so much happiness that I almost spontaneously combusted on the spot.

She made this cutesie wee shriek-squeak-squeal sound thing and then clapped her hands on her mouth, her big eyes shining with tears.I frowned. "Wait, why are you crying? Don't cry. Don't cry, okay? This is supposed to be happy.""Ben," she said, her voice muffled under her hands. "I'm...I want to hug you. Is it okay if I hug you? Because I really want to, and I'm going to do it anyway, even if you say no, so-"She cut herself off by catapulting off the ground into my arms with such grace that I was taken completely by surprise. Her arms locked around my neck and she buried her face against the base of my throat, wrapping her legs around my waist and clinging on like a little baby monkey.I couldn't help but smile goofily at the position we were in, and I walked inside her house as I hugged her tightly. I'd have to thank Ginny again for giving me Lottie's address.

And then I'd have to thank Clark for calling this kid named Zach who had Ginny's number which I used to call her.Lottie brought her face up and stared at me solemnly for a few moments, her eyes boring into mine like she was trying to look for something. "I keep telling you again and again what a lovely person you are, why can't you believe it?"My mouth puckered. God, she was too good for me. What did I even do to deserve this? "I just like hearing you say it," I murmured, nudging her nose with mine.She laughed that high, clear laugh of hers that had slowly but surely charmed the hell out of me. "You're lovely," she said, kissing my cheek. My face immediately began to grow hot. "You're lovely!" she said again, and kissed my other cheek. "Ben, you are the loveliest," forehead, "kindest," nose, "weirdest," one eyelid, "most wonderful," the other eyelid, "guy I have ever met!" She smiled at me, her eyes crinkling and her dimples surfacing.I cleared my throat so that I wouldn't to something I'd regret, but then cringed back when my eyes saw something over her shoulder.A man of medium height, thinning hair the colour of Lottie's, and a slight potbelly stared at us with his mouth agape. I looked frantically down at Lottie, who furrowed her eyebrows and let go of me.

She turned around, and upon spotting her father, she jumped and accidentally crashed into me. I put my hands on her shoulders to steady her."Hey Papa," she said awkwardly. "This is...er...this is Ben. He's my...he's my fr-friend."God, and there she went throwing around that damn word.What exactly do you call somebody you've kissed and wanted to keep kissing?NOT A FRIEND, THAT'S WHAT."Nice to meet you, sir," I said hesitantly, moving around Lottie so that I could shake his offering hand."Alright, Ben?" Mr Carter said, sounding surprised. "What are you doing here?"I coughed and scratched my nose. "Well, tomorrow is Lottie's birthday, so I just thought I'd - I don't know - come and see her?

I apologise if I'm intruding."As I spoke, Mr Carter frowned deeper, and then he looked at Lottie, who was watching us with a cocked head.

"Tomorrow is my baby girl's birthday," he said quietly. He blinked and walked over to her, putting his hands on her shoulders.She smiled at him, the kind of smile that was meant to reassure. "Don't worry about it, Papa."He bent his head, and I couldn't see the expression on his face, but his voice became extremely gruff. "I'd forgotten my daughter's birthday. I'm sorry, Charlie. I'm really sorry."Lottie patted his hand. "Birthdays aren't that great, Papa. It's really okay.""No, it's not. I'll make it up to you, poppet, I promise."And that girl, ever the selfless angel, just smiled soothingly. "You don't have to. Besides, Ben just got me the best present ever."She winked at me when I looked at her curiously. Mr Carter glanced at me and then back at her. "What did he get?" he asked.Lottie laughed, as though he was being funny. "Don't be silly, Papa. He didn't get anything. He came here, isn't that so cool?" A small smile quirked up one corner of my lips, and I felt myself fill up with an overwhelming feeling of affection for her.Her father just stood there, making me shuffle awkward. "Yeah...that's cool," he agreed, and then turned to me.

His stern gaze made me anxious. I didn't normally feel like this, but this was Lottie's father. I needed to make a good impression. "Thank you, son," he finally said, surprising me.I nodded. "I wanted to, so it wasn't like I was going out of my way or anything."He wrapped his arm around Lottie and grinned, breaking his aura of austerity. "Well...I give you my full permission to woo my daughter." Lottie's and my eyes popped out of our heads, but he kept on speaking. "But first you're going to help her make dinner and then we're going to eat it together while I ask you questions."His sudden shift back to sternness threw me off for a second. "O-okay," I said. "No problem."Lottie smiled shyly at me. "And Benjamin," Mr Carter said."Yeah?""Hurt her, and I won't hesitate to take out our two foot Nutcracker figurine that my girlfriend bought us and put it to good use."I grimaced. "Got it.""Good. Now you kids be safe. I'm gonna head out to Delia's. I forgot to pick up my medicine from her!"Lottie kissed his cheek, her face flaming red from his previous statements. "Bye Papa. We'll be fine."Mr Carter squinted his eyes at me as he walked over to the front door.

"You're lucky that I trust my daughter," he said, then quickly added, "and also that I had to listen to her gushing about you for a full thirty minutes!""Papa!" Lottie exclaimed, but he'd already slammed the door shut.I looked at her extremely embarrassed face and my amusement grew. "A full thirty minutes, huh?" I said smugly. My chest felt like it was expanding and I straightened my back.She hid her face in her hands. "Don't tease me," she moaned into her hands.I walked over to her and touched her soft hair. "Don't be lame."Lottie peeked up at me and when she saw my wicked expression, she turned her back to me. "Don't say anything, I don't want to hear it!""Lottie, what did you tell him?" I asked, putting my hand on her back and looking at her from over her shoulder. Her face was so red.

"How unbelievably handsome I am? My down-to-earth personality? My expansive intellect?"Her hands covered her ears and she shut her eyes. "Nope, nope, nope, nope," she chanted. I enjoyed seeing her so shy too much.I bent near her ear and said softly, "Or maybe how good I am at kissing?"Lottie squeaked and shoved me away. "Stop!" she said, running away from me."Come back here! I was just kidding!" I followed quickly behind her, down the hall of her house and into a room with a different coloured door than the rest. It was a very light blue, and I guessed it was her room.I stepped inside and looked around.

The room was small and airy, and decorated with lights and pictures. "Lottie," I said in a sing-song voice. "I know you're in here." I dropped to my knees and checked under her lavender coloured canopy bed. She wasn't there, so I stood up and walked over to the closet. "Lottie," I sang again .There was no response.I flung open the closet and scanned the small, half-empty space. I bent and pushed aside some pea coats to check near the floor.I furrowed my eyebrows. Nothing."Boo.""Fuck!" I jumped and swore again, leaping to my feet and spinning around.And there she stood demurely, her hands clasped behind her back, her big green eyes wide and wondering, her smile soft and sweet.

"I believe that's one to three," she said primly. "We're almost at a draw."I rubbed my hand over my face, feeling embarrassed. Jesus Christ, I hadn't been expecting that.She punched my shoulder. "Hey, wanna go make dinner now?"I shrugged, unable to keep a straight face. She was more excitable than usual, and she seemed genuinely delighted that I was here. Just seeing her like that did wonders to my primarily sullen mood."Come on," she said, grabbing my hand and pulling me out of her room.

"We'll cook dinner, and then I'll give you a tour!"I thought back to the cake I'd made that was just chilling in a cooler in my car. I didn't want anything to happen to it, but I also didn't want Lottie to see. I'd have to wait for her dad so that he could distract her while I sneak it in. "What are we making?" I asked, knowing full well that I refused to ever touch anything cooking-related ever again. Never again."I don't know. We'll see what junk my dad has holed up in the fridge." She squeezed my hand excitedly and I tugged her so that she was pressed up against my side.

I didn't like not being close to her.I followed her into the kitchen, which was this wide open area with an island counter in the middle, a dining table and chairs beside it."Ben," she said suddenly, in a noticeably less enthusiastic tone.I frowned. "What?""Are you okay?""What?""You talked to your dad, right? Did you guys patch anything up?" The amount of worry she held for me made me feel strangely vulnerable. She didn't know it, but she held quite a bit of my self-esteem and heart right in her hands."Maybe you should sit down, Lottie. I've got a story to tell you."

Chapter 35

I started laughing. "Ben, that's a potato peeler."

He looked at peeler and then back at me with raised eyebrows. "So what?"

"I asked you to cut the carrots," I said.

"But shouldn't I peel them first?" He frowned and stared intently at the cutting board, where'd I'd put the freshly washed and cleaned carrots.

"I'm sure you would've had to, if I hadn't already done it, Ben."

Ben pursed his lips, turning his face away from me. I clapped a hand to my mouth in an attempt to not burst into laughter. "Oh," is all he said.

I paused to keep from laughing at his annoyed expression. He really wasn't a cook, was he? How did he even function at his apartment? "So...are you going to, you know, cut them any time soon?"

"Just keep the sass coming, Lottie," he grumbled, putting down the potato peeler in exchange for the knife I handed him. "Keep it coming, I have a thick head. I can take it."

I smiled at him. "Thanks, Ben."

He didn't say anything, just reached out and touched my cheek, running his thumb across my cheekbones before nodding and facing the cutting board. I noticed his mouth thinning and his face turning pink, and that made me grin.

I opened the freezer and stuck my head inside as I searched for frozen beans, hoping that I could cool off the rising heat in my own cheeks. It didn't work though. I pinched my elbow and breathed deeply.

I wished he could be happy. I wished that permanent crease between his eyebrows would smooth out. But with his dad acting like such a...

I wanted to know more about Ben. I wanted to learn more about him than just his general likes and dislikes or his overall personality. I wanted to know his story.

I sighed and closed the fridge, my mouth turning down. I looked over my shoulder at his back. His broad shoulders moved up and down with each chop of the knife, and his head was bent over.

Would he ever let me in? He'd said he would tell me a story, but he ended up saying he wanted to wait until after dinner or something. He was avoiding the subject.

"You working hard there, pal?" I asked.

"Who's your pal?" he said sullenly.

I ignored that and skipped over to him, peeking around at the cutting board. The small circles of carrot he chopped weren't the same size, but the cuts were smooth. I beamed. "Beautiful," I said cheerfully. "You could be a professional carrot chopper, Ben."

He glanced down at me, and I was sure that he was about to smile. That made my grin grow, and I patted him on the arm before pouring the beans into a pot. "Where should I put these?" he asked.

"In the pot, if you please."

I stirred the pan that held the chicken and spices and then dumped the chicken into the pot with the beans and carrots. I hummed a little while I stirred the pot around, and then once the carrots cooked, I took the pot of cheesy roux and poured it in as well.

"It smells good." I jumped in surprise at the sound of Ben's voice right next to my ear, my heartbeat immediately skyrocketing. I turned my head and saw him standing right beside me, smirking. He wiggled his eyebrows and pinched my nose closed.

I laughed and shoved him away, even as I tried to control my erratic breathing. "Don't do that."

Ben straightened and shoved his hands in his pockets, watching as I took out a pot and filled it with water.

"Do you know how to make mashed potatoes?" I asked hopefully, spinning around to meet his gaze.

He scoffed. "Not unless they come out of a box."

I stuck out my tongue and shook my head. "That's gross. You're gross. Don't eat that stuff." He scowled at me for three seconds and then lunged.

Before I knew it, Ben had me in a headlock, knuckling my hair frantically. "Take it back!" he ordered.

I twisted and tried to push him off, laughter bubbling in my throat. "Get off me, you oaf!" I grabbed his hand and tugged on it, but he had me in the tightest hold imaginable, and I couldn't even turn around to see his face.

"Not until you take it back." He shoved me gently, so that my knees were on the floor. My face warmed at the awkward position he'd put me in.

I could feel his warm chest against my back, and closed my eyes. "Ben, the food's going to burn!"

"Then apologise for calling me gross and an oaf."

I felt him breath right on my neck, and I froze, my eyes snapping open. "B-but you don't want me to lie, do you?" I teased, stuttering slightly. Being so close to him still had me going crazy.

"Don't be nervous, Lottie. Am I making you nervous?" he cooed softly.

"Yeah, when you say creepy things like that!"

In the span of one second, Ben had let go of me and flipped me over so that I was lying on my back, and then he pinned me in place with his hands while he sat down right on my stomach.

My chest started to hurt from laughing so hard. "Ben!"

"Yes?" he said loftily, stretching out his legs and leaning back on his palms.

I tried to shove him off. "Get off me!"

"All you have to do is apologise, babe."

My heart fluttered in my chest when he turned to look at me and grinned. It made his dark eyes crinkle up at the corners and made his already strong cheekbones stand out more. My eyes literally glazed over from being so in awe of him.

"I'm waiting," he said, patting my cheek.

I wondered how on earth I could stand him sitting right on top of my stomach, and then I noticed that he held most of his weight on his arms. I sucked in a breath and looked away from his arms to his face, but immediately regretted it. He looked so smug that I started blushing immediately. "I'm sorry for calling you gross," I said in a monotone, struggling to keep straight-faced when he frowned at me.

"Say it with meani-"

Before he could finish his sentence, I reached out and shoved him hard. He tumbled right off my stomach and I shot to my feet, running out of the kitchen. "Make sure you turn off the heat!" I called.

"What the fu-"

I laughed and ran into my room, locking the door and jumping on my bed. I liked it when Ben was being all playful.

The knob jiggled and I heard Ben's exasperated groan. "Goddammit, Lottie."

"Sorry, not sorry."

"Are you really going to make me do something drastic like break down the door?"

"I don't think you're strong enough," I said absentminded-ly, wandering over to my old desk. I hadn't been in here in months, but everything was exactly how I'd left it. Subconsciously, I paid attention to the violent jiggling my door was going through, but in reality I stared at the picture frames lining the edge of my desk.

I leant over and blew, and dust flew in all directions. I picked up one frame in particular and smiled, wiping the glass with the corner of my sleeve.

"That's your mum?"

I wasn't even surprised that Ben had managed to fit the key to his flat's bathroom in my bedroom door to open it. "Yeah," I said. The picture was of when she had first been admitted into the hospital, when she still glowed and shined like a star. I had her lovely smile, I hoped, and her soft, round features.

"She looks kind of like you," he said. His voice was low and hesitant, and it made my chest swell at how careful he was being.

"We do share the same DNA." I put the picture frame down and smiled. "You never told me your story, Ben."

He sat down on my bed and frowned. "What?"

I waved my hand around. "About your dad. About you. About what happened."

His hands moved to cup his elbows and he shifted awkwardly, hunching over his lap. He avoided my gaze and starting shuffling his feet. I watched him carefully. Ben wore his heart on his sleeve without even knowing it.

I sat down beside him, just a few inches away. He stared at the space in between us dazedly. "You don't have to," I said, looking at my hands. I was wringing them like a worried mother and I didn't know why. "But I just..." I leant my head on his shoulder. It was big and broad, and it was very, very comfortable. "Ben, are you going to tell me about you?"

His arm flexed next to my waist and he shifted so that his arm was draped around me. "What do you want to know?"

Ben's chest moved up and down with each breath, and I matched my own breathing to the sound of his steadily beating heart. "I want to know about what makes you you. And I want to know about your family, and Archer, and I want to know what's going on with your parents."

"Nosy git," he muttered, but I knew him enough by now to know that he was just teasing me.

I reached across his lap and grabbed his other hand. "Tell me about you, Ben," I said.

"You have to promise me that your opinion of me won't change," he responded, his tone quiet and serious. "Or at least don't judge me."

I squeezed his hand tightly, trying to transfer a bit of the faith I held to him. I trusted Ben as much as I trusted Ginny or Zach or my dad, and I wanted him to know that. He seemed to understand, because he began to speak.

For probably the first time, Ben Fisher spoke to me. He spoke to me, and I knew it was hard for him. Sometimes he would stop and sigh, as if he was tired, and sometimes he would pause and glance at me to make sure I was listening.

And I listened.

I listened as he described his childhood, made bright and sunny by only by Archer and Clark, but dampened by his father's constant disapproval and his mother's inability to go against his father. His expression was smooth, as if he didn't mind anymore.

When he started to talk about his destructive teenage years, his muscles tensed, and he began to glance at me every few seconds. He was worried about what I'd think of him, and I didn't know why. I mean, I fell in love with him because of everything about him. I loved every little bit of him, and I loved what made him himself now. Not then.

He was a bit of a plonker a few years ago, but I didn't mind. Those years had matured him and had shaped him. They had caused him a pain that I could feel as he talked about it, and my opinion didn't change.

I loved the way he spoke. His voice, gruff and hesitant, painted a picture with his words. He never assumed an arrogant tone, or said anything that seemed conceited or depressing. He didn't downplay or overplay anything. As always, he was honest.

I didn't loosen my grip on his hand. If anything, I clutched on tighter when he started talking about his parents.

"Mum never liked to do anything Dad didn't like," Ben said. Somewhere along his tale, I had thrown my legs over his thighs, and then he'd moved me so that I was sitting on his lap. He held me like a teddy bear, and tucked my head at the base of his neck. His heartbeat quickened, but he carried on speaking without a hint of a stammer. "And my dad never liked anything I did."

I frowned. I hadn't spoken up once, but I wasn't sure how long I could keep still while he talked about his dad. Who, by the way, I still wasn't keen on.

"But when I was over there, he said he'd welcome me back, and not disown me anymore."

I brought my head up and examined his expression. He didn't look happy, but he didn't look sad, either. "Really?" I asked, confused.

"He said he was sorry for throwing me out, and he asked to come back and help him with his company. He said he would help me."

I breathed in. That was good news, it really was, but... "What about uni?"

Ben's eyebrows furrowed and his jaw locked. "He wants me to transfer to University of York, where I would've gone if...that hadn't happened."

"York," I echoed. That was a brilliant school, and my eyes widened. But... "That's kind of far away." Ben didn't say anything.

I blinked harshly. Okay, Ben was going to York. That was a lovely school, and he deserved it! And his father was trying, I supposed. My head felt foggy thinking about it. Seriously, what was up with me and my selfishness? I had to be happy for him.

"That's wonderful, Ben," I said honestly. "That's so, so wonderful."

His expression changed, and I didn't understand it. "I guess," he said reluctantly.

I wondered why he suddenly seemed upset. I didn't like it. "That's good, right?" I asked, kind of desperately. "Don't you want that?" He didn't say anything, and I started panicking.

If he even had the slightest inclination to not go there, I'd do everything in my power to make him stay. I didn't want him to leave, I didn't want him to leave me. But I also didn't want to be the reason he split from his family, the reason that he didn't go to the university of his choice.

I grabbed his face and turned him to look at me. I was wide-eyed and my eyebrows were raised so high that they disappeared into my hairline. "Ben," I said slowly.

"Lottie, just say it," he said.

My heart thumped loudly in my chest. "Say what?" I asked, confused. What did he want me to say?

His gaze drilled right into my eyes. "Whatever you want to say about this, your completely honest feeling, I want to hear it." He wanted me to say something specific, but I didn't know what he wanted me to say.

Was I supposed to wish him off like the selfless person I tried to be? Or was I going to try and take the only thing I've wanted since wishing my mother didn't die?

I peered right at him, my face so close to his that I could feel him breathing on me. His hands tightened and a flicker of uncertainty passed through his expression.

My eyes began to burn, and I laughed the short, breathless kind of laugh that you make when you've got so many pent-up emotions inside you that the only way to release them was a laugh. Ben looked confused at my reaction. I blinked rapidly and my hands trembled. I didn't know what I wanted to say. I had so many things to say to him.

"I'm in love with you."

Chapter 36

I didn't have time to even react the words Lottie had said before she sprang off my lap and held her hands to her mouth, looking horrified. My eyes widened in confusion. She didn't say that. She couldn't have said that. "Pardon?" I asked.

"I-I...uh, I'm-ah-" She restarted her sentence too many times to count, and then frantically back-pedalled, moving to the door.

I got to my feet, and felt my heart plummet to my feet. She was in love with me? Then why did she look as if she wanted to throw up?

"Lottie," I said. I started to walk towards her, but she held up her hands. I stopped abruptly. A flicker of hurt pricked my chest.

"I'm sorry," she whispered. She rubbed her face and looked at me with forlorn eyes. "York is a lovely place and I'm very glad for you. Plus, Uni of York is a really good school," she continued. "Don't mind me." A proud smile grew on her face, and it irritated me because the one time somebody ever looked proud of me was the one time I didn't fucking want it.

I furrowed my eyebrows. The muscles in my arms tensed in complete and utter annoyance. How exactly was she able to look so genuinely happy for me, but at the same time look like I had just fucking stabbed her through the heart?

"You turned off the cooker, right?" she asked when I didn't respond.

"Yes," I said through clenched teeth. I heard the blood pump in my ears, and knew that my expression was growing steadily darker.

Lottie didn't notice, because she'd turned her back to me and ran away. What was she doing?

I stalked out of her room with my back flat as a board and my hands shaking from the effort I was going through to not punch the nearest thing I saw. I stopped at the entrance of the kitchen, slightly out of sight, and spotted her leaning against the fridge. She had her eyes tightly shut, and then took a deep breath and stood upright.

I edged back and leant against the back wall, tipping my head back. She could bounce back so easily when I couldn't. I felt like there was a spidery, metal-fingered hand wrapped like a band around my chest, making it hard to think.

Did she even love me? The doubt started creeping into my mind.

Fucking fuckity fuck fuck.

How could I claim I loved her when I questioned her like that? She was just being regular, selfless, considerate Charlotte Carter.

And I had never hated it more.

I wanted her to be selfish. I wanted her to ask me to stay, because by now, I'd do anything for her. I didn't want to go to York. I liked my classes at Manchester. I liked my apartment and I liked being near Clark. Mrs Wallace needed me to take care of Queenie. I wouldn't be staying just for her, but I needed some push.

I stepped quietly into the kitchen, where Lottie had her head down, quietly peeling potatoes on the island counter. I swallowed and strode over to her, slamming my hands on the counter opposite her. She jumped and glanced at me. Her eyes didn't have that sparkle in them, but she still managed a smile.

Fucking Lottie. Jesus Christ.

"Tell me what you want," I said, staring at her. Her eyes crinkled at the corners and she looked away.

"I want to finish making this chicken pie," she said primly.

That just pissed me off even more. "Tell me what you want, Lottie," I said in a quieter voice. I saw panic in her expression, and I frowned. I had just told her my entire life story. I thought she'd understand that I couldn't handle any more abandonment. I thought she'd understand that what I wanted was her.

"I want to finish making this chicken pie," she repeated, not meeting my eyes.

I blew out in frustration. "Lottie," I said, just short of a plea. Could she hear my underlying message?

Did she want me? Or did she want me to leave her?

She bit her lip. "I want you to go wherever makes you happier," she said quietly.

I watched carefully as she gathered up the peeled potatoes and dumped them into a pot of boiling water, and then as she grabbed a box of puff pastry from the fridge. I looked at my hands and swore under my breath. She affected me so much, and she didn't even realise it.

Lottie looked so small standing near the stove with her shoulders hunched like that, and it made me deflate. "Ask me what I want," I dared loudly.

She paused. "What?"

"You told me to do what made me happy, but you never asked me what I want." I walked towards her as I spoke.

Her shoulders slumped even more. "Look, Ben, I know I'm not that great, but that's kind of a mean thing to ask me to do, you know?"

I took her by the shoulders and gently turned her around. "Ask me," I said.

She sighed, and it took her longer than normal to cover up the sad look on her face. I didn't like that I'd put that sadness there. "Ben, what do you want?"

Instead of answering, I moved my hands to cup her face, and I bent down, kissing her. She stilled for a moment, and then I moved one hand to her curly hair and she melted. Her hands held tightly onto my hips, and I felt the spatula she'd been holding press into my skin.

I moved her away from the stove and pushed her against the island counter, wrapping my arms around her back and pulling her closer. She squeaked into my mouth, and every sane thought flew out of my head and I lost it, and all I knew was that I was kissing Charlotte Carter. I could feel her heart rocketing around in her chest just like mine, and it made me happy because I wasn't the only one affected.

"I love you," I mumbled in between kisses, but it was faint and garbled and I didn't think she heard me.

She finally broke it off and rested her head against my chest. I heard her heavy breathing, and the sound made me smile smugly.

"I don't want to go," I whispered. "And you should've known that."

I felt her shake in my arms, and I tightened my grip. "I shouldn't have said anything, I'm sorry," she cried. "I'm sorry, please, just go, I know you want to!"

I leant my chin on her head and internally cringed at her behaviour. She shouldn't have said she was in love with me? Was she serious? "I don't want to," I said flatly. "I literally just told you that, so stop questioning me."

"But it's such a good opportunity," she said. "And your dad-"

"I don't give two shits. He'll get over it. I'm starting to think you don't want me around." I frowned. I hoped she wasn't just trying to get rid of me in the nicest way possible. It was Charlotte, after all, letting down men in a way that they couldn't even tell.

"That's not it," she whispered, and I believed her. She hid her face against my chest, so her next words came out muffled.

"What did you say?" I asked.

"I love you," she said shyly, hesitantly. It made my heart ache - the good kind of ache.

"Can you look at me and say it?"

Lottie peeked up at me. "Do you promise that you don't want to go to York? Do you promise that your dad won't act like a...thing anymore? I don't want to be the reason you hold back," she said. Her eyes were big and curious and guarded.

I could see her reserved excitement, and that excited me. "Yes I promise. I'm not sure about my dad, but he'll get over it. Archer's the one who's into the whole business scene." She searched my face for a minute, her eyebrows furrowing in concentration. I knew she was trying to figure out if I was lying or not. I wasn't lying. "You're not holding me back, Lottie, you nutcase."

Lottie's hands let go of my waist, and she tossed the spatula behind her. Then she looked at me long and hard, contemplating something. "I love you!" she exclaimed, jumping up to hug around my neck. Like before, her legs wrapped around my waist and I gripped her tightly. She laughed bashfully, the sound warm and light and happy, and I couldn't help but grin.

I made her happy, and the feeling of that was indescribable.

"I love you," she said again, and laughed some more. "I am in love with you." Every time she said it, a little thrill shot down my back. Not to be arrogant, but quite a few girls had told me the same, but they never meant it. But with Lottie, sincerity seeping out of her tone, it made me feel different.

But fact that she was almost one hundred percent willing to blow me off just because she thought I'd be happier without her slightly worried me. Lottie would never fight for me if it meant making me happy, but she made me happy. I didn't think she knew that, though, but she always thought she knew best about what made people smile the most.

"Don't assume what will make me happy, Lottie," I said firmly. "You always choose the thing that isn't you."

She looked up and smiled, and the dead look was gone. Her thousand-watt beam was back, and I couldn't help but bend down to kiss her again. I loved kissing her.

So...what did that make us?

Had I even told her I loved her yet?

Wait, did I?

Oh fuck, what must she be thinking?

"Lottie," I started, but then stopped at the sound of splashing water and hissing.

Lottie's eyes widened and she let go of me. "The potatoes!" she cried, running over to turn off the heat.

I scowled and crossed my arms. Those fucking potatoes.

She used a hand towel to take hold of the pot of potatoes and drain it in the sink, and then grabbed this weird spoon thing that wasn't really a spoon but was some sort of mashy thing. I'd seen Clark use something like it before. "Do you want to mash the potatoes while I make the pie?" Lottie asked hopefully. She didn't even know how impossible it was for me to say no when she scrunched her nose like that and squinted her eyes.

I took the mashy spoon thing from her hand and stared at it while she fumbled around in some drawers for a pie dish. There was a little metal grid at the bottom that I assumed was for crushing the potatoes. "How do I...?" I muttered to myself, twisting the thing in my hand. Was I just supposed to go for it?

Lottie popped up from behind the counter and watched me with confused eyes. "What are you doing?" she asked.

"I have no clue, to be honest."

She stood up and showed me how the weird spoon mashy thing worked. "It's pretty simple. Make sure there's no lumps, okay?"

"Okay."

I held onto of the pot handles and slowly pulverised the steaming potatoes, my hands becoming wet from condensation. My eyes were trained on Lottie, however, as she bustled around and assembled the pie. I badly wanted to tell her how I felt, but I really didn't know how. As cheesy as it sounded, I'd never felt anything this before for anybody in existence. There was just something about her that had sunk deep into the holes in my chest and filled them up - however fucking weird that sounded.

It was a strange feeling, and I didn't know what to do with it. I didn't even have the excuse of rejection. She'd already said she loved me.

Cue stilling of heartbeat.

I thought back to the cake nestled in the icebox in my car. Tomorrow was her birthday. I could give her the cake and the other thing I'd gotten for her, and maybe figure something out for that?

Lottie peeked at me from over her shoulder, and her smile softened when I winked at her. "You doing alright, Ben?" she asked.

I looked down at the contents of the pot and nodded. "Yup, looks pretty mashed to me."

She abandoned the pie without folding the puff pastry on top and came to admire my work. "Sweet!" she said happily. "Lemme just put in the milk and butter, and then we can put salt and pepper."

I watched as she dashed some milk into the pot and then grabbed a stick of butter from the fridge. "How much should I put?" she mused to herself. She cut off a decently sized chunk and threw it in. "Now mix it, Benny!"

I obeyed while she cracked some black pepper and sprinkled salt into the mashed potatoes. My stomach growled and I frowned. "I'm hungry."

Lottie spooned out some of the potatoes. "Try some," she urged, offering the spoon to me.

Instead of taking the spoon from her like she implied, I bent down and let her feed me. My insides glowed when I saw her amused expression. "More pepper," I said.

"I'm home!" we heard, and I stood upright. Lottie jumped and moved away from me just as her dad came wandering into the kitchen.

She waved to him. "Alright, Papa?"

He nodded, and when his eyes turned to me, I smiled politely and asked him how he was.

"Well, dinner smells lovely. Thanks for helping Charlie out, Ben."

"It wasn't an issue."

We both looked over at Lottie, whose face, for some reason, had turned bright red. I raised my eyebrows, and she coughed awkwardly, avoiding our eyes.

Mr. Carter smirked. "I take it I'm not wanted here? Don't worry, I'll just be watching some footie in the living room. Call me when it's time for supper!"

Oh sweet baby Jesus, now my face was red. "What's wrong with you?" I asked her, wondering what exactly was going on in her mind.

She ignored me and finished making the creases in the pie shell, and then put it in the oven.

I rolled my eyes. "Do you want me to lock you in the loo?"

Lottie laughed. "Don't be stupid, it locks from the inside."

She just called me stupid. Lottie had just called me stupid. "Rude," I muttered, hiding my amused smile. I watched her for a while, and for just a moment, her lighthearted expression dropped. I frowned. "What's wrong?"

Lottie didn't reply, just smiled reassuringly at me. I didn't feel reassured. I wished she wouldn't do that.

I took her hand as she walked by to grab the potatoes. "Would you please stop doubting me?" I asked. I spilt my whole heart to her, and she still didn't believe me?

"I'm not doubting you," she argued. "I just don't want to be the reason you don't go to such a good school and fix things with your dad."

She really was too good for me.

I tugged her gently towards me and wrapped my arms around her in a bear hug. She pressed her face into my chest and breathed deeply. "As lovely as you are," I said. "You're not the only reason I'm staying. Should I feel responsible for giving you a big head?"

She laughed this cute, embarrassed laugh that warmed me to the tips of my toes. "Sorry, sorry, sorry, sorry," she apologised in quick succession. "I didn't mean to, I just-"

"I know," I said quietly. I knew why she did the things she did and said the things she said. Because she wanted the best for everyone but herself.

But I wanted the best for her too.

Chapter 37

I literally could not stop looking at him.

Ben was sitting at the kitchen table, waiting for me to finish making the pie that Papa wanted me to make for dessert. He thought I was almost finished, but I had barely just put the dough in the fridge to chill. I leant against the counter, putting my elbows on the top and my chin in my palms. Ben was on his mobile, and hadn't looked up in about ten minutes.

I felt a little creepy just watching him and smiling, but I couldn't help it.

"Lottie, what flavour pie are you cooking up?" he asked suddenly, glancing up.

My elbows slipped and I accidentally smacked my head against the marble. "Oh," I said, half in pain and half in surprise. I rubbed my forehead.

When I looked at Ben, he had his eyebrows raised and his mouth pursed in amusement. "Are you okay?"

I closed my eyes, feeling my head throb. That was what I got for being a creepy thing. "Just splendid, thank you," I said cheerfully. Then I thought about what I did and slapped the counter, giggles escaping my mouth.

I rubbed my head again, tears slipping out of my eyes from the throbbing and the laughter. "Jesus Christ, Lottie, what's wrong with you?" he asked. When I glanced at him, his twitching mouth had morphed into a full-blown smile, and he shook his head.

I smiled back at him, and my heart seemed to fall out of my mouth. "A lot of things," I told him. He stood up and walked up to me, putting his hands on my shoulders and bending down to look at my eyes. I blinked at him in confusion when he frowned. "What's wrong with you?" I asked.

Ben managed to keep a straight face for about three seconds before he sagged his head and started laughing. His hands gripped my shoulders so tightly that I could feel his body shaking, which in turn shook me.

I loved his laugh. It came all the way from his belly and was a deep and satisfying sound that hung in the air and made me want to laugh as well. Soon we were both falling all over each other with laughter, and I didn't know what was funny, but I just loved hearing him go at it.

My voice faded off, but Ben was practically gripping me to his chest and crying with laughter. "Y-y-you just-" I furrowed my eyebrows and just watched him. I beamed affectionately, not knowing what to do.

I poked his shoulder to try and get his attention, but he just rested his head on my shoulder and kept laughing. "Benjamin Fisher," I said, tapping his cheek.

"You just fell against the counter!" he exclaimed. "Lottie, what-"

I cupped his cheeks with both of my hands and turned him to face me, pressing my smiling mouth against his. That definitely got him to stop, and he kind of froze against me. I giggled and he moved his hands from my shoulders to my hair and started responding. I felt his heart beating wildly, and it made me smile wider.

I really loved him.

I moved back and grinned, wiggling my eyebrows. "Don't make fun of me," I said, pinching his cheeks and stretching them out.

"Jesus Christ, Lottie," he breathed, straightening up. His face was flushed, and that made me want to tease him really badly. "I just wanted to know what damn flavour your damn pie was."

I beamed at him and stepped back. "Strawberry and blueberry, is that alright?"

Ben squinted at me. "How much sugar are you putting it?"

"Just a pinch - the fruit is sweet enough. Okay with you?"

"I'm sure if you make it, it'll be fine."

I paused and my eyes widened at his words. He'd said it with a straight face, still looking a little grumpy from me teasing him. Did he really compliment me like that? "Oh," was all I could say.

He rolled his eyes and kissed my cheek, ruffled my hair, and walked back to the kitchen table. My goofy smile refused to fall. Ben sat at the table and glanced at me like he didn't know what to do now.

I sighed happily and took the cartons of strawberries and blueberries from the fridge. I washed them and put them in a pan with some cornstarch and a wee bit of sugar, but my head was in the clouds and I couldn't really think. While the fruit cooked, I took the dough from the fridge and rolled it into a pie pan. "Ben," I sang to myself. "Ben, Ben, Ben, Ben."

"What are you saying?"

I ignored him and kept working until the pie was ready to put in the oven. I loved him, I really, really loved him, and the fact that he didn't want to go to York had me unable to frown.

I hoped he wasn't going to give anything up for me, though. I really hoped he didn't, because then I wouldn't be able to forgive myself. But maybe to think that was exceptionally conceited of me, because what if he didn't feel anything for me like I did for him?

I mean, I didn't mind that he hadn't responded to my I love you, but it was kind of a downer. Maybe he hadn't said anything because he didn't want to lie.

I closed my eyes. I was seriously going to hurt myself with all this self-deprecation.

Suddenly, Ben stood up. I jumped and looked at him, puzzled. "I left my laptop in the car," he explained, walking out of the kitchen. I stared after him, but shrugged and went back to work.

Papa came into the kitchen just then and he beckoned to me. "Charlie, can you come here for a minute? I can't get the damn telly to change programmes."

I giggled and followed him to the living room. "I'm surprised that you were even able to turn it on in the first place." He rolled his eyes and gave me the remote, pointing to the telly. I saw that the footie was still on, and I frowned. "You want to switch away from football?" I asked. My dad didn't watch anything but football. He literally would watch the matches, and then would watch them again, and then would rewatch segments of old World Cups and follow his favourite players to see what they were up to.

Papa stared at me blankly until we heard the sound of the front door opening. I glanced back to see Ben hurrying to the kitchen, and I was about to go after him when Papa propelled me to the front of the TV and pointed at the screen. "I'm feeling like Food Network," he said.

My mouth opened in disbelief. "You want to watch Nigella Lawson?"

"Don't forget Jamie Oliver." Papa grinned widely and falsely, and I didn't know what to think, but I just shook my head and changed the programme for him.

I looked at my dad again and at his suspiciously ruddy and pinched face. "Papa?"

"Yes, poppet?" he asked. His voice pitched a little higher than usual, and I began to worry.

"This thing you're worrying about - is it serious?"

He seemed to relax, and just shook his head. "Don't you worry, Charlie. It's nothing of consequence."

I watched him for a few more seconds before handing him the remote and shuffling back over to the kitchen. Since everything was already baking and getting ready and the salad was in the fridge, I pulled up a chair beside Ben and sat down. "Whatcha up to, Benny?" I asked cheerily.

Ben gestured to his phone. "Just checking my marks from my last exam."

That seemed innocent enough, but I looked down at the table and pursed my lips. The only things on it were the tablecloth and a tissue box. "Where's your laptop?" I asked curiously. Wasn't that what he went to his car to get?

It didn't escape my notice how Ben stilled momentarily before shrugging and avoiding my gaze. "I didn't need it. I don't want to be working right now."

I nodded and smiled. "That's good! You can just relax and hang out with me tonight."

Ben didn't change his stoic expression, but he did reach out and gripped one of my hands, bringing it near his mouth so he could press a small kiss on my knuckles. My face flamed when he winked.

My poor heart didn't stand a chance.

"Where are you from, Ben?" Papa asked. He sat across from me and Ben, but had his eyes trained on his plate of chicken pie.

"Manchester, like you two," he said smoothly.

I grinned inwardly. I loved how I knew that Ben was nervous only by the brusque quality of his voice. I was sure barely anybody else could tell that him being gruff and manly served as a cover for his anxiety. "And what's your major?"

"Computer science."

Papa looked up, impressed with him. That was the best thing Ben could've said, because Papa had majored in that in uni too. "Brilliant. So are you taking calculus? Which kind?"

"It's multivariable."

Papa winked at me. "Smart chap, eh, Charlie?"

I laughed. "He's extremely smart, Papa."

We spent a couple of minutes just eating. I peeked at Ben, and noticed his tight expression. I tapped his shoulder, and when he glanced at me, I smiled reassuringly. His shoulders eased almost imperceptibly, and his eyes crinkled at the corners.

"So, you liking the food, Ben?" Papa said a while later.

"Lottie made it, so I really do."

Upon hearing that, I accidentally hit my thigh against the underside of the table and closed my eyes at the sudden, sharp pain. I gripped my leg and sighed slightly.

Papa just grunted affirmatively at Ben's response, not noticing my current state. I opened my eyes and straightened, rubbing the sore spot gently.

"Are you okay?" Ben whispered in my ear. I could sense the beginnings of a laugh in his voice.

"I'll kiss you in front of my dad if you make fun of me," I warned. He couldn't take me by surprise like that! It literally wasn't good for my physical health.

Ben just touched my shoulder and turned back to his plate in time for my dad's next question.

"What do your parents do?"

Without flinching, Ben said, "My dad owns an automobile company and my mum helps manage it."

"You got a plan for the future?"

"Not currently, but I'm working on it."

"Any ideas?"

"I'm thinking about becoming a teacher." My eyebrows raised - a computer science teacher? Like in university? I hadn't known that. But then again, I hadn't asked.

"You have any siblings?"

"Just one wee brother."

"How old is he?"

"Seventeen."

"How old are you?"

"Twenty." I was impressed with the ease at which he answered every question my dad threw at him, because they came in rapid succession and were confusing me.

"Do you have a job?"

He nodded. "I watch over a little girl most days."

Papa grinned. "Like a nanny?"

Ben winced slightly. "Kind of?"

"There you go, Charlie! He likes kids! That's great for you, right? Haven't you always said that you want a lad who-"

"Papa," I interrupted, feeling mortified. Ben pursed his lips, and I just knew he was trying to stop from chuckling. I pinched his hip under the table, and he swatted me away.

My dad's grin just widened. "What's this little girl like, Ben?"

"Er...well she's really cheeky. She's really hyper all the time and loves sweets, like Lottie." I looked down at my plate to hide my smile. You could tell how much he cared about

Queenie just by listening to him. "And she's pretty nice for a kid, always sharing her toys and playing with the loners at the park."

Papa looked from me to Ben a few times, his grin gone. I furrowed my eyebrows. Why was he making that face? He stood up and gathered his empty plate and utensils and stared menacingly at us. I reached under the table and grabbed Ben's hand, which was mildly sweaty. I would've laughed at his nerves had I not been worried too.

Abruptly, Papa broke into a wide grin "I like you, boy." Then he turned around and strode into the kitchen.

I breathed out and beamed. "Good job, Ben! You handled my dad really well!"

He squeezed my hand. "Are you sure?"

"He said he likes you. He's never said that to any boy he's ever met before!"

"Has there been a lot?" he asked, frowning.

I shook my head rapidly. "No, just when we go out to the shops or for dinner and boys talk to me, he never likes them. But he likes you. I knew he would!"

"Parents don't usually like me, so how did you know?"

"Obviously they have impaired judgment, then," I said impatiently. "And my dad doesn't."

Ben looked at me, and all the creases on his face smoothed out, and he let go of my hand only to lean towards me and wrap me in a hug. "Thanks," he murmured.

"For what?"

"I don't really know," he said. "I guess thanks for being you."

Chapter 38

I watched Lottie taking blankets and pillows from a cupboard in the hall near her room. She was dressed in a big shirt and a pair of trackie trousers like a normal person about to sleep. I, on the other hand, still wore my normal clothes in order to not make her uncomfortable. Even though I was pretty sure that she liked me wearing less clothes...

But that was besides the point.

"Where should I sleep?" I asked her. I reached out to take most of the pile from her arms, because she looked like she was being swallowed by the five pillows and the blankets she held.

She peeked at me from over the top of the three neatly folded blankets she held and smiled. "How do you feel about building a fort in the living room?" she asked. She raised her eyebrows and did this sweet little smile thing, and I just knew she knew that I wouldn't be able to resist that look.

"How old are you?" I asked in an attempt to show that I could hold my own against her. But let's be real, the second she smiled at me like that, I was a goner.

Lottie laughed and took my elbow, tugging me down the stairs. "Come on, tomorrow's my birthday," she sang. "Humour me!"

I let her lead me because it made her happy. She turned around and looked at me as she walked down, but then she tripped, and her eyes widened. My hands immediately dropped the pillows and grabbed her by the waist. "What the fuck!" I exclaimed.

"Oh, I didn't expect that," she breathed, clinging onto my neck like a scared baby monkey. I could feel her heart beating fast, and she rested her head on my shoulder.

"What's wrong with you?" I grumbled. The pillows and blankets were now scattered all around us, and she suddenly started laughing. I frowned and said, "I don't trust you to walk properly anymore."

"Wha-" Lottie squeaked when I adjusted her so that she was draped over my shoulder and back. "What are you doing?"

I walked downstairs and deposited her on the floor, and as she gave me a bemused look, I went back upstairs and shoved all of the things we dropped towards her. "You don't even know how to walk properly." She pouted.

"It was just a mistake!"

"First you fall on a counter, and now you're falling down stairs-"

"Benny!"

"What?"

I squatted down and stared at her. She stared back with her expressive doe-eyes, and I gave her a sort of smile and ruffled her hair. Despite the fact that she nearly gave me a panic attack, she was still fucking cute."How do we make a fort?" I asked to see if it would make her happier.

That brightened her up out of her pout and she shot to her feet, grabbing pillows at random. "Come on, then," she urged, smiling excitably.

I gathered up the rest of the blankets and followed her to the living room, wondering how on earth she could get me to do things that I really didn't want to do. She beamed at me and immediately jogged over to the biggest sofa that lay in front of the telly.

"Pass me the Winnie the Pooh blanket, will you?"

I wrinkled my nose in distaste. "I like this one," I said sarcastically, grimacing at the sight of the bright pink background and mismatched orange stitching.

Lottie ignored me and took the big Winnie the Pooh blanket, draping it over the back of the sofa. She did this weird thing with the pillows where she used them as stoppers for the blanket to create this tent-like shape while I watched with furrowed eyebrows. I wasn't sure how she did what she did, but it was fascinating to watch.

While spreading some more blankets on the inside of the fort thing, she glanced at me and shook her head. "Lazy bum," she said.

"What do you want me to do? You've practically finished it all!"

"You could offer to help?" she suggested, trying to look mad, but I could see that she was holding back a grin.

I sighed and got to my knees. "Would you like some help, love?"

I didn't even know until I said it, but the 'love' slipped out so naturally that it surprised me. Lottie paused, giving me a strange look. I returned her look blankly until she just laughed nervously and reached out to grab my hand and tug me nearer.

"Come put the pillows inside while I make some hot chocolate."

It took me a while to register what she said, but once I registered it, my brain went into some sort of seizure mode. Making hot chocolate required her access to the fridge, and in the fridge was her cake, so in a frenzy, I wrapped my arms around her waist and hugged her.

"What are you doing?" she asked, highly amused as I nuzzled her neck and pulled her onto my lap.

My cheeks heated slightly when after a moment's hesitation, Lottie started stroking my hair. I really liked it when she touched my hair. It felt nice, and her fingers were really gentle.

"Ben, as lovely as you are, I really want some hot chocolate."

I panicked again and clutched her tighter when she went to stand up. "Wait," I said, and paused. What was I supposed to say to stall? "Er...let me go make it." She couldn't go into the kitchen, because she'd open the fridge and see the cake.

"Really?"

I internally groaned my displeasure at the idea of having to be in the kitchen for something other than eating, but nodded my head anyway. "Yes, I'll make it. You fix up the pillows here."

"Really?" she asked again. She looked so skeptical that it made me want to laugh. She was suspicious, and I had to think of something quick.

"Lottie," I said.

She cocked her head in confusion. "Why do you want to make the hot chocolate? You wouldn't even whip the cream-"

She was getting too suspicious and it was psyching me out. "Stop talking," I muttered.

"Wha-" I cut her off by cupping her face and kissing her. She made a surprised noise and fell over, and I followed, moving my hands to her hair and hovering right over her.

When I pulled back, her eyes were unfocused and dazed and her lips were bright pink, and even though my breathing was uneven and all I wanted to do was keep kissing her, I got to my feet and ran to the kitchen. I let out a relieved breath.

Oh fuck, now what do I do?

How do you make hot chocolate?

I stood in the middle of the kitchen and scowled.

I took a carton of milk from the fridge and had to look through all of the damn cabinets just to find a mug and hot chocolate powder. I poured the milk into the mug, spilling a little, and then put it in the microwave. "What the hell am I supposed to do now?" I asked myself, eyeing the buttons angrily.

"Ben?" a small voice said.

I turned around and saw Lottie leaning against the door-frame. "Hi," I said.

"Do you need help?" she asked softly. She smiled and skipped over to me when I nodded frantically.

I watched as she pressed some random buttons on the microwave that made multiple beeping noises that I didn't understand. "How are you doing that?" I asked.

"How am I heating up milk?" she asked, raising her eyebrows. She took her mug out of the microwave and laughed that lovely laugh of hers. "You're seriously hopeless. How are you living by yourself?"

I rolled my eyes, but couldn't help but laugh with her. "Clark's the next Masterchef, Lottie."

Once she'd made her hot chocolate, she took my hand and took me back into the living room. Her hand was really warm from holding her mug, but mine was probably even warmer from nerves, not to mention disgusting and sweaty. She either didn't seem to mind or didn't notice it. She stopped us in front of the fort and knelt down to prepare to crawl inside.

"Lottie, I don't think I'll fit in there," I said. The blanket creating the fort wasn't all that large, and I wasn't sure how I felt about sleeping while Winnie the Pooh's enlarged face stared at me.

"Don't be silly, you will," she said, beckoning to me.

We stared each other down for a minute until I groaned and crouched down so I could sit beside her.

The inside was dark, and all I could make out was the shape of Lottie's body and the giant smile on her face. "Isn't this fun?" she asked.

I leant back against the mounds of pillows. "If I'm being honest, not really."

"I knew you'd say that," she said. "Do you want to watch a movie or something?"

I looked at her hopeful expression and felt myself crumble into a pile of lame Ben crumbles. "Okay," I said, and had to take a deep breath when she cheered quietly.

"Give me a minute." She crawled out of the fort thing and I could hear her pattering away. I sighed and then sat up, pulling off my shirt, socks and belt.

I wanted to be comfortable, for Chrissakes.

I closed my eyes and relaxed against the pillows and blankets. It was actually really comfortable, but I still felt like a giant in a baby's house. But it made Lottie happy to do this, not to mention it was her birthday tomorrow.

And it had absolutely nothing to do with the fact that we got to sleep beside each other. Nothing at all.

"What shall we watch?" I heard her say, and I grunted in response. I felt her lying down beside me, and then she jumped up. "You took off your shirt."

I opened my eyes and balanced myself on my elbows. "Keen observation, Lottie," I said. "Does it make you nervous?"

I couldn't really see her expression in the dark, but she coughed a little, and the shining laptop I saw in her hands shook. "No," she said, laughing. "You're very fit, and I know that already."

I bit my lip to keep in my smile as she plopped down beside me. She didn't even flinch when I rested my arm under her neck and pulled her head onto my chest. She even snuggled closer, which made me nervous because I worried she could feel how fast my heart was beating.

"My dad leant me his laptop," she said, opening the lid. "What do you want to watch?"

"Whatever is available," I said vaguely. I rested my cheek against the top of her head and closed my eyes. Her hair was so soft, and was funny to feel because of the mound of curls and waves.

I shifted my body so that it was slightly turned towards her, and she giggled. "You're tickling me," she whispered.

"What am I even doing?"

"Your chest needs a shave, you're gross."

"I'm not gross, don't be rude."

The artificial light from the laptop illuminated her face in a slightly creepy way, but she still looked absolutely beautiful. Even when she wrinkled her nose in disgust like that.

"You need to wax your whole body, I bet, you hairy bear," she teased, making me want to laugh. I watched her log into Netflix and browse the different films.

I scoffed. "I'm gorgeous the way I am."

"Okay," is all she said. There was this extremely cheeky grin on her face, and I just wanted to poke her dimples.

"Let's watch that," I said, pointing at the screen randomly.

"You want to watch a cheesy horror film?"

I pursed my lips. "Why not?"

"Aw, Ben, is it going to scare you? Do you want me to protect you?" Her tone was completely serious, but she couldn't last even two seconds before she started laughing.

"Brat."

"You love it though," she laughed.

My whole body seemed to fill with an unbelievably over-whelming sense of compassion for the girl in my arms as I listened to her giggle, and it made me realise that I hadn't told her yet. Suddenly, my hands started sweating and I found it hard to breathe, and I wasn't sure whether I was just having issues or I was losing my voice.

Lottie had started the cheesy horror film I had picked and positioned the laptop so that we both had a clear shot. "If you get frightened, just let me know. I'll hold your hand."

"Who wants to hold your grimy hand?" I mumbled, still thinking about when I was supposed to tell her how much I adored her.

She craned her neck so I could see her wink at me. "You do, Ben."

Well, she wasn't wrong.

We watched that stupid, not at all scary film from start to finish, and I'll be honest. I didn't think Lottie was the type to criticise how weird paranormal ghost things killed their victims, but she was. I thought she'd get scared, but she didn't, just pretended to throw up on me.

"That was gross," she said in a sleepy voice, yawning into her hand. "Too much blood, right?"

"Right," I agreed.

"I didn't know ghosts could hold knives."

"Me neither."

Lottie closed the laptop and yawned again. "Are you okay?"

"Yeah, why wouldn't I be?"

She snuggled close enough to me that I could feel her light breathing on my chest. "You're just being quieter than usual."

Sorry, I was just trying to figure out how to confess my love to you. "I'm okay," I said. "There's nothing the matter."

"Ben?" I heard a few minutes later. Her voice was soft and quiet, and I almost didn't hear her.

"Yeah?"

She patted my chest and sighed tiredly. "I just wanted to remind you that I think you're lovely. Don't think any different."

I closed my eyes and breathed in and out four times. "I love you, God, I really, really love you," I said, the words tumbling out of my mouth in a rapid, garbled mess.

But she was already asleep.

Chapter 39

"Lottie," I heard.

"Go away."

"Lottie."

My mind was foggy and I couldn't make sense of what was going on. I stretched and pressed my face into my pillow. "No, go away," I said sleepily.

I heard a couple of thuds and sighed, trying to fall asleep again. But then I felt a soft tickling on my face and wrinkled my nose. "Why?" I whined, opening my eyes. "Who even-"

"Happy birthday," Ben said. He had on a conical paper hat that fastened under his chin and was decorated with poorly drawn blue balloons. He looked extremely uncomfortable and that made me want to laugh.

"You look great," I said, smiling at him. He leant down so that instead of kneeling, he was on his elbows and eye-level with me.

"I always look great," he replied and patted my head like I was a dog. "Your dad made it."

I stretched out my aching arms and accidentally smacked Ben in the face. "Oops, sorry," I said, patting his cheek. He just laughed and sat up, pulling me with him. I yawned and said, "I'm so tired."

"Your dad made you breakfast, so you should get up."

I cocked my head. "What did he do? Defrost the waffles or put the bread in the toaster?"

"It's a special day, I think he made both."

Abruptly, I leant forward and kissed Ben's cheek, then I stood up, scratching the back of my head. "Let's go then, I'm hungry." Ben stood up as well and yanked the adorable birthday hat off of his head, jamming it onto mine instead.

"That thing was giving me a double chin," he grumbled, running his hand across his jaw.

"Don't blame the hat, Benny," I teased. He just scoffed and nudged my shoulder. I noticed he had put his shirt back on, but I wasn't sure whether that was a good thing or not. I shook my head fiercely to get rid of the image.

"Charlotte!" Papa exclaimed when I entered the kitchen. I grinned at him and ran up to him, giving him a big hug. "Happy birthday, poppet," he said, holding me tightly.

"I heard you cooked me breakfast?"

He let go of me and chuckled. "The very loose definition of 'cooked,' Charlie."

Ben suddenly came up behind me and touched the small of my back. "By cooked he means he went to the bakery and brought back croissants and muffins," he said.

Papa and I laughed, and I saw the big white box from the local bakery and made a beeline for it. I grinned when I saw my favourite chocolate-filled croissant waiting for me, still warm and buttery from the oven.

"You look like a hungry wolf," Ben said, but I ignored his stupid jokes and started eating it. I should've changed and brushed my bird's nest hair before having breakfast, but I was starved.

Papa rubbed my head as I ate and said, "I'm going to Delia's house for a bit, okay? Charlie, Ben said you and him can spend the day however you want, but come home for dinner and presents with Delia and I."

"Okay, Papa," I mumbled. He shook his head and left, and then Ben sat down next to me. "Do you want any?" I asked after I finished the bite in my mouth. He just stared at me, and I frowned and wiped at my mouth self-consciously. "What?"

"What do you want to do today?" he asked.

I smiled dopily and shrugged. "I'm going to say it."

Ben rolled his eyes. "Shut up, don't say it."

"I will."

"No, please, Lottie. Don't."

"Ben, it doesn't matter what we do-"

"Please shut the fuck up."

"-as long as we do it together." I started giggling at the fed-up expression on Ben's face. We had watched a movie a while ago where the couple would say the same such sickly-sweet things, and Ben had hated it.

"Lottie, why do you hate me?" he groaned while I laughed at him.

I shoved the rest of the croissant in my mouth and grinned. Once I'd swallowed, I said, "I'm sorry, but not really." When he just stared at me flatly, I stood up. "Do you want eggs and toast for breakfast?"

Ben pursed his lips and smiled slightly at me, making me return it tenfold. "Yes please."

As I passed his chair on my way to the fridge, I ruffled his hair playfully. "How many eggs?" I asked, turning around to look at him.

Ben looked at me for a second, and then his eyes widened and his hand twitched. "I actually forgot that I'm deathly allergic to eggs and toast."

My eyebrows furrowed. "What?"

"Come here, Lottie."

I just stared at him, confused. "How can you be allergic to eggs and toast? You've been eating my baked goods for weeks and you're not dead. You do know that most cakes have eggs?"

Ben leapt out of his chair and grabbed my hand, tugging me out of the kitchen and upstairs. "Go change, we're going out to do something."

I froze and squirmed in his hold. "But you haven't eaten breakfast."

"There's some stuff left in the box, I'll eat one of the scones or something. Just go get ready. Something kind of warm."

"Ben, make sure you eat breakfast!"

He kept pulling me upstairs and then shoved me in my room. "Yeah, I will, don't worry."

The door to my room closed and I stared at it, confused. Deathly allergic to eggs and toast? How dumb did he think I was?

I decided to let it go for the moment, because I was sure that he couldn't be hiding anything bad from me. So I just grabbed some old clothes from the pile I'd left behind when I went to university and took them to my bathroom, where I showered and changed.

Ben was waiting by the front door when I trailed downstairs, and I skipped over to him. His bored expression softened when he saw me, and I smiled at him.

"Where are we going?" I asked.

"Do you like ice skating?"

I slipped my feet in my shoes and nodded eagerly. "Yeah, are we going to the ice rink in the town centre?"

Ben wrapped his arm around my shoulders and I cuddled against his side as he led me to his car. "Yeah. There's nothing much else to do in this place."

"You're right," I said. "I mean, we could go vandalise something-"

"No," Ben said firmly, shoving me inside and starting up the car.

"I know, Dad," I scoffed, but inside I was kind of disappointed. I'd never done anything particularly bad before, except for not reading my assigned reading books in school, but maybe that was for good reason.

Ben seemed to know his way to the town centre quite well, and we got there faster than I would've gone, mainly because he drove like a speed demon.

"Benny, this isn't NASCAR, slow down please."

He dropped maybe 3mph, but kept going super fast. "We need to get there before ten, otherwise we won't get the free ticket for your birthday."

"How'd you know about that?"

"I just looked it up."

"Did you just look up cheap birthday deals?"

There was a pause, and he glanced at me worriedly. "Yes."

I stared at him blankly, trying to psych him out as if I'd expected him to pay a lot of money for me. Then I beamed and raised my hand. "My kind of guy!" Ben rolled his eyes, noticeably more relaxed, but gave me a high five anyway.

When we reached the town centre and had taken advantage of the fact that it was my birthday, Ben turned to me and adjusted my coat so that it was covering me a bit more.

I smiled, amused. "Ben, I live in England. Cold doesn't affect me that much."

He ignored me and placed his hands over my ears like muffs. "You didn't bring a hat," he said disapprovingly.

I frowned at him and pointed at his thin jacket and lack of hat. "Neither did you, silly." I reached up and flicked his ears. They were already tinged slightly pink from the cold, and we hadn't even entered the ice rink yet.

He stepped back and made a rude face at me. I put my hands on my hips and made a ruder face back. "Real mature," he said.

"Says you!" I replied in a sing-song voice. I bit my lip in an attempt to stop from laughing at his dumb expression, but I couldn't hold it and started giggling.

Ben rolled his eyes and grabbed my hand, pulling me to the ice rink, which was awkward because of the ice skates we wore.

"Do you know how to ice skate?" I asked.

"That would've been more helpful if you'd asked me before we got here," Ben sassed me.

"Considering you're the one who asked if we should come here!"

"Lottie, ask yourself, can I ice skate?"

We got to the actual rink part, and I shoved him hard, causing him to topple over onto the frozen floor. I clapped my hands over my mouth to stop myself from laughing. "I guess not," I said.

"Lottie, what the fuck," he moaned.

I raised my eyebrows. "Are you hurt?" I asked worriedly.

"No, but-"

"Then bye!" I squeaked and spun around seeing that he was struggling to get up and get me back.

"Wait, Lottie-"

"Sorry, I can't hear you!" I spun around a little and started skating backwards, watching him carefully as he got to his feet and then slipped again. I smiled and skidded to a stop, watching him struggle.

Ben was seriously such a cutie!

I hastily slid back to him while he was on his bum and then bent at the waist, wrapping my arms around his neck and squeezing tightly. "Cute!" I said.

Ben froze in my arms, and I stayed like that until I was sure that he was too dazed to try and push me down as well. "What are you doing?" he asked.

I laughed at him and let go. "Oh I don't know, Benny. What is it called when a person puts their arms around another person?"

"Strangling," he said with a perfectly straight face.

I held up a finger. "Ding ding ding! A*, you got it!" I stretched out my hands to him and he took them, pulling himself up.

"Now can we actually skate?" he grumbled, brushing off spare bits of ice from his front.

"Of course, madam."

Ben glared at me, but there was no heart behind it. I grinned cheekily, and he just shook his head.

Antagonising him was so fun.

"Do you think they give out free things on people's birthdays?" Ben asked thoughtfully.

I stared at the shop he pointed at. "We don't have an animal, that's a pet grooming salon."

"I've got you," he said.

"Good joke."

We'd already gotten a free ticket at the ice rink, then a free coffee at the coffee shop, and then a free kid's ice cream scoop at a random ice cream shop, and then went to a Italian restaurant and got five percent off the total bill.

"What else should we do?" I asked. I'd really had a wonderful time with Ben, and he'd made it such a wonderful birthday. Perhaps my very best birthday ever. I missed Ginny, but we'd arranged to have a nice, long phone chat once Ben and I reached Papa's house.

"We've done pretty much everything. Shall we go somewhere else and see if this little village has any other things to do?"

"Unless you're up for smoking cigarettes behind buildings, there's nothing," I said.

"Let's do it," he said unenthusiastically. I looked at him and he sighed. "Let's go back, Lottie."

I grinned and pulled up his hand that I held and kissed his knuckles. "Okay," I said. I really loved holding his hand.

His expression was a little softer when he glanced at me, and he started pulling me towards the entrance.

I felt light, happy, so glad to be here in this place at this time with Ben. And then, out of the corner of my eye, I spotted that creepy man from the bus. Rick.

A few seconds later, he saw me and smiled widely, and then he saw Ben, and the smile became a glare. I blinked and shuffled closer to Ben, and when I glanced back, Rick was gone.

And I was worried.

Chapter 40

"**W**hat the hell are you doing?"

Lottie blinked at me, perplexed. "What do you mean?"

I raised my eyebrows. "You've been looking over your shoulder for the past hour. What's the problem?"

She shrugged and looked at her feet. I sighed. You'd think that by now she'd know to tell me when she was bothered.

"Tell me, Lottie," I pressed, nudging her shoulder. Lottie just smiled sweetly at me and patted my hand, but didn't respond. "Come on, what's wrong?"

"Girl problems, Ben," she said quietly. I opened my mouth to speak then snapped it shut. Oh.

After a minute of awkwardness, I spoke. "Do you...do you need anything?"

She shook her head while grinning. "Not at all. Thank you."

"You sure? Alright, then should we get back to your place?" I asked, steering her back to my car. I wanted to show her the cake I had made before the day was over.

"Okay!" she exclaimed, grabbing my hand and skipping over. I rolled my eyes, but still smiled when she wasn't looking.

By the time we got back, the sun was close to setting, but there was still enough light to look around. It had begun to sprinkle a while back, but was not much compared to a regular winter's day in England. It was almost like it was summer, and the Earth was smiling down on Lottie's birthday. How fuckin' cheesy am I?

I was just about to herd her inside before she got soaked when something stopped me.

"Charlie, babe, there you are!" a loud, obnoxious voice yelled. Lottie and I turned around and saw a man staggering down the sidewalk to Lottie's house. She squinted, and when the man got closer, she jumped and half hid behind me.

"Who are you?" I asked rudely, moving my hand back to cover Lottie. "Go inside, sweetheart," I said to her.

"I'm her boyfriend. My name is Rick, how are you?"

I heard Lottie take in a sharp breath of air, and she stepped around my arms and stared at him. "Rick who?" she asked.

"Rick Bienvenue, I'm hurt you don't remember. We have been together since we were sixteen, after all," he simpered, touching his chest. I hated the shifty way he looked at her, and I reached out to pull Lottie closer to me, and then I comprehended their words.

I cocked my head, confused. Who the fuck was this guy? "Lottie?" I asked, expecting her to deny what that guy was saying. It was bogus, lies. I knew it was.

She blinked those huge eyes at me, wide with shock and a hint of fear. She didn't respond. She just stared, as if she was realising something.

"Come on, tell this guy he's insane," I said, not even recognising my own voice. It sounded separate from my body.

"She can't say anything because she knows it's true."

My head snapped to that guy, who wore a smirk that I itched to punch straight off his face. "Shut the fuck up, am I talking to you?"

"Temper, temper," he cooed, wagging his finger at me. His condescending tone baffled me and infuriated me at the same time. Who the fuck did he think he was to talk to me like that?

"Would you shut the fuck up?"

"I'll see you at home, baby," Rick sneered, waving his hand. "I can see when I'm not wanted."

I breathed in and out so that I wouldn't pounce on him and fucking clobber his face in. "At least you're not fucking blind," I hissed. His smirk widened, and I almost lost it when he reached out and patted Lottie's cheek, and then sauntered away. My eyes fixed themselves on his back, and I knew my face was becoming bright red.

"Ben..." Lottie whispered finally.

"What is going on?" I asked. My eyes widened worriedly, wondering why she hadn't interrupted him while he was speaking. Because he was obviously lying, there was no way they were dating. "He's lying, isn't he?"

"I mean, I couldn't exactly say that-"

"What?" I blinked, taken aback. "What do you mean?" My chest all of a sudden felt tight, and I had to blink rapidly to see straight.

"By that I mean that I do know Rick and I have dated him, but that's not all, I need to tell you-"

"Lottie, stop," I said, my jaw locked, my head in my hands.

She stood her ground, staring at me defiantly. "No. You should trust me, not some idiot off the street!"

"For what? For me to figure out you're dating somebody already?"

"Ben, just listen to me!"

"I've heard enough," I grunted, turning my back to her. "And anyway, what do I care?"

That seemed to take her by surprise. "What?"

I spun back around, trying hard to look more angry than hurt. Because, fuck, I hated how it felt more like I was getting stabbed in the heart, because that was how much I cared. I fucking cared about her, I loved her, and of course this would happen. "I don't care, Charlotte. I don't care, why would I care?"

"I-I don't-"

I wanted to take everything back when I saw the hurt on the face, but I didn't. I kept going and I didn't know why. "Think, Lottie. Did I ever tell you that I loved you?"

Lottie's hands shook, and I had to lock my jaw and look away. "No," she whispered. "You didn't."

"And why do you think that was?" My voice was cruel, reminiscent of how I used to be before I met her.

I saw a spark of stubborn Lottie come up, and she snapped, "Because you are a dumb fuck."

I wanted to laugh at her profanity . I wanted to sweep her off her feet and listen to her side and tell her I loved her, but I kept seeing Rick's face, and I kept seeing how at loss for words she was when he said he was her boyfriend. And the gigantic asshole inside me was able to spit those horrible, untrue words: "Because I don't love you."

I didn't think I had ever done anything that had hurt her as much as when I spoke those last five words, and it killed me. "That's a lie, Benjamin Fisher, and you know it," she said, but her voice shook.

"And so was your 'I love you,'" I shot back. "I'm done, Lottie. I'm done, okay?" I held up my hands and started backing up to my car.

She put her hands on her hips and her eyes flashed. "So at the very beginning of conflict, you're going to run away? What's wrong with you? Why won't you listen to me?"

"I watched as some man told you how much he loved you and how you were going to go home to him later, and how you denied none of it. I think I've listened to enough."

"Well you know what I think?"

"I don't care."

She ignored me and kept speaking. "I think you're just looking for a way out! Because you're scared, aren't you?"

"Oh, so you're a psychologist too? Why don't you analyse my mind some more and tell me exactly what my problem is?"

"I just did, and you know it's true!"

I clenched my fists and threw open my car door. I couldn't think anymore. I had to get out of here. "Bye Charlotte. Have a nice life."

"Ben, wait, please." When I heard her voice break, I lost it. I knew that if I looked at her, I would drop everything and run to her. I couldn't do that, though. I couldn't just stand by and listen as someone else I loved chose something else over me. It had happened too many times, and I didn't know how much more I could take. I had to get out.

And so I did. I started up the engine and drove, not looking back once.

"I hope you know that you're an idiot," Clark said in a deadpan.

My head ached and so did my heart but I refused to admit it. "Yeah, how did it take me so long to figure out the girl already had a fucking boyfriend?" It made my insides churn. I'd kissed her and held her. I'd spilled my guts to her. I'd laid myself bare to her and after all that? A boyfriend. Jesus Christ.

Her scoffed. "Honestly, Benjamin, you're a jackass."

"We just established that, and you're an insensitive prick," I snapped.

"You didn't stay to hear what she had to say?"

I collapsed onto the sofa and crossed my arms. "No."

"God, Ben, why?"

I glared at him. The one time I needed him to be sympathetic was the one time he wasn't. "Shut up."

"Ben, stop being a child for just a second, please? You fucking love the girl, and clearly she had something to tell you. But you just drove the fuck away."

"Clark, what part of 'she has a boyfriend,' is so hard for you to understand? I couldn't stay there and listen to her tell me that I'm stupid for even falling for her, for thinking I could ever be good enough for her. That guy was a prick, but I've heard of him. Rick Bienvenue. His father owns a huge oil corporation and he goes to this really expensive private university that his grandfather founded and he's studying to be a fucking lawyer. And what do I have to offer her? Nothing."

Clark stared at me for a moment. "Poor bastard," he muttered. I moved to punch his stomach, but he grabbed my arm and sat on me so that I wouldn't move. "There's seriously nobody who was ever gotten you as flustered as Charlie, huh?"

I looked down, and a small sigh escaped me. "Yeah," I said quietly. I felt exhausted and drained and didn't know what to do. I wanted to just sleep for twelve years. What was this feeling?

"Heartbreak. It's never easy, but you should have been the bigger person and listened to her side," Clark said.

Heartbreak. No girl has ever broken my heart before, and now it was from literally the sweetest person on the planet? What were the odds? "I probably should've," I agreed, just so he would shut up. But no matter how I replayed it in my mind, I couldn't think I could have ever stayed there after hearing what I did. But I wouldn't have said so many cruel things.

I wouldn't have. Lottie's hurt face hurt more than actually being hurt. If that made sense.

Clark stared at me with a goofy smile. "You've gone soft," he observed.

I folded my arms. "Have not."

"Have so! You think I've forgotten the way you look at her?"

There was no way it could be that obvious. "And how do I look at her?"

"You get super gentle and soft. It's really weird and a bit disgusting, to be honest."

I looked away and shrugged. "Well, that never helped me, did it?"

"Don't fuck with me, Ben. She's always looked at you the same way. I know there's an explanation to this."

I scoffed, waving the hope aside. "Are you kidding me right now, Clark? She looks at everyone like that, that's how she is." I couldn't even pretend anymore that I had been any different. I was probably being dramatic, but I didn't care. I was feeling dramatic and sad and felt that it was warranted.

"Yeah, but there's a big difference between the way she looks at you and the way she looks at everyone else."

"There is no big difference, stop trying to make me feel better. She's got a boyfriend."

"But I bet she doesn't look at him like he's her whole world."

My jaw clicked. "She never looked at me like that either."

Clark glared at me. "Don't even, mate. You know it. She looks at you like you're the centre of her universe. She looks at you like everything's okay because you're there, so why don't you grow a pair and show her that the feeling's mutual? Go and find her, you great galoot! Listen to her! Don't let go."

Maybe there was an explanation to all of this. Lottie wouldn't just lie so blatantly. She wasn't a cheater, right? There was no way everything we'd been through had shown anything but her true self. I knew Lottie, and I knew that I knew her. She wasn't a liar, and she wasn't unfaithful. I had been an idiot and not trusted her.

I jumped to my feet and began to pace back and forth. She would never answer her phone if she saw it was from me now. Where would she be? Still at her father's? "I'll be back soon, Clark," I said hurriedly, grabbing my car keys and heading for the door.

"Good boy," I heard him say.

I yanked open the door and almost toppled over in surprise when I saw a dripping wet Lottie standing there, holding a big silver tin, one of her hands raised to knock. "Lottie? Oh shit, come it, you're soaked."

"Excellent observation, my good man," she said, but most of the cheekiness was lost amidst her chattering. My eyes widened and I grabbed her arm, pulling her inside into our heated apartment. "Hello, Clark!"

"Alright, Lottie?" he replied casually, a giant grin on his face.

"I'll grab a towel," I muttered, kind of at loss for words. How did she get here without a ride? Why would she come back? After I was such a dick, I wasn't sure why she would come back. I jogged over to the bathroom and picked up the cleanest, driest towel I could find, as well as a shirt and sweats from my room.

"I'll give you guys some privacy," Clark sang, grabbing his coat and walking out. I stared at Lottie shivering on the sofa where I had been wallowing in self-pity just a few minutes ago, and I walk up to her with my head hanging.

"Here," I said, my voice low.

She smiled politely and takes the clothes from my hand. "I'll be out in a minute," she said. I nod in agreement and watched as she scampered to the bathroom. Already, I felt myself warm up at the sight of her, as if I'd already forgiven her. As if I needed to forgive her in the first place? But before I could touch her again, I really needed to know what was going on.

I waited impatiently for a few minutes, and when Lottie emerged from the loo, I sprung to my feet. My mouth went dry when I saw her in my clothes, my towel in her hair, and I swallowed hard. I didn't have the right. "I think..." I said. "I think I owe you an apology."

Lottie looked at my under her eyelashes and sat cross-legged on the floor, her back against the sofa. "Why?" she asked curiously.

I took a deep breath. "Because I said some horrible things, and I was really horrible. I'm sorry, Lottie, really, I am."

"No, no, it's alright. It's me who should be apologising to you."

I looked at her in disbelief, and knew that if she really already had a boyfriend, I would probably just wallow in self-pity for the next one hundred years. "Why?" I echoed her.

"I should have cut to the chase and told you exactly what was going on."

"Well, if you could tell me now..."

She giggled, and I drank in the sound. At least she didn't sound so horribly hurt by what I'd said. "Alright, Ben. If you want the short version, when I was sixteen, I met Rick Bienvenue. He was a nice guy, and really sweet, so when he asked me out, I said yes." I closed my eyes, not wanting to listen to this. "But then, right before I moved to Manchester for uni, he got in this horrible car accident. It was kept very down-low, because the hitter was his father and they didn't want a scandal out. Rick lost his memory, and so he lost all memory of me. His doctor didn't want me around, because he said Rick needed family, not outsiders to help him heal. So I told Rick that I was breaking up with him when he had no idea what was going on, and I guess he just got his memory back."

"Do you...love him?" I asked, coaching my voice to keep low and even, and not crack.

Lottie smiled at me. "No. I just liked him, and now, after seeing how crude he's become, I don't. I couldn't even recognise him at first, because he was dressed so differently and had dyed his hair. You should know that I don't love him, Benny."

Hearing her say that made me feel more and more like a fucking disgusting jackass. "God, I'm sorry, Lottie. I'm sorry," I said, my face in my hands.

"Oh, it's okay. I'm just glad you're not calling me Charlotte anymore." I looked up and saw her smiling gently at me.

"How come you came back when I was so terrible to you? Why didn't you stay with your dad?"

"I wasn't going to," she said absentmindedly, picking up the silver tin she'd brought in with her. "I was really hurt, so I went to the fridge to stuff my face like any other hormonal, menstruating female."

I gulped at her choice of words, and then my eyes widened when I realised what she'd brought in the tin. "You didn't-"

"Remember how you said you never loved me? That was a lie," she said. "You shouldn't lie, Benjamin." Lottie opened the top of the tin, and I saw my lopsided, sad excuse for a cake inside, with the messy white icing on the top spelling, 'I love you.'

I bit my lip. "I'm so sorry."

"That's not what I wanted to hear from you, Ben," she said expectantly.

I blinked and then realised what she wanted. "Charlotte Carter," I said, scooting over and throwing my arm around her shoulders.

"Hm?" She closed her eyes and rested her head on my chest and I knew she could feel my accelerated heartbeat.

"Lottie..."

"I once said I loved writing more than anything else in the entire world," she whispered. "But there is one thing even better than that."

"Hm?" I asked softly.

"It's you."

Chapter 41

"Huh? Huh? Huh?" Ginny whacked me repeatedly with her towel, chasing me around the shop.

"Ginny, stop," I said, pushing her away from me.

She smirked in a way that scared the bejesus out of me. I slowly started backing away. "You think I'm going to let you off when you said one day and you've been gone one week? Get the fuck back here, you tramp!"

I squeaked and ducked behind the front counter. "Come on, Ginny, I'm sorry," I said, pouting at her.

"Don't give me that look. You didn't even call me!"

"I did, but you didn't answer." I slapped my hands on the counter and stood up slowly, staring at her.

Ginny raised her eyebrows and popped one hip sassily. "What?"

"Zachary answered your phone when I called. Tell me, Ginny. What's been going on with you two?"

She scoffed. "Nothing at all. Why would you expect any-thing more from the King of Being a Scared and Immature Brat?"

I sighed. Zach was an idiot. "Oh," I said. "Nothing at all?" I made a mental note to call Zach and ask him what was going on and figure out what stupid thing he'd done this time.

"Nothing at all. Don't go running off to him, either, Charlie. Maybe I had fancied him a little before, but I'm actually perfectly fine without him."

I smiled. "Really?"

Ginny smiled back, shoving the surprisingly stinging hand towel in her apron pocket. "Really, I swear. It's way different than your ooey-gooey, die-without-you thing you've got go-ing with Lover Boy."

I ducked my head to hide how quickly my face turned red. "Stop it!" I laughed, covering my face with my hands.

"Aw, are you embarrassed?" she cooed. "Aww, don't worry Charlie, Benny-wenny wuvs you!"

Even though she was teasing me, her words made me beam. Ben loved me, he really did love me. There wasn't a thing in the world that could describe how I felt when I opened the fridge after Ben left and saw that adorable cake in its crushed cardboard box, just chilling there on the top shelf.

"Charlie, I hope this romantic business won't affect your work schedule, because God knows I am going to work you like the dog you are-"

"Dog?" I asked curiously.

Ginny rolled her eyes and threw up her arms. "You're a bitch, Charlie. Honestly, do I have to spell out everything for you?"

I shrugged and smiled. "I'm sorry, Ginny."

"But are you really?"

"I'm sorry for making you cover all my shifts," I said sincerely. "And for not calling you."

"Especially on your birthday," she muttered. "I tried to call you but it kept saying your phone was disconnected or some shit. And then what was I supposed to do? My best friend's birthday. Dammit."

"I did come back at seven," I tried, feeling really guilty when I saw how annoyed she was. "And you made the rest of my day amazing."

"Yeah?"

I grinned and ran around the counter to give her a big hug. "Yes, best friend!"

Ginny rolled her eyes, but hugged me back anyway. "I'll forgive you if you cover me now, I've got a date at half past twelve."

I giggled and let her go. Same old Ginny. "Okay! Just make sure you don't drink too much and get a taxi to bring you back! Also, if you're going to sleep over, call me!"

"Alright, Dad," she snapped. "Jesus, who needs annoying-ass parents when I've got you?"

"Thank you!" I sang out.

She just muttered, "Whatever," and disappeared into the back room. Meanwhile, the door tinkled, and I looked up and smiled at Clark, who was holding hands with Queenie.

Ginny stormed out from behind me and past Clark. He raised his eyebrows. "Ooh, someone's in a bad mood!"

"I'll kill you!" she shouted.

He laughed and walked up to me. "What did you do, Charlie?"

I shrugged. "Who knows? Hey there, Princess!"

"Charlie!" Queenie giggled, her curls bouncing everywhere in her excitement. "Do you have anything special for me?"

"Queenie," Clark scolded. She didn't seem the slightest bit abashed, which made me laugh.

"Where's Ben?" I asked curiously.

"Wow, sorry for disappointing you with my appearance," he said, raising his eyebrows.

"Oh, come off it!" I said teasingly, lightly smacking his arm.

Clark chuckled. "Don't worry, Lover Boy is on his way, he just had to grab some-"

Ben entered the bakery at that moment, a small bouquet of beautiful sunflowers in his hand. He wore his standard bored expression as he swaggered in, but don't think I didn't notice how his eyes crinkled happily.

"Hello!" I said cheerily, waving energetically.

"I'm offended, I didn't get that kind of greeting. I'm telling the manager," Clark joked.

I laughed, and nudged him. "Don't be sore, I'll give you a cupcake for free, okay?"

Ben shoved Clark. "Not on your life, he'll pay for it."

"I'm with child," Clark complained, picking up Queenie. "Don't abuse me, you brutes."

Ben rolled his eyes. "'With child' means you're pregnant, you ignoramus."

"Don't you have a girl to be wooing?" Clark grumbled.

Ben's cheeks flushed, and I had to cover my mouth with my hands to keep from laughing out loud. "Be quiet!" Ben said.

"It's not like she's blind. Who else are the flowers for? Me?"

"Honestly, Clark, you'd think you'd know not to pick on Ben," I said.

"I'm holding a child, what's he gonna do?"

Ben glared at Clark. "Queenie, come here, honey."

She giggled and jumped into his arms, and he put her and the sunflowers on the front counter. In the next two seconds, Clark's face was pressed into the floor, and Ben was knuckling his hair.

"Oh, do be careful! Don't hurt each other!" I said worriedly.

"Each other?" Clark choked out. "Yeah, poor Ben can hardly stand this beating I'm giving him!"

"Ben!" I exclaimed, clapping my hands over Queenie's eyes. He glanced at me, and upon seeing my expression, he rolled his eyes and got up.

"Get up, Clark," he told his friend, stretching his hand out. Clark allowed Ben to pull him up, but grumbled all the way.

"Don't you have something to ask your Lover Girl?" Clark mocked. I laughed at Ben's annoyance.

"Can we go somewhere...private?" he asked.

"Why?"

"He wants to shag," Clark said.

Ben smacked the back of his head. "Clark! Can you please?" I coughed and blinked in Queenie's direction.

She stared at us with wide, innocent eyes. "Like in Scooby Doo?"

"Exactly like that, baby," I said cheerily. "Clark?"

"Fine, I'll be on my way. Just give me two cupcakes for my effort."

"They're three pounds each," Ben said sternly.

"I know, I know. Jesus, calm down." He dug in his pocket and counted out six one pound notes. "One for beauty and one for the beast." I grinned when Clark flicked Queenie's nose, making her squirm.

I took out two of the double chocolate mint cupcakes and put them in a mini box. "Here you go, love."

"Cheers," Clark said, taking the box in one hand and Queenie in the other arm. Before he left, he met Ben's eyes, and they seemed to have some sort of exchange with their eyes.

It was quiet for a moment. "I'm going to lock up I think. It's my break."

Ben smiled slightly at me, and I drank in the sight of his cute dimples and sparkling eyes. "Alright. Need some help?"

I smiled happily and grabbed the keyring from inside the till. "Can you use this key to lock up front and turn the Open sign off? I'm going to clean up a bit in the back."

"Sure thing, babe." He chucked my chin and took the key from me. I went into the back room and started to clean up the used bowls and whisks, and then I realised that it was strangely cold.

I frowned and looked around. "Oh man, Ginny left the freezer room door open."

I walked inside the huge freezer room and started to check to make sure that nothing had defrosted.

"Lottie?"

"In here!" I called, my back to the door. I heard footsteps approaching, and then I remembered something, my eyes widening. "Wait, don't let the door clo-"

Ben stared at me, the sunflowers in his hand again. "Wait, why?"

I groaned. "It locks from the outside."

"Oh God, are we-"

"Locked in? Yeah."

Chapter 42

"Look, I'm not one to point fingers," Lottie said cheerfully after half a minute of dead silence, "but this is totally, completely your fault."

I turned around and shot her a flat look. "Who came in here in the first place?"

"I told you not to shut the door!"

"So you're saying this is my fault?"

She laughed. "I literally did just say that, Ben." She walked over to the door and jiggled the handle, as if that would help at all. "Do you have a credit card on you or something?" she asked me.

I dug in my pocket and took out my wallet, handing her one of my credit cards. "Do you know how to unlock locked doors like that?"

"No, but now I have your credit card," she replied, grinning at me. I scoffed while she slid the card between the door and the frame and wiggled it around to no avail. "Okay, this isn't working. Can you call Clark or Ginny? I left my mobile in the back room."

I pulled out my phone, but then clenched my fists and blew out air in frustration. "I definitely could, but I locked the front door like you told me to, so I don't think either of them would be able to get in."

Lottie turned and blinked at me, her eyes filming over kind of vacantly. "Oh swell," she said blankly. "We're stuck in here? Yikes, yikes, yikes."

I waved a hand in front of her face. Should I do it now? Maybe I should do it now. While we were waiting, possibly left to freeze to death, just go ahead and do it. No time like the present, I always so. Even though I never say that. Because I don't do things like this. "Charlotte, listen to me."

She blinked again, looking like she didn't know what exactly to do. When she breathed out, a small cloud of fog gathered around her face because of the cold.

"Lottie, come on. Someone will get us, okay? Just chill out and look at me for a second."

After a second, her mouth twitched, and just like that she was grinning again. I felt relieved because I really didn't know what to do when she got all stiff like that. "Chill out?" she repeated. "Poor choice of words given we're stuck in a freezer unit, Benny, don't you think?"

I rolled my eyes but couldn't stop the smile, and I handed her the sunflowers that were in my hand. I'd accidentally crushed the stems a bit, and they were quite small since our part of England didn't generally have the ideal climate for wildflowers. However, their bright yellow colour reminded me of her, and so I couldn't help but buy them to accompany the question I had for her. I was going to get roses, but along with being pretty much bankrupt, I thought she'd appreciate the sunflowers more.

"Ben!" she exclaimed, burying her face into the sunflowers. She sheepishly looked up and wiped the pollen off her nose, and I smiled softly at her astounded expression. A fucking doll, she was. "These are sticky," she said, but smiled widely. "I love them. Oh, thank you, Ben! Thank you!"

I scratched the back of my head nervously and looked at the floor. I could feel the cool starting to creep in under my skin even though I was wearing a big jacket, since it was winter and all. But Lottie wasn't properly clothed, she was just staring at her flowers happily wearing a dress that looked like it couldn't keep her warm no matter how much she tried. "Lottie, I have a question for you."

She looked at me, her eyes crinkling at the corners in a way that made my heart unconsciously clench up. "Yes, precious person?"

Her words caught me off guard for a second, so much so that it took me a second to remember what I was going to ask. I opened my mouth, but then I noticed that she was shivering slightly. "Are you cold?" Dammit, that wasn't my question. I wanted to ask her if she wanted to be my fucking official girlfriend, but of course I had to chicken out.

She kept smiling even though her teeth were chattering. I started to feel really bad, because it really was my fault we were locked in here with no foresight of release. "A little, but you just gotta look at this in a positive light, you know what I mean?"

I stared at her. "How can you see getting trapped in a freezing storage room in a positive light?" I asked, questioning her already on-the-brink sanity.

Lottie sat down and pursed her pink lips thoughtfully, drawing her knees into her chest. I watched her carefully, aware of every single move she made. My mind whirred and I just wanted to ask her my original question to see what she would say. "Well," she started. I sat down beside her.

I raised my eyebrows expectantly as she rubbed her arms self-consciously, her shivering becoming more obvious the more she tried to hide it. "See," I told her. "There's no positive way to look at this. We're trapped in a freezing cold room with nobody to come look for us for hours." All of which was my fault, if we were being honest.

She showed me one of her breathtaking grins. "C'mon, Benny. You should stop being so cynical all the time! Just think, now you get to spend time with me!" she exclaimed cheerfully, pulling herself even tighter into a human ball.

"That's not a good thing to be stuck with an annoying splodge like you," I taunted, even though I was lying through my teeth. I scooted closer to her, my eyes taking in the subtle way she shivered so that I wouldn't notice how cold she really was.

"Y-you're lying," she giggled, her teeth chattering slightly. "You know you adore me. Dare I say, you looove me."

I faltered, my throat closing up. God help me. Instead of answering, I rolled my eyes. "Just shut up and come here," I suggested.

"Wha-" She didn't even have time to protest before I grabbed her elbow and yanked her onto my lap.

"You're cold," I said when I saw her shocked face. "And I'm wearing a coat. Hopefully this will at least warm you up a little bit."

She smiled adoringly up at me, making my heart clench painfully at the beautiful sight I had in front of me. "Thank you," she said softly. "Hey, can I see your phone for a sec? I wanna see if there's any reception."

"What about spending all this time with me? You're such a poser," I teased, but gave her my mobile anyway.

"As much as I love you, and love taking up all your body heat, I would rather take up all your body heat while not inside the bakery's freezer."

I chuckled and rubbed my hand down her back. She curled into me, and I tried to remember it was because she was cold, not because she liked me. And then I remembered I didn't have to think self-deprecating thoughts like that because she'd already admitted she loved me. "Fair enough."

"Ginny, you answered! Oh my goodness, Ginny, I'm so sorry for interrupting your date, but Ben and I got locked in the freezer, and the front of the bakery is locked. We don't know what to do, do you have a key? Can you please come help us?" She listened for a bit, and laughed. "Okay, I promise, I will. I will! Oh my god, please stop talking! Please, for Chrissakes, just come! Bring your date too if you want!"

Another pause. "Okay, I love you, Ginny, you're awesome! Thanks, best frieeend."

"She coming?" I asked.

Lottie gave me my mobile back and laughed. "Yes, and I feel gross saying this, but Ginny told me to tell you that you..." She stopped, her face turning red.

I raised my eyebrows, always interested in whatever insults Virginia had to give to me. "What is it that she told you to tell me, Lottie? Tell me, I want to know."

She covered her bright red face with her hands, and that made me start laughing. "I can't!" she wailed.

"No way, you gotta do say it now!" I said, poking her sides. She giggled, and I started full-on tickling her. "What did she say, Lottie? What did she say? Come on, come on, tell me!"

"Oh my God, no, no, stop!" She laughed so hard tears came out of her eyes, and she clutched onto me like a monkey so that she wouldn't fall down on the freezing cold floor. "Beeeeen!"

"Beautiful little princess, please tell me what that leviathan friend of yours said about me so that I can return the favour when she comes to get us."

Lottie buried her cold face into my neck. "Ginny's not a leviathan," she scolded me. "You guys should be nicer to each other."

"Don't change the subject, what did she say?"

"Fine!" She was quiet for a moment, and then she looked at me. Her face started turning red again as soon as she met my eyes. "Oh my god, I can't even looking at you. She said, youbettermakemefeelgoodandnotjustfinishyourselfoff."

I furrowed my eyebrows. "What? I didn't quite catch that."

"Argh," she groaned. "Ginny said, you better make me feel good and not just finish yourself off, oh my God, I have to go take a shower now, I can't believe that just came out of my mouth."

While she sat scolding herself, I, meanwhile, was laughing my ass off. "Ginny doesn't have to worry about that one bit," I told Lottie, even though she was hiding her face from me and covering her eyes. I bent over and put my mouth right next to her right ear. "I will take very good care of you."

"Ben!" she complained.

"What?" I said innocently, even as I myself had to fight down the blood rushing to my face at the thought of having sex with Lottie. If it would ever happen and I didn't screw things up, of course, as I was liable to do. "Did I say something wrong?"

She wouldn't respond to me, and lucky for her, she didn't have to, because just then, the freezer door slammed open. We sprang to our feet. "Ginny!" Lottie exclaimed happily, her face still red from embarrassment. "You got in!"

"Yeah, you're lucky the back door was open otherwise you would've been stuck here until our demon boss got back from Hell, or wherever she is, I don't know." I didn't know whether to be grateful or annoyed at Lottie's crazy-eyed friend for interrupting us, but she did open the door when poor Lottie was probably freezing to death.

Lottie ran and gave Ginny a big hug, who returned it while glaring at me. I glared right back at her. What the fuck was her problem this time? "I'm sorry you had to miss out on your date!"

"It's whatever, Charlie. He's out front waiting for me, and we'll probably going to do it later." I gagged, and unfortunately she noticed and shot daggers at me. "Speaking of doing it, did you tell that human garbage bag what I told you to tell him?"

I grinned to myself despite her calling me a garbage bag as Lottie said, "Yes," with a meek expression on her face. She definitely did tell me.

"So, are you okay to lock up, or are you going to do something stupid again?"

"I won't do anything stupid," Lottie promised. "I'll see you when you get back from your date?"

Ginny smiled at her, which took me aback for a second because I forgot the she-devil knew how to smile, or even doing anything remotely human other than bark at me. "Yeah, actually, do you wanna meet him? He's a writer, too. But don't get attached, I don't wanna feel guilty for dumping him later."

Lottie laughed and agreed, and then looked at me. "Come on, Ben!"

"No way!" Ginny shrieked, shoving me back into the freezer and slamming the door shut.

"What the fuck!" I yelled angrily. "What the hell is wrong with you, you fucking frizzy-haired behemoth? Lottie, get me out of here!"

"Ginny, come on," I heard Lottie say. "Be nice to Ben! I love him, and I love you, and I want you guys to get along."

"Don't make me get along with that freak of nature," she muttered. "How could you fall in love with someone who looks like Grendel and his mother?"

"Virginia."

"Oh, for Chrissakes, stop scolding me, Dad, I'll open the damn door." The door opened, revealing Ginny pouting and Lottie with her arms crossed. I closed and locked the damn thing behind me, vowing to never set foot in there ever again.

I smirked at Ginny, throwing my arm around Lottie's shoulders. "She loves me more," I taunted her, sticking out my tongue.

"Charlie! Are you even hearing him?"

My smirk widened and I raised my eyebrows. Lottie shoved me playfully. "Come on, let's just go meet Ginny's date, okay, Ben?"

"Okay," I agreed, pulling her back to my side.

Ginny shot me one last deathly glare before leading us to the front of the bakery. "There he is, I just met him like last night or something. Rick, Rick, come over here! Come meet Charlie and her stupid boyfriend Ben!"

I had no time to revel over the fact that even Ginny called me Lottie's boyfriend before the man even turned around, I knew who it was by the way Lottie tensed up and let out a breath beside me. Her hand tightened on my arm.

I felt anger bubbling in my chest and red began to enter my vision. "Are you fucking kidding me?"

Rick smirked. "Hello Charlie. Hello Ben. Nice to see you two again."

Chapter 43

I felt my expression twist into shock and a little bit of fear when I realised exactly who it was that Ginny was on a date with.

Ginny looked between me and Rick suspiciously. She had never met Rick, and she didn't know about my experiences with him because I wanted to forget that it ever happened. He never made me feel anything, and I'd never even kissed him! Plus, we were in Year 11 when we dated, so it wasn't even anything serious.

"H-hello Rick," I stuttered. My fingers clenched Ben's arm until I was pretty sure I was cutting off his circulation, but he didn't move. In fact, he had gone completely still.

"Do you know him already?" Ginny asked. I couldn't ever hide anything from her, and I didn't know what to say. I looked at her with wide eyes, pleading with her, and she shook her head in confusion. "Rick, you know Ben and Charlie already?"

"You could say that, sweetcheeks," Rick said, his voice grating on my ears just enough for me to shudder and press myself nearer to Ben. There was literally nothing outwardly wrong him, but the memories and the feeling I got from him were enough to make me want to curl up and cry.

Ginny scowled. She'd never dated even a halfway decent guy, and I always wondered why she did it when she didn't like them. Whenever I asked, she would say she was just having a wee bit of fun. "Shut it," she said severely. "And give us a moment."

She grabbed me by the arm, but since I was already completely attached to Ben and kind of in a daze, it took a good while for her to separate us. "Lottie-" Ben started. I looked at him with wide eyes and furrowed eyebrows, and he frowned at me.

Sorry, I mouthed, and followed Ginny to the back. I felt bad about leaving Ben with Rick, but he could definitely handle himself. Actually, I was more worried that he would knock the lights out of Rick than I was that Rick would try anything with him.

"What was that about?" she asked as soon as we were out of earshot. Her hands came up to grip my shoulders, and her scowl deepened.

I smiled weakly. "What was what about?" I asked, as if I had no idea what she was talking about.

"You are the worst liar, idiot," she snapped. My smile widened, and I was about to laugh when her withering look stopped me. "You and that ugly moth know Rick, don't you?"

"I-I would say..." My heart thumped, and I focused my eyes on a stain on the back wall. "Yes," I finally admitted. "Yes, I know him."

Ginny let go of me and ran a hand through her hair, shaking her head. "That weird energy in there, I don't get what's going on. Did he do something to you?" Her eyes widened as if she had just thought of something, and she took hold of my shoulders again. "Oh god, did he do something to you, Charlie? Just tell me, okay? Say the word and he's dead-"

I ruffled her hair and grinned nervously. I didn't really know what to tell her. "A few years ago, we dated, that's it," I blurted out. "In Year 11."

Her worried scowl smoothed out, and she grinned back at me. "Oh, that's it?" she said brightly. "Thank God, that means it'll be easier for dump him faster."

I chuckled, still nervous. Okay, good, she believed me when I told her that was it. "How'd you even find him? And why are you going out with him if you don't like him?"

"Honestly, he's cute, but kind of creepy. I saw him hanging around outside that pizza place down the corner last night, and he asked me out then."

My lip curled in shock. "Are you serious, Ginny? Why on earth would you agree to a date to some creep in the dark?"

She laughed but I wasn't amused. "Well, you dated him, so how bad could he be?"

"Ginny, come on! I know you like doing this kind of thing. What, is it like a thrill or something? Whatever, whatever it is, that's dangerous!"

"Oh, shut up, Mother," she said, rolling her eyes.

I blinked rapidly, already used to Ginny being like this. But since I actually knew who Rick was and that he was not a good guy, it put it into perspective for me that maybe a lot of the guys she dated weren't either. I breathed in and out, starting to become more and more nervous. I couldn't focus on Ginny's face, and I think I may have swayed a little. Poor Ginny, poor Ginny has a bad friend like me. Did I ever think about her? Her safety?

"Charlie? Charlie! Charlie! Ah, fuck, should I call Hellboy in here?"

"What the fuck is going on?" I recognised the voice, but I still didn't stop shaking.

"I don't know, Needle Dick, I don't know! Can you do something, I don't know, to calm her down? Please!"

I felt a pair of arms wrap around me, and a warm hand pushed my head into a warmer chest. I gripped his shirt and focused on my breathing. "Lottie," said Ben, in a gentle voice that I wasn't accustomed to hearing from him. "You're okay, babe." Fingers brushed through my hair, and as I concentrated on the rising and falling of Ben's chest, I very slowly stopped shaking.

I pulled back and looked up at him with wide eyes. His eyebrows were furrowed worriedly in a rare moment of showing his emotions, and he brought one of his hands up to the side of my head. "Thanks Benny." I looked around for Ginny, and when I couldn't find her, my eyes unconsciously started filling up. "Where's Ginny?" I asked tearfully. I still needed to talk to her.

"She's waiting out front," he said, still in that gentle voice. "Are you okay?"

I nodded, but he looked like he didn't believe me. "I want to talk to her." He stared at me for a moment, unconvinced, but then leant down and kissed my forehead. I breathed deeply, and despite myself, I smiled, my cheeks turning pink. "Thank you," I said again.

He didn't smile, but the wrinkles around his eyes told me that he was happy, and that cheered me up a little. We walked into the front, and Ginny instantly sprang up from beside Rick, who looked annoyed that she'd completely interrupted their conversation.

"Charlie," she said, speeding towards me. She shoved Ben away to hug me, who stumbled back in shock. He opened his mouth to snap, but I shook my head slightly and he just scowled. "Are you okay?" she asked, holding my head and turning it in all directions.

I shook her hands off me. "I'm fine, I'm sorry," I replied softly. "Are you okay?"

"Why are you asking me?" she growled in a low voice. "What happened? Tell me honestly, are you okay?"

"Yeah," I said. "I'm sorry, I just got a little overwhelmed. I...I just want you to be safe. I don't tell you enough, but I need you to be careful when you...date. Not all guys-"

"-are your stupid, ugly raccoon Benjamin, I know," she said. At my surprised look, she added, "The only reason I haven't beaten him up yet is because he's nice to you. And don't worry, Charlie, I know how to handle myself, so don't feel bad, okay? You do enough for me as it is, for God's sakes."

I felt like Ben and Ginny were treating me like a child, and I sighed heavily. I did act like a child a lot of the time, but I wasn't an idiot. "I just need you to tell me you'll be careful. Do you have mace? Or a pocket knife? I'll get you one-"

"Shut up," she said. "I'm on a date, you interrupted me enough. We're going!"

"Ginny-" I started, but she already grabbed Rick's hand and tugged him out, but not before he winked at me. I frowned and threw my head back, my eyes rolling back to stare at the ceiling in annoyance. She would be the death of me.

"She can handle herself," Ben said from behind me. "If she can shove me around and not die, she'll be okay with that twiglet."

I laughed a little. "The only reason you let her shove you around is because of me, isn't it?" He didn't respond, but I knew I was right. "Give me one second, okay?" I ran back into the back room and picked up the sunflowers he'd brought for me.

When he saw what I held in my hand, the tips of his ears turned pink, and I grinned. "Do you like them?" he asked, scratching the back of his head.

"I already told you I did!" I said, sniffing them again even though they didn't smell like anything. But they were beautiful and bright, and just looking at them perked me up. "You didn't have to get me anything though, Ben!"

He cleared his throat not once, but three times. "Lottie?"

"Yeah?" I said distractedly.

"Do you want to go out with me?"

"What?" I said, not totally comprehending what he just said. "Wait, what?" I turned to look at him, and saw that his expression was tight with worry. I wasn't used to seeing him so nervous, and it made me want to pat his head reassuringly.

"Lottie, do you want to go out with me?" he said again, and this time I understood. My eyes widened and I bit my lip so as to not look like a complete and total fool, but I could feel my cheeks heating up and my hands shaking.

"Are you being serious?" I asked happily. When he nodded, my face split into a wide beam, my eyes crinkling so much that they became slits. "Ben, are you really asking me out?"

He crossed his arms and scowled in embarrassment, turning his face away from me. "For Chrissakes, who else am I asking? The fucking cupcakes?"

I laughed delightedly. "Okay!" He asked me out! This handsome lad just asked me out on a date! I didn't know whether to play it off cool or show just how excited that made me, but when was I ever known for playing it cool? "Yes, I want to go out with you!" I exclaimed.

Ben's entire face turned a bright red that made me want to laugh even harder, but I couldn't tease him more than I already had. "Cool," he said, using the other tactic of playing it cool. But I saw the way his lips twitched up and how his eyes twinkled. I saw how excited he was, too!

"Cool," I repeated. And I couldn't help it. I jumped up on my toes and kissed him right on the mouth.

After Ben asked me out, I locked up the bakery, and he walked me back to my flat. The entire time, I was having trouble not bouncing around like the Energiser Bunny, and he strolled along beside me, actually smiling. His smile warmed me from my head to my toes, and I all but forgot about Rick, especially after Ginny texted me to tell me that she'd dumped him.

"Bye Benny!" I said cheerfully, waving at him. I blew him a kiss, and that made him look down to try and hide a smile that I clearly saw.

He waved back without saying anything, and turned around to walk away. I didn't know when or where our date would be, but I didn't care. I just knew that Ben Fisher had asked me out! That definitely meant he liked me at least a little, right? Because he never said he loved me back when I said it any of the times, but he must like me.

My mood refused to damper throughout the rest of the day, even when I realised that there was absolutely no food in the fridge and freezer except ketchup and some ice cream. What did Ginny even eat? I shook my head. She could always get guys, and girls even, to feed her. Her flirting was so useful sometimes.

Ginny hadn't come back yet, and I was hungry, so I texted Ben that I was going to the shops in case he needed something. I grabbed my wallet, keys, and mobile and skipped out the door, heading to the bus stop.

When I reached my stop, I hopped off the bus and started to walk the remaining few minutes to Safeway.

"Hey Charlie," I heard someone say ahead of me. When I saw Rick, my eyes bulged out of my head, and I felt my heartbeat speed up. What was he doing here, loitering around like a creep? He didn't even live here! Right?

"Oh, I have to go," I said slowly, backing away as he walked forward with a confused expression on his face.

"Go? Weren't you just coming? Where are you going?" From the slur of his words, I could tell he was intoxicated, and that made me even more worried.

"Er...not here," I mumbled, turning around to walk away fast. Even if he was nice to me when we dated, which he wasn't really, his eyes didn't have the gentle look that Ben's did.

"Hey, wait!" he called, latching onto my elbow.

I started to panic, my eyes widening in shock at the painful grip he had on me. "Please let go, you're hurting me!"

"Not until you tell me why you're running away from me!" he snapped. "We dated, Charlie! You were my girlfriend, and then you left me? Just because I was sick?" So he knew, he knew all about it? How? Who told him? And what was he doing here? "What kind of girlfriend are you?"

I flinched at his tone. "Not yours," I whispered.

Suddenly, a look of comprehension dawned on his face. "Benjamin told you to stay away from me, didn't he?" he sneered.

I trembled in his grasp, trying to twist away. "Unfortunately, it's not of your business," I replied as nicely as I could.

"He did! Dammit, I knew he would try to spoil my fun."

"Fun?" I repeated. "What fun?"

His eyes snapped to me and he leered, making his pleasant features morph into something ugly. "When did you become

Benjamin's little bitch, doing whatever he says, huh? Don't you want to make your own decisions?"

"Not that it's any of your business, but he never said anything about it to me. I think it's best for me to stay away from you," I replied stiffly.

"Oh really?" he said, as though he didn't believe me. "Why don't you figure out if I'm a bad guy yourself? You know me, we fucking dated!"

I tugged on my arm harshly. "I'm sorry, but I trust Ben, and I don't think it's a good idea to stay near you."

"You trust him? You trust him?" he snarled, his voice rising to a shout. "Why the hell do you trust him? He's been nothing but horrible to you! Don't you think that would stretch to lying? Benjamin Fisher isn't a good guy, no matter what you think! He's capable of anything! He doesn't care about you."

Rick's words were like a punch in the stomach. A look of glee enveloped his face, as though he thought he could sway my belief in my best friend with only a few words.

I couldn't believe I ever dated this piece of...

"Excuse me," I said in a very calm and patient voice. "Maybe Ben doesn't care about me, maybe you're right about that. But don't you dare speak of him like that!"

He looked shocked at the words that were flying out of my mouth.

"Ben is a thousand times the man you'll ever be! Maybe he's a little vulgar, but I don't care! Maybe he says hurtful things, but I don't care! Maybe he does bad things sometimes, but I. Don't. Care!"

Rick laughed mockingly, getting over his initial shock of me standing up to him. "You don't care? You're blind, Charlotte. You're blind if you can't see what kind of person he really is!"

My eyes widened as I felt an emotion I haven't felt in a long time. Fury. "I know what kind of person he is!" I shouted angrily my hands curling into fists and my eyes blinking rapidly from the sudden onslaught of tears. "And he's better than you!" Suddenly, my head whipped to the side, making my neck crack.

It took me a few seconds to realise that the stinging pain I felt in my cheek was from the slap Rick had just given me. And from the looks of it, he had more where that came from.

My free hand touched my throbbing cheek gently. "I-I can't believe I ever dated you," I murmured.

"Oh, you better believe it, you stupid whore," he muttered, raising his hand again.

I flinched away, pulling at my arm frantically, but he was too strong. "Leave me be!" I cried. "I never did anything to you!"

He laughed, a crazy glint in his eye. Even when he was drunk, he was stronger than me, and that was absolutely terrifying. I sucked in a breath, astounded at how manic he looked. Just as he was about to slap me, a deep voice made him freeze.

"Don't touch her."

"Benny!" I cried in relief, struggling against Rick again.

Ben's dark, furious face was directed at Rick, his hands clenched tightly. "Let go of her, Dick."

Rick growled, pulling me violently towards him. I yelped in disgust as he wrapped his arm around my neck so tightly that I couldn't breath. "Not until I have my fun with her. I promise, Benjamin, you can have her when I'm through."

I whimpered, making Ben's gaze snap to me. His eyes darkened with concern and he took a confident step forward. "If you don't let her go right now, I can't promise you'll leave here without a few broken bones." I shivered at the sound of his deadly voice, but I knew Ben would never, ever hurt me.

Rick's hold tightened on my neck, getting a shocked gasp from my mouth at the sensation of my eyeballs almost popping out. "You come any closer, and I'll kill her, Fisher," he threatened.

Ben's expression darkened with anguish as he looked at poor, little, defenceless me. What would Jackie Chan do in a situation like this?

He'd probably do a flip and knock Rick out with one little flick to the forehead.

Unfortunately, I wasn't a karate master, so I'd have to deal with my girlish survival instincts.

I glanced at Ben and smiled before slamming my foot up behind me into Rick's little junior, causing him to let go of me as he fell to the ground in pain.

I scrambled away from him to Ben, who was running towards Rick. "No, we have to go," I urged, grabbing onto his steady hand.

Ben took one last, disgusted glance at Rick, before kicking his balls again and taking my hand back up. I laughed as he pulled me away quickly.

"Was that really necessary? I thought I got him pretty good," I complimented myself as we ran.

He glanced back at me, the anger not yet leaving his face. "You have a girlish kick. That would've only kept him down for a little while," he mocked.

"I hope you stopped his ability to have babies," I told him teasingly.

"Lottie, come on," he said. "You were freaking out earlier because your crazy friend Ginny wasn't being careful, but here you are, completely brushing off what happened to you! What if he had done something, Lottie? What if you weren't able to kick him down in time? What would I have done without you?"

I touched his shoulder, almost jogging to keep up with him. "Ben," I said softly. "I-I'm sorry. I just don't know how to...how to deal...with what just happened." I shuddered and started rubbing my eyes to get rid of the tears that started prickling at the corners. I took a deep breath. He was right. What if Rick had gotten to do what he wanted? Where would I be?

"Don't be sorry," he said, sighing. "I'm sorry, I should be taking care of you. Are you okay?"

"I'm okay, Benny. Thank you for helping me. You saved me."

Ben suddenly stopped, causing me to crash into him. "What you said back there..." he said nervously, scratching the back of his head.

He glanced a look at me, and turned away quickly at the curious smile that I had on my lips. "Yes?" I urged. "What did I say?"

"A-about the trusting me and stuff," he muttered, not looking at me.

I pursed my lips at the cute expression on his face, but managed to keep it in because I knew he would probably not appreciate that.

"Did you mean it?" he asked, almost hopefully.

I looked at him, almost incredulously. I've told this boy I loved him and he still had to make sure I meant it? "Of course I mean it."

"Lottie, can I tell you something?"

I took his hand and smiled. "What's up?"

"I love you."

Chapter 44

"You know, Benny, I have a question," Lottie said. Even after what had just happened, she still wanted to get her food, so I was following her through Safeway while she picked out everything she needed.

"Yes?"

"How did you hear all that stuff I said to Rick?" she asked, turning to look at me. Her eyebrows furrowed. "Were you already there?"

I frowned when I realised what she was thinking. "I wasn't just watching you get hit, Lottie. I heard the screaming, so I ran up and got there as he tried to hit you again."

She smiled and took my hand, giving it a squeeze. I covered it with my other hand and saw her face flush a little bit, which made me inwardly grin. "Okay," she said, visibly relaxing. "I just-"

"I know," I said. "You texted me about shopping, so I was coming to meet you." I rolled my eyes. "I'm not stupid enough to just watch that piece of shit lay his filthy hand on you."

Thinking about it made me shake with anger all over again. He fucking slapped Lottie, why was he not dead?

Lottie laughed. Noticing me starting to shake again, she kissed my knuckle as if I was a princess. "But you're a little stupid, right?" she teased.

She stopped in front of the cereal aisle, which gave me the opportunity to examine her face. She seemed perfectly okay, but she always did that when she was upset. I could see that his slap had irritated her face, and her cheek was red. I breathed in and out, trying to calm myself down enough so that I wouldn't stop back out to the bus stop and beat the life out of that stupid piece of shit.

Rick Bienvenue. Ugh, maybe he was rich, but his ugly mug showed both on the outside and the inside. I never wanted him near Lottie again, and if I ever saw him again, I don't think even Lottie could pull me back.

Well, to be honest, she probably could, but that was besides the point.

I slung my arm around Lottie's shoulders and scooted closer to her while she debated between Frosted Flakes and Cocoa Krispies. "If you ever see that motherfucker again, put aside your stupid morals and kick him in the wanker again," I said.

"My stupid morals?" she repeated, amused. "Don't worry, Benny, he probably won't bother me again in fear that you'll rip off his face."

"Okay...gross, but true."

"What do we do about him?"

I pursed my lips. "What can we do? Anything we try, his precious daddy will just bail him out." Rick Bienvenue Senior, CEO of Bienvenue Oil. A face everybody in England knew. Untouchable.

Lottie chose the Cocoa Krispies. "He used to not be like this. He was okay. Not great, kind of arrogant, but he couldn't even hurt a fly. I haven't seen him since his accident, though, so I can't say what that did to him."

I shook my head. "Whatever, he's a prick, and he deserves my fist in his face."

"It's okay, Ben," Lottie said vaguely, strolling down the aisle. "Not everything bad that happens needs revenge. I'm just going to leave it."

Once again, I was floored by the amount of forgiveness and love this tiny princess held in her heart. It would've sickened me once upon a time, but now I just wondered how I could ever deserve her. "But he hit you!" I argued.

"He's not himself. He just got over his amnesia, it seems like. Brain damage always changes people."

"That doesn't excuse being a complete and total arse."

She shrugged. "It's okay. Look at me, it's okay." She grabbed my hand again and used her other hand to turn my face towards her. I scowled, and she grinned. "He'll leave us, and we'll leave him. And that's that. We already kicked him twice...down there...so it's even, right?"

I looked away, and my scowl deepened. "Not really," I muttered. "But if you just want to leave it, I suppose-"

"Charlie."

"Oh for fuck's sake!" I growled. Lottie made a surprised noise and tightened her grip on my hand. I pulled her behind the trolley and stretched my arm out in front of her. "Do you ever let up?"

Rick, covered in dirt and slumped over with red eyes, stared at Lottie. I gritted my teeth. "Chill out, Benjamin," he said. "I'm not drunk anymore."

"You being drunk isn't an excuse." I had to remind myself to keep breathing and keep focusing, otherwise I would fucking lose it. "Are you having a laugh, mate? Want me to finish the job off of kicking off your testicals?"

"Just shut up, I'm not talking to you!" he snapped.

"What's up, Rick?" Lottie piped up. I wanted to groan out loud at her for all eternity. How could someone be so forgiving and kind and just...I'm going to lose my fucking mind.

He opened his mouth, attempting to speak several different times. I glared at him, my arms crossed and my foot tapping the ground impatiently. "Fuck, Charlie, I can't speak with your new boyfriend staring at me like he's going to fucking run me through with a butter knife!"

Lottie raised her eyebrows, but she didn't deny the 'new boyfriend' remark. I had to hide my smirk so I could continue to stare menacingly at Rick. "Can you blame him?" she asked softly and pointed at the cheek that he had slapped. "Just say it. What do you need?"

He looked like he was in extreme pain, which confused me enough that I dropped my glare. What the fuck was he waiting for? Did he know that the longer he stood around here, the more likely I was to throw a punch at his stupid fucking head? "Okay, I'll just say it. Charlie, I'm sorry."

Lottie's eyes widened. "Er...okay?"

"Look, that's all I have to say. You don't have to accept it, but that kick to the dick kind of knocked some sense into me." He paused, staring at the ground. I couldn't believe what was hearing, and it seemed like Lottie couldn't either.

"You kind of threatened to rape me," she said, her voice cracking. I gulped, worried for her. "You hit me. And you said all those horrible things about Ben. Come on, Rick. You can't blame it all on the alcohol."

"I know. I just wanted to tell you before I left. I'm going back home, and I'll leave you guys alone now. I just...sorry, Charlie. Bye." He turned around to leave, but then turned around to look at me. "Also, I said a bunch of random shit about you to Charlie, and she didn't believe it for a second. You should probably know that." And then he hobbled away.

I looked at Lottie, who smiled sheepishly at me. I felt my tiny, shrivelled heart expand as I looked at her embarrassed expression. "That was weird," she said cheerfully.

I smiled at her. "You're weird," I said. "I still want to punch him in the neck."

"Yeah, I know."

"Throttle him."

"Yup."

"Throw him into a volcano."

Lottie patted my arm and started searching for her groceries again. She put a bag of oranges in the trolley, and I just kept following and watching her. Dammit, she was such a good person.

"Do you forgive him, Lottie?" I finally asked.

"He said sorry," she said, as a way of answering. "I feel kind of bad for him."

I snorted. "Why?"

She shrugged. "He's rich, but I mean, look at his dad. He put his son in a coma, and all he cared about was covering it up so his reputation wouldn't be destroyed." She shook her head sadly, and I wondered where all this unconditional love was coming from. Rick didn't deserve it, I didn't deserve it. Nobody did.

"But that doesn't excuse-"

"It doesn't," she interrupted. "It doesn't, but he said sorry and I forgive him. And now we never have to think about it again, because he's leaving." She smiled brightly and stopped walking. "I think I have everything."

I looked into the trolley that was literally full to the brim. "Why do you have so much stuff?"

"Some of it is for you and Clark," she said without skipping a beat.

I didn't know why every time she did things like this I was shocked, but I still was. "You do know I'm not letting you pay for all of this?"

She looked at me with wide, puppy-dog eyes and pouted very slightly. I blinked and had to take a step back. "Come on, Ben! Let me pay!"

"No, no, no, you can't do that, that's not fair!" I complained. She knew, she knew if she did that thing with her eyes and cocked her head like that I would give in. I covered my eyes with one hand and grabbed the trolley with the other.

"I love you," she said softly.

I shook my head, even as I felt my ears become hot and a smile emerge. "I love you, too."

Lottie tugged my hand away from my face and smiled gently at me. I stared at her, not sure what spell she was putting me under. "Will you let me pay?"

I leant forward so that my mouth was right next to her head. I grinned when I felt her go still as I breathed in her ear. Two can play at this game. "Lottie," I said. I touched her face very lightly.

"Y-yeah?"

"No." I grabbed the trolley and started sprinting towards the checkout, thankful that Lottie was still innocent enough that stuff like what I just did was enough to shock her into staying put.

"W-wait, what? Ben!"

I reached the cashier way before her and was able to hand in my credit card just as she reached. She bent over, breathing heavily and coughing. I laughed at her. "Nice try, babe," I said.

"I'll get you next time," she tried to threaten, but she was wheezing too much for me to take her seriously.

I just kept laughing and put all the bags back into the trolley. "Come on, I'll drive you back."

She shook her head, frowning at me, but followed anyway. "I can't believe you did that," she muttered.

"Don't be sad, princess. We both know who's the smarter one here," I teased. I patted her head like a dog and she shoved me away, laughing. She could never be annoyed for very long.

"Oh, you be quiet!"

"Not until you admit that I defeated you," I said.

She crossed her arms and shook her head firmly. "I'll get you," she said. "Watch your back, Ben!"

And it turned out I was wrong, and she was right, because after I dropped her and all of her groceries off, I dug my hands in my pockets and realised that she'd shoved four twenty pound notes inside without me noticing.

Lottie would be the death of me.

Chapter 45

Ben wouldn't tell me where he was taking me for our first date, but I expected as much. He wouldn't even meet up with me beforehand because he wanted to build the suspense, and something about not being able to keep a secret when I stared at him like he was a murderer. I didn't know what he meant by that, but then again Ben said a lot of things that took me a while to comprehend.

I didn't really know what to do throughout the day, though. I was so used to hanging out with somebody, like Ben or Ginny or even Zach that being alone was the epitome of boring. I thumped my head against my bed for a minute before I realised that wasn't taking up as much time as I hoped.

I picked up my phone and called Clark, because I was running out of options. "Hey, Charlie!" he greeted. "What's up?"

"I'm bored and Benny won't hang out with me," I said.

"Aw, is Benny being a real meaner?" he teased, and I heard a thump on the other end, followed by Clark's rather high-pitched cry.

"Don't fucking call me Benny, jackass," Ben growled, his voice muffled through the phone. I smiled at the sound of his characteristic violence. One day, he'd try and beat up someone who'd turn out to be a black belt in karate and would then beat him up, and I wouldn't do anything but laugh. Maybe cry a little if he got hurt, but mostly laugh.

"How come she can call you Benny and I can't?" Clark whined. I giggled, because he sounded rather out of breath, as if Ben was sitting on his poor chest.

"She just can, okay?" Ben muttered. My smile widened at that, and I had to bury my face in my pillow to keep from squealing like a high school girl. To be fair, that had never stopped me before, but at this particular moment, I didn't want to embarrass Ben.

"Sorry, Charlie-poo, but Benny-boy over here is threatening to eviscerate me, and I do rather like my nether region, so I gotta blast!"

"Do. Not. Call. Me-" The call ended before I could hear the rest of Ben's fury-filled sentence, and I shook my head, laughing.

But now what to do? I didn't know where Ginny was. As per usual. Maybe I could call Zach? I haven't heard from him in a while.

I felt guilt crawl up my chest. Okay, maybe that was my fault for neglecting him. I rolled over onto my side and dialed his number, but it took a while for someone to pick up. "Hey, Zach," I said softly. "How are you?"

"Er...sorry, who is this?"

I blinked, perplexed to her this confused feminine voice on the other end. She sounded American, actually. That was cool. "Sorry," I apologised quickly. "Is Zach there?"

"Yeah...but still. Who is this?"

"Carie, who is that?" I heard Zach's familiar grumble and I sighed in relief.

"I don't know. Some girl," Carie said. I bit my lip, trying to hold back my laughter.

The line was blank for a minute before Zach said, "Hello?"

"Zach, it's Charlie."

"Oh! Hey, Charlie!" he exclaimed, surprised. "How are you?"

"I'm okay, I just called to see what was up. Is Carie a new girlfriend?"

He chortled. "I really shouldn't say anything here, when," and here his voice became a whisper, "when she's right here."

"You're so weird," I said cheerily. "Why don't you date somebody you like, like Ginny?"

"Ah, Charlie, how I missed your nosiness."

"Come on, Zach!"

"I'll text you, okay?" His voice lowered into a whisper again. "I can't talk about this in front of Carie."

I burst out laughing, unable to take it anymore. "Zach and Carie!" I cried. "Zach-Carie, oh, it's perfect!" I couldn't stop laughing, because the perfection of the two names put together was doing me in. It was too good. Zachary. Zach-Carie. Amazing. "There's no way you can break up, now! You'll be missing an opportunity!"

"Shut up, pest," he said, amused. "How's little ol' Grumps?"

Of course I immediately knew who he was talking about. "Ben," I emphasised, even though I couldn't help but giggle at the nickname, "is doing great. We're going on a date tonight!" I said the last part almost as a shout, because I was just so excited! It was exciting!

He made a weird sound at my screech, but returned the favour by screaming, "Wow!" right back.

I jumped a little, my ear buzzing. "Oh, you be quiet," I said.

"Sorry, Charlie, but seriously, that's awesome. He finally grew some balls."

"He always had them," I defended Ben. He always was protecting me, and even though it sometimes bugged me that I couldn't usually do it myself without dying, I appreciated it.

Zach laughed. "Yes, I know he does, I'm aware how biology works." My cheeks turned warm at his comment, and even though he wasn't actually here, I had to hide my face. "Anyways, it was good talking to you, pest, but I need to drop Carie off at work."

"Okay," I said, sighing that the second person I tried to talk to had to leave so soon.

"But I'll talk to you soon, okay? No forgetting me because of that hairy beast, right?"

"Zach!"

His laughter was too loud, and I had to pull the phone away from my ear. "Okay, okay, I'll keep from insulting him. But I'm serious! Call me later!"

"Okay, cheers, Zach-Carie," I said cheekily. He chuckled one more time before hanging up.

I groaned out loud when I realised again that I had no one to talk to and nothing to do. My essay was written, my math problems completed, and my final exams studied for. I had nothing else to do. I groaned again.

"Oh my God, Charlie, did you bring a man home? Finally?" Ginny squealed, rushing into my room.

I gaped at her, my cheeks turning bright red. "Ginny!" I exclaimed, clapping my hands over my cheeks. "If you thought I brought back a man - which, why would you think that, by the way? - why would you run into the room?"

Ginny scowled at me, disappointed, and crossed her arms. "I just got carried away when I heard those sex sounds, Lottie. I thought you were finally doing exciting."

"That doesn't explain anything," I said, half-amused and half-concerned. "If I had been having sex, what would you have done?"

She shrugged, coming to lie down on the bed beside me. She shoved me aside a little, and I almost fell before I clamped onto her arm. "Probably throw a party for you or something. I don't know."

I grinned at the same time as being slightly disturbed. But I should've been used to it by now. "You, my friend, are something else. Hey, where were you?"

"In class. I do that sometimes," she said vaguely. "My parents want me to come home for the weekend, so I gotta leave you for on Friday."

"That's okay," I said, leaning my cheek against her shoulder. She patted my tummy. "Are you doing anything else the rest of the day?"

"I don't think so."

"Wanna have a girl's day?" I asked, my grin growing.

She smiled. "Sure, I need a break from guys anyway. I'm so sorry, Charlie, that Rick guy was a total mistake." I ignored that last statement for my own sanity, because I didn't want to hear about Rick for the next...ever. "Pride and Prejudice and cupcakes, then?"

"I'll get the cupcakes," I said at the same time as she said, "I'll rent Pride and Prejudice." We high-fived and dispersed to our own task, returning at around the same time.

"Double chocolate mint, and orange-cranberry," I said, setting the two boxes on Ginny's bed. Her bed was bigger than mine, so we hooked up her laptop to the big monitor she had mounted on the wall and inserted the DVD into the DVD drive.

We settled comfortably against the backboard of her bed, and Ginny rested her head on my shoulder. "So I heard from a little birdy that your date with Piglet is tonight?" Ginny asked, as the film began.

I giggled, shoving her gently. "I'm the one who told you that!"

She grinned. "I know. Are you excited?"

I threw my hands in the air. "I'm so excited, Ginny! I don't know what to wear, though, because he won't tell me where we're going, but it doesn't matter, because whatever he chooses will be great!"

Her chest moved almost violently from how hard she laughed. "Jeez, how big do you inflate his ego, Charlie?"

"Not that much," I said sheepishly. I thought he needed it, though. He was kind of depressingly self-deprecating.

"I guess it doesn't matter," she said. "He's totally different with you than with anyone else, anyways, so it's not like you notice."

I huffed. "What do you mean?"

"Haven't you noticed? When he looks at you, he becomes so gentle, he becomes so...disgustingly happy. Ugh, I could vomit. It's like he's transformed into an entirely different person. And that's all you, Charlie. I don't know how you did it, but you got that ugly manbeast to be somewhat passable."

My heart fluttered in my chest at her words. Was she right? Because I knew he treated me very kindly, and it was so much different than when I first met him, all brusque and cold. I smiled.

Ginny cuddled my arm. "You love him, right?"

"Yeah," I said, softly. "Very much so."

"He loves you, too," she said. "It's very easy to tell."

"I know," I said, even softer. I wasn't trying to be cocky or anything, but I did know. He told me, and I knew that he was telling the truth because of his actions. He loved me. Oh, what a thought, that little Charlotte Carter could ever be the object of the beautiful Ben Fisher's affection.

"I wish I had that," Ginny said, almost silently, but I still heard her.

I leant into her more. "You will get it," I said firmly, wondering whether I should bring up Zach. As much as I adored the prospects of the name Zach-Carie, maybe it was time for a rerun of Zachinny. But I'd think of a better name later. "You should talk to Zach," I blurted before I could stop myself.

"Charlie," she sighed. "We're not-"

"I don't believe that," I said stubbornly. "Can you at least just talk to him? Please? Please?"

She groaned loudly at my persistence. "If you'll let us watch the rest of the film in peace, then yes, I'll talk to him."

"Promise?" I held out my pinky, and she stared at it for a minute before rolling her eyes and hooking pinkies with me. I grinned.

"Promise," she said.

"What do I wear?" I wailed, flailing around in my closet. It was almost time for Ben to come pick me up, and I wasn't even dressed yet.

Ginny lay on my bed, casually texting someone while I was drowning in a sea of bright colours. Why did I have so many floral prints?

"Ginny!" I whined, sinking down so I was sitting on the floor of my closet.

She rolled her eyes and sat up. "Get off the floor, idiot," she snapped. "All you have to do is pick a nice dress, for Chrissakes. Something less girly than usual, though. Just one colour. Two colours max."

I pouted but listened to her regardless, flicking through my hangers. "How about this one?" I asked, holding out a cute navy blue dress with a sweetheart neckline.

She eyed it critically. "Yes," she finally said. "I'll get you my white kitten heels to wear with it."

I smiled as she left. "I love you, Ginny!" I called.

"Yeah, yeah, whatever," she grumbled, which made me smile wider. She didn't even realise how similar she and Ben were. It was hilarious.

She was the best friend I'd ever had in my entire life, so I hoped she would call Zach. I firmly believed they were perfect for each other and just didn't realise it yet.

Plus, Zach had texted me earlier, telling me Carie was actually his friend's sister. So Zach-Carie wasn't even a thing to begin with. But the thought with Zach with Ginny made up for the perfect lost ship name, so I would survive.

He hadn't told me, but I thought he liked Ginny already. Or at least was still stuck up on her. I mean, I'd known him since even before Rick. I knew what he was like.

Ginny returned with her cute white heels, and I thanked her as I slipped them on. They were comfy and the heel wasn't even that big, so I'd probably be okay for the whole night.

Ginny scanned me over and smirked. "He's gonna die when he sees you," she declared.

I raised my eyebrows and lifted the ends of the dress a little. "But I look the same."

"My previous statement stands," she said dryly. "Clearly you've never noticed what Ben is like when you're in the same room together."

I looked away so that she wouldn't see me turn red. " Stop embarrassing me, Mother," I joked.

She snapped her fingers. "Speaking of which, Loverboy does know he has to get through me before he can take you out?"

"Ginny, come on," I said. "Haven't you put the poor guy through enough?"

She smirked evilly and shook her head. "Never!" she cackled. "Your parents aren't here, so I'm going to sit in as the intimidating guardian this time."

I snorted a laugh and decided to wait with her for Ben to arrive. I felt at peace, I felt very calm. At first, I was a bundle of nerves, but it really didn't matter what the date was or anything like that. As cheesy as this is, and I'm known for being a cheeseball, Ben was all that mattered.

But it was our first date.

When we heard a knock on our dorm room, I literally jumped out of my skin and clutched onto Ginny's arms. Suddenly, my heart was thundering, jumping out of my chest. "Chill out," she said. "It's just a slimy little worm who loves you, you have nothing to worry about."

"You're right!" I cried, jumping to my feet and skipping to the door. I took a deep breath, straightened out my dress, patted down my hair, and finally opened the door.

"Good evening," Ben said, dropping his voice down about three octaves.

I smiled giddily at him. He was dressed semi-formally like I was in a pair of khaki trousers and a black button up shirt with the sleeves rolled up. If I was a weaker woman, I would drool probably, because he looked really, really good. "Good evening," I replied in a silly voice.

And then I noticed he was holding out a bouquet of beautiful red roses to me that gave off a light fragrance that was starting to fill up our suite. Ben scratched the back of his head. "Er...are you going to take them, or...?"

"Oh!" I said, shaking myself out of my daze. "Wow, Ben, thank you!" I carefully took the flowers from his grasp and buried my face in them much like I did with the sunflowers from before, which were now dried and placed by my bed. I inhaled once, closing my eyes and taking it all in. These must've been so expensive. "You didn't have to get me flowers," I said, glancing back up at him.

He snorted. "What kind of first date would this be if I didn't get you flowers?"

I bit my lip to keep my smiling too much. "Well, thank you," I whispered, my eyes crinkling at the corners. "You're so nice!"

"Wow, this is so awkward!" Ginny screamed from somewhere inside the room, and I whipped around, looking for her.

"Be quiet!" I laughed.

"You look beautiful," he said, and it was just a simple sentence, but the way he said it made my stomach flip and made me feel all sorts of different things. His eyes went from my head to my toes and back up again, and then he smiled his sparkling smile at me. I wanted to stare, I did stare. He was too much.

"So do you," I squeaked out by mistake.

"Well, my mum always did want a girl," he chuckled, amused. I laughed as well, because I couldn't help it when he looked so happy.

"Are you just gonna let him freeze to death outside?" Ginny asked. "Because I think that would be fine, but close the door so we don't get a draft."

I shook my head. "Come inside, my mum wants to meet you."

He frowned, confused. "Your mum? But-" He stopped himself and shook his head when he saw my eager expression. "Okay, I guess."

"It's just Ginny," I whispered, and he nodded in understanding. I did wish that my actual mum could be here to meet Ben, but at least I had my dad. And now Delia too, I guess. And Ginny, of course.

"Alright, young man," Ginny said when I sat Ben down on the sofa opposite of Ginny, who had her arms crossed, one foot tapping the ground. "Where are you taking my girl?"

Ben raised his eyebrows. "You're not scary," he stated.

Ginny growled almost animalistically, and I had to hide my face in embarrassment at what she was doing. Might as well invite Papa over, right? He could get on this too. "So this is the kind of riffraff you bring home, Charlie? That's it. Get him out!"

"Are you serious?" Ben asked in annoyance.

"Get him out, Charlie!" Ginny said. "I won't have you dating him!"

"She's kidding," I muttered, even though I wasn't exactly sure. "Let's just go."

"Wait!" she cried. "Let me at least take pictures!"

"No, we're going," I said. "I'll see you later!"

She smirked suggestively, and I wished I had the force so I could force-shut her mouth before she said anything creepy. "Is this going to be one of those sleepover-type situations, or should I wait up?"

"Neither," I said, trying to force any and all inappropriate images out of my mind before my head exploded from all the blood rushing to my cheeks. "I'll get back when I get back, okay?"

"Don't do anything I wouldn't do!" she sang. But I didn't think she understood what her words meant, because she would do pretty much anything. Regardless, I waved good-bye to hear and tugged Ben out the door.

"Where are we going?" I asked brightly once we were outside in the nippy weather.

"Nothing crazy, just a nice restaurant," he said. "And then hang out afterwards?" He looked at me with hopeful eyes and I felt myself practically melt into the ground. I nodded, which made him grip my hand tighter and look away to smile.

He helped me into his car like the perfect gentleman, and then we were off. "How's your mum and dad?" I asked. "Oh, and Archer!"

He shrugged. "They're doing good. Mum and Dad still want me to go back, but I told them no."

I looked down at my lap at his words. "Oh," I said quietly.

"I'm here because I want to be," he said. "I'm not there because I don't want to be there. Do you understand?"

I nodded and smiled. He reached out to me, his eyes still on the road, and I took his hand. "What did I do to deserve you?"

Ben scoffed. "You're asking that question with the wrong tone," he said. "Right now, you're saying it as if I'm a reward, but you should be saying it as if you've done something horribly bad, let's say homicide, and now you're being punished."

I laughed at his ridiculousness. "Don't be thick," I said.

"You don't be thick," he said. "What did I do to deserve you?"

I shook my head. "You're asking that with the wrong tone," I repeated. "You're saying it as if I'm a reward, but you should be saying it as if you've done something awful, like let's say embezzlement, and now you're being punished. With me."

"Lottie, come on-" he started to argue.

"Do you hear how ridiculous it sounds?" I interrupted. I sighed. "I don't know what I have to do to convince you that you're exactly good the way you are. You're a wonderful person."

He was silent for a moment. "Every girl I've ever dated has tried to change me, tame me, whatever. You never tried that. Why?"

I hit my head against the seat. "I just told you," I said, feeling myself become exasperated. Ben couldn't understand anything I was saying, or he wasn't listening.

"You didn't. Just tell me."

His strong hand held mine tighter, protectively. I revelled in the warmth that came from our connected fingers, my eyes focused on his scarred knuckles so that I wouldn't blush like a complete dunce. "I just..."

"There must be a reason why you put up with me," he urged. "I just want to understand. I want to know why."

"Benny," I said, rubbing my thumb over his knuckles. "I don't think I would've fallen in love with you if you were a different person. Falling in love with you meant falling in love with every part of you, and I don't want to take any part of that away."

As I spoke, his face blanked as if my words horrified him. I gulped nervously, trying to pull my hand away. I hoped I didn't say anything wrong. I didn't dare to look at his face for fear of what I'd discover.

"I-I'm sorry," I stuttered, as I tugged my hand away. He hadn't responded, making me fear the worst. I chanced a glance up, my heart rocketing in my chest like a hyper three year old.

"Oh quit with the 'sorry' business," he said, and I could hear a smile in his voice. I let myself relax. "And you say I doubt myself? Man, I'm becoming a giant sap, Clark was right. You didn't try changing me, but it happened anyway, I guess. Just so I could maybe one day deserve you."

I didn't know what to say to that. Everything he said just made my heart dance and made me want him to pull over so that I could kiss him. "All this 'you don't deserve me I don't deserve you' rubbish," I said. "We're both idiots, I think, and we both belong to each other. Two big idiots." Ben laughed, and I laughed with him.

Two big idiots. Two big, happy idiots. I didn't think I'd ever been more happy in my entire life, and hopefully Ben, the absolute love of my life, felt the same.

"You, my love," Ben said, pulling up my hand to kiss my knuckles, "are sweet as a strawberry."

Chapter 46

"Where's Daddy?" Amity asked me with her adorable lisp, peeking over the counter at where I was icing some mint chocolate cupcakes.

I smiled at the little cutie pie and passed her the spoon. "He's hiding," I told her. "He knows Mummy will beat him up if I find him." Unlucky Ben, he couldn't escape from me today because we both had a day off - him from his software development job and me from my bakery. Plus, our car was in service, so he couldn't drive away and hide in the safety of Clark's, or Ginny and Zach's house.

She giggled, her pigtails bobbing. "Silly Daddy," she said fondly, smearing chocolate all over her face.

"Yes," I said, moving around the counter to ruffle her hair. I licked my thumb and wiped away a smear of chocolate that she'd somehow gotten on her nose. "Want to help me find him?"

"Can I help beat him up?" she asked eagerly. Maybe that was bad parenting on my part, but she was only three years old, so I figured Ben could handle a little beating from his pint-sized daughter.

"Of course," I agreed warmly, reaching out my hand to her. She grabbed it, and again I marvelled that Ben and I were able to create such a wonderful little girl with half of his knucklehead genes. "Where shall we look first?"

"My room!" She tugged me upstairs.

"We need to make a plan," I whispered.

Amity clapped her hands. "Plan!" she repeated, and I chuckled when I realised she had no clue what I was going on about.

"I'm going to wait outside, and if you find your dad, don't tell him I'm waiting, okay?" She nodded furiously, her pigtails going wild. She had my hair, but Ben's beautiful dark eyes. "And then we attack!"

She giggled, but then clasped her hands to her mouth in horror. "Sh!" she said. "We need to shhh!"

"Right," I said. "We do need to be quiet, we need to be sneaky! Can you tiptoe, angel?" She proudly showed me that she couldn't in fact tiptoe and didn't know what I meant by tiptoe, but she was such a tiny little thing that it didn't even matter. "Perfect," I exclaimed, and we high-fived. "Okay, now check your room."

I leant against the doorframe and watched in amusement as she checked under all her toys for her enormous father. "He's not here, Mummy!" she whispered loudly, disappointed.

"It's okay, angel, we'll check somewhere else." She ran up to take my hand, but then I noticed something out of the corner of my eye. "Wait," I whispered. "Amity, look under your bed." How the heck did he fit under there?

Amity ran over to her bed and dropped to her hands and knees. I shook my head when a hand shot out from under the bed and grabbed her, pulling her underneath. She screamed happily. "Daddy!"

"Give up the chase, my love!" Ben yelled, his voice muffled. "I've got your precious daughter in my grasp and there's nothing you can do about it!"

Amity laughed, and I knelt down, seeing her tucked comfortably under her dad's arm. "She's your daughter, too," I reminded him, just in case he forgot. Even from back here I could see his eyes twinkling challengingly, a smirk plastered on his face. His handsome face looked just as it had back when we were in uni, except more rugged, with his dark beard and sharp features.

"Come and get her," he taunted.

I rolled my eyes and crawled over to my little family. I dropped down to my stomach. "Want to come to Mummy, angel?" I asked, holding out my arms.

Amity beamed at me, her round face softening even further, and carefully wriggled out of Ben's grasp to hug me. I smiled smugly at Ben, who returned it with a grumpy look. "Look at Daddy's face!" Amity said with a cheeky smile.

"Hardy hardy har," Ben said, slightly amused. "What's wrong with my face, Amity?"

"You look silly!"

"Go play with your toys, angel," I said. She scrambled up immediately and ran to the newest doll her doting father had bought for her for absolutely no reason other than the fact that she had him wrapped around her chubby little finger. I lay on my stomach, propped up on my elbows. "Hello, hubby," I said slowly. "What are you doing, hiding under our daughter's bed?"

"Trying not to be killed by my little wife," he said sheepishly.

"And why is that?" I asked in a sing-song voice.

"Oh," he drew out, twiddling his fingers. "No reason."

I pointed at him. I was more amused than annoyed now, but he didn't have to know that. "Out. Now." It took him awhile to scoot his body out from under there, and I watched, a slight smile on my face. By the time he was all the way out, he rolled onto his back, gasping for breath.

"Lottie, you know I love you, right?" he tried, staring at me pleadingly.

I pushed myself up and sat on his stomach, causing him to let out a soft oof. "I love you, too," I had to say back. "But that doesn't let you off for offering up my baking for Queenie's birthday party tonight when you know I have to go see my dad at the hospital!"

"I'm sorry," he said. "I'm sorry, my love, I completely forgot!" He grabbed my hands and put them on his cheeks, closing his eyes. I watched his handsome face crease worriedly, and I felt my heart expand.

"It's okay," I said softly. "Anyways, I already finished, so it's not that big a deal."

"I didn't mean to cause more work for you," he said, opening his eyes. "Queenie just kept saying they were getting cupcakes from Safeway, but that she liked yours so much more!"

"It's okay," I repeated, shaking my head. I smiled at him, and his wrinkles smoothed so that he could send me one of his panty-dropping smiles.

Do you know what a lot of couples do after they fight?" I stared at him, not having any idea what he was saying, because we didn't even fight. "Make up sex."

"Benjamin," I gasped. "Your daughter is right here!"

"Want to give her a brother or sister?" he asked in a whisper. Then, louder, "Amity, angel, do you want a brother or sister?"

I whipped my head around to see Amity staring at us with wide eyes. "Yes!" she squealed excitedly. "I want a little sister! I want to be a big sister!" She spoke so fast that her lisp made it almost impossible for me to understand what she said.

"You heard the girl," Ben said with finality. He rolled us over and stood up with me still clutching onto him. "Mummy and Daddy have some work to do if you want that sister."

Amity squealed again, dancing around and waving her hands about, absolutely ecstatic. "I'm going to tell Vivian tomorrow that Mummy and Daddy are giving me a little sister!"

"Ben," I groaned, burying my face in his neck. "What have you done?"

"Careful, my love," he said. "If you say my name like that again, we might have to be a little...late to Queenie's party."

My face turned bright red at his words, and I gasped when he squeezed my thighs. Even after eight years of being with

him, I wasn't prepared for when he'd say something suggestive. "I swear, Ben, I'm going to kill you," I muttered.

He hugged me closer to him and swiftly exited Amity's
room. "Angel, just knock on Mummy and Daddy's door if you
need anything!" he called.

"We can't leave our daughter alone," I said, rolling my eyes.
But we could, because she was content to play by herself
for hours. I thought perhaps she was more mature than her
father.

"She'll be fine," he said. "I would say this'll be quick, but we
both know, from my stamina, that that isn't the case." I didn't
have time to tell him off, because he kicked our door closed
behind him, throwing me onto our bed and climbing up on
top of me.

I wrapped my arms around his neck and smiled. He leant
down to kiss me, but I quickly put a finger on his lips. "Just let
me give her a snack," I said.

He groaned and fell off me onto his back. "Fuck me," he
muttered sullenly.

I rolled onto my side, facing him. "In a minute," I whispered
cheekily and then sprang up off the bed.

"Charlotte!" he yelled, but I just laughed and skipped outside.

Once I grabbed a juice box and a packet of cheese crackers
from the kitchen, I went to Amity's room, where she was
innocently playing with her Ironman and Captain America
figurines. I crouched down beside her and lay the snacks
beside her. "Angel, if you get hungry, just have these, okay?"

She grinned at me, showing me her cute baby teeth. "Okay, Mummy."

I smiled and brushed a stray curl away from her eyes. "Love you, angel."

"Love you, too, Mummy."

I stared at her for a minute. I couldn't leave her alone, she was just too cute! I mean, Love you, too, Mummy? That was killer. "I'll be back, okay? Knock on my door if you need anything."

"Okay, Mummy," she said, starting to get annoyed that I was still there, interrupting her playtime. I shook my head and kissed her head.

Now to attend to my other baby.

I slowly opened the door to mine and Ben's room. He was still lying on his back, covering his face with his hands, but when he heard the door opening, he immediately sat up. His eagerness would've made me laugh if I wasn't feeling the same.

I wiggled my eyebrows and closed to door, locking it. "Hey, hubby," I said, smiling.

"Are you going to come here, or do I need to come get you?" he asked, aggravated.

My smile widened, and I slowly zipped down just enough of the front of my dress to make my husband's face turn a bright red. Over the past few years, I'd learnt some tricks, and I knew what to do that would make Ben want to throttle me if he didn't have other things on his mind.

"Charlotte," he warned.

I walked over him and shoved him hard onto his back. "You're so sour," I said, amused. "Sour as a lemon, you are!"

"I'll show you sour," he muttered, swiftly kicking my legs out from beneath me so that I was sprawled across him. "Nice to see you down here," he said, winking.

I smiled. "Want to make a baby with me?"

Epilogue

"I'm going to vomit if you make me eat that," Lottie said, slowly backing away from me, her eyes trained on the brownie I held in my hand.

I frowned at her. She didn't want a brownie, her complete ultimate favourite thing in the entire world besides me? "What's wrong with you?" I asked. She looked like she was going to burst into tears, so I hurriedly put the brownie back on the plate and wiped my hands off.

"Ben!" she wailed.

I narrowed my eyes and scooped her up, feeling her tremble in my grip. She sniffled into my shoulder. "Lottie, what's the matter?"

"I-I...I don't know!"

I put her down and placed my hands on her cheeks, moving her face so that she was looking at me. I cleared my throat once, then again, and then a third time. "Hey, do you need me to run down to the shops and get you...anything?"

Her cheeks burned under my palms, and she looked up at the ceiling so she wouldn't make eye contact with me. She frowned, her forehead furrowed thoughtfully. "No, Ben, you know I'm a just little late."

I grinned. I did know. A week's wait every month, but it was always worth it at the end, once I...you know, got some. But then I focused in on Lottie's trembling lip, and my smile fell off my face. "Then what's the matter, babe?"

She didn't say anything and that worried me. My brow creased and I rubbed my thumb along her cheek. "I really don't know," she said finally. "I'm just feeling a bit emotional."

"Why?" I asked. Her lip trembled even more, and I felt myself starting to crumble at her feet. No, no, no, I didn't want her to cry.

"I don't know!" she suddenly sobbed, throwing her arms back around my neck.

I stared at the top of her head, absolutely flummoxed. I honestly had no idea what to do. Should I call Ginny? Was this something that I didn't understand? "Should I call Ginny?" I voiced my thoughts.

"No! I don't want to bother her, she's three hours away!" I felt a wetness on my shirt, and I almost collapsed when I realised she was crying. "I don't want to bother her!"

"It's okay, Lottie," I said softly, rubbing her back. "You're fine. Come on, don't you want a brownie?"

"No!" she snapped, which couldn't even technically be described as snapping, because she still spoke gently. But for Lottie, it was snapping, and that made me raise my eyebrows. "I already said I didn't want a brownie!"

Okay, Ben, keep your dumb mouth shut, then. I sighed and picked her up, carrying her to our sofa. I sat down and settled her on my lap, and she whimpered slightly. The sound broke my heart clean in two, and even though I was sure nothing horrible had happened, I was still worried about her. Why was she acting like this? Was she sick? Did I need to take her to the hospital?

After a few minutes, I realised she had fallen asleep on me. I shifted so that I was laying against the armrest and swung my feet up on the cushions. I felt her breathing steadily and pushed her hair out of her face. She looked worried even as she slept, and I hoped this was just a weird thing and she'd sleep it off and be okay after her nap.

But she wasn't. She woke up after an hour, looking extremely queasy. "Ben?" she said worriedly, eyes half-open and arms stretched out, looking for me.

I pulled her closer. "Right here, my love." I bit my lip. I had to go to work soon. I'd already missed half of the day, but I didn't want to leave Lottie alone when she was like this. "Are you okay?" I asked carefully.

She rubbed her eyes and yawned. "I'm okay," she said. "Why aren't you at work?"

I didn't answer truthfully, because she would probably get mad at me for staying here with her. "Took the day off," I said.

She saw right through me, though. "No, you didn't," she said, narrowing her eyes. "I'm not going to be the reason you're fired, Ben."

"I won't be fired," I assured her.

"Just go, okay? I'll be fine. You're already dressed anyways."

I glanced down at my shirt and slacks. I'd been ready to leave when Lottie got a little emotional, but now I just wanted to lounge around home with her. "I don't wanna," I whined.

She smiled at me. "I'll be fine, I promise. I can take care of myself."

I stared at her. I hated when she tried to use her loveliness against me, because she knew I could never refuse her. Whatever magic it was she held over me, I had no idea. I'd married a sorcerer. "If one thing happens, one thing, you better call me," I warned. "If I find out something happened while I wasn't here, I'll smother you for a month!"

Lottie laughed. "Okay, easy, tiger. I'll be right here when you get back."

"You're not going to work, right?" I asked.

"Nope," she said. "I closed it for today. Bernice had to go to her mother's for the day." Bernice, the manager of Lottie's bakery, pretty much held the place together. Honestly, Lottie was incredible, but she wouldn't be able to manage a business if my business guru of a dad didn't do it for her.

"Okay," I said, relieved that she didn't have to do anything. "I'll be back around five. Remember to eat lunch." I straightened out my clothes and my hair that had gotten a little ruffled, and then I bent to kiss Lottie. "Love you."

"I love you," she echoed. She followed me to the front door and waved as I got into my car.

I frowned, feeling really bad about leaving her alone. But she seemed okay now, and I'd be home soon. Maybe I'd pick up some flowers on the way back. Yeah, I'd do that.

I unlocked and opened the front door and stepped inside. "Lottie, my love, where are you?" I set the sunflowers I'd bought on the coffee table and went to go look for Lottie. She was sitting on the sofa, reading a book. I felt relieved. She looked fine.

Lottie glanced up at me, and I realised her expression was anything but fine. "Ben, before you sit down, can you go fetch the buns that are in the oven?" she asked in a wobbly voice.

Oh no, was she going to cry again? Fuck, fuck, fuck, I shouldn't have left her alone. "Okay," I said, moving to kiss her on the forehead before heading to the kitchen. I frowned. I couldn't smell anything cooking.

I looked back at the sofa, where Lottie had her eyes closed. Was she going crazy? I shook my head and opened the oven anyway. Just like I thought. Nothing in there. Got me worked up to eat her bread for nothing.

"There's nothing in here," I called.

"Check again," she insisted. She looked over at me with pleading eyes.

I shook my head. Of course I would check the clearly empty oven again when she looked at me like that. I wasn't a monster. "There's still nothing ther-" I paused, noticing something on the bottom rack. A piece of cloth? I picked it up without looking and strode over to Lottie. "Why's this in the oven?" I asked. If she was going to tell me this was the "buns," I was going to have to force her to go to bed.

Lottie smiled nervously and gestured to me. "Look at it."

I unrolled the cloth, realising immediately that it was actually a tiny white onesie. Baby clothes? My eyes widened as I read the curly black script: 'Sorry ladies, my daddy's taken.' My heart starting pounding wildly. "Y-you...this isn't for you, is it?" I asked idiotically.

Her hand moved to her stomach and she shook her head. "Not for me, dummy."

I gaped at her, my eyes wide, my mouth opening and closing like a stupid fish. "A-are you...are you serious?" I looked from my wife's face to her belly several times, not comprehending what was going on. The onesie in my hands fell on the sofa.

She nodded, a beautiful little smile blossoming on her face. "Bun in the oven," she joked softly.

"M-mine?"

Lottie looked at me like I was an idiot and then rolled her eyes. "Obviously."

I didn't know what to say. I didn't know what to do. "Oh," I said stupidly. My mind was blank.

Her face fell. "Oh," she repeated.

I stared at her and she stared back for maybe a whole minute. Her big doe-eyes pleaded with me to say something else, but my throat had closed up and I was starting to hyper-ventilate. What did this mean? I was going to be a...father? I blinked. "Oh!" I screamed.

Lottie jumped about a foot in the air, her hand going to her heart in shock at my sudden yelp. "Ben!" she exclaimed.

"I'm going to be a dad!" I yelled, bouncing to her and gently picking her up. She giggled as I twirled her around once and then set her down for fear I might cause her an upset stomach. "I'm going to be a dad! You're going to be a mum!"

"Yes," she said. She sniffled, wiping her face and smiling a watery smile that almost killed me. "That is what this means."

I sunk down beside her and took her hand. I was going to be a dad? My mind whirred. We needed to go shopping, we needed to book a doctor's appointment, we needed to start baby-proofing everything. "I need to call my parents," I said.